HIGHEST BIDDER

Highest Bidder

Book 1

CHARLOTTE BYRD

Byrd Books

Visit my website at www.charlotte-byrd.com

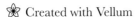 Created with Vellum

Praise for Charlotte Byrd

"Twisted, gripping story full of heat, tension and action. Once again we are caught up in this phenomenal , dark passionate love story that is full of mystery, secrets, suspense and intrigue that continues to keep you on edge!" (Goodreads) ⭑⭑⭑⭑⭑

"Must read!" (Goodreads) ⭑⭑⭑⭑⭑

"Charlotte will keep you in suspense!" (Goodreads) ⭑⭑⭑⭑⭑

"Twisted love story full of power and control!" (Goodreads) ⭑⭑⭑⭑⭑

"Just WOW...no one can weave a story quite like Charlotte. This series has me enthralled, with such great story lines and characters." (Goodreads) ⭑⭑⭑⭑⭑

"Charlotte Byrd is one of the best authors I have had the pleasure of reading, she spins her storylines around believable characters, and keeps you on the edge of your seat. Five star rating does not do this book/series justice." (Goodreads) ⭐⭐⭐⭐⭐

"Suspenseful romance!" (Goodreads) ⭐⭐⭐⭐⭐

"Amazing. Scintillating. Drama times 10. Love and heartbreak. They say what you don't know can't hurt you, but that's not true in this book." (Goodreads) ⭐⭐⭐⭐⭐

"I loved this book, it is fast paced on the crime plot, and super-hot on the drama, I would say the perfect mix. This suspense will have your heart racing and your blood pumping. I am happy to recommend this thrilling and exciting book, that I just could not stop reading once I started. This story will keep you glued to the pages and you will find yourself cheering this couple on to finding their happiness. This book is filled with energy, intensity and heat. I loved this book so much. It was super easy to get swept up into and once there, I was very happy to stay." (*Goodreads*) ⭐⭐⭐⭐⭐

"BEST AUTHOR YET! Charlotte has done it again! There is a reason she is an amazing author and she continues to prove it! I was definitely not disappointed in this series!!" (*Goodreads*) ⭐⭐⭐⭐⭐

"LOVE!!! I loved this book and the whole series!!! I just wish it didn't have to end. I am definitely a fan for life!!! (*Goodreads*) ⭐⭐⭐⭐⭐

"Extremely captivating, sexy, steamy, intriguing, and intense!" (*Goodreads*) ⭐⭐⭐⭐⭐

"Addictive and impossible to put down." (*Goodreads*) ⭐⭐⭐⭐⭐

"What a magnificent story from the 1st book through book 6 it never slowed down always surprising the reader in one way or the other. Nicholas and Olive's paths crossed in a most unorthodox way and that's how their story begins it's exhilarating with that nail biting suspense that keeps you riding on the edge the whole series. You'll love it!" (*Goodreads*) ⭐⭐⭐⭐⭐

"What is Love Worth. This is a great epic ending to this series. Nicholas and Olive have a deep connection and the mystery surrounding the deaths of the people he is accused of murdering is to be read. Olive is one strong woman with deep convictions. The twists, angst, confusion is all put together to make this worth-while read." (*Goodreads*) ⭐⭐⭐⭐⭐

"Fast-paced romantic suspense filled with twists and turns, danger, betrayal, and so much more." (*Goodreads*) ⭐⭐⭐⭐⭐

"Decadent, delicious, & dangerously addictive!" (*Goodreads*) ⭐⭐⭐⭐⭐

"Titillation so masterfully woven, no reader can resist its pull. A MUST-BUY!" (*Goodreads*) ⭐⭐⭐⭐⭐

"Captivating!" (*Goodreads*) ⭐⭐⭐⭐⭐

"Sexy, secretive, pulsating chemistry…" (*Goodreads*) ⭐⭐⭐⭐⭐

"Charlotte Byrd is a brilliant writer. I've read loads and I've laughed and cried. She writes a balanced book with brilliant characters. Well done!" (*Goodreads*) ⭐⭐⭐⭐⭐

"Hot, steamy, and a great storyline." (*Goodreads*) ⭐⭐⭐⭐⭐

"My oh my....Charlotte has made me a fan for life." (*Goodreads*) ⭐⭐⭐⭐⭐

"Wow. Just wow. Charlotte Byrd leaves me speechless and humble... It definitely kept me on the edge of my seat. Once you pick it up, you won't put it down." (*Goodreads*) ⭐⭐⭐⭐⭐

" Intrigue, lust, and great characters...what more could you ask for?!" (*Goodreads*) ⭐⭐⭐⭐⭐

Want to be the first to know
about my upcoming sales,
new releases and exclusive
giveaways?

Sign up for my newsletter and get a FREE
book: https://dl.bookfunnel.com/gp3o8yvmxd

Join my Facebook Group: https://www.
facebook.com/groups/276340079439433/

Bonus Points: Follow me on BookBub and
Goodreads!

About Charlotte Byrd

Charlotte Byrd is the bestselling author of romantic suspense novels. She has sold over 2 Million books and has been translated into five languages.

She lives near Palm Springs, California with her husband, son, a toy Australian Shepherd and a Ragdoll cat. Charlotte is addicted to books and Netflix, and she loves hot weather and crystal blue water.

Write her here:

charlotte@charlotte-byrd.com

Check out her books here:

www.charlotte-byrd.com

Connect with her here:

www.tiktok.com/charlottebyrdbooks

www.facebook.com/charlottebyrdbooks

www.instagram.com/charlottebyrdbooks

Want to hear about new releases, free books and get exclusive giveaways?

Sign up for my newsletter!

Sign up for my newsletter: https://www.
subscribepage.com/byrdVIPList

Join my Facebook Group: https://www.
facebook.com/groups/276340079439433/

Bonus Points: Follow me on BookBub and
Goodreads!

amazon.com/Charlotte-Byrd/e/B013M-
N45Q6

facebook.com/charlottebyrdbooks

tiktok.com/charlottebyrdbooks

bookbub.com/profile/charlotte-byrd

instagram.com/charlottebyrdbooks

x.com/byrdauthor

Also by Charlotte Byrd

All books are available at ALL major retailers! If you can't find it, please email me at charlotte@charlotte-byrd.com

Highest Bidder Series
Highest Bidder
Bidding War
Winning Bid

Hockey Why Choose
One Pucking Night (Novella)
Kiss and Puck
Pucking Disaster
Puck Me
Puck It

Tell me Series

Tell Me to Stop

Tell Me to Go

Tell Me to Stay

Tell Me to Run

Tell Me to Fight

Tell Me to Lie

Tell Me to Stop Box Set Books 1-6

Black Series

Black Edge

Black Rules

Black Bounds

Black Contract

Black Limit

Black Edge Box Set Books 1-5

Dark Intentions Series

Dark Intentions

Dark Redemption

Dark Sins

Dark Temptations

Dark Inheritance

Dark Intentions Box Set Books 1-5

Tangled Series

Tangled up in Ice

Tangled up in Pain

Tangled up in Lace

Tangled up in Hate

Tangled up in Love

Tangled up in Ice Box Set Books 1-5

The Perfect Stranger Series

The Perfect Stranger

The Perfect Cover

The Perfect Lie

The Perfect Life

The Perfect Getaway

The Perfect Stranger Box Set Books 1-5

Wedlocked Trilogy

Dangerous Engagement

Lethal Wedding

Fatal Wedding

Dangerous Engagement Box Set Books 1-3

Lavish Trilogy

Lavish Lies

Lavish Betrayal

Lavish Obsession

Lavish Lies Box Set Books 1-3

Somerset Harbor

Hate Mate (Cargill Brothers 1)

Best Laid Plans (Cargill Brothers 2)

Picture Perfect (Cargill Brothers 3)

Always Never (Cargill Brothers 4)

Kiss Me Again (Macmillan Brothers 1)

Say You'll Stay (Macmillan Brothers 2)

Never Let Go (Macmillan Brothers 3)

Keep Me Close (Macmillan Brothers 4)

All the Lies Series

All the Lies

All the Secrets

All the Doubts

All the Lies Box Set Books 1-3

Not into you Duet

Not into you

Still not into you

Standalone Novels

Dressing Mr. Dalton

Debt

Offer

Unknown

About Highest Bidder

The auction is an opportunity of a lifetime…or so I thought.

After a bad breakup, a busy career and no time for a personal life, I went to a bougie party and auctioned myself.

The highest bidder would get one night with me.

I've slept with plenty of bad dates for free, why not make it worth my while?

One night with a billionaire would pay off all three years of my law school student loans. Afterwards, I could quit my thankless soul-crushing corporate job and focus my legal work on people who really need me.

Little do I know that the man who buys me is my worst enemy.

Anderson West is arrogant, obnoxious, but also incredibly easy on the eyes. He was my biggest bully growing up, and my primary rival at law school. He hates everything about me and will stop at nothing to make my life miserable.

What happens when I find out he's the highest bidder when I'm naked in bed waiting for him?

Chapter 1

JUNE

The whir of the radiator is more meaningful than anything coming out of Madi's mouth. Another unending meeting that could have been an email. But at least doodling on my notepad makes it look like I'm paying attention. Never mind that I'm just drawing that guy that hangs his nose and fingers over the edge of something.

What's his name? Conroy? Leroy?

Doesn't matter. He's just a way to kill time.

I almost wince when I realize I'm using the poor doodle man that way. It's what my most recent ex said about me. After two years, Trent said I was a way to kill time until his real life started. Just what every girl wants to hear.

"Exactly, June," Madi sternly says. "A terrible use of resources."

I give a polite smile and a curt nod, realizing she thinks the face I made was about her presentation. On resource management? How did I get roped into a meeting on resource management? I swear I get needlessly cc'ed on everything.

My doodle's name is bugging me. My dad used to draw him on random things like doctor's notes and grocery lists just to make Mom smile. Why the hell can't I remember his name?

Walroy? Is that even a name? Or am I thinking about my boss?

Wallace, my boss, wants me to attend every meeting I can to get a better feel for operations. I'm two years out of law school, and he threatened me with getting onto the fast track for partner, so now I'm hooked into all the meetings, no matter how mundane. If I tell Wallace I am not interested in micromanaging every detail of the firm, I'm off the partner track, which would be ideal. But it'll disappoint my mom, and I can't do that to her. Not again.

She liked Trent. When I told her we broke up, *she* was the one who cried. Disappointing her again is not an option.

Thinking about her crying gives me the same guilty, sinking feeling I had when I was a kid and I saw her upset. Will I ever grow out of that? Hope so. But that feeling was the reason I tried so hard in school. The first time I brought home a bad grade, I wasn't punished in the technical sense, but I saw the look on her face. Not mad. Disappointed. After that, I did everything I could to avoid that face. Straight As from fourth grade on.

Bobroy? Pretty sure the doodle's name is Bobroy. Who decided to name someone Bobroy?

Behind Madi stands the best window in the entire law firm. It overlooks the harbor, but today is a gray and rainy autumn day. Just the way I like it. This morning's pumpkin spice coffee had given me the hope of a good day until I saw my calendar. Meeting after meeting, working through lunch, and none of that counts toward my two thousand billable hours for the year.

When I was a girl dreaming of law school, I did not count on this.

TV lawyers were dashing, well-dressed, articulate people with full lives. I am a soft, sort of okay dresser with mild social anxiety who couldn't deliver a closing argument if her life depended on it. My life is full of Cheers reruns and calling my mom. The TV shows never talk about student loans or rent that outpaces income, even when you work sixty-plus hours a week.

It wasn't just the glamor that drew me to the law. The money was a tremendous incentive, as was helping people. These days, my bank account could be best described as a desolate void from which I attempt to pay rent, and I don't help people. I help corporations. Though, according to the Supreme Court, I guess I *am* helping people. Ugh.

Maybe I'm naïve, but I don't think you should be twenty-nine and counting the days until retirement. This morning, my calendar reminded me I have just over ten thousand days to go, so I scraped myself out of bed and got moving. By the time retirement comes, I will have been stuck in a meeting with Madison Montague for thirty years.

I'm not sure I'll make it.

To my right, Garrett Edison taps my foot and subtly shows me his notepad. It reads, "Nice Kilroy."

"*That's* his name!" I declare in the middle of the meeting. Garrett snorts a laugh, and Madi quirks her head at me. A human record scratch. I blink half a dozen times and point to the slide,

"Uh, Evan Wilcox. I was trying to think of him the other day. Thanks for putting him in the presentation, Madi. Good timing."

"The entire presentation is on Evan, June."

"Right. Just hit me I was trying to think of him. The other day. Like I said."

She gives a tight smile. "Moving on. If you see here …" She droned on, and I tuned out again.

Garrett barely conceals his laughter—his shoulders give it away. He scribbles on his notepad, "Smooth."

So, I doodle a hand with the middle finger raised, and he grins at me. Eighty-four years later, we break for lunch. "Hey, do you want to come with me and Callie? We're hitting the new brew pub two blocks over."

He arches a curious brow. Garrett is Japanese American, with a permanent charming smile and a cool confidence about him. I have always envied that. "Thought you were working through lunch again."

"If I do that again, I might explode from the sheer fun of it, so I'm skipping that meeting."

"Ah, well thanks for the invitation, but I have a lunch date … thing."

"Good for you. Becca in accounting again?"

He smirks, shakes his head, and says, "See you later."

"I want details after."

"I never kiss and tell."

"You always kiss and tell, and that's why we're friends."

He grins. "Better get moving. Madi's coming your way."

"Thanks." I grab my gear and bolt for Callie's desk. "Let's go. Now."

"I need a minute—"

"Madi is trying to find me."

Callie smiles brightly. "Right behind you."

We bounce as fast as possible while not looking like we're running away. Thankfully, the walk is short, because the rain is really coming down now. More rain, more frizz for me. But not Callie. Her perfect, stick-straight, shiny blond hair would be enough for me to hate her if she weren't also a wonderful person with an enormous heart. She's white and I'm pretty sure her family was on the Mayflower. She folds her umbrella neatly, while I jam mine into my side of the booth. After ordering, she asks, "What did you do to piss Madi off this time?"

"I did not give her my undivided attention, and it showed."

She rolls her big brown eyes. "How dare you be so rude to a princess?"

I laugh and shake my head. "I know, right? How're things in property law?"

"Oh, you know me. I love it. VC?"

"My venture capital courses in school gave me the idea I'd make a lot of money doing good things for people. Turns out, that's a big fat lie. But being surrounded by people with too much money and not enough sense means I'm expected to dress and look like one of them, so not only do I have school loans to pay, but I also have credit card debt that makes me feel like I'm doing my part to increase the national debt."

"It'll get better, June. We're both new at this. It just takes time."

"You're going to give me a sunburn, Callie. Stop being so sunny."

She giggles and soon, our veggie burgers arrive. "Any word from Trent?"

"Why would I hear from him? We broke up a month ago."

"I thought maybe he'd come to his senses."

"Even if he had, I'm not interested."

She shrugs and nibbles.

"What about you and Daniel Fisher? How are things there?"

Her smile grows brighter every time I say the man's name. It's sickening, but also kind of adorable. "We're good. Actually, we're going to a ball tonight."

"An actual ball? Like with ballgowns and shit?"

"Formalwear, but yeah. It's a charity auction to preserve an old Victorian mansion."

"Sounds like …" *A snooze fest.* "… a good way to network."

"It's an excuse to dress up and drink champagne and spend time with Daniel and his friends."

"Isn't that weird, though? They're all so old, and he's a senior partner."

"You make it sound like he's the crypt keeper," she says, laughing. "He is in his forties, and we don't talk about work. It's not that deep."

"Lucky bastard. He's halfway to retirement."

Callie sighs at me. A rare moment. "All you think about is work. Do you think that's why you struggle with men?"

I sigh at her. A nearly present state of being. "I struggle with men because they're men. But I'm done with all that. Work won't tell you that you're a way to kill time. It won't divorce you. It won't keel over from a heart attack. Work is the only thing I have going for me right now."

"But work won't love you back."

"Love is overrated. I'm done with it."

-

Chapter 2
JUNE

Back at work, I long to be tied to a desk in an old movie. Not in a kinky way, but because when someone was busy back then, everyone knew it. Work was literally piled on their desk, so people bothered them less. My work is mostly on my computer, making it invisible, so no one sees an obstacle to their conversation.

Especially not Madi. Though I doubt a pile of work would persuade her to leave me alone.

She clicks her fake nails on my desk, and I swear they are pointier every time I see them. Without looking up from my typing, I groan internally and shove my glasses back up my nose before they slide down again. "Yes, Madi?"

"Wallace wants you to stay late to finish up the proposal for the Banks account."

"It's not due until next week. I have plenty of time—"

"He wants to look over it before you officially turn it in to him, so it needs to be completed before the morning."

I frown up at her. "Why does he need to look at it before I officially turn it in?"

She smiles sinisterly. "Because we've noticed your lack of focus lately, and before he discusses it with the client next week, he wants to look at it and make sure you've dotted all the I's."

I can hear the translation in my head. "Because I'm sleeping with him and you embarrassed me today, so I whined until I could get you punished."

"Uh sure, Madi. I'll just skip the meeting at four—"

"Oh, but you can't. It's an all-hands."

She's right. Which means I'm not getting out of here until eight. Or later. "Hell. Whatever. I'll take care of it."

Her smile slides from sinister to self-congratulatory. "Such a team player. I'll be sure to mention your respectful attitude to Wallace. See you at four." She saunters off, and I'm struck by how much I wish one of her high heels would break while I watch. I'm also struck by a wadded up ball of paper on the back of my head.

I roll my eyes and turn around. "Good date?"

Garrett grins. "Nah. Just thought you needed a distraction from eye daggering Madi's back."

"Gee, thanks. So, are you going to tell me about your date?"

"I hate her, but I love her fake nails. They match her personality."

"The store-bought illusion of sharpness? Agreed. What happened with your lunch—"

"So, has Trent called yet?"

I narrow my gaze at him. "Why aren't you telling me about your date? Since when don't you share?"

Garrett pauses, then joins me right by my desk. With an open floor plan office, it's hard to get anything resembling privacy, and we don't even have cubicles. When I'd asked Wallace about it, he said they interrupt the look of the place. But really, it was an excuse to monitor everyone.

He quietly says, "I'm less inclined to discuss this in front of everyone, because people can get weird about things. I know you're fine about these things, but other people might not be. My date was with a man."

"I don't think anyone here will care."

He shrugs and glances around. "You never know, and I don't want to rock any boats just yet."

"Well, how'd it go?"

He smiles. "Good. Really good. We're seeing each other again this weekend."

"That's awesome."

"We really click, you know? I mean, it was just a first date, so who knows, but I like what I've seen so far."

"I'm happy for you, Garrett."

He almost flinches when he asks, "So, seriously, Trent?"

"Why does everyone keep bringing him up today? First Callie, now you. I'm done with Trent. Forever."

"Oh. Okay. Well, there's more fish in the—"

"Not for me. I'm done with all that."

He folds his arms. "You've seemed *done* with everything lately. What's up with you?"

Shaking my head, I don't even want to get into it. But Garrett's a great guy, and I could probably use more than one person to talk to. Maybe his perspective would help. "I just … I thought once I was a lawyer, I'd have everything all figured out, you know? I'm staring down the barrel of thirty years old, and I feel just as lost as when I was a teenager."

He chuckles. "When I was a teenager, I wanted to be a pilot. What about you?"

"A lawyer. But not really. TV lawyers had all the money, so I went with that. What I really wanted to do was photography."

"What's stopping you?"

I laugh. "A mountain of school loans. The usual."

"And now, you help venture capitalists dodge taxes—"

"Find appropriate places to store their otherwise taxable income," I parrot the party line, and we both roll our eyes. "Yeah. Not exactly a dream job."

"Could be worse."

"How so?"

"You could be Madi."

I snort a laugh. "Uh no. Not in a million years. Could you just imagine me in her heels? It'd be like a foal trying to walk on its first day."

He laughs, too. "I'd pay to see that."

"I wouldn't hate everything here if maybe the clients were decent people, trying to catch a break. But I cannot describe a single client of ours that way. Here, it's multimillionaires, their questionable actions, and their shell corporations. Yuck."

"At least today is one more day off your retirement calendar."

"Yeah, I guess so."

We part ways, and the next few hours are a blur of meetings and proposals until I realize eight o'clock came and went. By nine, I'm on my way home. TGIF never felt as real as it does now, and I feel it in my bones by the time I turn the key to my apartment. Just as I step inside, my phone blows up with Callie's number. "Hey, what—"

"Daniel stood me up!"

"Oh shit. What happened?"

"Okay, not exactly stood me up, but damn near. I'm all dressed up with no place to go, because one of his kids is having a dental emergency and Daniel's ex-wife can't deal with oral surgery, so he has to be there for them. He feels bad, so he sent a limo to pick me up and take me wherever I want to go tonight. So, now, I have a limo, two tickets to a ball, and no date. Be my date. Pleeeease?"

I am so tired that I want to cry, but I can't disappoint Callie. It would be like scolding a golden retriever. How could I ever look her in the eye after that? Plus, she never asks for favors. I can't say no. After a deep breath, I gently try to get out of it. "That sounds amazing, but Callie, I don't have a dress nice enough for a ball."

"Everyone has a little black cocktail dress, June."

I laugh my retort. "Guess I'm no one, then."

"We'll figure something out. It'll be fine."

"None of my fancy shoes have a heel the right height for formalwear—"

She laughs. "Is that the best you can do?"

No. The best I could do is to tell you no. But even I'm not that heartless. Still, I don't want to do this. "It's been raining all day."

Silence. Nothing but silence.

"Callie? You still there?"

"*It's been raining all day* is your excuse for not going to a ball tonight? I distinctly recall you barreling down the sidewalk for lunch today in the middle of a downpour, June."

"I was very hungry, and if I don't hurry in the rain, I get it on my glasses, which you know I hate."

She giggles. "Here's what we'll do. Since you're obviously reluctant to go, I'll come over and we'll go through your closet together to find a suitable outfit. If I can't find one, then we will order in and watch your favorite scary movies—"

"You hate scary movies. You only like James Bond films."

"Yes, well, other adventure movies, too, but I am willing to suffer for you, if you're willing to suffer for me and go to this thing. But you have to give an honest opinion about the outfits I pick for you. You can't just say you hate everything."

I shrug. "I don't hate what's in my closet."

"Good. I'll be right over."

"Wait, um—"

But she's already hung up. There is no stopping Callie on a mission, and I know I'm getting roped into this. A ball. For fuck's sake, I'm going to a ball. Mom will be so happy when I call her on Sunday and tell her I went to a ball. I should probably at least talk to a guy while I'm there, so I can give her some hope of grandchildren.

The thought unsettles my stomach, so I grab

a ginger ale and crackers before Callie arrives. Then I'm off to my closet to pick something before Callie arrives. The sooner I get in a dress, the sooner this night is over.

-

Chapter 3
JUNE

"What are you wearing?" Callie spits the moment she sees me.

"You said to wear a little black dress."

"You look like you're going to a funeral, not a formal."

"Are you going to critique me from the hall all night?"

She rolls her eyes and walks in wearing a slinky, but classy red dress that hugs her lithe body. "You have crumbs on the boobs of your sweater dress, June."

"Crackers. They'll shake off." I pull at the material a few times, and they crumble to the floor. "See?"

"You're hopeless," she says it in a way that

doesn't make me feel bad. More like she's here to take care of me.

I follow her to my bedroom and flop onto the bed while she digs through my closet. "This is the only black dress I own, so I'm not sure what else you think you'll find in there."

"This wardrobe is a time capsule, June. When was the last time you cleaned out your closet?"

"1986."

She peeks around the corner at me. "You weren't alive in 1986."

"This apartment was my grandmother's. Half that stuff was hers. I've never had the heart to get rid of it, and going by the Golden Girls esthetic of shoulder pads and muumuus, I'm thinking that's the last time she cleaned it out."

She rolls her eyes, then dives back in. "Well, your grandmother had an interesting eye for—god, that's a lot of sequins."

"If you're into the sequins, then you're out of my size. Grandma was tiny." If I spent more time at the gym, I could probably get into her clothes. Not that I wanted to do either of those things. Fifteen-hour days are not conducive to going to the gym, and her clothes are a vintage that is not my style. It's a pity the apartment isn't rent controlled, though. I wouldn't mind paying eighties rent prices. $2500 a month is steep, even for Boston.

Maybe now that I'm not dating anymore, I'll have more time for the gym. Still not wearing Grandma's clothes, though.

"Found it!" The squeaks of hangers announce she's coming out from the rear of the closet and fill me with trepidation. There is nothing good that far back.

"Not sure what—"

The bridesmaid's dress I wore last summer dangles in her hand when she emerges. How she got all the way back there without ruining her hair, I will never know. The dress is a deep blue —not quite navy, but near enough—and has spaghetti straps with a low neckline and a slit up the thigh. Far sexier than anything I normally wear, but my cousin insisted all her bridesmaids wear the same thing.

Callie grins. "You've been holding out on me."

"That is hardly warm enough for this weather."

"We are going from a limo to a mansion and back again. You'll be chilly for a minute, tops."

"I don't have the shoes for it."

She smirks at me. "I already found the pair of nude pumps you wore all of one time ever. The bottoms aren't even scuffed. They'll work just fine."

My final objection sputters out. "You want me in a strapless bra for hours?"

"Or you can go braless. Whatever you like."

I huff and grab the dress. "I'll need your help with my hair and makeup—"

She squeals and claps like a seal. "Yay! Okay, let's get you ready for the party."

My only strapless bra is nude, so I grab the matching underwear, too, and inside of thirty minutes, I'm dressed and sitting in front of my bathroom mirror with Callie doing something painful to my head. But I can't see it yet—she promises it will look nice, but when I was watching her, I kept fidgeting, so she made me turn around. "Your frizz is no joke, June."

"Believe me when I tell you, I know."

"But I am a miracle worker, even with your lack of product. Take a look."

My frizzy curls are straightened and tamed low bun with a few tendrils out to frame my face. She did my makeup, too, and it's under-stated and classy—winged black eyeliner I could never do on my own, and a classic red lip. Nothing over the top, nothing garish. I look polished and elegant.

In short, I look nothing like myself.

"Wow, Callie. If you ever want to quit property law, you could do makeovers."

She giggles, but it's short-lived. "One more thing."

"What's that?"

"No glasses tonight. Contacts only."

"What? Why?"

Callie takes a breath, and I know I'm not going to like what I'm about to hear. "Think of any James Bond movie you have ever seen."

"Huh?"

"Which of the femme fatales wore glasses?"

"That's easy. Ruby Bartlett."

She frowns. "Who?"

"From On Her Majesty's Secret Service."

"Everyone knows the Lazenby one doesn't count, so neither does Ruby Bartlett. Contacts. I know you have them."

In all fairness to Callie, she had too many good points there for me to argue. So, I made the best of it and popped them in, grabbing a bottle of eye drops for the ridiculously tiny purse I have to bring. Honestly, it's an insult to purses to call this black satiny thing a purse. More like a pocket on a thin silver chain. "And I'm no femme fatale. I'm a femme ChapStick at best."

She giggles and practically shoves me out the door. True to her word, there's a limo waiting for us outside. I'd kind of hoped they had driven off—my last escape plan. Instead, we sat in the rear of the luxury car and she poured us two flutes of pricy champagne. "To a wild night of high society fun."

I clink my glass to hers and drink. The good stuff is, in fact, good. "Not sure it'll be a wild night, Callie. I picture little old ladies with tiny purse dogs and wrinkled men with erectile dysfunction in tuxedos."

"Oh, I'm sure they'll be there, too, but that doesn't mean it can't be fun."

"Always with the positivity. Even in this weather."

She laughs. "I love this weather."

"Easy for you to say. You have a shawl."

She slips it off and passes it to me. "It'll look better with your dress than mine, anyway."

"I wasn't saying that to get your shawl, Callie."

"I'm aware. But honestly, it doesn't go with

my neckline and I'm not as cold as you are. Take it."

The black fur was so soft I never wanted to take it off. "It's faux, right?"

"I imagine so. But it was a gift from Daniel, so I never asked."

"I can't wear his gift—"

"Oh, you can and you will, silly. Stay warm while I show off the goods."

I giggle at her. "Right. Like you're trying to attract anyone but Daniel Fisher. I have never seen you so into a guy before."

She smiles like she's on cloud nine. "I'm not sure I've ever been this into a guy before, June. He's a little stodgy at the office, but outside of there, he's …" she sighs. "Well, he's honestly perfect."

"Neglecting to point out that you're dateless because of him tonight—

"So he can be there for his child. I can't fault him for that."

I shrug. "Fair enough. Do you think he's the one?"

She can hardly contain her glee. "I don't know. Maybe? Feels like it's too soon to say, but when I'm with him, it's perfect. We get along great. We like the same things for the most part, but not enough to be boring. And the sex—"

"I do not need to know."

Her smile tells me more than I ever wanted to know. "It should be one of the Seven Deadly Sins, June. It's that good."

I sigh deeply and drink deeper. There is one thing I miss men for, and it is not their conversation skills. "I'm happy for you."

"Then why do you look like you could claw my eyes right out?"

"I swear I am, but your whole giddy school girl vibe is reminding me just how much I miss sex. "

"Even sex with Trent?"

I almost snort-laugh my champagne out of my nose when I choke on that thought. "Uh no. Not with Trent. Maybe that's why I don't miss him. That man could not kiss worth a damn, and the sex … it did not qualify as one of the Seven Deadlies. In fact, it may have qualified as penance for jaywalking."

She giggles. "Sex with Trent was the equivalent of jay walking?"

"No … come to think of it, it sex with Trent was the equivalent of pulling a mattress tag off. Not illegal. Not even a little naughty. It was something no one would even notice unless they were really, really paying attention."

"And you were with him for how long again?"

"Two years. Remember, he broke up with me on our anniversary—"

"When you thought he was going to propose. Right. Sorry to bring it up."

I shrug. "that's the weird thing about it. I should be more pissed off about that, shouldn't I?"

"I gave up *should* a long time ago. Feel how you feel. If you feel numb about it—"

"Not numb. Apathetic. Like, I hope he has a decent life, as long as it's far away from me."

The limo slows to a stop, and I realize I hadn't paid any attention to where we are. But Callie grins and stares out the window. "We have arrived."

-

Chapter 4

JUNE

I'm not sure of the dimensions, but the mansion is enormous by huge, and it's surrounded by a thick forest. We had driven for at least a half an hour, and we're outside of Boston. I'm pretty sure we're in Newton, but without paying attention, I can't say. The mansion is Victorian and dark, but that might just be because it's night. Hard to tell with the minimal lights aimed for walkways and driveways instead of the building itself, so it's underlit and ominous.

"If it weren't for all the people standing around in formalwear, I'd swear this is where Scooby Doo and the gang would find the masked villain."

Callie giggles, and we get out of the limo to stand in the entry line. Thankfully, it's swift, and we're inside the warm, opulent mansion in no time flat. The foyer features a golden and pearl chandelier that makes the entire room glow. Ivory walls with mahogany wainscotting rise to a domed ceiling. The floors are mahogany, too, or at least, they look like it. I was never one for architecture or interior design. But the dark wood floors gleam in the warm light. Black velvet ropes line a path from the entrance to guide us to the left.

It's crowded inside and we're ushered off to the left, slowly shuffling with the crowd to the west wing, according to the hosts who stand by the velvet ropes. To get there, we travel down a wide hall that mimics the look of the foyer. Enormous paintings hang in the hallway. Real art. No reproductions. I have a sneaking suspicion I'm about to be kicked out at any moment, and if I touched one of the paintings, I'd be sent to a deep, dark prison for life.

"This place is like a museum."

Callie laughs, then sees I'm serious. "You read the sign outside, right?"

"No."

"Oh. This is the Chamberlain Museum. It's a historical landmark. The auction is to benefit it."

Glancing around, I note, "Pretty sure they don't need *more* money."

"All of what you see is carefully maintained. If it weren't, this place would fall apart. Buildings this old need a lot of care."

I neglect to point out the money could go to a worthier cause, because Callie is into this. "The museum would be a nice venue for a wedding or something. The pictures would be stunning."

Her head bobs in agreement. "To be honest, I'd sort of hoped to steer the conversation that way with Daniel. Maybe get him to start thinking of weddings. And *me*."

"Callie! It's that serious?"

She takes a long, nervous pause. "I think so."

"Be sure before you start that talk. You can't unstart it."

"I know, I know."

The west wing has several rooms, and a sign marks the location of the auction itself. We walk into a ballroom, and inside, the auction is already active. It's a silent auction, thankfully. Not as brash as a stressful verbal auction with gavel banging and rapid fire bidders. Instead, the walls are lined with tables, featuring their items up for bids. Some have people standing nearby—local celebrities and a politician or two.

"Ballsy to offer yourself up for an auction."

She titters, "Quiet. They'll hear you."

"I'm just saying, Callie. I mean, I know it's for a good cause, but who wants to bid for a lunch with a local news anchor?"

"Look at his bid sheet."

I casually glanced over, trying not to be obvious about it. There was a stack of filled bid sheets in front of him. "I'll be damned."

"You never know what rich people want."

"Speaking of what rich people want, are you bidding on anything?"

"No. I'm saving up for a summer share in the Hamptons for next year."

"Tired of Nantucket?"

She shrugs. "More like, I'm tired of summering with my family every year. I love them to pieces, but if I have to spend another summer listening to my sister whine about everything, I'll *tear* her to pieces."

"A murder in Nantucket?" I feign a gasp. "What would the neighbors say?"

"As if it'd be the first murder there?"

"Of course not, but I imagined you people

brush that sort of thing under the Persian rug. Murder being so impolite, and all that."

She snickers. "I promise not to get her blood on the Persian rugs."

"Pretty sure we passed by a bar on our way in here."

"Shall we?"

"We shall."

So we make our way to the bar two rooms down from the auction ballroom. It is darker than the other rooms—the wainscotting travels up forest green walls instead of ivory and the chandeliers are turned down low. Small high-top tables litter the space, and each of the spindly things is better quality than anything in my home. The bar itself is a long, dark wood thing with a thickly glossed top. After we order, it's time for people watching.

A woman in her mid-thirties comes next to us, ignoring the men ogling her. She orders some kind of whiskey I've never heard of, then turns to face the crowd like we have. Her dress is a floor length nude-toned number that is impossible to ignore.

Callie gives her a quick glance. "Your dress is Matiradonna?"

"You have an eye for fashion. I just returned from Paris last week."

Her lips pinch in curiosity. "She's out of New York."

"Not for her private clients."

It takes a lot to impress Callie, and this woman has done it. "It is all but impossible to get on her list."

"The Maestra has become a good friend over the years. Admittedly, it took some persistence. But I'm no quitter."

"I'm Callie Brown." She thrusts her hand out to the beautiful stranger. "This is June Devlin."

"Camille Cardo. A pleasure to meet you," she says, as she looks us over. Her gaze lingers on me. "Both of you."

"Likewise," I tell her, unsure of what to say to her. Callie is a high-class woman who comes from a good family. A beautiful, preppy girl next door, if that door belonged to a home on Nantucket.

Camille is something else. White, very thin, with glimmering long brown hair that wreaks of money. Her bright green eyes smile even when she doesn't. There's something exotic about her, and I can't put my finger on it.

She knocks back her drink. "That should get me ready for the next auction."

"There's a second auction?" Callie asks.

"Yes, and I'll be taking part, so I'm glad they carry my brand of whiskey. Helps to set the mood."

Now, I'm the nosy one. "Set the mood?"

Her red lips form a perfect O and she stops herself from speaking for a breath. But then she smiles. It's feline and seductive, and if I were a man, I'd be on my knees for this woman. She is wild—it's written all over her. But she tells us, "Never mind. Forget I mentioned it."

Callie laughs. "As if we could now. Come on, you can tell us. We don't know anyone here, anyway."

"The auction is …" She leans forward to speak quietly. "Rather illicit. It's not for you."

I'm halfway to rolling my eyes, but curiosity is a beast. "Camille, we're lawyers. Pretend you gave us a dollar so you have attorney-client privilege."

She laughs musically, then sighs as she smiles. "Very well, then. I suppose I can tell my attorneys anything. This evening, I will be auctioning myself off to some gentleman who will pay an exorbitant fee for my … *time*."

"You're a sex worker?" I whisper, fascinated. I'd always wanted to meet one, but had been too scared to call one up. Not that I wanted to use their services. The idea of sex as an occupation had always intrigued me, though.

"That is one way of seeing it. But I work one night a year, so it's hard to call it that."

"One night a year? That's too good to be true."

She smiles. "You know, they would eat the two of you up at the auction. You have a … freshness about you."

Callie frowns, and I'm not sure if I'm flattered by that depiction or not, but my curiosity has grown into a full thirst-for-knowledge.

-

Chapter 5

ANDERSON

"This is lame. Wanna bounce?" Tag McAllister asks.

"You say that about anything that doesn't involve speed or women," I say, brushing off his whining. We'd come to the bar to dawdle until we could make a well-timed exit. Too many people knew me for us to leave early.

Word would get back to my father, and I'd hear all about it. I could hear him now, "Anderson, your actions reflect on the firm, and we are known for our charity work. When you leave early, it reflects poorly on our family..." He'd go on and I'd tune out, and it would blow up into another argument about familial duty. What I wanted in that regard was immaterial to the old man. It didn't matter that I was bored by the law, or that he knew it. I had responsibilities.

I'd heard the lecture my whole life. Hearing it again was not worth leaving a few hours early.

"Nothing worth bidding on," Tag mutters. "The weather girl is pretty enough, but they always have that plastered, mannequin look to them. Not my thing."

"You'd be bidding on a lunch with her. Not fucking her."

He laughs. "I'd hit it in an hour, tops."

"You've always been so sophisticated, Tag. Hard to imagine why you're single." The truth is Tag was my best friend from childhood, but our styles had diverged in high school in that I grew up, and he opted not to. Not that he needed to. As the youngest son in his family, no one expected much of him.

Not like me.

He shakes off the comment with a laugh. "Single by choice, my friend. Why tie myself down—wait. That doesn't sound so bad." He waggles his brows, then laughs harder.

I chuckle and glance around the bar. The same boring people I see at most charitable functions. Senator Briggs, Mrs. Goldfarb, a stunning woman in a dress designed to make her appear naked…I don't know her. I jut my chin her way subtly, and Tag's quick to look.

He mutters, "Dibs."

"She's all yours."

"Seriously?"

"Have you ever seen me with someone that bony? I mean, she's beautiful, but—"

"Great. More for me." He walks up to her, so I'm on my own.

Finally, a moment of peace.

I have always been a lucky man. Born with a silver spoon, I went to the most exclusive schools, had the best nannies, and I could have gotten into any university I wanted. As the eldest son of Harold West, life came easy to me, though it was packaged with responsibilities. So, perhaps I shouldn't have been taken completely off-guard when I spotted June Devlin at the Chamberlain Charity Auction. Luck had always been on my side, after all.

Except when it came to her. I'd never gotten lucky when it came to June. Figuratively or literally. And it was all my own fault.

We had attended Appleton Academy together, and unfortunately my teenaged self did not understand the racing heart and sweaty palms I had around her. It made me feel awkward and unprepared, and unaccustomed to such things, I made an ass of myself with her.

No. That's too generous. I had been an asshole to her.

She was there on a scholarship, so that had been the first thing I zeroed in on, but it wasn't the last. Her hair, her body, her clothes, anything I could pick apart, I did. I made sport of her, and looking back now, I loathed my younger self.

I'd been cruel to someone who did not remotely deserve it.

To her credit, though, she fought back.

June was not the kind of woman to take criticism. Not even as an awkward teenager herself. She gave it right back to me, and that only deepened my relentless crush. She was witty and sharp, and I adored that about her. Given my privilege, I wasn't used to someone who stood up to me. She was a breath of fresh air.

Now, as a grown man, I still feel like that uncomfortable teenager when I look at her. Over the years, she's become more breathtaking. Her body has curved out with full hips and breasts that own her blue dress. I'm happy to see she isn't shy about showing herself off anymore. At Appleton, her uniform had always been a size or two too big, so she could hide. Something I blamed myself for.

Funny how, had I not picked on her, she probably would have dressed in her correct size, and I could have appreciated her body even more back then. But stupid teenaged boys do stupid teenaged things, I guess.

I need a closer look.

So, I carefully mix into the crowd so she won't see me. With my back to her and her blond friend, I overhear their conversation.

The blond asks, "You can't be thinking about this. Not seriously."

"Callie, what else can I do to make that kind of money?"

Money?

"But … an auction? *That* kind of auction? There has to be a better way."

Out of the corner of my eye, the nude dress woman joins June and Callie. "So, have you thought about it?"

"Pretty much all I can think about right now, Camille," June says, her voice tight.

"Think of it this way. It's one night with some random man, and whatever you want the money for is yours, no questions asked. It's a better return on investment than any date I've ever had."

That auction? She can't seriously be thinking about it. She's a lawyer, for god's sake.

Callie sighs. "I hate to admit it, but she has a point. You wasted two years with Trent with nothing to show for it. In one night, you could pay off your student loans—"

"And my credit card debt. And have money left over. In theory."

Camille adds, "Last year, I made over five hundred thousand dollars. One of the things you have to do going into this is to be honest with yourself. I'm thirty-five this year and I've been doing this for close to a decade, so I don't expect to hit that kind of money again. But I'm hoping for the mid-four hundreds. You're young and new, and those men love novelty. I would think you'd hit at least three hundred, easy."

"Why so low for me compared to you? What is it they like?"

"I was a runway model for a few years. That gets me some clout. You're a lawyer, and forgive me, but there are plenty of people who do not like lawyers."

June nods and shrugs. "Are the men … gross or desperate or something?"

The thought of some other man with his hands on her ... renting her ... it boils my blood. This cannot be happening. I won't allow it.

Camille laughs. "No, not at all. Well, some of them aren't the most attractive, others are well past their prime. But they're respectful and appreciative of us."

"These guys," Callie says, "they're wealthy enough to do this. So, why resort to it?"

"People pay for company for all kinds of reasons. The transactional nature means it's honest—"

"Honest?" she asks incredulously. "They're paying you to pretend to like them."

"Sometimes. But it's not like going on a date where he's not sure why the other person is there. For men of a certain echelon, it's hard for them to know if someone likes them for them or for their money. Difficult to build trust that way. So, when he pays for a night, he knows precisely why we're there, and so do we. But it's not always for physical intimacy."

June frowns at that. "What else?"

"One year, a man asked me to simply hold him while we talked about his life. It was my favorite. Not that I don't enjoy the other kinds of attention, but it was different. Sweeter."

June turns to Callie. "That doesn't sound so bad."

"If you want to do it, I stand by you."

She takes a moment, then chugs Callie's drink. "I want to do this."

"Good. Because the auction is about to start," Camille says. "Let's go." The three of them leave the bar, and I follow.

There is no way on this Earth that I will let some other man pay to put his paws on June Devlin. Tonight, she's mine.

"Thought we weren't leaving yet," Tag says from behind me.

Fuck. I force a smile on when I turn around, but I keep an eye on where the women went to. I had been invited to take part a couple of times over the years, but I am not sure where it is held. The mansion is expansive. I'd never been interested before now—it seemed in poor taste. But at the moment, I don't care. June will not fall into some other man's clutches.

Now to cook up a lie. "I just saw someone I have to speak to. Work stuff. Don't wait up."

"Another merger?"

If I play my cards right. "It remains to be seen. I won't bore you with the details." Knowing what I know now about the woman in the naked dress, I wonder how it went. "You and the bony woman in the nude dress? Did you get her number?"

"Nah. She's taken."

Not yet. "Too bad. Talk to you tomorrow?"

"Yeah. Good luck with your work thing."

"Thanks. I'll take all the luck I can get."

-

Chapter 6
JUNE

I can't believe I'm doing this.

"I can't believe you're doing this," Callie says enthusiastically.

Camille had taken us to what she called a sitting room. Apparently, Victorians believed in a room for everything. This one hosts a few sofas, a chaise, heavy dark brocade curtains, a fireplace which is thankfully burning hot, and short chandeliers for a little more light. The rugs beneath our feet are patterned with flowers of some kind, but I'm too nervous to figure them out. I'd guess roses, considering the era, but right now, they could be cacti for all the attention I can give them.

"Yeah. Um. Me either." My mouth is so dry, no matter how much I drink.

She giggles. "I'm so excited for you. This is wild."

"Not really the wild part that's got me nervous, Callie. It's the sex part. And the judging."

"The sex part I get, but the judging? What judging?"

"Well, aside from society's opinion of this kind of thing, Camille said I'd be on a stage. In front of bidders. Letting them judge whether I'm worth their money. What if I don't make anything? What if no one likes what they see? Wh—"

"Oh, stop! You're so pretty. I know you'll make money."

"Camille was a fucking model, Cal. I am not in her league. We don't even play the same game!"

She giggles at me. "You're psyching yourself out for no good reason."

"No good reason? I'm twice her size!"

"You are exaggerating, and since when are you so self-conscious?"

I huff. "It's not that. Any normal day, I like how I look. But this isn't a normal day. Not even close. I'm going into a room full of strangers and asking them for money so they can have sex with me. If that isn't the ultimate act of ego, I don't know what is. And since Camille is my competition … I must have lost my damn mind."

"First of all, she's not your competition. One guy will go with her. That leaves the rest of them looking for another woman. And the kind of guy who is into her is probably not the kind of guy who is into you. She's thin, you're curvy. Those two types usually result in two different kinds of men, so really, she's not your competition. She's just there."

My worry balloon deflates some. "Okay. You have a good point."

"Second, it's like Camille said. This isn't that different from a date, except you both know what's expected of you, so in reality, that takes a lot of the pressure off. You both know you're getting laid, which means there's no point in worrying about that, and you're not expected to necessarily make small talk and you look fabulous tonight, so you don't have to fret over your appearance. That's like half the work done already. And since you're going into this with your eyes open, it's not like you're meeting the man of your dreams tonight, so again, no pressure to be clever or sexy." She sighs. "Honestly,

I'm a little jealous because that sounds like the best date ever."

I laugh. "What?"

"No pressure to be perfect. You're getting laid. And you go home with a boatload of cash."

"You could sign up, too, you know."

But she shakes her head. "I couldn't do that to Daniel. The bidder could be one of his friends and I wouldn't even know it until I ran into him at a dinner party or something—"

I laugh harder this time. "Oh god. That would be awkward. I can just imagine now. You running into the bidder, the bidder recognizing you, and Daniel asking how you two know each other … worst night ever."

She nods, smiling. "So, I'll have to live vicariously through you. You have to tell me everything afterwards. You know that, right?"

"Pretty sure I'll be signing an NDA for this. I doubt they do this kind of thing without some sort of coverage." With my background, it's hard to ignore the legalities involved here, but I'm trying. I'm also trying to ignore the way my heart keeps clenching in my chest. Not a full-on palpitation, but close. I shouldn't be here—I should be at a cardiologist. Or a neurologist.

Who in their right mind does this? But then Callie's here, acting as though there's nothing to worry about. Maybe she's right.

"Good point about the NDA, but it'd be totally unenforceable."

I shrug. "This whole thing is unenforceable. If Camille hadn't sworn for the validity of this, I'd think it was a scam for rich guys to trick women into bed and not pay them."

She shrugs. "Seems legit, though."

"Camille said my number is six to keep things as anonymous as I want. I don't even have to tell him my name. Do you think the bidders do the same thing?"

She shrugs her slender shoulders again. "Maybe. Or maybe they use code names or something. A pity your number isn't seven."

"Huh?"

"Well, it's almost like you're a spy, and you could have been—"

"Double-oh-seven?" I cannot believe she's Bonding this.

She grins and nods.

And I can't help but laugh at her. "You're such a goober."

"Come on! Think about it. This is the perfect cover for a spy or a sexy assassin. You can totally think of him as some enemy intelligence officer you have to sleep with to get information, and—"

"Did I just get a peek into your sex life with Daniel?"

Her cheeks redden fast. "Um. No."

I snort a laugh at her unconvincing lie. "Uh, huh. Sure. Okay."

"My point is, you can make tonight into whatever you want in your head. He doesn't need to know, and you can pretend he's anyone. I mean, what kind of guy does this?"

"The same could be said for the women. Let's not go there."

"Oh please. Everyone wants money. It's easy to think of what kind of woman would do this. But the guys?" She drifts off for a moment. "They could be here for any reason, really. Hell, maybe they just get off on the idea of paying for it. Or they like outcompeting the other men in the room for the woman they want. Or maybe they hope the woman will do things their wife won't—

"Shit," I bite my lip, "my bidder could be married." Great, so now am I not only freaking out, but also there's the possible guilt to consider. This night just keeps getting better and better.

"Yeah, but I wouldn't worry about it."

"How come?"

"These kinds of people … well, I've known this sort of person my whole life, June. As much as we all try to ignore it, a certain amount of indiscretion is swept under the rug. Wives and their tennis instructors, husbands and their executive assistants, it happens all the time. If he is married, this isn't the first time and it won't be his last, and it's likely that if he's doing this, his wife is doing something just as iffy."

I peer into her eyes and for the first time, I see something less than cheery. "Callie, your parents—

"Oh, right as rain. Not my parents. But my aunts and uncles have all had their own … let's say, *hobbies*. There's a reason my Uncle Marcus spends so much time at the office and Aunt Regina is so good at tennis, and the rest of my aunts and uncles are just as distracted with their own hobbies."

I wonder if she's purposefully ignoring her own parents' affairs, or if they truly are the exception to her rule. But bringing that up now seems cruel. "Ah. Well, I guess it doesn't matter then. Or well, that's what I'll be telling myself, because if I could make enough tonight to pay off my student loans, I'll be thrilled. I might even be able to do what I've always really wanted to do."

"What's that?"

"Start a photography business. It's lame, I know, but—"

"Oh my gosh, that's a great idea!"

I blink at her. "Really?"

"Well, you take the best selfies of anyone I know, and normally, you have that plain-dressed, simple makeup thing going that every genius photographer does. What else do you need?"

"Actually, I looked into it. I have a list of things I need, but as businesses go, it's one with a very low start-up cost. I figure I'd start off with wedding portraiture to get my feet wet, and go from there."

She hugs my shoulders. "I am so proud of you for doing this."

"Really?"

"You're going after what you want, June. Maybe in an unconventional way, but still. Too many people never take this kind of a leap. Or any kind of leap. They just do what's expected of them their whole life and give up on their dreams."

I take a breath. A full one. Since agreeing to this, a weird sense of shame has twisted me up, but hearing that from Callie—the sweetest, most moral person I know—makes all of this easier somehow. "Thank you. That means a lot coming from you."

"Plus, Camille said she works one night a year and makes nearly a half million dollars to live on for the rest of the year. If this goes well, maybe you could do that and live retired for the rest of the year."

"I'll be happy if I can pay off my loans and start a business. I'm not sure I'm up for doing this again." But she has a point. Still, it might not be for me. I'm so nervous I could pee myself right now. "We'll see how tonight goes. Once is a wild night. Annually is a career, and I'm not sure I'm down for that."

"Well, no negative judgment from me either way. I just hope you have a fabulous time and make a ton of cash."

"Me too."

-

Chapter 7

JUNE

"Number six?" A man asks when he walks in.

I glance at Callie, startled. Is this how it works? Camille said we walk on a stage so they can see us. Did he just bid on whoever, sight unseen? "Uh, yes?"

"No need to be nervous yet, dearie. I'm Cesar, and I am the stage manager for the auction, not a bidder. Say goodbye to your friend and follow me, please."

Callie gives my hand a supportive squeeze, then she turns to him. "How long will she be?"

"All night. Are you her ride?"

"I am."

"No need. We will see her home."

Callie's eyes flash with worry. "I am not leaving her here."

He smiles smoothly. In fact, everything about him is smooth. His dark brown skin gleams in the firelight, and he's bald. His charcoal suit is custom—it has to be. It fits him like a second skin. He steps into the room like a dancer on a stage, as though every eye is always on him. He could be in his late twenties or early sixties. It's impossible for me to tell. When he smiles, he dazzles.

"It is good you are such a concerned friend. After she is paid, she will be driven wherever she likes by one of our people. There are no cell phones permitted in the rooms—that could lead to legal issues we all prefer to avoid. The dubious nature of our auction could lead to many unfortunate issues, so to guarantee the anonymity of all involved, everyone is screened before entering the room. But security guards are posted outside the door. If there is any reason whatsoever that she is uncomfortable, all she must do is call out. Nothing is allowed which might stop her from doing so. Safety is our number one priority. Anonymity is also number one."

Callie smirks. "You have two number ones?"

His cheeky smile sets me at ease. "What can I say? I'm greedy. If you'd like to observe the auction, you are welcome to. No sense in making you worry that it's seedy."

"Thank you." She turns to me. "You're absolutely sure about this?"

I want to shout, "No!" and run away, but it's not true. Not completely. I need the money, and unless I want to wait three decades to live the life that I want to live, this is my only option. Somehow, my body is light and heavy at the same time. Thankfully, the nausea has abated, but my heart still thumps my ribs each time I think of what I'm doing. Do I even know what I'm doing? This is nuts. This is not what sane people do.

Oof. That was judgmental. Get your head out of your ass, June. Quit being a chicken and own your choice.

I nod. "It's okay. You can go. I'll text you in the morning to let you know how I am."

"Alright. I'd like to watch the auction."

I'm not sure if that's better or worse. If I make a fool of myself and Callie sees … best not to think about it. Standing on shaking legs, I'm sure I might pass out from nervousness. But I tell him, "Ready."

"Follow me, Six and friend." We travel through a hall into a library. Books line the shelves and a few desks take up the middle of the room. One has a single slip of paper and a pen. But we don't go there. Instead, we go to a bookshelf. He tugs a tome, and the whole bookshelf slides into the floor.

I laugh. "An honest-to-God secret passageway?"

"I love my job." He grins. "Once we go in that hall, you must refrain from commenting. We'll be seeing the auction in progress, and people can hear us if we speak."

Nodding, we follow him into the hallway. It's narrow and dark, and I'd be claustrophobic if I weren't already a bit of a wreck. At the end of the hall, I pick up on voices. He pulls back a sliver of a curtain, and I see it all.

Camille struts and poses on stage—her back is to us, but her nude dress is a dead giveaway. Flattering rose gold lights shine down on her to make her look even more enticing. The audience isn't as well lit. In fact, it's hard to see anyone out there. They're all in shadow, presumably to prevent recognition. Smart. It's not a fast-paced bidding war, or if it is, I can't see it. No paddles go up, but the auctioneer at the left of the stage runs a play-by-play on the microphone as he stares at something in his hand.

"Gray, four-eighty. Diamond, five hundred. Timber, five-twenty-five. Beach, are you certain?" He pauses, as if reading something. "Beach, six hundred…going once. Going twice. Sold to Beach for six hundred." He strikes a gavel, and that is that.

Camille blows a kiss toward the audience.

Cesar turns to me and quietly asks, "You're certain of this?"

"Did she just make six hundred thousand dollars?"

"Yes."

The thought of that kind of money is enough to mute some of my anxiety. "Then I am very certain. Yes."

"Back to the library, then." We make our way back through the secret passageway and to the desk I'd noticed before. Cesar says, "This is a contract, stipulating that fifteen percent of your fee will be paid to the Chamberlain Charity Auction. As you know, historical homes do not preserve themselves."

Callie points out, "This is a lot of liability for just fifteen percent."

"If she would like to donate more, she is more than welcome to."

I chuckle and shake my head. "No, we just think about things from a legal standpoint. We're—"

But he shakes his head. "No identifying details, please. I don't need your occupation, your name, none of that. Not for your first time. You'll sign an X on the line there. It's more of a symbol than a true contract, of course. We cannot legally come after you for the money, considering how it is gained. But given what we do and who we are, we can make life challenging for anyone who wishes to break the contract."

I gulp. "Make life challenging? How?"

He's a mind reader. "Nothing like physical harm, if that's what you're worried about, dearie. But it is easy enough to sort out who is who—the rest of the mansion has security footage of everyone, so identifying our guests is rather simple. After that, it's just a matter of figuring out how to *socially* destroy someone. The wrong thing said in the right ear can make the world fall down around them. Promotions can vanish in the blink of an eye. Things of that nature."

Callie asks, "How often have you had to enforce that part of things?"

"Not even once, and I am grateful for it. I prefer to keep things as friendly as possible."

My hand shakes when I pick up the pen. Symbolic or not, it feels meaningful. My X comes out like two lightning bolts crossing. "Is that clear enough for your purposes?"

He bends down behind the desk and produces a bottle of champagnc and three flutes. As he pours, he says, "Every first timer's is just as scribbled. It's perfectly fine." Then he passes us some champagne. "To Hell. May the way there be as fun as the stay there."

We giggle as we clink our flutes. After a sip, I ask, "So what do *you* get out of all of this?"

"I find the whole thing fascinating, truth be told. To me, the only thing worth understanding is the psychology of why. Why anyone does anything. In a world where sex and money are so readily accessible, why do we still resort to this sort of arrangement? It boggles the mind, really. But the allure of trading money for sex has been with us since time immemorial. One might argue there is a primal desire to do so—that we trade the results of our effort—money—for the one thing we cannot do for ourselves—

sex." He pauses. "Well, sex with someone else, that is."

The champagne must be going to my head, because I giggle again. Callie, too. I shrug. "I guess so."

She says, "What was up with the names out there? It didn't sound like real names."

"Because they are not. They pick their own identities out there. Anonymity."

I nod. "Makes sense. Why don't we?"

"Numbers are easier to keep in order."

"Can I have more champagne?"

He smiles. "Of course, dearie." After filling my flute, he asks, "Without details, can you explain why you are interested in this exchange?"

"The money."

"Not the sex?"

Another giggle pops out of me. "I mean, it could be great or it could be terrible or anything in between, I guess. But the idea of spending one night and making the kind of money that's being thrown around here … that's the draw for me. Is it sex for the other women?"

"Sometimes. Anonymous sex has its own appeal, and the money is a fun bonus for them."

"Am I supposed to call myself Six to my bidder? Like, will he moan, oh, Six, in my ear?"

He laughs. "That is the first time I've been asked that in such a way. You are welcome to call yourself whatever you like, or even let him pick a name for you. But we advise you not to give your real name for obvious reasons."

Callie wonders aloud, "How did the auctioneer know who was bidding what? I didn't see paddles or hear anything."

"It is done through text on burner phones the bidders are given when they walk in." He looks at his phone. "Speaking of, it's time for number six to go on stage. Ready?"

"For this? No. But let's go, anyway."

-

Chapter 8
JUNE

Walking down that dark hall again, my palms are so sweaty I'm convinced they'll drip on stage and my humiliation will be complete. Doesn't matter that it's cool in the hall. My nerves don't understand the temperature. While my palms are pouring, my mouth is dry. I haven't been this anxious since taking the bar.

Cesar smiles. "Last chance to turn back, Six."

It takes everything in me not to take him up on the offer. But I'm facing twenty-eight years of utter drudgery before retirement versus starting a real life of following my dreams, all in exchange for one night of work. The tired feeling I'd begun my night with vanished the moment I chose to do this. The very idea has invigorated me and given me hope. How could I possibly turn my back on it now? "I'm not turning back."

"I'll pull back the curtain and you will step out there. Strut the stage like you own it, because when you're out there, you do. All eyes are on you, and they are grateful for the opportunity to see you. Each of the men in the audience is fascinated by you. Every one of them wants you. All you have to do is show them they are right to want you."

I nod once, trying to let his words soak in.

"When the—"

Footsteps come from behind us, and soon Camille's face comes into view. She beams at me. "I'm so glad you're doing this. You'll have the best time."

Cesar snarks, "Wonderful timing as always, Five."

"Thank you, Cesar," she says, flirting.

He rolls his eyes and smiles. "As I was saying, when it's over, you'll come right back here. We will be watching."

"Why didn't Cam—Five come right back here after?" Callie asks.

"Because this path is for first timers," he

explains. "I always like to check in before they go off with their bidder."

She notes, "Oh. That's nice of you."

"Six, ready?"

I gulp and nod with all the confidence I don't have. "Yes."

He smiles, then pulls back the curtain with himself and the others behind it.

My feet feel like lead. But I do my best to glide out here. What did he say again? They're fascinated. They're here for me … something. I never got a pep talk in a locker room before, but that's what I pictured when he said all of that stuff, and now, I'm in the bright lights on a stage in front of an unknown number of men all ogling me, and I've forgotten everything.

Camille whisper-shouts, "Strut!"

Right. So, I do an imitation of her walk, and I might as well be a baby duck for all the grace I have. A sweaty baby duck, for that matter. God, is my dress clinging to me?

The auctioneer says, "We begin our bidding at the customary fifty."

Shit, we start at fifty? Even if I don't make Camille's money, fifty would be enough to take a good chunk out of my loans.

"Timber, seventy-five."

I got one of Camille's bidders? So much for Callie's theory about us not having any crossover.

"Roswell, one twenty-five."

Interesting name and a good jump.

But then, there's a lull, and I'm instantly humiliated. Should I strut harder? Really put myself out there? God, I feel like an idiot, parading myself back and forth on the stage. Camille looked glamorous doing it. I'm not Camille.

"Apologies, gents, it appears I had a technical difficulty. Brown, one fifty. East, one seventy-five, Marker, two hundred."

Two hundred? Wow!

"Chocolate, two twenty-five. Ambergris, two thirty."

Okay, I'm hovering. But this is one hell of a haul for a night, and my loans would be almost totally paid off. It'll take another year before I can start my business, but I can work with that.

"Timber, two forty-five."

This is so weird. But I think I like it. I get the appeal now. Camille is right—this is fun. Awkward as fuck, but it's fun to know what men think of me. How much of their fortune they are willing to part with just for a single night of my company? That's a turn-on. It's not like being at a bar where you're comparing yourself to every woman around, thinking of them as the enemy. This takes all of that out of the equation. It's brutal, but honest, and I can respect that.

"Roswell, two fifty."

Okay, yeah. Looks like I'm staying at a quarter of a million. Oh my god, some guy wants to pay a quarter of a million to sleep with me. This is the strangest night of my life.

"East, are you sure?" He pauses. "Very well. East, three fifty."

"What the fuck?" I bark.

A few of the bidders laugh at my shock.

The auctioneer ignores me and quickly says, "Timber, three sixty. Roswell, three seventy, East, three eighty." He pauses. "Timber, three eighty-five. East, three ninety."

Oh, my god. What the hell is going on? I'm stuck in the middle of the stage, still too shocked to wrap my brain around what's happening. How did I go from a quarter of a million to three ninety in a matter of seconds?

He waits again, before declaring, "East, you are the winner." He knocks the gavel, and the auction is over.

I'm numb and walking with a numb body is even more awkward than walking with a sweaty one. But Cesar whispers, "Six," and I know where I'm supposed to go. I wobble my way back there, and I'm swallowed up by the curtain and back in the hallway.

Camille pulls me in for a hug, and vaguely, my body registers that it's a little painful. Her ribs dig into my softness. "I'm so happy for you. That was amazing. Clearly East saw something he wanted."

"To make a hundred thousand dollar jump?" Callie asks rhetorically. "Yeah, I'd say so."

"Come along, ladies." Cesar gently corrals us back to the library. Once the bookshelf closes, he asks, "How are you, Six?"

"I'm really not sure. Kinda numb."

"Perfectly normal," Camille declares. "I was too on my first night."

"Really?"

She nods. "It's nerve-wracking to be out there the first time. You never know what to expect. But girl, you killed it."

Callie grins at me. "I am so fucking happy for you."

It's still hitting me in waves. Numb, then

nervous, then numb again. "I'll be done with … with everything I hate about my life. My school loans. My job." I turn to Camille. "Thank you for getting me involved in this."

"Don't thank me yet. You haven't met your bidder."

"Do you think he's gross? Have you met East?"

Cesar says, "They choose a new name every year. She wouldn't know if she's met him."

"Oh."

Callie, ever the girl scout, asks, "What are the next steps? I presume they use condoms—"

"Of course," he says with a nod. "No one wants any unfortunate outcomes. All other details are listed in a letter in a folder in your room. Six, you have the presidential suite for the evening. We like all our first timers to have the best room for their experience. If—"

"It's beautiful," Camille says reassuringly. "You'll love it."

"As I was saying," Cesar tells us, cutting her off with a look, "if you have any needs, we will see to them. Food, water, new clothes, all you have to do is pick up the phone and someone will answer. No need to dial a number. The phone works as an intercom more than a phone—if you dialed out, it would not work."

"I see." But I didn't. "Why not let people dial out?"

"All we need is one person to dial up their friend and tell them about what they're doing for all of this to blow up in everyone's face." He shakes his head. "No sense in risking such a thing."

"Ah."

"You will enter the room first. You will have ten minutes to follow the instructions in the folder. Then, East will join you."

I gulp and let that thought pass through me. Can't focus on him. One thing at a time.

"After the evening has been completed, your money will be delivered to your bank account."

Callie asks, "And how is this handled by the IRS?"

"How she decides to tell them she earned the money is between her, her accountants, and her lawyers. It is not our concern."

"I got a guy," Camille says. "I'll hook you up with him. He can take care of anything."

Numbly, I nod. "Um, okay." Now there's money laundering? Better than the alternative, I guess. Hell, I practically do that on a regular basis at work, but in a legal capacity with appropriate tax shelters.

Cesar passes me one more flute of champagne, and I chug it. "Stay hydrated. Some of our bidders enjoy using enhancement drugs to get their money's worth out of the auction."

"Oh. Well, that makes sense, I guess." Nothing like worrying about my stamina at a time like this. As if I didn't have enough on my mind.

"I will escort you to the presidential suite now."

Nodding, I hug Callie first, and she mumbles into my hair, "Be careful and have a wonderful time."

"I will." I hope.

Camille hugs me next, and her bones dig once more, but I hardly feel them. Another wave of numbness has hit me. She says, "I'll give Callie my info so I can hook you up with my guy for your taxes."

"Thanks again. For all of this."

"I haven't done anything. This is all on you now."

It really, really is, isn't it? I smile stiffly and follow Cesar out to the next bizarre part of my night. Part of me wants to dissociate from all of this and pretend it's not happening, but the bigger part of me wants to be absolutely present for the entire experience. I'm turned on, confused, still kind of numb, and definitely on the verge of something, but I can't tell what.

"Where are we in the mansion? This whole place is disorienting."

"The south wing. Don't worry—when you're in the halls, you're not going to be alone. No one expects you to know where you're going."

I nod and we go down a long hall. It's elegant and ornate, but mostly what I notice are the guards. Two posted at each door. We stop in front of a gilded door.

"Enjoy the presidential suite, Six. This is where I leave you. Remember, you have ten minutes before your bidder arrives. Enjoy." He presses his finger to a lock mechanism, and the door clicks open. I take a deep breath and walk in.

-

Chapter 9

JUNE

The first thing I notice is the smell, probably because I'm on the verge of hyperventilating. The air smells like cinnamon, and it triggers the memory of a sex tips article I'd read once that talked about cinnamon enhancing the blood flow for male genitalia, so it encouraged women to bake something with cinnamon in it when a guy comes to visit.

My memory is clicking along weirdly tonight, but given the circumstances, it gets a pass.

I'd thought the rest of the place was opulent. This room gives new meaning to the word. It's like stepping into a royal bedroom. It's grand and luxurious, down to the last detail. I want to absorb them all, but then Cesar's words ring in my head. Ten minutes before my bidder arrives.

A red folder sits on the ornate ivory desk in the corner. It's small and thick, like the kind restaurants use to conceal the bill. Inside, I learn President Grover Cleveland had once slept here. Huh. I'm instructed to go to the attached bathroom and prepare myself in whatever way I desire, which I take to mean to quickly swab off for hygiene.

I hope he has to do that, too. *Nothing worse than a sweaty dude climbing all over you. Oh my god. Some dude is going to be climbing all over me soon. There goes the dry mouth again.*

Per the list, check out is at seven in the morning, but if he wants to leave earlier, he can. A grandfather clock says it's midnight now, and I struggle not to get lost in calculating my hourly rate.

Stay present.

The instructions say I've signed up to do whatever he wants, and there are a variety of lubricants and toys in the nightstands, but absolutely no bondage is permitted for safety reasons.

They really have thought of everything, haven't they?

Also, no extra people will be involved. I

hadn't thought of that, but I guess it's a relief. Tonight is going to be strange enough without adding a three-way into the mix. But with him being able to leave whenever he wants, I wonder if that means he could have bid on more than one woman. I mean, no reason not to—not like he's mine for the night or something. But since he'll be here in ten—no, nine minutes now—I wonder if I get first dibs or if he's already been with someone else tonight.

Huh. Not sure if that bugs me. But it doesn't really matter, does it?

At the very bottom of the instructions, it reads, "You are to be completely nude when your bidder arrives."

Somehow that line makes all of this realer than real. I take a deep breath, blow it out in a puff, and hurry to the bathroom. It's pretty and elegant, and I have absolutely no bandwidth to revel in any of it, because I'm in a panicked hurry. I pee and use the softest towels I have ever touched to wipe down the rest of my body. Once that's done, I'm already naked, so I hang my clothes in the closet and dash to the bed to shove under the covers. An appropriate place to hide, I think.

Thankfully, the mattress is much more

modern than the rest of the furniture. In fact, I doubt it's ever been slept on. No divots and it's super comfy. The sheets are smooth and cool, and if I weren't so nervous, I'd think I was in for a night of the best sleep of my life.

But I am nervous and I'm sure I won't get any sleep tonight. Not if he's got erectile dysfunction pills.

From the bed, I can take in my surroundings. Everything is old as dirt. I'm guessing it's all Victorian, like the rest of the place. There's scrollwork on the corners of things and gold accents abound. The bed itself has a curtain thing behind the headboard, as though I am on a different kind of stage and about to perform.

Which, in some ways, I am.

The rug beneath the bed had been super soft, and it had a pattern at the edges—some kind of old timey vine thing. It's all so old that I'm starting to worry about my bidder. Do they keep all of this antique stuff around so he won't feel so old?

An unsettling thought.

Or maybe it's so pretty in here so the women can have something nice to look at instead of her ugly bidder. Maybe that's why the lights are so low. Because wealthy men can obviously get laid easily, so why else would they have to resort to this?

On a whim, I dart out of the bed and lower the lights more. I'm not sure I want to know what he looks like. Not that I'm shallow—not much, anyway—but, besides the possibility of him being unattractive, some added anonymity seems like a good thing. Unfortunately, I cannot figure out how to lower the lights over the bed. They're dim enough to be flattering, but not low enough to make me invisible. Hopefully, he'll climb on top of me and remain backlit, so I don't have to know who he is.

Thankfully, there's no chance he's someone I know. I don't know anyone with this kind of money. Sure, there's the clientele at the law firm, but most of them are so old they wouldn't possibly—

Oh god. What if it's a client?

Then, I definitely don't want to know if it is. I'm glad I turned the lights down. Not dark enough to stumble, but dark enough to conceal. Better for everyone involved, really. And hell, does it really matter if it's a work client? I'm quitting the law firm, anyway.

With that thought, I'm grinning. My first smile since I walked into the presidential suite to sell my body to a stranger. Huh. I wonder how long this auction has been going on. Maybe President Cleveland slept here because he was a bidder. Wouldn't that be an interesting historical footnote?

My smile dies when I wonder if this is going to be terrible. He could have bad breath or be a bad kisser, or worse, not want to kiss at all. What if he's too rough or not rough enough? Maybe he's a biter. Security is out there, but—

I am panicking over nothing. This will be great. Camille wouldn't do this every year if it sucked. She doesn't strike me as the kind of woman to put up with anything she doesn't like.

Besides, if the sex is bad, who cares? I've had plenty of bad sex, especially in the last two years. *Thanks, Trent, for lowering my standards when it comes to sex.* At least I'm getting paid for it this time.

Three ninety. I'll pay off my loans, quit my job, and start my real life as a photographer. Mom will ask how I did all that, and I'll lie and tell her I got a bonus at work. I don't enjoy lying to her, but if I told her the truth, I'd never hear the end of it, and she doesn't need to know about any of this.

Ever.

She doesn't need to know her daughter had sex for money. I'd thought it was awkward when Mom caught me making out with Billy Crane in my room when we were supposed to be studying. I'm not sure what level of awkward comes from her finding out something like this, but it would be much worse than that, I am sure of it.

Sitting alone and naked in the bed reminds me of every gynecology visit I've ever had. There's a sexy thought to get me in the mood. Better sarcastic than so anxious I might pass out, though, and no joking will shake this clinical feeling.

I'm under a drape, a little cold, and very, very uncomfortable. Just like the doctor's office. I don't know how Camille does this every year. Sure, the money is amazing and I'm kind of aroused in a weird way at the moment, but doing this more than once would be too much. I'd make a terrible professional escort. Those women are amazing to me. So much braver than I am.

I've read accounts of their lives. It tracks with what Camille said—every guy likes something different. Some like feet, some like you to pet their head and tell them they're a good boy, others want to get straight to business. I'm kind of hoping for the latter, because I don't think I could stop giggling if he wanted to lick my feet. Maybe that's why they make the room smell like cinnamon. So we don't feel self-conscious when a guy wants to lick our feet.

My champagne buzz makes me giggle at the oddness of the thought and of my night, when a knock at the door makes me jump. Show time.

-

Chapter 10

JUNE

I expect him to barge in, not knock. What the hell do I say?

But instead, he asks through the door, "May I come in?"

I want to tell him something tacky like, "It's your dime," but instead, my heart lodges in my throat, and I can't get anything out for a breath. What the fuck am I doing with my life? I'm naked and trembling and about to see a strange man in the dark who paid a ridiculous amount of money to sleep with me. It feels like the last chance to get off this crazy train.

But I need that money.

And some naughty part of me is way more into this than I want to admit.

I clear my throat. "Yes, come in."

The door opens and the faint light from the hall frames him so I can't see his face. All I can make out are the outlines of a black tuxedo and short hair. At least he has hair. Probably not a thousand years old. Thank God. He's quite tall, with narrow hips and broad shoulders, but that's all I can tell about him. He closes the door behind himself, and I'm alone in the room with a complete stranger.

Security is just outside. Relax.

He doesn't march to the bed to have his filthy way with me. Instead, he stays near the door, like he might run out of the room. He liked me well enough to bid. Now that he has me, what does he want to do with me?

His voice is deep. "Before things progress, I have some questions."

"Okay."

"You are a beautiful woman. You could have any man you wanted. Why resort to such an arrangement?"

I could tell him it's the money, but that seems cheap and I doubt that's a turn-on for him. It's also a little embarrassing. Here's this man with all the money in the world. He wouldn't understand the reasons people would sell themselves. He's never struggled in his life,

I'm sure of it. How could he understand the truth?

Besides, it's not the only reason. Not really. Just sitting here, waiting for him to make his move, I'm on edge, and I kind of like it. But it's embarrassing to admit that to myself and makes my stomach flip when I think about it.

So, I pull my shoulders back to let the sheet hang on my tits. Covered, but revealing at the same time. Let him think I'm into this. Because a part of me is. I try for a seductive register in my voice and hope the words don't squeak out of me. "It sounded like something fun to do. Life is short. Might as well enjoy it while we can, right?"

"I suppose that's true." He strolls to the desk and leans on the edge with his arms folded over his chest. "But is that the only reason? Life is short?"

What is he driving at? "Do I need another?"

"No."

"Why did *you* agree to this arrangement?" Maybe I shouldn't ask that question, but I'm curious and he brought it up.

He takes a beat, and I'm not sure he'll answer me. "You strike me as the kind of woman who enjoys a mystery. Perhaps I should keep that detail to myself."

Not answering. Great. I'll die of curiosity. "Generally, I prefer answers."

"Have you always?"

Odd question. "Well, yes."

"Hmm." He shifts his stance, arms at his sides. "I recognize this is a peculiar situation. But for me to fully enjoy myself, I'd like to know some things about you, if you'll permit it."

"That depends on the questions."

"Favorite movie genre?"

"Horror."

Favorite color?

"Green."

"Green like mint or green like a prep school uniform?"

That question stops me in my tracks. My prep school uniform was green plaid. There's no way he could know that, but the question gives me pause. "Mint."

He nods once. "Did you have a cat or a dog as a child?"

A cat. "A dog."

"Is that mattress as firm as it looks?"

Now we're getting somewhere. Maybe. Do I want this to get somewhere? "Yes."

"Are you a cop?"

I laugh. "After all the hoops you've gone through to get me here, that's your question?"

"Answer it, please."

"No. I'm not. But speaking as someone with an extensive legal background, even if I were a cop, I could lie to you about it, so that question wouldn't save you from legalities."

"I'm aware. Mostly, I wanted to know if you'd tell me." His voice has a taunting tone to it, and for some reason, that triggers a memory.

I can't sort it out, though. Is it the teasing that's jogging my memory, or is it something else? I used to get bullied a lot when I was younger, so it's probably just the teasing aspect of his voice. Hard to be the poor kid in a pricy prep school. Those mental scars don't ever really go away. Thankfully, they fade with years and distance, and all my bullies were too fabulously wealthy to stay in Boston for long after graduation.

"Can I ask you a question?"

He shrugs, and even though he's in the dark and in a tux, I can tell his shoulders are huge. "Go ahead."

"Your favorite movie genre."

"I like mysteries."

"Favorite color?"

He lets out a slight chuckle. "I hesitate to say it."

"Your favorite color is too personal or something?"

By his tone, I'd swear he's smirking. "My favorite color is the faint pink from when a woman blushes. It tells you the color of certain other parts of her when she's excited. If you can get her to blush, you can see her *everywhere*, all at once."

And with that, my cheeks flush. Dammit. Well, it's not like he wasn't going to see me *every-where*, anyway. "You're quite the pervert."

He laughs, and it triggers something else in my mind. I'd swear I know that laugh. He says, "I prefer to think of myself as an aficionado of women. But that is also why I hesitated to answer the question. Some take offense."

"Given the circumstances surrounding our meeting, I'd say it's hard to offend me."

His voice slips even deeper. Almost ominous when he says, "I hope that's true."

"What's that mean?" What kinky shit is this guy into? Somehow, my champagne buzz vanishes completely with the worry of what he may want from me.

"A trifle, nothing more," he says as he stands straight. "I have two more questions and then we can decide how to proceed."

"Um, okay."

"What would you like me to call you for the evening?"

I swallow and try to think of a name. But my brain is utterly blank at the moment. It goes alongside the waves of numbness, though they've slowed down. Right now, most of what I feel is trepidation. The only thought that comes to mind is, "Six."

"Why did you lie to me about having a dog?"

How in the fuck does he know I lied? "What makes you think I lied about that? I have no reason to lie to you."

"You have a tell, Six. You said horror movies with no hesitation. Same for green. But when you said you'd had a dog, you sat up straighter, like you were trying to convince me with your confidence. You've never done this before, have you?"

"Does it matter?"

He pauses. His voice is tight when he says, "It matters to me."

Whatever else he's said tonight, *that* I believe.

"So what if I haven't? Does that ruin it for you? I'm not as experienced in this realm as you'd hoped?"

He shakes his head. "Not at all."

"So, you're *more* into it if I haven't done this before? Some kind of conquest thing for you?"

He laughs. "No. Far from it."

"Then why do you care if I've done this before?"

He steps out of the shadows, and I know why he cares. He's here to torture me.

Chapter 11

JUNE

My heart stops, and when it starts up again, blood rushes through me in a tsunami. I struggle to remain on the bed. I want to run out the door, but being naked stops me from doing so. If this had happened the last time I saw him, I would have been utterly humiliated. Right now, though, all I feel is rage.

I tighten the sheets around me. There should be miles between us, oceans would be better. Right now, the only thing between us is this thin sheet, so I cling to it. "Get the fuck out!"

"No, I won't be doing that just yet, thank you."

"What are you doing here, Anderson?"

"You know what I'm doing here, June," he

says with that easy confidence that sets my teeth on edge.

He always had that confidence. Even when we were teenagers in prep school. Back then, he had bullied me into making my teenage years the most miserable they could possibly be. Picking on my frizzy hair, my ample curves, my name. June Devlin became June the Devil, Junior Mints, June bug, and one particularly mean day at lunch, Spoon, for how I was shoveling it in. Anything to make me feel less-than.

Everything Anderson West did, he did it to torture me. I was his favorite to pick on, and I couldn't tell if it was because I was just that lucky or because I fought back. The other kids he picked on didn't. But I couldn't just sit there and take it.

And I'm not taking it today.

"What I know is you better leave right now, or I will call security to drag you out before my date gets here."

He smirks and shakes his head before running his fingers through his thick, black hair. That smirk makes his bright blue eyes sparkle and a dimple on his cheek deepen. The bastard has grown into his looks—there is no denying that. His tux is missing a bowtie, his shirt open at his throat, framing his muscular neck. From his strong jaw to his athletic body, Anderson West is the quintessential handsome multimillionaire—

Wait. No. He can't be my bidder. Life can't be that cruel. Can it?

"I hate to be the bearer of bad news, June, but I am your winning bidder."

The news is almost enough to get me out of the sheet, naked or not. I gulp and ask, "You're East?"

He boyishly shrugs. "I'd worried such a pseudonym might give me away, but I was in a cheeky mood."

"Why the fuck are you here, Anderson?"

"I bought you. For the night. I thought they explained what the auction was for—"

"Don't be a smart ass. Tell me why you really did it."

His smirk still penetrates me. Just like when we were younger. He was this handsome, wealthy boy who I'd have had a crush on, had he not been an utter asshole back then. I always felt insufficient around him. Either I wasn't pretty enough or rich enough to be in his presence.

There was the time he called me a loud

breather—like I breathed wrong. What the fuck does that even mean? At the time, I merely asked, "Oh, like your mom?" and walked away.

Anderson shifts his weight. "Is it so unbelievable that I'd want to spend the night with you?"

"You weren't funny back in the day, and you're not funny now. Is that what this is? This is all just a big joke to you? Did you do this to point out how poor I am in comparison to *you*? To make fun of me for resorting to this?"

His lips smooth into a patient line, and he comes toward the bed, unbuttoning his tuxedo jacket. I curl my feet up from the end of the bed as he sits there. Taking up my space. Like he's owed it. Screw that. I nudge him with my feet beneath the blanket, so he gets up, then moves to the other side and sits next to me.

This is worse. I shouldn't have kicked him. He'd be further away if I hadn't kicked him. Now he's close enough for me to smell his oceany cologne.

"I didn't do this to make fun of you in any way, June. Not at all."

"Then why?" I blurt between gritted teeth.

"Would you believe me if I said I did it to spend time with you?"

A sharp cackle jumps out of my soul.

"Would you believe me if I said there is a unicorn in the room with us right now?"

"I've missed that wit, June."

"You know what, Anderson? I always knew you were a sadistic bastard, but this is a new low. Even for you."

His rough voice purrs, "Even for *me*?"

"You are the guy who had his friend call the school to tell me my cat had died as a joke. So yeah, even for you, this is fucking low."

"I am sorry for that, June. And for so much more. I—"

"This isn't the time for your confession, Anderson! Do you think I give a shit about your guilt? After everything you put me through?"

To his credit, he blinks and stays silent for a solid minute. "Probably not. But I won the auction to spend time with you. That's real."

"I don't believe you."

He takes a deep breath and forces it out in a huff. "I—"

"What do you want?"

"Nothing."

"I don't believe you."

He laughs and shakes his head at me. "You were always smarter."

"And kinder."

"No, not to me, you weren't—"

"You didn't deserve kindness. You deserved wrath."

"Yeah. I did." He rakes his fingers through his hair. "I earned whatever shit you gave me, June. And more. I was an asshole to you. A punk kid who didn't understand—"

"I. Don't. Fucking. Care. Your excuses are just that. Excuses. You didn't see anyone else being that awful to other people. Just you and that twerp who followed you around all the time—"

"Tag."

I roll my eyes at him. "Like that's even his real name."

"Oh, it is. Well, it's his name, anyway."

"Sure, whatever. You two were nightmare fuel for me for years. And then, to see you at college? It was like being stalked by my own personal bully. Because that's what it was. So, to have you come in here and try to talk to me like you're a human being now … no. Just no."

"If—"

"Throwing your money around doesn't get you my time. Not my forgiveness, either."

He closes his eyes and takes another breath to steady himself.

His lips pull into another smirk. "You always had a mouth on you." His eyes flicker to my lips before he meets my gaze. "A pity I didn't appreciate that more when we were younger."

Why is he being so soft on me right now? It makes no sense. Anderson couldn't keep a prank going this long back then. That was why he had to have Tag call the school about my cat—when a joke had gone on too long, Anderson would always start laughing. It was the only reason I survived his bullshit back then. He was all malice, but had no stamina to keep going. He preferred the hit-and-run style. A bra strap pull here, an insult there. Nothing that took this kind of planning.

Maybe he's developed more of a backbone for this kind of thing.

"Are there cameras in the room or something?" I ask as I look around. "Some kind of feed going to the internet so you can broadcast my desperate disgrace around the world? Because if so, I've already run to the bed naked, so you can stop this bullshit regretful act. You got me. I'm naked and embarrassed for the world. Congratulations, asshole."

"No. Nothing like that."

If that's true, good. If not, fuck him. But

also, if not, then why? I still need that money, as much as I'd like to leave. Of course, then the question becomes, if he's here for real, then can I even do this? With *him*, of all people? A night with my bully in exchange for twenty-eight years of my life … can I say no to that just for the sake of my pride?

"You still haven't told me why you're here, Anderson. The real reason."

"I came for you, June."

Either he's learned how to be a better liar over the years, or something else is going on.

Chapter 12
ANDERSON

"Yeah, you keep saying that, but why?" she snaps.

Even the snap in her voice gets to me. When she's angry, her deep brown eyes smolder. Her voice gets low, and there's a growl to it that makes me want to grab her for a kiss. The angrier I make her, the more she reacts, and the more she reacts, the more I want her.

It's a vicious cycle. How can I explain this to her succinctly?

"The answer remains the same. I'm here for you, June."

"Liar!"

It's my own fault that she hates me. I am self-aware enough to know that. I had tormented her for years, and though she always gave as good as she got, it left a mark. Clearly. Otherwise, she wouldn't spit venom at me with every word coming out of her perfect mouth.

"If I could wring the neck of my teenaged self for what he did to you, I would—"

"Don't do me any favors."

"I mean it."

She rolls her eyes and glances away. "And don't talk about your teenaged self like it's someone else. You're one and the same. You're still the boy who tried to make me hate myself."

"I never wanted that—

"Then why did you treat me like garbage?" she snarls when she whips her head around.

Because I was a foolish boy who liked you and didn't know how to handle it. "Because I was a stereotypical rich kid who was an asshole to everyone."

She studies me for a moment. The snarl is gone from her voice, replaced by ice. "You and I are little more than strangers, Anderson. So, if you lie to me, so be it. But don't lie to yourself, too."

"I am being honest."

"Not even close. If you think you were an asshole to everyone, then you're wrong." June

Devlin has not only grown more beautiful over the years but also more baffling.

"Being an expert on myself, I must say you've read me wrong. I made it my mission to be an asshole to everyone at school. I'm surprised you don't remember that. You, of all people, should."

She stares into my eyes and says, "Kalen Black."

How does she even know about that? I force myself not to react. "What's that? A new Porsche color?"

"Don't. Don't play the role of the rich playboy with me. I know about what you did for Kalen. How you found out about his family being unable to pay for his tuition, how you got your father to secretly pay for it, and how your father made you work the entire summer after graduation to repay him, all so Kalen could graduate on time. You missed an extravagant trip to Paris with your snooty friends because of working for your dad that summer." She knows everything. But how?

I mumble, "Not just Paris. Athens and Rome, too."

"So telling *me* you were just some cliched,

asshole, rich kid is a lie. Telling *yourself* that story is delusional."

"How do you even know about all that?"

She flashes a wicked smile, and god, the curve of her lips sends a throb through me that is hard to deny. June slyly says, "I might be poor compared to you, but I still have my resources."

It helps that the sheet clings to her breasts like custom lingerie. Her smirk, her tits, knowing she's naked under there, it's all enough to make me hard. I shift in my seat to relieve the pressure, but it doesn't work, so I get up and pace with my back to her. Can't let her see how much she affects me. "You shouldn't know this. Kalen doesn't even know who did it."

"No. He doesn't. I never told him."

"So—'

"Since I've proved you weren't the self-centered asshole you pretended to be, tell me the truth for once in your life, Anderson. Why were you cruel to me?"

I can't do that. The thought of telling her the truth makes my erection die. If I tell her, then she holds all the cards in this, and I am not one to give someone else the upper hand. Ever. So, I face her and shrug. "Why not?"

Her face twists into something like rage

given human form. "Why not? That's all it took for you to make my life a living hell? A whim?"

"Can't we just chalk it up to me being an asshole kid who didn't understand what he was doing at the time?" Because I sure as hell didn't. Not really.

"No! You knew exactly what you were doing!"

"Truly, I did not. I was fifteen! How could I have known how much this would haunt you—"

"We were surrounded by anti-bullying PSAs! It was everywhere in school! You weren't as smart as me, but you were smart enough to read the signs!" As she shouts, her breasts heave with every word, and I know I was trying to make a point a minute ago, but damn if I can remember it. She snaps her fingers. "Are you even in there?"

"Uh, yeah. Look—"

"No, you look. Tell me why you helped Kalen."

"We're back on that?"

She stares up at me. "I'm waiting."

Another uncomfortable memory. "He didn't deserve not to graduate on time. Our private school was small. It didn't feel right for the rest of us to graduate without him. He was a good kid, and he worked hard. Just needed a break."

"He wasn't your friend. You didn't know him. So, I ask again. Why?"

"Exactly what I just said."

"You did a good deed that cost you something important to you, strictly because you could. That's what you're saying?"

I gulp and shrug. "Yeah."

"Then explain to me why he got your mercy, and I got your torture from the moment I met you. The first thing you ever said to me was, 'Nice shirt. Does it come in women's?' How come Kalen got this other side of you when I didn't?" Her voice cracks, but she holds it together to add the stinger, "Was I just that *special*?"

I want to say *yes, in every way imaginable.*

But she's close to something she doesn't want to do, and I will stop her from it. June would hate herself forever if she cried in front of me. She has too much pride for that. I have to redirect her, and the fastest way to do that is to be the arrogant asshole she thinks I am.

But just in case she needs to wipe a tear, I turn my back to her again. I slip off my tuxedo coat and drape it over the back of the desk chair long enough for her to straighten herself up, and tell her, "I tormented you and became your nightmare fuel. I made you hate school, hate life, too, I'm sure. With a single sentence, I ruined every moment between us. But for me, it was … any other day." I give a half shrug as I turn to her. "You weren't special, June. You were just another target."

Her tears have cleared. The rage is back. Good. She can hate me as much as she wants. She always has. But at least she won't hate herself in the morning.

"You're lying again."

"I am not—"

"Yes, you are."

"This conversation will get us nowhere fast."

She huffs a laugh. "We weren't going anywhere, anyway."

A shameful fact. I shouldn't be trading barbs with her or dodging questions. I should be seducing her. Isn't that the point of all this? But I can't do that. She's not just some woman to seduce and disregard. She's June. The girl I crushed on for years. The woman I wanted in college. How could I just fuck her and leave her behind like all the rest?

So, I muster an excuse to keep her here. "Are you hungry?"

"What?"

"We're not going anywhere, as you pointed out, and I'm famished. Everything is included in your asking price, so it's on me, so to speak." I smirk at her. "Let me buy you breakfast."

She laughs once, incredulously. "This has got to be the weirdest prank you have ever pulled."

"What?"

"Why do you think I brought up the stuff with Kalen? Besides proving my point that you actually knew what you were doing back then, I wanted to get it out there, in case this *is* all being broadcast online."

I grin. Can't help it. "Clever girl."

"So, it *is*—"

"No. I'm just impressed that you thought to do that. Telling the one thing that could have ruined my reputation as the class jerk ... well done. But this isn't being broadcast, and it's not some over-the-top, elaborate hoax to embarrass you, June. This is just a night brought on by strange coincidences."

I want to ask how she afforded the ticket to the fundraiser in the first place. It's very exclusive, and obviously, she didn't bring a date or she wouldn't be here with me now. But if I ask anything about money, she'll get even more pissed off, and not the good kind.

"So, breakfast?"

"Sure. I could eat." But her brow furrows in suspicion.

That's fine. I can work with suspicion. I call down and order whatever normal people eat for breakfast. June doesn't seem the type to enjoy my usual protein shake and power bar combo for breakfast. Especially when she adds, "And French toast, too."

"You got it." I add that, two bottles of champagne, and hang up, content that she'll at least stay for breakfast.

"Did you order all of that to see me stuff myself?"

I laugh and shake my head. "I ordered all of that because I like variety."

"Yeah, I bet. You look like you've never tasted bacon in your life. No wonder you were such a miserable asshole in school."

Her snarky side makes me smile. "I do, in fact, enjoy bacon on occasion, but usually on a burger. Not for breakfast."

"A burger? I thought that was peasant food.

That's what you told me when I got one in the cafeteria."

"Your memory is impressive. You ever think of going on a game show or something?"

She laughs. "I cannot believe I'm sitting here and talking to you. While I'm naked."

"You're not naked. You're in a sheet. It's practically a dress." I shrug.

"It's white, and I am aware of how thin the material is, Anderson."

"So am I."

Her cheeks flush pink, and I memorize the color. It's as close as I'll ever get to seeing her naked for real. There's no way she'd ever … but the look in her eyes says something else. An unspoken tension builds frisson in the air, and I am dying to make a move. Just then, someone knocks, shattering the moment.

"I'll get that." Turning the lights up a little, I reach for the door.

"You better. I'm not leaving this bed this naked."

Not *yet*. I roll the food cart from the hall into the room. No sense in embarrassing her further by letting the attendant bring it in. By the time I look up, she's tucked the sheet in on itself around her body.

Should I tell her to get dressed? If I do that, she might think I'm not interested in getting what I paid for, which is not, strictly speaking, the truth. But I'd rather *earn* sex with June, not just pay for it. Hell, I'd give her the money if she asked for it. A small price to pay for what I'd done to her.

Am I a lech for keeping her scantily clad? Meh. I've been called worse. By her. So, instead of offering her clothes, I make her a plate, then one for myself, and sit on the bed bedside her to eat.

"What made you come to Boston U? You could have gone anywhere, Anderson. You had the grades, the money. Why there?"

Because you were there. "Because my father wanted another Harvard man in the family, and at the time, I lived to disappoint him."

She laughs, and it might be the first time I've ever earned a genuine laugh from her. It's nice. Especially because it makes the sheet slip a little. So, I pour her some champagne to keep her laughing.

Chapter 13
JUNE

"Does being daddy's little disappointment still satisfy your urge to be bad, Anderson?" Okay, that was more flirtatious than I meant it to be. Maybe the champagne buzz hasn't worn off. In fact, after two glasses with him on a nearly empty stomach, it's hitting me more than I care to admit. At least the French toast doesn't come with any sexual connotations.

He arches a brow at me, then smirks, and dammit, he's gotta stop doing that. It's starting to curl my toes. "I gave up on rebellion against him a long time ago. Mostly. In fact, I work at the family firm now. Just like he always wanted."

"My god, you? Doing something normal? Say it isn't so."

He laughs, and when he laughs without his

trademark teasing edge to it, it's sexy. "I'll have you know I do all kinds of normal things these days. I clean my apartment—"

"Yourself?"

"Well, not the deep cleaning, but I *do* pick up after myself. I grocery shop, I pay my taxes … it's almost as if I'm an adult."

I roughly snort a laugh, which I'm sure makes me the sexiest call girl ever. Burying my face in my hands, I laugh again. "Oh my god. Let me have it. I know you want to say something about that."

"Nah. Too easy."

He laughs again. "Who knew pancakes were this good?"

"Um, everyone without abs."

He grins and dips his finger into the left-over maple syrup and butter from my French toast on my plate before sucking it clean. "Clearly, abs are overrated. If normal food tastes this good, I'm ready to lose them."

"Don't go doing anything rash."

"Oh, I don't know about that. One naughty night of doing whatever I want doesn't seem like enough to bring such dire consequences." At this point, I'm not sure if he means the abs or me, but I'm pretty sure there's no air in the room anymore.

I finish my flute, and he's filling it before I can even object. Oh well. More for me.

"Let me take that," he says it as he grabs my plate. Then he takes it to the trolley. "Do you want some more? There's fruit and whipped cream, if you want something sweet."

I gulp. "Berries with whipped cream, if they have them."

"Coming right up."

"Why are you waiting on me?"

"Because I didn't think you'd want to leave the bed in that sheer sheet."

I look down. Yup. He's definitely seen the outline of, well, everything. Oh well. More champagne will make this less embarrassing. I hope.

When he sits next to me, he's delivered a plate full of the biggest, reddest strawberries I've ever seen and a bowl of fresh whipped cream. I'm not even hungry anymore, but my mouth waters at the sight. Swiping a berry through the cream, I tell him, "It's thoughtful of you to get my plates for me, Anderson."

"I'm trying something new."

"No, you're not. See, I don't think you were

as much of an asshole as I would have liked you to be."

"You wanted me to be an asshole?"

I shrug, and can't help but notice that when I do, his eyes focus on my chest. Bully or not, he likes some parts of me. "If you were just a pure asshole, then I could hate you. But you're a complicated asshole, and that makes everything else complicated, too."

"You're seeing what you think you should see. I'm a purebred, grade A asshole, June."

"Do you want me to bring up Kalen again?"

He looks away and grabs a berry for himself. After dipping it into the whipped cream and taking a bite, his eyes roll back. "My god, that's delicious."

I giggle. "A tasty way to change the topic?"

"Only if you let it stay changed."

"I suppose I can do that for you. But you'll have to do something for me."

He swallows, then looks me over. When his eyes drag over my chest, my nipples harden from the attention. Stupid body. Finally, he meets my gaze. "Name it."

"Unbutton the next button on your shirt. It's practically strangling me from here."

He laughs and unbuttons it. "Better?"

"Yes. Thank you."

"Stud, by the way."

I blink at him, then take another swig of champagne. "Excuse me?"

"On a tuxedo shirt, the buttons are called studs. Not buttons."

"Oh. The buttons. Right."

He smirks, and my libido stirs. *Seriously, body, we hate this guy. Stop that.* But it might make things easier if I give in to what my body wants. If I just go with the flow. This isn't some elaborate prank—I'm almost completely sure of that. We've been in here for over an hour—nearly two now—and nothing's happened.

Which is also a problem.

If I don't do this soon, he can claim breach of contract, such as it is. Sure, Camille said she had that cuddle guy, but this is my first time doing this, and I'm sure they don't give a free pass to first timers. Either we have sex and I get my money, or we don't and I won't.

But after all the bickering, is he even in the mood?

Anderson, the man I hated for almost half my life, cants his head to the side as he smirks at me. "Are you in there?"

"Um, yes. I am."

He reaches up for my face, and at first, I start to pull back. But then I remember I'm supposed to be here for him to touch. So, I just freeze. When his fingertips touch my cheek, I fight a shiver. His thumb runs over my bottom lip and when he pulls away, there's whipped cream there. He licks it off. "You had a little cream there. Thought I'd help."

That was the most satisfying sexual thing to happen to me in over two years. Dear God. What in the hell.

I gulp and lightly joke, "Can't take me anywhere, can you?"

His wry smile sets me on edge. But it falls quickly. "Are you finished?"

I haven't even begun. "Yeah. I think so."

Again, he takes my plate to the trolley, then his own, but this time, he sets the silver domes on them. "I presume you're done with every-thing? Unless you want more. I'll load up your plate, if you like—"

"No. I'm good."

He putters with things there, and it's only then that I see it. He's stalling. *Oh my god, he's nervous, too.* It's not as though he has to clean anything in this situation, yet he's organizing and reorganizing the plates. After everything, he's not sure how to start this.

Clearly, he's interested in me that way. He wouldn't have spent all this money to get me alone in a room otherwise. And given this isn't a prank of some kind, he's … he's here for a reason. *I'm* the reason. But he won't make the first move. Maybe I was too abrasive, or he thinks I truly hate him.

None of that matters right now. I need the money. I can't wait for him to get off his ass about this. There's less than five hours left to go, and if I wait for him, I do not know if he will give up.

It doesn't hurt that he's only gotten better looking with age. And that damned smirk thing … why does that work for me? It's like a naughty smile that tells me exactly what he's thinking, and what he's thinking about is the dirtiest thing I can conjure.

That's it. I have to make the first move. I'm done waiting.

So, I get out of the bed and pad over to him, wrapping my arms around him from behind. His whole body stiffens up in my arms. He murmurs, "What are you doing?"

"I thought I'd see if you wanted to do what … we're both here for."

Slowly, he turns around to face me. It is impossible to admit that I have always found him attractive, even when he was an asshole. Admitting that felt wrong. But I did back then. Now, though, when all arrogance has fallen from his face and a line of confusion forms between his brows, he's even more attractive.

Every other guy I've been with, the moment I brought up sex, that was that. It was time for sex. But Anderson isn't jumping my bones. In fact, he looks concerned more than anything else. "June, you don't have to do this. I promise."

I smirk up at him. "And you're going to pay me almost four hundred thousand dollars just for a nearly naked breakfast?"

He half-smiles as he thinks of what to say, so I pull him to my lips for a kiss. It's tentative at first, just to see if he's for real. I think I surprised him —it's like he's being careful as he kisses me back.

After a moment, though, he wraps me in his arms and slants his mouth over mine, deepening the kiss. His fingers weave into my hair, gently tugging to tip my head back more for him. The touch sends sparks through me. His tongue sweeps into my mouth, and before I know it, I'm gone. It is the best kiss of my life.

Whatever confusing, psychological damage this might do to me in the future, tonight, I don't care. I want the man who haunted my nightmares.

Chapter 14
JUNE

Anderson presses his forehead to mine and breaks the kiss. "Are you sure this is what you want, June?"

"Yes."

With that, all his caution is gone. He holds me tighter to him, kissing me roughly. *Fuck, finally.* I dig my fingernails against his tuxedo shirt to find his thick shoulders. It makes him growl into my mouth. That growl spikes my pulse, and that pulse swims through a river of champagne, so I'm warm and supple all over.

I'd hated myself for the secret attraction I'd harbored for him all this time, and something about this feels so wrong, and that only makes me hotter right now. I've never done anything remotely like this. Every guy I've been with only got to this point with me after at least a few dates, and with the intention of carrying on a relationship. I was not the one-night stand girl, and certainly not the sells-sex girl.

Selling myself to Anderson West is wrong on every level. And that is what makes it so right.

He grabs my ass over the sheet and bites my neck, and I'm delirious from the pleasure of him. I try to maintain some grip on reality, but this feels too fucking good. When he licks up my throat, I moan from his touch. He kisses me again and as he does, he backs me up to the bed, before nudging me onto it and laying on top of me. The weight of him pins me to the bed.

Anderson is hard and kissing me, and this is too surreal, but I'm not willing to stop. I murmur, "Take off your clothes."

He smirks again and stands up. With his eyes on me, he unbuttons his shirt and peels it away. Scant dark chest hair shades his musculature. The man has an eight-pack, and I'd be in awe of that if he weren't already reaching for his pants.

But I sit up with him between my feet and swat his hands away to do it myself. I want to see him close up. Without a word, he lets me undress him. Black satiny boxer briefs tickle my fingertips before I palm him over them. His abs tighten from my touch. Never thought I'd have that effect on Anderson West.

His hips thrust against my hand a little, almost like he can't help himself. My mouth waters for him, but I'm trying to be good. Ish. I tug his boxer briefs down, and find he's more than I realized. A lot more. I'm not sure how this will work. But I'm happy to try.

He bends down, kissing me again as he wraps his arm beneath me. Pulling me tight to him, he carries us up the mattress until we're both on it comfortably. Anderson kisses down my body before pausing at the sheet. Instead of asking for permission, he bites the sheet in his teeth and looks me in the eye. I smirk and nod, and he pulls it down, barely waiting for it to be gone before his mouth is on my tits.

He's all over me there, sucking, licking, biting, trailing his devil tongue around my soft flesh. I'm groaning for more, but I can't do much because the damned sheet is in my way. It's the border between us fitted to me like a pencil skirt from all our shifting around and stopping him from mounting me fully. But he grinds against me, like he's inside already. I'm on edge and shaking from his every touch.

His hand slides beneath the sheet between my thighs and when his fingertips touch me there, I jump because I'm so tense. His tongue flicks my nipples as his fingers massage my clit, and I am ready to die happy. "Mm, that feels so good."

He goes after me harder as a finger glides into me. His thumb keeps at my clit, and I struggle to get the sheet out from between us. He kisses down my newly exposed stomach, just as lovingly as my breasts. When I've peeled the sheet away fully, though, he takes a moment to look me over. His head drops against me as he murmurs, "More beautiful than I ever imagined." Then he adds a second finger, and I'm catapulted into some other level of pleasure.

It's been a long, long time since anyone paid this kind of attention to me. Trent never did. Not even when we first started dating. But I figured as guys get older, they get lazier, and that's just how things were. He wasn't the first guy who treated my pleasure as optional.

Apparently not to Anderson.

He kisses me lower and lower until he's parked between my thighs and about to go down on me. But my lawyer brain kicks in. Breathlessly, I pant, "The contract."

"Hmm?"

"There's a part in the contract … no bodily fluid transfer. You should stop."

He pauses, but his fingers keep going. "Do you want me to stop?"

"Well, no but—"

"Are you going to turn me in for tasting you?"

"No."

He smirks. "Neither will I. Be bad with me, June."

How in the hell can I say no to that?

So, I nod, and he yanks my legs over his shoulder right before his tongue strikes out for my clit, sending electricity through me. There's no holding back my moans anymore. I don't care if I'm loud. Let the guards hear me. I'm sure they've heard it all.

Pleasure pools in my core, and it's deliciously too much. Perfectly too much. My thighs clench around his shoulders, and he growls into me. His fingers hit the spot inside, and my back bows from the mattress. Heat rides me. It's all I can do not to scream when he sucks my clit into his mouth. I erupt on his lips, coming and clenching and crying out for more, and he doesn't stop until I blurt, "Please, fuck me!"

At that, he leans over me and grabs a condom from the nightstand, quickly sheathing himself with it. Once in place, he dips the tip against me, just gliding over my wet, sensitive flesh. He smirks. "No turning back?"

"Anderson, now!"

He notches himself into me, just the tip to let me adjust to the stretch. But when I thrust myself to him, he takes that for a sign and thrusts halfway in. We both groan from the intensity, and soon he climbs over me, kissing as he slowly works the rest of himself into my center. It's so much. The stretch, the feel of his body on mine. I'm back on the edge again already. Bliss takes hold. It's like I'm flying, but he has me safe beneath him.

I hook my hands under his arms and over his shoulders for leverage. Easy to move this way. Working myself against him makes his handsome face go rugged. More determined. He kisses me dizzier. His growls in my mouth make me yearn to see him come. I want him unhinged by me.

I plant my foot on the bed and roll us over, so he takes the hint and lays back, pulling me with him. Before I can even think about it, I'm on top of Anderson and riding his cock with abandon. It's got a curve to it, and he fits me just right. He hits my spot on every thrust and has me shaking for him in no time at all.

His large hands cup my breasts as I ride him, and I pull his forefinger up and suck it into my mouth. He groans, "Fuck, you're so sexy."

I bend down and kiss him for that, and this whole new angle is even more intense. He cocks his body up, bouncing me on his length and driving me back to the edge again.

Some small voice in my head keeps chirping, "This is so wrong." But I don't care. It's never felt like this before.

His stubble burns me on every kiss, and I love it. One more bit of stimulation to memorize. Another pleasure to savor. When he cups my ass and smacks me there, I ride him harder, faster. I love that, and I didn't know I ever would. There is nothing he does that doesn't bring me on. He swats me there again, and somehow that little sting of pain launches me over the edge, and I'm coming again. He lays down a few more while I come, each one stealing my breath. When it's over, he holds me tight and kisses me.

Until he tips me off of him.

Anderson kisses me while he turns me onto my hands and knees. He tucks a pillow beneath my hips, bringing me on full display to him as he kneels between my legs. I can only imagine what he's looking at—me, bent over for his viewing pleasure, wet and aching. He spreads me wide before licking me all over. I whimper for more, too beholden to my body to do anything else. He's made me his for the night. No doubt about it.

I hope I give him what he paid for.

When his cock presses against me from behind, I purr, "Oh, fuck yes!" as he shoves into me all at once. I bounce back to meet his thrusts, but he takes my wrists and pins them in the small of my back. I'm at his mercy—the mercy of a man I thought had none. But while he holds me like that, he reaches beneath my hip and plays with my clit, matching his thrusts to his touch. The sounds that pour out of me are not language. It's utter gibberish.

"Come again," he demands.

"Close!"

He bucks into me harder until I'm right there, so close I can taste it. My body clenches on him. Then, he slams his full length into me, our bodies slap together, and I'm coming so hard I see stars. He's got me screaming for him, as he releases me to grip my hips tight and snarls, "Oh fuck yes!"

His cock throbs inside of me—even with everything happening, I still feel it almost trigger another orgasm for me. But his snarl becomes a roar as he hammers into me like a mad beast. The bed slams into the wall over and over until finally, he buries himself as deep as he can, pulls out, yanks the condom off, and marks me as his by coming on my ass.

Anderson collapses next to me, as breathless and pink-faced from exertion as I am. But I'm stuck on the pillow hill he made for my hips. I can't move yet. I don't want to. Lying right here is all I have the strength for.

He almost smiles and says, "That was one hell of an appetizer. Hope you're hungry for the main course." Then he disappears behind me again, and I realize my night has just begun.

Chapter 15
JUNE

It's not waking up in an empty bed that bugs me. It's that he didn't say he was leaving first thing in the morning.

Not that he owes me anything. Other than my payday, that is. But still. Isn't it just good manners to mention leaving first thing? But then I laugh at myself for thinking Anderson West might have good manners. Still, though, he is nothing like I thought he was.

And maybe neither am I.

I sold my body. Granted, it was for an absolute ton of money, but still. Maybe it's societal programming or some other thing, I'm not sure. But I sold my body, and something about it feels wrong. Deliciously wrong. Does that make me some sort of deviant? Maybe. But how much do I really care about that?

I'm not sure.

Whatever the case, I have to get out of here. I'm the lucky associate who gets Saturday meetings, because international venture capitalists don't really care what day of the week it is. Standing up is a feat. My hangover rings through my head like a bell, and every muscle in my body aches like I ran a marathon. Even my toes are tired, but I blame Anderson's smirk for that.

By the time I'm dressed and looking halfway presentable, Cesar is at the door with my purse and phone. He smiles politely. "Was it what you thought it would be?"

I laugh harder than I thought possible and discover my abdominal muscles are so angry from all the exercises of last night that laughing feels like punishment. My cheeks hurt, too, so laughing and smiling are pretty much out for the day. "Uh, no. Not even close. Nothing like what I expected."

"Yet you smile as though the unexpected is a good thing."

"In this case, it is."

"I am glad to hear it. Follow me." He leads

me out of the mansion through a warren of tunnels that lead to a garage. The garage has several cars, and he takes me to a Bentley with black tinted windows and a driver. Cesar instructs him, "Wherever she wants to go."

The man behind the wheel merely nods.

Cesar says, "This is where I leave you, Six." He passes me a card with information on it. "Go to that website, type in the passcode, and the transfer will hit in three business days. I wish you all the best. If you are interested, feel free to return for next year's auction."

Next year's auction? Pretty sure this was the only auction I had in me. Probably.

"Thank you, Cesar." I give the driver my home address, wondering if that's a bad idea. But it doesn't matter now if they know who I am. What am I thinking? Of course, they know who I am. There's no way they haven't checked me out to see if I'm with law enforcement. I wonder if I even needed to give the driver my address or if it was plugged into his navigation before I got into the car. Classical music plays low during the drive, and I use my phone to follow Cesar's instructions. I'm three business days from my dreams coming true.

On my way from the car to my apartment

building, it is freezing cold. I should have taken Cesar up on last night's offer of clothing. But I'm inside fast, and take a blitz of a shower, pin my hair up, and dress within ten minutes, then it's back to work.

After such a long day and an even longer night, by the time I reach my desk, I am almost dead. Last night's sleep was really this morning's sleep, and that was less than two hours. Anderson was a machine with no stop button. If I'd wanted to go again, he was ready, willing, and able. But I was a boneless mess by five in the morning, and he let me drift off in his arms.

It's almost uncomfortable to admit to myself just how comfortable I was falling asleep in his arms.

I'm in my second meeting by the time I realize I haven't eaten anything all morning. Between the champagne hangover and a total lack of food, not to mention all of the last twenty-four hours' activities, it's a wonder I can string two sentences together to discuss risk and tax shelters.

Not to mention that my head isn't in the game. I keep flashing back to last night. From fear to rage to curiosity to denial, and finally, to the best sex of my life. There is no denying that part of things. Anderson West is an animal in the best way possible. The way he moved and kissed and touched, it all worked for me, and not only because it had been so long since I'd gotten laid. He is amazing at sex. A simple fact.

Funny how he's paying me for it. I feel like I should have been the one paying for everything he did last night.

The thought makes me smile, but the smile fades fast. It's a strange sort of feeling—knowing what I'd done. *Conflicted* doesn't even begin to describe how I feel. I'm not sure if the conflict in my mind is more the hangover or the fact that I'd slept with Anderson West—my sworn enemy —or the fact that I'd sold my body. *To* Anderson West. Whatever the case, I am too foggy to be at work.

The whole situation feels messier than I like my drama, but focusing on what's important will get me through the day. I hope. After another meeting, I check my emails and find one from my student loan servicer. Those numbers used to give me indigestion. Now, they seem small. If—

"Oh my gosh," Callie whispers behind me.

I spin around. "What?"

She giggles, looking at me. "Did you get any sleep last night?"

"For all intents and purposes, no. No, I did not."

"For a good reason, I hope."

Slowly, I nod as my cheeks burn. "And in three days, this," I point to my loan email, "will be history."

She eyes the page. "God, is that really the size of loan people take for law school?"

"And mine isn't even all that bad. I had some scholarships and grants to help."

"Damn."

I nod. "Soon, last night will be in my rearview, and so will this place. You'll still text me after I leave, right?"

"Of course, silly. Just because I won't be able to see you here all the time doesn't mean we're not friends."

"Wait, why are you here on a Saturday? You're never here on the weekends."

She laughs. "I had to know how it went, and you haven't returned my texts."

"Oh, shit." I grab my phone and look. There's a dozen from her. "I'm so sorry. I'm not really here right now—"

"No worries, I promise. I was hoping good sex was the reason."

"Not just good. Life altering."

She giggles. "I'm so happy for you!"

And right now, so am I. "Three business days before the money hits … so, like, Wednesday at the latest?"

"I guess so. But considering everything, maybe wait until Thursday before worrying about it."

Nodding, I wonder aloud, "And Daniel? Did he text you this morning?"

She smiles. "After he made sure three dozen roses showed up at my door."

"Are you kidding me?" I'd once sent a dozen roses to my mom for Mother's Day when I couldn't be there, and it cost me damn near a car payment. Three for missing a date? Good god. "Wait, why three?"

"One dozen for every month he's loved me."

"Oh. My. God."

"I know, right?"

"That is the sappiest thing I have ever heard."

She giggles and nods. "And I love it. He's a big romantic."

Wonder what that's like. Last night was not exactly the stuff fairytale romances were made of. What am I thinking? I do not want a fairytale romance. Especially not with Anderson. Never him.

Love is a minefield as it is, and fairytale romances never appealed to me, even as a girl. The reason they always ended once the prince, and the girl got married was because, "Happily Ever After," was easier to write than, "Over the years, he grew to hate how loudly she chewed, and she loathed that he left his socks on the floor." Fairytales are not real life.

But the googly eyes Callie has when she speaks about Daniel are real enough. I'm worried her fairytale romance will end in tears.

So, I give a simple, "I'm happy for you, hon."

Chapter 16
JUNE

Wednesday came and went without a payday, and by Thursday, I am freaking out to Callie at lunch. "I knew it. I fucking knew it. This always happens."

"You knew what?"

"No money from the weekend."

Her eyes widen. "Well, maybe it's—"

"No. This is some cosmic punishment for doing what I did. I never do anything wrong. I am a rule follower. When I was a kid and I saw a friend cheating on a test, do you know what I did?"

"What?"

"I turned them in and lost a friend. And do you know why?"

She sighs. "Why?"

"Because the rules are in place for a reason. Or well … that's what I was raised to believe. I don't cheat. I don't lie. Most of the time, anyway. And I don't, under any circumstances," I lean over the table and whisper, "have sex for money. I am being punished for what I did. I know I am. It always happens like this. I do the slightest thing out of line, and boom. Instant punishment."

Callie smiles her "You're being silly" smile, and I want to growl at her for it. "There are a million reasons the money might not be there just yet. You are overreacting."

"I am not overreacting. That money is earmarked for my future, Cal. A beautiful future, where I'm happy and fulfilled and relaxed. Right now, it is the only reason I haven't lost my mind at work. Can you honestly tell me you plan to sit in the office for the next twenty-eight years pushing papers?"

"Well, no, but—"

"And that's because you have the money to do something else. Money is freedom, and without it, you're stuck suffocating on the boot heel of bitches like Madi for decades. I can't. I won't. That cannot happen. I will lose my mind. I—"

"Breathe. You're turning colors."

I close my eyes and try to force a deep breath, but it hurts. My chest is so tight that I can't do it. It's been like that all week, though a part of that is probably from how sore I was over the weekend. Who knew hours and hours of sex were such a workout? "I'm trying to breathe."

"Good. This isn't over, June. You can contact the auction house for information."

"Okay, yeah, but it's not like I can take them to court over this, since what I did is not legal."

"Right, but like Cesar said, there are other ways to enforce a contract."

My brows bunch together in confusion. "How could I do anything socially to hurt the Chamberlain mansion?"

"Old buildings are highly flammable."

I snort a laugh, and she merely smiles at me, as if she had just suggested getting a pedicure. "You cannot be serious, Callie."

Half a shrug is all I get before she dips back into her salad.

"Callie—"

"All I'm saying is, there is more than one way to skin a cat." She makes a face. "That is an awful saying, if you think about it."

"I'd rather not. And I'm not threatening arson—"

"Who said anything about a mere threat?"

"Callie!"

She giggles. "You get my meaning. There are always ways around obstacles. You just have to be willing to do the work."

"I was. I did the work. And now, I'm not getting paid." I huff and sip my hot tea, wishing it were something much stronger. "This sucks. I shouldn't have to chase down my money. This was supposed to be a fun little adventure with a huge payday. Not a hassle."

"In my experience, the people with the most money are the least willing to part with it. So, perhaps your date is stalling. I'd put money on it that Cesar is freaking out, too."

"What makes you think so?"

She thinks for a moment. "If we take Camille at face value, that her auction stories are true, then that means she's done this several times, and there's a good chance she's not the only one. Which means Cesar would work to keep all the women happy, so they are more likely to return. If he finds out one of his bidders hasn't paid—"

"Then he might socially destroy him for me," I say slowly as she nods.

"Cesar might be your best hope of taking care of this."

"Except I don't have a way to contact him. And I'd kind of like to handle this myself. The less of a stink I make about it, the fewer people will catch wind of what I did." Plus, I made my bed. Seems fitting I lie in it.

She shrugs. "Understandable. But keep calling the Chamberlain mansion in your back pocket. It's likely they can reach out to Cesar for you."

I nod and choke down a bite of burger. Ever since the weekend, it seems like that's all I want. Comfort food. Not breakfast foods, though. Just thinking about pancakes makes me tense. "Still can't believe I did something this drastic on a whim."

"I was surprised about that myself, to be honest."

"You practically talked me into it."

She smiles sweetly. "I gave you a nudge. That was it. You were halfway there on your own." She's not wrong.

"I guess so. Still. This was so unlike me."

"Mm, hmm. But even if it all goes sideways, I still think it was good for you."

"What makes you say that?"

Callie sits back and looks me over. "You said it yourself. The best sex of your life. And since you've returned from your naughty night, you've been a lot less careful about things. In a good way, I mean."

"What do you mean?"

"You snapped at Madi when she told you to get a move on for a meeting. The old you would have snarked behind her back or made a face when she wasn't looking. But you snarled, and I quote, 'I'll get there when I get there.' I've never seen Madi speechless before. It was awesome."

I chuckle and shake my head. "It was insubordinate."

"That is part of why it was awesome. Whatever this weekend was in your head, I think it uncorked something in you that's been bottled up for too long." She's not wrong.

All week, I've been more direct with people, and while it's gotten some good reactions, it's also gotten some bad ones. When I speak to people—even to clients—it's like I have no filter. I haven't exactly been fire-worthy unprofessional, but it feels like it's coming. I just don't give a shit like I used to. All thanks to Anderson West.

Great. He fucked me for free, and now he's going to get me fired. Just what I need.

But it's almost like facing him and calling him out broke something in me. Something that's been holding me back this whole time. Maybe it's closure regarding what had happened when we were younger … I don't know. Or maybe it's that I finally accepted that, despite his teasing and all the rest of it, I had always harbored an attraction to him. It wasn't the meanness that got me—that was a huge turn-off because I'm not a masochist—it was that he was hot and he always seemed like he had more going on beneath the surface than he'd let anyone know.

Kalen Black was proof of that.

Maybe Callie's right. I needed this weekend for more than just the money. It was a strange kind of therapy that I could have never bought. Not to mention all the orgasms. I lost count after twelve. An odd thing to count, but I couldn't believe how my body responded to him, given all our baggage. The way he touched me was practically worshipful. There was no cruelty, no malice. More proof that there was far more to Anderson than he ever let on. He gave me things I didn't even know I needed.

Still, though, I also need the money.

"I don't know what I'm going to do, Callie."

"Focus on work and get yourself through the day. It may just be a weird banking thing—you know how some deposits don't go in until after a certain time?"

I nod.

"So, it could be that. When we get back to work, dive into it and shut everything else out. This will all settle itself. You'll see." Her cheery tone is betrayed by the look in her eyes. She's as unsure as I am.

I take another bite of my burger, not willing to call her out for her fake cheer.

-

Chapter 17

ANDERSON

Sitting outside of Christophe's for my monthly lunch with my father, I watch the freezing rain come down in sheets. One more barrier between me and him. One more reason not to be here. But I know he's already inside, likely nursing his martini. Punctuality is another of his virtues, alongside honesty and commitment to duty.

I am not looking forward to another lunch where he tells me about how I fall short of his legacy.

I swear, he books these things on Fridays just so he can ruin one of my weekends every month. Weekends I use to enjoy the Boston nightlife or spend in the company of some woman I've only just met. With Dad spoiling my mood of the Friday beforehand, I'm down to three fun weekends a month.

And if he had his druthers, he'd ruin those, too.

But he is not the only reason I'm still in my car. I can fiddle with the radio and the settings until I die of thirst, but none of that will distract me from what's really on my mind.

June Devlin is a maniac in the best way.

I sit back, trying not to get another erection just from thinking about her. It's not fair that she has such a hold on me. I'd thought to protect her from lecherous men at the auction, but I failed at that. That woman is human Viagra. She brought out the wolf in me. I could not stop touching her, not even when I knew she was falling asleep. I had to hold her, at the very least.

It's never been like that before for me. She is dangerous.

Not that it matters now. I don't have her number. I purposefully did not ask for it. Best I cannot reach out to her, or she'd have me over a barrel in a week. There is nothing I wouldn't have given that woman a week ago. Now, with time and distance between us, nothing's changed.

In fact, it might be worse now, because I cannot stop thinking about that night.

Get it together, Anderson. Dad's inside.

That thought is enough to quell my body's newest addiction, it seems. I'm dressed for the weather, so stepping out of my car is little more than an inconvenience. Even so, I don't enjoy it. Boston is wonderful for many things, but her weather is not one of them.

Once inside the restaurant, I know where to go. The same table he always takes. Right by the window, overlooking the harbor. We are such regulars that when the hostess sees who just walked in, she offers a smile and a nod, and takes my coat and hat. But I am on my own when I go to the table. I don't blame her. Dad is not the friendliest man to staff.

The restaurant itself is lovely. He's always had good, classic taste. White tablecloths, glass and wood in every direction. The music is present, but not overwhelming. Given the weather, though, most of the restaurant is empty. No people watching for me today. I can give Dad my full attention. Hoorah.

Before I can even sit, he begins, "Anderson. Nice of you to show up."

I sit across from him, noting his half empty martini glass. "Nice of you to be sober."

He ignores the slight. "Enjoying the weather?"

Wonderful. He's stalling. "It's my favorite."

The server pops by for our orders and vanishes as quickly as he can. Dad notes, "The service here has fallen off a cliff."

"You picked it."

His eyes narrow, and it's like being glared at by my future self. I hate how much we look alike. I've seen pictures of him when he was younger, and it's uncanny. But I refuse to end up as miserable and angry as he is. No one with his kind of privilege should be this much of a crabby bastard.

"I have something important to discuss, Anderson. Can you keep your barbed tongue to yourself, or do you wish to lose another argument today?"

I clench my jaw, trying to rein myself in. "I didn't lose the Johnson case this week. The jury was bought."

"Keep telling yourself that. I'm sure it'll make Mr. Johnson feel better about losing."

"Dad—"

"Never mind all that. Johnson was a loser in

the first place. You didn't have much to work with." He concedes with a shrug, and I'm shocked. Elliot West is not one to forgive anything. Ever. "You vanished at the Chamberlain auction last weekend. It's all anyone is talking about. I want to know why."

As if I'll ever tell him. "You know how Tag is. I had to get him out of there."

He arches his brow and sneers, before taking another swig of martini. "I don't like that boy. Never have. You have to stop taking him to everything. A woman would be a more suitable date for important functions."

Perhaps agreeing with him will confuse him and shorten the discussion. "Certainly."

When he frowns, there's no confusion. Damn. "But you'd have to commit to *one* first. A steady. Someone bright and beautiful to lull people into a secure feeling in their dealings with you. The right partner is essential in business, Anderson."

Stellar. We're having this talk. Again. "I am more than aware of your thoughts on the matter."

"You have the reputation of a man unwilling to commit. How can clients trust you, *commit* to you, if you cannot commit to a woman?"

"Having a girlfriend is not representative of my capacity as a lawyer."

"On the contrary—"

My cocktail arrives with no fanfare from the server. He simply places it and flees. I wish I could go with him.

Dad continues as I sip my Maker's old-fashioned, "If you have a girlfriend, it shows clients you can commit to someone, something, a plan, at the very least. How am I supposed to relinquish the firm to you if you can't even do the most basic thing?"

"You know who I am. You know what I can do. But you're stalling because retirement freaks you out."

"A West does not stall. A West commits. He protects what is his. If you can't commit to a woman, how do you expect me to think you are faithful to the firm's employees and shareholders?"

"That is hardly the same thing."

But he shakes his head once. "The man who sits at the top must be, above all else, reliable and trustworthy. You have proven to be neither in your affections, and that is where you play at commitment without a net. It is the easiest thing in the world to find a woman who wants to be with a wealthy, attractive man. Find one. Commit to her. Then I will reconsider my options."

This is the same song and dance I get at least once a quarter. Every lunch is some version of a speech on inadequacies. How I lack direction or foresight or some other skill he mastered in the crib. Nothing is ever good enough for Elliot West. I'd long ago given up whining about how unfair he was—whining showed a lack of character, according to him, and I was sick of hearing how I'd never measure up.

One of the few times I'd ever received his praise was when I wanted to help Kalen Black. But he didn't give it right away. He paid for Kalen's tuition under the strict agreement that I'd work at the firm the entire summer and miss out on the trip I'd planned with my friends between graduation and starting college. So, I worked my ass off that whole summer without getting paid, without complaint. When my friends posted pics of the trip, I never mooned over them. Just kept my nose to the grindstone. At the end of the summer, when my debt to him was finally paid off, he said, "Good show," and firmly shook my hand.

It was as close to a hug or a genuine compliment as I'd ever received from him, and it meant the world to me at the time.

Thinking of Kalen makes me think of June, because after last Friday, the two are inextricably linked in my mind, and now that I've started thinking of her, a convenient story pops into my head. "Well, on that matter, I've actually started seeing someone."

A few of the lines in his face fade. His version of being surprised. "You have?"

I nod. "And it's been getting serious."

"Why haven't you mentioned her before?"

"You know better than most that this is unfamiliar territory for me, Dad. I'm not exactly sure what the proper milestones are in this."

"Very well. How did you meet?"

"At a fundraiser. Well, that's where we re-met. I knew her back at Appleton and ran into her at Boston U, as well. But we never hit it off back then." All true, though omitting the details may qualify that statement as a lie. It's all he's getting out of me, though. No sense in explaining the auction.

He smiles, and it's such an unusual event

that I'm not sure how to interpret it. "What's her name?"

I can tell him that because I'm sure I've never mentioned her before. "June Devlin."

"What clubs does she belong to?"

I almost laugh at the question. "I don't think she does, actually."

"Devlin … I don't know that name. Is she from Boston originally?"

"I believe so—"

"You believe so? You don't know? How serious can you be if you don't know the basics? *Think*, Anderson."

I force a smile. "I know the important things about her. She likes French toast over pancakes. She laughs like there's music inside of her. When she says my name, it's all I can think about."

"God help us, my son is in love."

I laugh hard at that. "Not sure I'd go that far—"

"It's all over you. No wonder you were late."

"You're getting ahead of yourself, Dad. I like her. A lot." Probably more than I should. "Things are getting serious, but I'm not in danger of losing myself in this. It's like you always say, love is a child's emotion. It's not for men like us."

"No, it is not. Watch yourself with her."

"I will—"

"Better yet, *I'll* watch you with her. Bring her to Sunday supper. Your mother will be overjoyed. She's always going on about how you need to settle down, and this will put her mind at ease."

Shit. This was a bad idea. Abort. "I'm not sure she will be available on such short notice."

"Make her available, Anderson. I want to meet this June Devlin and see if my boy has lost his heart to her."

He never calls me *his boy*. My mouth goes dry, and I flash back to the end of that fateful summer and that feeling of pride again. I cannot believe it. He's actually proud of me for having a girlfriend. All this time, I had thought he used the girlfriend thing as an excuse to never retire. It's a strange feeling to see him proud of me, but I like it. I want to keep this going, no matter the consequences. "I'll do my best, Dad." Now, how do I get June's number?

-

Chapter 18
JUNE

Friday, on our way back to the office, we are dodging the rain, and I'm practically vibrating. Callie has been trying to keep me calm this whole time, but I'm done. When we get to our office building, I stop and she notices. "What?"

"You go on without me. I'm calling the Chamberlain mansion. Now."

"It's pouring cats and dogs out here, and it's freezing."

"Is it? I hadn't noticed."

She rolls her eyes. "At least come inside. You'll catch pneumonia out here."

But I shake my head. "Can't let anyone in there know about this. Go ahead. I'll catch up."

Her lips smooth to a line as she thinks about

it. "Alright. But don't do anything I wouldn't do."

"Too late."

She giggles, rolls her eyes, and jogs into the building.

On the streets of Boston, there aren't too many places to have a private conversation. But the weather has kept a lot of people indoors, and building awnings provide enough cover to stay as close to dry as I can. I'm sure I'll be soaked through by the end of the conversation, though. The rain is blowing a little sideways today, and it's icy because my day couldn't possibly get worse.

I dial them up and, to my surprise, a man answers. I'd expected to go round robin on a phone tree system like every other place I call. "Chamberlain Museum. How may I direct your call?"

"Uh, well, I'm not sure. I was at the auction last Friday, and—

"Please hold, and I will connect you to our auction acquisitions department."

"But—"

Nope. Hold music. I huff a puff of foggy air in frustration. This is already going wrong.

"Acquisitions, Miranda speaking."

"Yes, hi. I was there for the auction—"

"And you're missing an item? Your name?"

"June Devlin, but I—"

"You're not in our system. Did you win or lose your bid?"

I groan my irritation. "Neither. I was there for the first auction and the *second* one. If you catch my drift."

"I am afraid I do not. There was only one auction here last Friday. A silent one. Are you certain you have the right establishment?"

I want to scream at her, but it's entirely possible she has no idea what I'm talking about. "Does a man named Cesar work there? He knows all about this."

"No one by that name, I'm afraid."

"Fuck." I lean on the brick building behind me.

"There is no need for that kind of language—"

"Sorry, sorry. That wasn't directed at you. Thanks for your help." I hang up and want to throw my phone, but I can't because it's expensive and unless I get my money, I cannot afford to go throwing phones around.

I need my money. My life cannot change without it. Moreover, I earned it, dammit. And at this point, it's the principle of the matter. How dare they set this up so that people who need money the most get taken advantage of by people who can afford it the most? This is just wrong, and I'm not standing for it.

A quick Google search tells me something I didn't want to know. Anderson West's family firm is within walking distance of my office. I'm marching down the sidewalk before I can talk myself out of this.

I hate when people show up unannounced to see me. It is one of my top five stress triggers. An unexpected knock at my door, a phone ringing, a text from an unknown number, any time someone tries to get my attention without some kind of warning, it all makes me flash back to when Anderson used to sneak up and pop my bra strap, and I fucking hate it.

So, I'm going to sneak up and pop his metaphorical bra strap.

By the time I reach his father's steel and glass building, I'm soggy and I don't give a shit. I'm so pissed off I might actually spit nails at Anderson. But I'll have to get past the security desk first. Two guards, both guys, one younger than me, and the other a few years older. They're wearing that cocky grin guys get when they look at a dirty magazine and are huddled over something interesting on the younger one's phone. The moment they notice me, the younger one shuts it off.

Great. Two horned up guys, and I need to get something from them. Huh. Good afternoon. Sorry to bother you—"

"Who are you here to see?"

"Anderson West, but it's a surprise. Is there any way you can skip buzzing up?"

"I'm afraid not, miss. Protocol."

"Of course. I understand. It's just that … if you buzz up," I heave my shoulders and let my voice shake as I quietly tell them, "then the surprise is ruined, and I'm already running late because of this awful weather." I untie my trench coat and my thin sweater dress is clinging to me, garnering their full attention. "I've never done this before, and I'm going to get fired if I ruin the surprise."

"You've never done what before?" the older one asks.

A faint smirk upturns my lips. "I'm a … *masseuse.*"

"Never seen a masseuse in a dress," he teases.

I giggle. "Well, I'm a special kind of masseuse."

"I'll bet you are."

"Anderson's friend Tag hired me as a surprise for him. It's his birthday, I think. I don't know. But I'm here as a surprise, and I got stuck in this weather—I'm sure I look awful. And I'm new to all of this. I'm just so nervous and now," I laugh at myself, "I'm rambling. So sorry to bother you." I grab the neckline of my dress and bend over a little to wring it into the plant sitting next to the desk, giving them both a view down my dress. Then, I hitch up the hem and do the same, flashing them way too much thigh. Desperate times, and all that. "I'm so fired if I don't get up there and surprise him."

The older one takes a second too long to pry his eyes off my body. "You'll, uh, want to freshen up before seeing him." He presses a button and the elevator near him opens. "It's the executive elevator. It'll take you right up to his floor. His office is at the end of the hall on the left. There's a ladies room, second door on your right. You can straighten yourself out there before going to give him a ... massage."

"Oh my gosh, really? You're a lifesaver! Thank you so much! I might actually make rent this month."

He chuckles. "Good luck with everything."

"You're my hero. Thanks again!" I give a flirty little wave as the doors shut and hold back from making a face. No idea if they can see the cameras in the elevator, and I can't let on that I duped them. It's all I can do not to tap my toe impatiently, but I have to make this look good.

When the door opens, I'm not sure how high up I am, but the nearest window says I'm at least twenty stories up. I dash into the bathroom first. Pretty sure that if the guards think I'm a sex worker and they have access to the cameras throughout the building, they will be watching me come in and out of here. After straightening up a little and re-tying my trench coat, I head for the end of the other hall.

In the vestibule, his admin sits there and her attention grows with my every step. "Good afternoon. Can I help you?" On the enormous door behind her is a sign with his name on it.

"Anderson is in his office, right?"

"Well, yes, but—"

"Thanks." I barge around her desk for the door.

"You can't go in there!"

"Try and stop me." I throw the door open and find Anderson with his back to the door. I snap, "What in the hell are you doing?"

He turns around, and I realize there are two other men in the room with him. They'd been gathered around a table and I hadn't even noticed them in there. It was like, the moment I saw him, I couldn't see anything else. But Anderson throws on a charming smile, even though I've clearly caught him off-guard. "A pleasure to see you, too."

His admin says, "I tried to stop her, Mr. West—"

"No worries, Angela. Hold my calls, will you?"

"Would you like me to call security?"

"That won't be necessary. Thank you. Sorry for the confusion."

She glares at me, then leaves.

I feel two feet tall right now, even though I'm not in the wrong on this. My cheeks burn, though, like I am the source of all the problems right now. This is more awkward than I thought it would be, but I need that money, and I'm not about to let him off the hook for embarrassing me yet again. For making the poor girl come after him for what she's owed. Nope. He's not getting off easy this time. If I have to humiliate him to get what's mine, then I will.

Chapter 19
JUNE

Anderson stands to guide his guests out. "Gentlemen, see Angela about getting on my schedule soon. My apologies, but emergencies wait for no one."

That's what he's calling this. An emergency. Well, it is to me. Glad to see he's taking it so seriously. If that is, in fact, what he's doing. The suits leave, and I close the door behind them. Anderson is within arm's length, and I can't tell if I want to kiss him or strangle him. Somehow, he manages to make a navy suit look more impressive than a tuxedo.

Get your head right. This is not a social call.

Right, right. I'm pissed off. He's nothing but a dollar sign to me, and I have no clue what I am to him. "Am I still a joke to you, Anderson?"

He looks like I slapped him. "What?"

"You were never this good of an actor back in the day. Did you take lessons? I don't remember you being in the drama club but I imagine men like you can afford lessons for anything."

"What are you talking about, June?"

I take a stroll around his office. It's expansive. The entire room reeks of way too much money. There's the sitting area where he had hosted his clients a moment ago. To the left of that is an oversized walnut wood desk and behind it, a wall of bookshelves loaded with books on the law. The outer wall is a solid glass pane, giving an unobstructed view of the city. Even now, with our gray, dreary weather, the view is spectacular.

"Why are you playing dumb? We both know that you know."

"That I know what?"

I run my finger down the edge of his desk while I speak. A dramatic mood has come over me, and since he's pissed me off, I'm going to take my time with this and enjoy seeing him twist in the wind. "That's all I've ever been to you, isn't it? A joke. A way to amuse yourself.

Another plaything. You saw me at the auction and thought, Oh look. A game I can win."

"Not even close."

"Right." I lean back over the desk, slightly jutting my chest out. He may not respect me, but he loved them. Maybe he'll pay up if I remind him of that. "I'm supposed to believe you saw me at the auction and actually wanted me?"

"Why else would I have bid that kind of money for you?"

"Funny you say bid and not *paid*."

He frowns. "Bid, pay, whatever. The point stands. You still think I paid that kind of money to pull a prank on you?"

"That's the thing, though, Andy. You didn't."

"Don't call me Andy."

"I'll call you whatever the hell I want until you actually pay me."

He pauses. "What are you talking about?"

"Cut the crap. You know damn well you haven't paid up. Or do you have so much money that you wouldn't notice *misplacing* that kind of cash? Did you leave it somewhere? Is it in your other wallet?" I can't help but mock him right now. I'm too pissed off. "Or is the little rich boy crying poor?"

"I paid you. Well, I paid the shell corporation they use for the auction, anyway."

"Bullshit! The money never hit my account because it was never wired because you never sent it!"

He huffs. "I'll call the mansion. Surely they have someone—

"I've already called them, trying to track this down. They pretended not to know anything. Stop stalling and pay me what you owe me."

"Given Friday night's events, you're worth every penny and more." He goes to his desk and sits behind his laptop, so I march around the desk myself and stand next to him to see whatever the hell he's doing. I tell myself it's because I don't trust him, but I like standing close to him. I've been conflicted for a week over this man, and it's not getting any easier by being near him. But he smells too good to wait on the other side of the desk.

I am hopeless. Truly.

As he types, he mutters, "Truth be told, I find you priceless, but if this is what it takes to settle things between us, then I'm happy to do it."

"I'm not here for more of your lies, Andy. Pay me."

He winces at that. "Must you, with the *Andy* of it all?"

"Your full name will cost you three hundred and ninety thousand dollars."

He smirks a little, and I force my toes to stay put. "A small price for such an incredible night." Then his smirk dies when he looks at the screen. "The hell …"

I struggle to remain unmoved, but the panic in his tone sets me on edge. If he's panicked, what the hell chance do I have? "What is it?"

"My account is frozen. This can't be right." He mashes some buttons.

"Oh, bullshit! You're such a con artist! I will destroy you, Andy West. I'm not sure how, but I will fucking end you. I have powerful friends who would love nothing more than to make me happy." Okay, I have Callie and that's about it, but given her whole arson plan, I wouldn't put it past her to do something awful to Anderson on my behalf.

He rakes his fingers through his hair, looking stressed as heck while he glares at the screen. "Before you bring the apocalypse down around me, do take a moment to look at my screen." He turns his laptop to face me.

Sure enough, it reads, "This bank account is now frozen to protect your financial interests. This bank account has been frozen due to unusual ACH activity. If you would like to unfreeze it, please contact our customer service line and provide the necessary information."

"You could have downloaded a screenshot of a frozen bank account, Andy. You think I'm buying this? This is amateur hour shit."

He loses a long sigh. "Wow. I mean, I appreciate how much of an evil mastermind you apparently think I am—it's rather flattering in a way—but, June, until I get this handled, I am fucked. So, I'd appreciate if you took this seriously."

"I have known you in one capacity or another for most of my life, and yet, your audacity never fails to take the wind right out of me. You are such a little shit."

"Excuse me?"

"You have more money than God himself, and you're lecturing *me* on taking this seriously? Do you even grasp the lengths I went to in order to get even a fraction of the kind of life you take for granted?" I bend down so I can growl this in his face. "Any man at the auction could have bought me. *Any*. Do you have a clue how much I put on the line that night? My health. My freedom. All so I might not have to be miserable for the next twenty-eight years. That is the kind of thing I had to do to get a tiny shred of your fortune."

"I'm…I'm sorry."

"Does it even occur to you to think before you speak?"

He takes a breath. "That was insensitive of me."

"It's almost as if your brain is not connected to your mouth, Andy."

"Fair point. I earned that. Look, I will get this taken care of—

"You still haven't even proved that this is something to get taken care of. How do I know this isn't some part of your plan? That you didn't fake this?"

Anderson sighs. "Give me your phone."

"What?"

"Give me your phone. You can watch me log into my bank account on your own phone, so you can see that this isn't something I faked."

If I get his banking information, then maybe I can … no. Having sex for money is one thing.

Banking fraud is a law I'm not willing to break. Not even for this.

I pass him my phone and watch as he logs in. Sure enough, the same screen pops up. "Now, do you believe me?"

I take a breath and let it out slowly as I nod.

"You look like you're going to vomit."

"A prank you can fix. But banking shit can get complicated."

"Well, things have never been easy between us before. Why would they be now?"

I huff a laugh and sink into myself. This just got so much worse. I want to believe this is all still some game he's running, though. I'd rather think the worst of him than believe this could be out of his control.

Chapter 20
ANDERSON

Even soggy from the rain and incredibly pissed off, June is gorgeous. Unexpectedly seeing her in the real world is something I hadn't dared to hope for—I'd actually considered hiring an actress to play her role at my parents' upcoming supper. An actress felt less awkward and dangerous than trying to see June again. Couldn't lose my head around a woman I didn't know. But June does something to me. It's as though my brain short circuits around her, and if my brain does that when we are at supper with my parents, then he will never retire.

My luck will not hold out, if that's the case.

But, then again, she did just show up here …

"Any idea why your account is frozen?" she asks in that sultry voice of hers.

Or maybe I just hear it as sultry and it's a perfectly normal voice. "Could be any number of things. It's a large sum of money—banks get angsty about that kind of thing."

"Yeah, okay. That makes sense. I just … I wish you knew more."

"As do I." The truth is, it's mortifying. I have never not paid a debt for any reason.

To have the bank get persnickety when I need my money the most?

The ultimate humiliation.

And June more than earned her wage. She deserves to be paid. Hell, she deserves that money for letting me peer into her deep brown eyes. If anger didn't simmer behind them, I might try to kiss her right now.

"I will make some calls and get the situation handled. The transaction will be marked as a donation to the Chamberlain charity and given that, I imagine they think there's an extra zero or some such. An assumed clerical error. Nothing more. I will handle it, and you will get your money, June. Regardless of what happens with the bank, you will get it. I promise you."

She sighs and sits on my desk, and it's all I can do not to run my hand up her dress. "You do not know how much this money means to me, Anderson. It is everything to me right now."

"I've never been in your position, so I'm sure you're right about that. When I tell you I'll do something, though, I do it. You'll have your money. And soon. As soon as I get all of this settled, you'll have it." I'm not sure what combination of words will make her smile again, but I'm willing to try them all.

No smile yet, but her brows lift, as though she's a little relieved. "Thanks. And I'm sorry about barging in here when you were with clients—

I wave her off. "No need for that. Your matter was far more urgent than a murder trial, and—"

She laughs in shock. "What?"

But I grin up at hcr. "Kidding. Just a run-of-the-mill property dispute."

"You dick," she says with a giggle.

"Just wanted to shake you up a bit. Give you a start, so you could unwind."

She smiles and rolls her eyes. "Yeah, okay, funny guy. Not my fault that I'm stressed out about all this."

"No, apparently it's mine. But like I said, I'll

handle it, and you will have your money as soon as possible."

My words appear to wash through her this time. The rigid line between her brows has lessened and the harsh set of her mouth falls. I'm glad to see it. She should have a simple life of luxuries, not one defined by stress. But June's entire life has been one of stress.

And I did not help matters. But I can now.

Well … can I? Why the hell is my account frozen? It makes no sense. I drop bundles of cash onto anything and for any reason. Sure, this is a higher sum than most, but it shouldn't be anything that would trigger a freeze. It's preposterous. I've made bigger donations to various organizations in the past. For this to trigger a freeze? It's downright degrading.

Maybe because Chamberlain has gone to a new bank? Something overseas for *these* transactions? What I'd told June wasn't that far off—banks get tetchy for all kinds of reasons. If Chamberlain's bank is flagged for something international or another reason, it may be the sole reason for all this hoopla. No need for me to get worried about it.

And yet.

Something about all of this rubs me the

wrong way. If I had never made larger donations in the past, I wouldn't be that worried about it. I'd think that was the cause of this. But given that I have, it's hard not to get lost in my own questions on the matter.

Whatever the case, I must call the bank.

"Here's what we're going to do. You can give me your number," and as I say the words, her brows leap up her forehead, "and once I get things settled on my end of this, I will phone you to let you know what is going on and when you can expect your payment. Agreed?"

She takes a breath and cautiously nods. "Yeah, okay. I guess so."

"You guess so? Is it really such a terrible idea for me to have your number?"

"Is it really such a strange idea for me to hesitate to give you my number?"

That stings. I take a breath and let it out slowly. "Forgive me, but I would have thought our last interaction bought me a sliver of grace."

Somehow, she manages to purse her lips and almost smile at the same time. She pauses to think about things. "Look, I want to believe this is all some banking error. That you're not the same jerk who tormented me throughout school, and that you're not playing some wildly elaborate hoax on me. That you're not going to rip me off somehow …"

"But?"

"But I learned a long time ago that a tiger can't change its stripes, and you've bitten me more times than I want to remember, Anderson. Yeah, we had a shockingly good night together, but one night compared to years of bullying isn't enough to balance the scales or tip them your way. So, forgive me for being suspicious of you. I have every right to be."

I hate that she's not wrong. A single night is not enough, though. As much as I'd have loved for that night to tip her scales in my favor, that would have meant she was a fool. And I don't harbor crushes on fools. "You're right. I shouldn't be insulted by your suspicion. If you weren't suspicious of me after all this time, then you'd be mentally deficient. But either way, I still need your number to contact you about the payment. And if I were a real bastard about things, I could have gotten your number years ago, if that was my angle."

"That makes sense. You have more money than you know what to do with. I'm sure getting my number wouldn't be too hard if you wanted to do something nefarious with it."

"Precisely."

"Thank you for understanding about me being suspicious of you." She gives me her number, and I give her mine. "And I hope you'll also be understanding about this." A moment later, my phone lights up with her number on the caller ID.

"About what, exactly?"

"Had to try it. To make sure you gave me your real number."

I laugh. "The depth of my imagined dastardliness is unfathomable in your mind, eh?"

"There are things I can forgive, but I never, ever forget."

So she can forgive some of the things I've done, but she'll never forget them? I'm unforgettable? I think I can live with that. Romance has started with less.

Wait? Romance?

I shake off the errant thought. Clearly, I'm under-caffeinated and my brain is rambling nonsense. It's afternoon, so I'm sure she needs to get back to work. I know I do. "I must make those calls, and I doubt you were doing nothing before you came here, so …"

"Right." She pauses and frowns. "Thought about sticking around to watch you make your calls."

"But you know how banks are. This could take hours, June."

"And that's why I'm not going to stick around." She stands up straight and pauses again. "I just wish … never mind. I look forward to hearing from you, Anderson." She heads for the door.

But she wants to stay. And I want her to stay.

"You don't have to go—"

"Yeah, I do. Like you said, I wasn't doing nothing. Have to get back to work."

"Alright, then." Damn. "Talk later."

She gives a nod and leaves.

That was clumsy of me. I should have insisted she stay for the calls. Or a coffee. Or some other excuse to spend time with her. It probably wouldn't have taken much of a reason for her to stay. Instead, my mind went to work and logistics.

I am my father's son. What a depressing thought.

-

Chapter 21
ANDERSON

But nothing is more depressing than being passed from one banker to another.

I'd thought of going with my father's personal banker, of course. Dad claims the man is a genius with money, and he prefers not to deal with financial issues himself. I, however, don't mind using the bank's people under normal circumstances, as they know my bank's rules more intimately than a personal banker would. This is not normal, though. Not by a long shot.

Once I finally get a hold of the right man, though, he has fewer answers than I'd hoped for. It's all I can do not to snap the pen in my hand as I speak. "What do you mean you were told to put a freeze on my account?"

"You see, all your accounts are attached to your family firm, and yours have been flagged for transactions over twenty-thousand by the CFO."

I drop the pen when I stretch my fingers in place of balling them into fists. "Alan Willhiser put a cap on my spending?"

His voice is low. "Yes, sir."

It's all I can do not to rage, but it's not the banker's fault. "And is there anything else you can do on your end to help with this?"

"I am afraid not. The CFO is the only one who—"

"Thanks." I hang up. It was rude maybe, but I don't want to hear another word about how Alan has control over my money. That worm has been pissed off and jealous about my inheritance ever since I got it, and he finally has his greasy fingers in my wallet. Wonder how he convinced Dad to let him have this kind of control over me. Not that it matters.

I will simply have to convince Alan to back off.

The elevator ride to Alan's floor is a short one, and when I arrive, his admin looks nervous. But she always looks nervous. Being the administrative assistant to the CFO comes with a lot of people yelling at her, I'm sure of it, so I try to speak politely when I get to her desk. Storming past her will only darken my mood. So, I flash my nicest smile. "Alan in?"

She gulps. "Yes."

"I'd like to see him."

Her smile is strained, and I almost feel bad asking her to do her job. But she buzzes in anyway. "Mr. Willhiser, Mr. West is here to see you."

"Elliot or Anderson?"

She gulps. "Anderson."

Not sure if this idiot knows I can hear him grumble under his breath. Not the words, but the tone of them. He's not happy about me showing up in his office. Good. I'm not happy about him showing up in my wallet.

"Show him in."

His office isn't as nice as my own, but given his position, it is appropriate for his standing. A CFO should have a decent office, after all. A view of the city, since Alan has always hated the water. Larger than mine, but the furnishings are less comfortable. Scandinavian design is better suited to style than company. Everything is severe and angular, much like Alan himself.

He sits behind a glass-topped desk on the far right, his eyes locking onto me. His smile could not be more forced. "Anderson. Thought I might see you today." He glances past me. "It's fine, Gillian."

"Sorry to interrupt your day, Alan. I'll try to keep this brief." I shut the door behind me.

"By all means, come in and have a seat."

A white man in his fifties, Alan Willhiser worked hard to get to the top, sacrificing marriages on the way there. A workaholic of the first order. Once he reached CFO, we'd thought he would finally breathe, but no. He turned his affinity for work into micromanaging anything in his purview.

On more than one occasion, Dad had told him he didn't need to keep up such a grueling schedule. But Alan insisted a good CFO watched every penny, and that if he didn't, who would? Dad, being a man who appreciates dedication above all else, has warmed up to the idea.

Micromanaging has become his specialty, which might be why he has wormed his way into my money. If he hadn't wrestled his way into Dad's good graces, I doubt I'd be in this mess now. This means I have to play nice, which I loathe.

Alan hates I was born with Future CEO written in my DNA. He hates even more that I was given my inheritance and a cushy job straight out of law school. Never mind the fact that I didn't ask for my inheritance, nor did I ask for the job and all the responsibilities that come with it. My father simply had a plan in place for me, and there was no arguing that. I would have been a moron to turn any of that down.

Even though he's near my father's age, I swear Alan wishes he were my father's heir apparent. I can't tell if it's jealousy that I've had things so easy, or if it's anger that anyone but *him* has it so easy.

Doesn't matter right now.

I've kept my charming smile on, hoping to set him at ease, but I'm not sure Alan has anything resembling ease. Everything about him is stiff, and it always has been. From his overly starched collars to his precision haircut, all details are Alan-perfect, which is to say stiff and unyielding. As I sit, I wonder if he's ever so much as taken a deep breath. "Thank you for seeing me on such short notice, Alan."

"Anything for the West family, of course. What can I do for you?"

"I wish I had an appointment on the books, but a very important matter has suddenly come up, and I need to discuss it with you."

"I'm all ears."

Keeping my smile exactly as it was is a challenge. Alan truly is all ears. In fact, I've often wondered if he's considered getting them pinned so he less resembled a cartoon character. But that was the old me. The me who teased people for their appearances. I'd like to think I've changed. At least a little.

"Yes, well, I attempted to make a donation a few days ago, only to find out today that the donation did not go through and my account is frozen under your guidance. Care to explain?"

"Ah, yes, that. Your father asked me to monitor your accounts. Your spending has gotten out of control."

"Excuse me?"

He smiles slyly. "Your father's words. Not mine."

"My money is my own. Not his. Not yours."

"I'm sure you see it that way, but a four-hundred thousand dollar donation to some random charity? Surely, Anderson, you must understand why we cannot allow that."

"Random? It's the Chamberlain Mansion. How can you call that random? It's a Boston institution." That's the whole point of hosting the auction there. To make this look legit.

"I could have allowed for a smaller dona-tion, understand? But such a large one?" He shakes his head, still smiling that slimy smirk. "I'm afraid that is out of the question."

Oh, he is fucking loving this. Me, having to come to him for permission to spend my own money? The asshole is eating this up. "You're being a bit ridiculous, don't you think?"

"A four-hundred-thousand dollar donation is ridiculous for a man who has never shown the slightest interest in building preservation, Anderson. Did you win one of their auctions or something?"

Yes. "That's rather small-minded of you. I know a worthy charity when I see it. Don't need to win an auction to want to help a good cause. I'm surprised you're not as charitable as I am, considering how hard you've worked all your life. I'd think seeing how much work goes into things would make you more altruistic, not less."

He cocks an eyebrow at me. "Let me guess —there was some pretty girl you wanted to impress with the size of your *wallet*?"

I am dangerously close to snapping at him. "What I do with my money is my business, Alan. Not yours."

"It might not be my business, but it is your

father's. I was only following Elliot's orders. If you want, you can take it up with him."

Giving me permission to speak to my father? He is weaving his way between us, isn't he? If Dad does not see the way he's attempting to control the situation, then I will show him.

Alan tries to maintain a cool exterior, but I see the cracks. The way his hand slowly inches toward his call button. The somehow stiffer position of his shoulders. A tightening wrinkle at his temple. He's waiting for me to bark at him or attack him some other way. He's been wanting a confrontation with me for a long time, and this gives him the perfect excuse. To prove I am not CEO material. If I escalate this, I'll look like the dangerous hothead he's always told Dad I am.

So, I laugh, and the sound makes him jump a little. "Good talk, Alan." I leave his office without another word. I should have known better than to argue with Alan. There is someone above him.

-

Chapter 22

ANDERSON

Dad's office is on the same floor as Alan's, but on the other side of it. When his secretary—Margaret insists the old school title is her preference—sees me, she smiles the way a grandmother beams at her naughtiest grandchild. But only an idiot would mistake her soft appearance for a soft heart. She chides, "What trouble are you stirring up today, laddie?" Her Irish accent is one of the things about her that makes me smile.

The other is her crochet.

Dad had always told her she could do whatever she wanted at her desk, so long as all of her work was done. I'd almost never seen her work. What I've always seen her do is knit. Didn't matter the time of day, Margaret Hannigan always had those needles in her hands unless she was typing, and I'd only rarely seen her do that. No clue how she got anything done, but after forty years at my father's and my grandfather's desks, she was on top of every detail. Margaret was an institution of West and Sons.

"I need to see my father. Is he in?"

Green eyes give me the once over, while her hands are busy at work. "He is. But that doesn't mean he's available."

I smirk and take a breath. She's not being rude. She's being purposefully obtuse to remind me of my manners. "Margaret, would you please be a dear and let him know I'd like to see him?"

She giggles and teases, "All you had to do was ask." Then she shifts in her seat, fingers still flying with her needles. "Mr. West, Anderson is here to see you."

"Excellent. Send him in."

Why is he happy about this? That can't be good. But I keep my smile in place.

She blows a gray curl from falling in front of her eyes. "Go on, love. And don't stress him. He's having a time with the accounting department about billable hours again."

"Thank you, Margaret." As I pass her, I

pause to ask, "How did you page him without moving?"

"Had this handy button installed a while ago." She gestures with her foot at a black pad beneath her desk. "Does the same thing. But if the others ask, tell them I'm just that good."

I laugh. "You are, dear. You are." Dad's office is the largest, of course. Expansive windows, an arched ceiling, plants to make it feel less lifeless and yet failing to do so. The entire room is gray, as if he's never tired of Boston's muted colors.

When I was a boy and imagined how I'd redecorate it, color was the first word that came to mind. A red wall behind my desk. Furniture with life to it. But over the years, I've wondered if I would splash color all over the place or not. Whatever choices I make, it will not be something Dad would like. Hell, I could keep it the same as him, and he'd find a reason to complain.

Dad sits at his desk, gesturing for me to sit in his guest chair. I hate that thing, but expected no different. It's even less comfortable than Alan's guest chair. Doesn't matter. Hopefully, I won't be here for long.

"What is going on, Anderson?"

"I made a donation to the Chamberlain Mansion, and Alan decided it wasn't up to his standards for giving. He says you gave him the reins on my accounts. Would you like to explain that?"

"I am not in the habit of explaining myself."

"No, you're not. But if you want me to follow in your footsteps one day, I should learn your thinking on matters like this, shouldn't I?"

A smile spreads his lips. "Splendid answer. Alan is correct. I gave him the reins on your accounts."

I grit out, "Why?"

"Understand, it is not that I do not have faith in you, Anderson. You have shown remarkable improvements over the years. But your spending has become reckless, and we must tone that down. You must be more responsible, not only in your work, but also in your personal matters. This includes your spending habits."

"What I do with my money is my business, Dad. No one else's."

He laughs once. "Come now. I did not raise you to be this naïve."

"You didn't raise me at all. That was the nannies and Mom."

"And they raised you under my guidance.

It's the same thing," he brushes off the possible parental guilt and moves on, just like always. "Running a company is just as much about what we do as it is about what people think we do. If you run around spending your money like you'll never run out of it, then your employees will see this and think you are spending their bonuses. The shareholders will think you are blowing through their investment."

"Ah," I nod my head, as if it's only just occurring to me, "so that's why you and Mom live in a shoebox apartment, wearing scraps from thrift stores and eating fast food, right?"

"Your petulance is tiresome, Anderson."

"So is the bullshit about how I spend my money."

He leans forward, steepling his fingers on his desk. "Tell me this. Every business, no matter how successful, goes through tough times. What happens when there are lay-offs and employees, carting out boxes of their belongings, ask how you could spend exorbitant sums on building preservation instead of their salaries? How will you tell someone we must cancel their project for a lack of funds, when you just bought the newest model of a car you don't need? Frivolity feels good in the moment. But I need you to think of the long term. Every person in this building needs you to think of it, too."

He always picks at me. Whatever I want, whatever I wear, whatever I say, none of it is ever good enough. It's a poor reflection on him. Or on the company. Or on the family name. My interests do not matter to him. They never have. When I took up archery, it wasn't proper enough to please him. He said I could have taken up falconry or polo if I wanted to pursue a true gentleman's sport. My clothes were designer, but not the designers he liked. It's always been this way. But now, he is fucking with my funds, and if I try to defend my past purchases, this will devolve into a hell of an argument. The one he is baiting me into.

I will not take the bait. I will not give him yet another reason to avoid retirement. We have played this game too many times for me to not know the rules and how to evade them.

"Understood. So, maybe you would do me the honor of listing who else has a CEO title and a money nanny."

"You are not CEO yet, son."

"As you keep reminding me," I mumble under my breath and pick an imaginary piece of lint from my trousers. But then I smile at him. "How am I to learn to manage my money in a responsible way, if I don't have access to it?"

"That is a better question." He smiles. "But the best question is, how will you become a reliable leader if you don't commit to a woman?"

I face palm, then scrub my hand over my face, as if I'd planned to all along. "We're back on this?"

"Until the point no longer remains, Anderson."

"I told you I am seeing someone."

"And I told you to bring her to supper. But did you? No. And I'll tell you why. Because there is no June Devlin. You made her up, didn't you? Just trying to get the old man off your back. I used to let your white lies slide when you were a boy, but you are a man, and I—"

"I didn't make her up, Dad. Is that what this is all about? You think I lied about June, so you had Alan put a hold on my accounts?"

He laughs. "The two are not related, I assure you. And if she is real, then why did you miss supper?"

Because she doesn't know you think she's my girlfriend. "Because she was busy. With her own family last weekend."

He smiles approvingly and nods, pointing at me. "*That* is a proper reason. People trust those who are involved with their families. You should take a page out of her book. I know you must be serious about her to some degree, since you've mentioned her to me."

As much as I hate lying to him, this is the only line of discussion that doesn't make me want to tear my hair out. "I am serious about her. Told you that."

"You did, but until I see it with my own two eyes, I won't believe it. Trust, but verify, remember?"

His saying should have been etched on my silver baby rattle. "I know, Dad."

"The company will trust you more when you settle down, and you cannot settle down with someone until we meet them. Bring her to supper, Anderson. I'm serious about this."

"I will, but I can't rush it—"

"This Sunday." My father's oratory gift is making non-threatening words feel like a noose.

"I'll see what I can do."

Chapter 23

JUNE

Pajamas? Check. A bowl of ice cream with chocolate sprinkles and chocolate sauce? Check. The money Anderson owes me? Pfft. Like that's gonna happen. Depression is far easier to come by than my fee.

I should have known. Flicking through Netflix on my bed while trying to keep my hair out of my ice cream is a challenge, but it's worth the effort, unlike other recent challenges. I'm pissed and poor and there's nothing I can do about it, so I'm wallowing.

It's not fair. But I've always known life isn't fair. It wasn't when I was a kid, and it's not fair now. One thumbnail blends into another—it's all horror, so the thumbnails are some version of a dark background and spooky lettering with a woman who is either in trouble or she is the trouble herself. Why is it horror, which is so often lauded for being empowering to women, is also the genre that kills the most of them?

Life isn't fair, even in movies.

Ugh. I push my iPad away and dig into the ice cream. At least that never lets me down. Sweet, creamy flawlessness. This one is peanut butter, perfect for chocolate toppings. I don't care what anyone says. Ice cream may not fix my life, but it will fix my mood for the moment.

Still, my head swirls around one question, no matter how much ice cream I shovel in. How could I have been so stupid as to believe Anderson West about anything?

He hasn't called. It's been three days, and he hasn't fucking called.

So, I called out from work. I am in no condition to see other people. Not when I feel like such an idiot. I can't be my sparkling work self while I feel sorry for myself. It just doesn't work that way in my head.

It's funny how angry you can be when you don't get something you never expected in the first place.

I had never thought I'd be able to quit my job so early, and then this shiny opportunity falls in my lap—or rather, I fell in Anderson's—and I'd thought all my dreams were coming true. God, I'm an idiot. Of course, it was a fucking scam. I don't know how he did it. The elaborate nature of it all is boggling me, but he did it, and I am furious.

And for all my fury, what do I have to show for it? Chocolate sauce on my sweatshirt and my hair springing out in every direction.

I've already harassed him at work, so I'm pretty sure I can't just show up there again without security bouncing my ass out. Once again, I'm the butt of his joke and he got the last laugh. It makes my blood boil, and there is nothing to be done with the steam.

Just like every other time he made fun of me, I have to swallow this down and move on. Only, I don't want to. I want to sue the fucker. And I can't. Because there is no way to go through legal channels. And when I contact the Chamberlain Mansion, they act like I'm insane until I give up.

The rich get to play by different rules, and they always will.

As much as I love the thought of starting a photography business, that pipe dream is dying in my heart, because now I want to start a business that helps the little guy get what he's owed from the big guy. I want to level the playing field for all of us who have been screwed over and don't have a leg to stand on. The farmer who gets sued for copyright infringement because patented crops blew onto his field. The small time business owner forced to take the fall for a mobster just to keep his family safe. Farm workers exposed to deadly pesticides. All the little people who need someone in their corner.

A text startles me out of my Robin Hood fantasy. It's Callie, *open the door*.

I roll my eyes, tuck my ice cream between two pillows, and get the door. She's still in her work clothes and looks amazing. I love the girl, but god, I hate her for that. "Hey, Cal—"

"Hey, Cal? Seriously? That's what you have to say to me?" She brushes past me. "Where's the ice cream?"

"What makes you think—"

"The chocolate sauce on your sweatshirt, dingus."

"Hiding behind the frozen peas."

She huffs and goes to the freezer. "Neither Ben nor Jerry is a substitute for a boyfriend, June."

"Toss that in the trash and I will set your hair on fire."

She giggles. "Fine." Closing the freezer drawer, she turns to face me. "But put on real clothes. We're going out."

"I can't go out. I'm sick."

"You are perfectly fine. You're just feeling sorry for yourself."

I stare directly into her eyes and let out the world's most feeble cough.

"I will flatiron your hair within an inch of your life if you don't get dressed right this instant."

Whining, I flop my way to my bedroom and she follows. "But why?"

"Because you need to be among other humans, and don't look at me like that. If you roll your eyes any harder, they will stick that way."

"Other humans are the ones who got me into this mess."

"No, it was one human. And he's an asshole. And if I can work my connections in the Chamberlain Mansion to get them to blacklist him, then I will. But it's a tricky situation, so that will take time. Meanwhile, you need to get out and see that not every man is a gigantic jerk. We are going to Leonard's, so you can meet eligible, hot men with jobs and maturity."

"Can't do it," I tell her firmly as I dive back into my ice cream. "By eligible, hot men with jobs and maturity, you mean lawyers because Leonard's is a lawyer bar, and I am fucking done with lawyers."

"You are a lawyer."

"Which is exactly how I know I'm done with them."

She plops onto the end of my bed and steals my spoon so she can have a bite. "That is spectacular. But it's not better than sex. Remember sex, June?"

"You mean the thing that got me into this mess in the first place?"

Her eyes glaze with sympathy, and there's a tiny part of me that wants to smack her for it. "You got burned. Let's not sugarcoat it. But that doesn't mean you give up on happiness. Or having a life. Anderson has already taken so much from you. Do you want to give him that, too?"

Click. All of a sudden, everything she just said makes something in my brain align. "Holy shit. You're fucking brilliant."

"Thank you for finally seeing—"

"No, I'm serious, Callie. I've been looking at this all wrong. I've been needy and pissed off and so angry that I couldn't see straight, so that's probably why I've been looking at this all wrong, but holy crap, I've been letting the same bastard, who ruined my childhood, also ruin my adulthood. This is ridiculous. Fuck that guy. Give me five minutes and I'm out the door with you."

On my way to the shower, I hear, "Take ten and do something with your hair."

"You got it." Turning the water to full hot, I strip faster than I ever have. Hatred is fuel, and my tank is topped off. The shower scalds, and I don't care. I've got a few days of filth to deal with. I scrub myself clean, nearly taking a layer of skin with the dirt. Every whoosh of my loofah is fueled by the fury of righteous anger.

Can't start a revenge business without getting out of the house. Those lawyers she wants me to meet? They can all help me get my business off the ground. Callie might want me to meet my next Mr. Right Now, but I'm thinking co-counsel.

I got screwed. Then I got screwed over. Now, I'm getting revenge.

Chapter 24
JUNE

Unfortunately, I am the only one who got the revenge memo.

I knew Leonard's was a lawyer bar. I did not know Leonard's was *corporate* lawyer bar. Sharks, but not the kind I need for my revenge plan. Not even close. These guys would take a look at outside-the-law revenge planning and pass out. None of them have the backbone for what I need in a co-counsel for my hypothetical-slash-fantasy Robin Hood firm.

But at least the cocktails are good.

Taking Callie to any bar is the ideal way to end up ignored. She's magnetic and conventionally beautiful, the perfect storm. So the corporate lawyers swarmed around her until a collection of four decided they'd try their hand at getting in good with her at the same time. She's having a splendid time discussing torts with them, and I am having a grand time chatting with my cocktail.

It's a far more interesting conversation.

I should probably pretend to be listening so I can get her cast-offs, but I can't be bothered. Not even correcting one of those boobs about the law will pull me out of my funk, and that is saying something. Part of me wants to say, "No, Bradley, tort reform is not, in fact, good for the average person. Oh, why, you ask? Because average people need to be able to sue those who take advantage of them!" But convincing one guy of the obvious will do nothing in the long-term, so the idea barely moves the needle on my mood. Can't even get my back into it.

Tonight is a bust.

But Callie made all this effort to come and get me and try to cheer me up by surrounding me with hot guys, and I feel like I should make an effort, too. So, I scroll through my social media to pass the time.

"Are you a redditor?"

I blink, taken from my reverie. "What?"

The guy next to me smiles, all friendly. I hadn't even realized he'd peeled off from the group to speak to me at the bar. "Noticed you'd rather be on your phone than talk with everyone else. Thought you might have been more involved than your average social media user." He's cute in a bland sort of way. Dark hair, dark eyes, good chin. "Do you moderate a Reddit page or something?"

And he does absolutely nothing for me.

"Uh no. I am here against my will, thanks to the good will of my friend."

He nods. "That explains the vacant expression you've been wearing. Let me guess. Not a lawyer?"

I laugh. "Well actually—"

"Most women who come here aren't. Don't feel bad. We can get pretty intense about all of this when we get going, and that tends to exclude other people. We don't mean to, though. Especially when the other people are so pretty."

That was a clumsy flirt, but I'll allow it. "So, why do most women come here, then?"

"To hook up with lawyers, mostly. Isn't that why you're here?"

"To be honest, I'm not entirely sure why I'm here right now."

"Some come here for free legal advice, too. So it varies a little," he goes on, kind of ignoring me until he turns his gaze sharper. It makes him cuter when he looks like he has actual thoughts in his head, so I don't mind it. "Let me guess what you do."

I smirk. Can't help it. "Sure. Go ahead."

"You teach eighth grade at a private school."

An unrestrained laugh pops out of me. "Hardly."

He looks me over. "Admin to a magazine executive?"

"Keep trying."

He leans in close. "Naughty librarian?"

"Strike three. Have a nice night. I'm going back to my phone—

"Come on. You'd be hot dressed up like a naughty librarian, all stuffy with a little lace showing. Bet you'd get into it, too. You liked to be spanked, right?"

"Gotta go." I weave through the patrons to get some distance between me and that dude, because damn, that got creepy fast. No matter what Callie says, I do not need contact with other humans, especially other lawyers. When I get to a quiet corner, I check my phone again, desperate for some distraction.

A text from Anderson. *Need to talk.*

It must be my lucky fucking night. From the guy who wants to spank me to the one who did. *I am out, can't talk.*

I'll come to you. This is urgent.

Either he's decided to pay up or he's figured out some way to drag this out to amuse himself. If he's actually in a paying mood, I need to see him. If it's the other thing, I can tell him to take a hike. Maybe I can get the Naughty Librarian Guy to kick his ass. He seemed drunk enough to try.

So, I respond, *I'm at Leonard's Bar. Do you know it?*

Be there in 5.

That's fast. Whatever he's on about must be important. Or he's readying the next phase of this prank. I wish I had a better history with Anderson; that he hadn't been such a fucking bastard for so many years. That I could believe he's on the up and up. It'd be nice to think this was all just one big banking error, and he's been working tirelessly to get it sorted out.

But I have a long memory, and it is scarred by that man.

I'm not naïve. Not anymore. I will not be sleeping with him ever again. That needs to be the first thing out of my mouth when he comes in. *If* he comes in. Or he'll stand me up, like a coward. Nah. He won't stand me up. He has too much fun dicking me over.

I half expect to see his friend Tag some place in here, ready to watch Anderson take me down and getting into position to hit me with a double zinger of his own. He used to do that— wait until Anderson's insults hit, then join in with one of his own. Tag was many things, but *original* was not one of them. Wonder what he's up to these days.

So, I check out his social. Pic after pic of him on yachts with bikini-clad women under his arms. Him in a race car. Him, playing golf in some exotic locale. It's all I can do not to barf. He's the kind of man my imaginary clients would need revenge on. His family is involved in law and real estate, and they own properties around the world, enabling him to travel on the company dime and call it work.

In short, I hate Tag McAllister.

I'm sure there is no end to the people he's screwed over. Like Anderson.

It's strange, though. As much as I want to loathe Anderson—and part of me actively does —I also think he was embarrassed by his account being frozen. If all of this is an act, it's a hell of an act. He never used to have the kind of acting chops it would take to pull all of this off, and he could have learned to be a better actor for sure, but it's hard to believe. I mean, I know he hated me back in the day, but for him to go to these lengths? Extreme, even for him.

And then, there's the Kalen Black of it all.

The one proof that Anderson West has more depth to him than I ever credited him with. If he hadn't helped that kid, then I could believe this was all just Anderson being the pompous piece of shit I always thought he was. But when I brought Kalen up, he was uncomfortable. It was as though he felt exposed. Vulnerable.

So, he's not a hundred percent grade-A asshole. So what? He's still screwing me out of my freedom. A freedom I didn't even think was possible.

When a dark-haired, tall man walks in, I find myself leaning to see if it's him. No. But I keep watching the door. I should rejoin the others—I'm sure Naughty Librarian Guy has moved on. I don't want Anderson thinking I'm antisocial, no matter how antisocial I am. He might get the right impression.

Not that his impression of me matters. I just need to look payable. Not fuckable. I am never fucking Anderson West again.

-

Chapter 25
ANDERSON

Leonard's is one of those downtown bars I tend to avoid. It's nice enough—has an old world feel to it. Brick or glass walls, brass fixtures, properly uniformed staff, all the details to make you think it's worth paying through the nose for a decent whisky drink. Thing is, it is worth paying it if you're a wannabe corporate attorney. The accessible connections alone are worth the fee.

But I don't require those kinds of connections and desperation hangs in the air like expensive cologne.

It's full of young-to-middle-aged people, all looking for the hookup. Either for work or for pleasure. The bartenders are swamped, too. No sense in remembering all the details of a shady business deal or a bathroom blowjob. If you're drunk, then you have plausible deniability. Each of the patrons is dressed as though they've just come from the office. Wall-to-wall suits and skirts.

All of them but me.

I'd hoped to see June at her apartment, so I'd changed into something a bit more casual. Black leather flight jacket, gray cashmere sweater, and jeans, black leather boots, something that hopefully says, "Responsible man not trying to continue to screw you over." If I'd worn my suit, she might think I was trying to appear intimidating.

Strange to overthink an outfit, but this whole situation has me overthinking.

Scanning through the crowd, I wonder if she lied. I don't see her anywhere. It's not as though she owes me the meeting. She is the one who is owed, not the other way around. Couldn't blame her if she took a spot of revenge on me by lying about her location. It's not more than I deserve.

But then I see her. She's tangled up with some blond and a crew of suitors. Of course, June is surrounded by men. Not as if she has a reason not to be. I'd imagine men swarm her wherever she goes. She has all the options in the world.

Getting to her is a task and a half. The place is packed like sardines, and her group sits near the bar itself. Easier for them to get drinks, but harder for me to get to her. Once I reach her, I'm relieved to see she appears to have no interest in the men around her. In fact, she is ignoring them. One in particular wears a dejected glare whenever he looks at her.

Good. June Devlin deserves more than some stuffed shirt corporate attorney. She looks incredible. Blue jacket over a black on black ensemble. She outshines every woman in here. When she feels eyes on her, she glances up from her phone.

I nod toward the back, hoping to extract her from the group. This is not a conversation for anyone else to hear.

But instead of following my lead, she leans back on the bar, arching a little. Her jacket falls open, revealing the black blouse beneath is a tight lace. Open enough to see a hint of her black bra, but not enough to be indecent.

How she does not have men on their knees before her, I will never understand.

The confident anger in her eyes sends an

aching heat to my balls. I swallow hard, trying to form thoughts again when all I want to do is bend her over the bar and make her see God. Clearing my throat, I lean in. "You don't want anyone else to hear what I'm about to tell you."

Recognition lights her eyes from within. "Ah. Fine." She grabs her purse, whispers to the blond, who looks me over. Then June says, "Come on, then," and parts her way through the crowd.

I follow her lead. It's easier than trying to maneuver through there myself. Besides, following means I get to watch her ass in those tight little pants.

We find our way to a corner that offers the kind of shared privacy found only in loud bars. It's so loud that no one else will hear us, yet it's so public that no one would assume the contents of our conversation. If staying here makes her feel better about meeting with me, so be it.

"No chance we could speak outside, eh?"

Her surliness curls her lip at me. "No. There isn't. You wanted this meeting, Anderson. What's all this about?"

"I know you're angry with me—"

She cuts me off with a haughty laugh. "Oh, am I? Please tell me more about me."

I take a breath to get past that. "It's been days since I should have called you. I'm sorry about that. I was trying to figure out some way to get through the red tape I am facing, and it galls me to admit that I failed. If—"

"Why have you failed, Anderson? You've always been the guy who could do anything he wanted, but now, suddenly, I am the one thing you can't buy?" She laughs bitterly. "I find that impossible to believe."

"Yes, well, my history of buying whatever the fuck I want is precisely why. My father thinks I spend recklessly, and he may be right about that, but that does not change the fact he's interfering with money that is rightfully mine." I huff. It pains me to say any of this out loud, but especially to the one woman I would like to impress. "He is the reason my accounts are frozen. I cannot get them unfrozen until I prove I am not some careless kid with too much money."

"Good god. That is one hell of an excuse. I would have thought you had more pride than to come up with a cover like that. You know, maybe something like, the government has frozen your assets due to some … I dunno, charge against your father. Or you were involved in espionage." She giggles at me. "You could have told me you were a spy, you know. Something good and fun, not that your father is running the show. How pedestrian."

Then it hits me. "You still think this is some kind of prank?"

"Well, what else would it be? This is you, Anderson. Am I supposed to take your word at face value?"

I should have gotten a drink before I started this conversation. "Fuck. Um, I guess not."

"I'm not an idiot—"

"Never thought you were. Far from it, June. You were at the top of the class for a reason."

She frowns and tilts her head. "You remember that?"

"I remember everything about you."

"Right, well then, you remember that I'm not the kind of girl you fuck over. I'm tired of this cat-and-mouse thing you've been playing out, and prank or not, this is getting old. I'd like my money so I can move on."

"And I would like nothing more than to give it to you."

She arches a brow and smirks.

"The *money*." Although if she wanted me to give her anything else, I'd do so happily.

"Then why don't you tell your dear old dad that you owe a debt and need to pay it?"

"Because sums of money that large raise questions neither of us want to answer publicly, let alone to our parents."

"So, lie. You're a lawyer."

I laugh. "True as that is, I don't like to lie to the old man. And I can't figure out a good enough lie on my own for him to unfreeze my accounts. I have to give him a reason to want to do it."

June thinks quietly for a moment, and part of me wishes she would land on the idea herself. If it's her suggestion, she's less likely to deny it. "What kind of reason would be good enough for him to unfreeze your account?"

Damn. I take a breath to steady myself, because I'm about to swing for the fences like Ted Williams when he came back from the war. "I have an idea, and I'm going to need your help."

Chapter 26
JUNE

Ugh. I hate this. I hate everything about this, and now, he wants my help to get me my money? This isn't right. I should walk away.

But I want my fucking money.

"Fine. I'm listening."

"So, you'll help?"

I laugh and sip my drink. I've already decided he's probably not lying. If he was, it would have been a more fanciful lie. Something far more interesting than his dad, wallet-blocking him. But I'm going to make him sweat it out a little. He more than deserves that.

"I will listen. Whether I help depends on this plan of yours."

"My father has this thing about me settling down. He thinks that if I've committed to a woman, then clients will see me as commitment-worthy. It's some old school bullshit, but he clings to it."

"Not a bad theory, I guess. People like stability—wait." *He's not about to suggest what I think he's about to suggest, is he?*

"That's where you come in."

Panic clutches at my throat, and it goes raspy. This cannot be happening. "Anderson—"

He puts his hands up to cut me off. "I know you're gonna say no, but hear me out."

I laugh and realize there is not enough alcohol in the bar for what he's about to say. "You're insane."

"And you were willing to fuck me for this money. Are you saying you won't do a little role-playing for it, too?"

"I mean, fair enough, but low blow."

"Didn't mean it as an insult, I promise. Just that, if you're willing to go to one extreme—

"Yeah, yeah, I get it. But lying to your family? This is a lot, even for you."

He nods once. "If you pretend to be my fiancée at Sunday supper with my parents, then I can all but guarantee he will unfreeze my accounts. What he needs is for me to feel stable.

That's it. And when he unfreezes them, I pay you."

"That's it? I show up for *one* family dinner, and," I snap my fingers, "poof, the money?"

He takes a stiff breath. "Not entirely. My father is not easy to impress. I've been trying my whole life and only managed the feat a handful of times. This will take you, at the top of your game. He will try to trip you up, to make you say or do the wrong thing. My mom is easier— she just wants to see me happy. But Dad is a beast. He will want to know what clubs you belong to—

"None."

"What books you read—"

"Do romance novels count?"

"No. He will want to know about your breeding."

I laugh so hard, I'm convinced whisky will burn a tunnel through my sinus cavity. My eyes burn, but I don't care, because that was funny as hell. "My breeding? Am I a cocker spaniel?"

"It just means he'll want to know about your family, June. Who your parents are, your grand-parents. He wants to know how stable you are, too. If you were pedigreed, he would have heard of you by now. This is good and bad. The thing you have over him is that you're an unknown entity, so you can be whatever he wants."

That sounds suspiciously like what Cesar and Camille had said about my fateful night. He can't possibly mean it that way … but I have to ask. "Are you saying you want me to sleep with your dad?"

He freezes for a moment like a deer in headlights, then bursts into a laugh with his very soul. When he catches his breath, he shakes his head. "Fuck no!"

"Okay. Look, it's not that funny, considering everything. This whole situation has been a roller coaster for me, so I'm not out of pocket for asking that."

He wipes his eyes. "I don't mean to laugh so much at that, but if he ever touched you like that, I will end him."

That's oddly touching to hear, and I can't put my finger on why. "Good to know."

"I want you to pretend to be my fiancée so I can get control of my fortune. Nothing more than that. The second I get my money, you get paid. That's the takeaway." He runs his fingers through his dark hair, and I remember doing that when we were together that night. The feel of his hair. It's softer than it looks. Touching him like that was a strange and wonderful thing. Makes it hard to hang onto my anger, but a minute ago, I thought he might sell me to his dad, so the anger comes right back.

Sharply, I ask, "So be an impressive fiancée, and I get my money. That's the deal?"

He nods.

To be clear, I tell him, "You know I'm not sleeping with you, either, right?"

His eye pinches at the corner like my words struck something. "I'd expect nothing less, June. Not after what you've been through on my behalf."

It's funny. Saying the words out loud to him struck something in me, too. Maybe it's the finality of it. Like I've closed a door I might have wanted to remain open. I'm not sure. But now that I've told him, I have the urge to take it back. Strange, that.

But the only reason it stings a little is the obvious. I mean, he is easily the hottest guy I've ever been with, and the sex? Oof. That was something. A memory that's inspired me to burn out the motor on my best vibrator. It's replacement will be the first thing I buy with my money when it comes in.

If. If it comes in.

I still want him sweating this out. "You realize this is a big ask, right?"

"Without question, and as such, I'll tack on another ten grand for whatever playacting you will do to accomplish our goal. Consider it a consultant's fee. It will top you off at an even four hundred thousand. It's always bugged me that we didn't get to even it out at the auction, but some of those bidders were too dumb to realize what was on that stage."

A flush of heat rolls through me. Since that night, he's only had the best things to say about me, and I've almost constantly thought the worst of him. Even with years of bullying behind us, I still feel guilty for thinking that way about Anderson West. Is this a weird kind of Stockholm Syndrome? Whatever it is, when he says things about me being worth more, or that he remembers everything about me, I'm taken aback. He's either the best actor in the world, or he's being honest.

I can't tell which frightens me more. But if this is all a prank, then I can hang onto my anger. It's all I've had for years. It's comfortable. Anger pushed me through school. It drove me to overachieve and earn scholarships and get an excellent position at the firm I'm with now.

Anger at Anderson West and Tag McAllister and all the other snobs who said I didn't belong with them. So, I hope this is a prank. It lets me stay angry.

And if this isn't a prank ... if he means what he says about me, then I am beyond confused about every interaction we have ever had. My mouth goes dry at the thought of it, so I take another swig. "Tell me what I need to do, Anderson. Prep me for this. How can I help?"

Chapter 27
JUNE

The text came in early Sunday morning. I'd expected it to be Anderson. Something about making sure I wear the right clothes or say the right thing or use the right fork. He's been tutoring me in etiquette lessons he's convinced I've never had. He's right about that, but a long time ago, I'd googled and YouTubed everything I could on etiquette to be able to mix with my high-end clientele. No sense in losing an account because I drank my soup the wrong way. I'm not new. But, I want to impress his dad, so I've put up with it for a couple of days.

Today, though, the text was from work.

One of our clients is having some sort of emotional breakdown, so it's all hands on deck. Hoorah. Catering to whiny babies is one of the many reasons I need out of the firm. Any other day, I could lie and say I love my job. Today, though, I'm nervous enough about supper with the West parents. I do not need this on top of that.

But no one asked me. No one ever does. Which means I have to muscle through today and muscle through tonight. I can have my own personal breakdown come Monday morning.

This would all be less grating if I had my money already. Of course, it would be. That would mean I could be done with this job. I groan in my bed and fling the covers off. Staying in bed longer and wallowing in my misfortune is not going to change anything.

Today changes things. It will change everything. It has to. I don't know what I'll do if this doesn't work.

No use thinking like that. Let's go.

I haul out of bed and get ready for work. Sunday should be a day of rest and relaxation, or in my case, it should be a day-long existential crisis about lying to a man I don't even know so I can get my ill-gotten gains. Either way, it should not be a day of work.

But maybe this is a blessing in disguise. Going to work will keep me from freaking out all day about tonight. Can't have an existential crisis while consoling a giant wealthy baby.

My day disproves my theory.

As I'm coaxing a man off a metaphorical ledge, I'm also wondering if he's wrong to be on said metaphorical ledge. In fact, maybe he's the sane one between us. Either way, I'm multi-tasking—work and personal crisis—all day long, and it is exhausting. Thankfully, they also brought in Callie for today, so I have her to whine to. "… it's a lot, Cal."

"That was him at the bar, wasn't it?"

I nod.

"Good god, honey. He's a keeper."

I laugh and shake my head. "I did tell you about the years and years of bullying, right?"

She nods. "But it sounds like he's doing everything in his power to make this right with you. Maybe he's changed."

"You're only saying this because he's a walking panty-wetter."

"Are you saying I'm shallow?"

"I love you, Callie, but you make saucers look deep."

She giggles hard at me. "Yeah, well. Just because I have my priorities in order doesn't mean I'm wrong."

"Oh, really?"

"I like my men hot, well moneyed, and smart. I don't think that's a detriment to anyone."

"You wouldn't."

"And besides, is it so wrong that I want you paired up with someone on Daniel's social rung? It would make double dating easier."

I smile at her. "You're hopeless, my dear."

"So, what are you wearing for the big night?"

I pull out the garment bag from my deep desk drawer to show her. "Nothing too flashy—I don't want to look like I'm trying too hard, you know?" After I unzip, I get her gaze of approval.

"That's perfect. Simple cream sweater dress, boots?"

I nod. "Brown knee boots."

"Classic, sexy without being over the top, respectable neckline … I'd say you nailed it."

"Thanks. That means a lot from you." I pack it all back again. "I just hope Anderson agrees."

"He will. He's probably more nervous than you are. Seeing you in that will calm him down some, I'm sure of it. And as far as you? What will you tell them that you do?"

"For that, we've decided to go with the truth. I have a good job, something that won't set off their alarm bells. For their intents and purposes, I am a financial catch, funny as that is."

"And what causes will you champion when the topic gets brought up?"

"Huh?"

She smiles. "Thought so. You have to be able to rattle off some charitable organization you're involved in. People like the Wests must be involved in the community. Rumor has it Elliot West rides Anderson hard because he wants a Senator in the family one day."

That idea starts a cascade of laughter that I cannot hold back. When I look up at her, I'm the only one in on the joke. "The Senator and the hooker. It's too much for my pea-sized brain to handle right now, Callie."

"Oh please, you're hardly that. Besides, high-end escorts are nothing to be ashamed of, you pulled in quite the haul."

"Theoretically."

She shrugs. "It's only a matter of time before he pays up. You said it yourself."

"Yeah, but believing that takes a lot of faith at the moment."

"Speaking of your interesting reunion night, what will you tell them about how you met?"

"School."

"Ah." She nods once.

"We figure sticking as close to the truth as possible will be the easiest tactic. Lying about little things would only muddy things up. No sense in that."

"That makes sense. You have enough going on without adding to it." She pauses. "Client gonna make it?"

I can't stop from rolling my eyes. "When their biggest worry is whether Uncle Sam will find a few hundred k to tax, it's hard for me to get my sympathy up for them. Yeah, he'll make it. He's looking at a smaller tax burden than most lawyers normally have, and he has several hundred million stashed around the world. Can't say I'll be up tonight worrying about him."

"Well, that's good. You have enough on your plate."

"Speaking of, I have to get ready. Anderson will be here soon to pick me up."

"Good luck tonight, June. Break a leg."

I chuckle to myself. "Guess I'm making my acting debut, huh?"

"Nah. Pretty sure that happened every night in bed with Trent."

That earns a laugh. A bitter, sad little laugh. "You're not wrong."

I grab the garment bag and my boots to change in the bathroom. Once everything is on, I check myself a dozen times in the mirror. Callie says it's a suitable outfit and I trust her on these things, but I'm still tugging the sweater dress to stop it from hugging my curves so much. It fits, but it's *fitted*, and I'm not used to that.

When I come out of the bathroom, though, I get a low whistle from her. "You'll knock him dead."

"Not before I get my money."

"Have fun tonight."

Fun? How can I think about having fun tonight? I'm going into the lion's den. But she means well. "I'll try."

The trip in the elevator feels like I'm sinking to Hell itself. Like when the doors open, there will be an inferno about to engulf me. I don't enjoy lying to parents. Little white lies? Sure. I'm fine, how are you? Sure, I caught that play. I love the Red Sox. Little white lies that mean nothing in the grand scheme of things.

But pretending to be Anderson's fiancée is a huge one. For all I know, his parents could be perfectly lovely people, excited to meet me because I'm the first girl he's brought home. Disappointing parents is something I am hard-wired to hate doing. Thanks, Mom. So this feels incredibly wrong.

But four-hundred thousand dollars feels incredibly right.

I've committed to this, and I'm doing it. I am not backing out because of guilt or any other pointless reason. When the doors open, there's no inferno. Only the lobby. Strolling through, I wave at the security guards like I always do, and walk out to the canopy in front of the building. The weather is freezing and wet, but I hardly notice it because Anderson is there, leaning on his shiny sports car. I don't know cars very well, but I've never seen its equal. The car is low to the ground and sleek beyond need. A showing off car. It's so black, it looks like it drinks the light. He smirks and opens the door. "Your chariot awaits."

I laugh and roll my eyes before stepping into the car. I hadn't thought it was built for comfort as well as speed, but I was wrong. The sumptuous black leather seats swallow me with ease, like sitting in a spa chair for a treatment.

He closes my door, then joins me in the driver's seat. Anderson's eyes rake over my body, making my thighs clench. What the hell. His deep voice rumbles, "Are you ready for this?"

"Only if you drive near the speed limit."

"Such a good girl, aren't you, June? For tonight, let's be bad."

His words caress every intrusively dangerous thought I've had about him since our night together. It's too close to what he said about going down on me, and I can't help but think he chose those words on purpose to do exactly what they are doing to me.

I clear my throat, trying to think. "The speed limit, Anderson. If you want me to be on my best behavior with your parents and not a frazzled wreck, then you will get me there in one sane piece."

"Have it your way."

I plan to.

Chapter 28

JUNE

"I'll be good," Anderson says. But the amusement in his eyes still worries me.

"I just don't want to be any more nervous than I already am—"

"Relax, June. You were born to play this role."

"Myself?"

He grins cheekily, while keeping his eyes on the road.

I roll my eyes. "You're a real funny guy when you want to be."

"Glad you're finally appreciating my sense of humor."

"Yes, well, being the butt of the joke for years put a damper on enjoying it."

His face darkens, and I immediately regret

saying that. "For what it's worth, June, I am deeply sorry for all of that. Truly. I hate—"

"Don't flog yourself on my account, Anderson. I'm fine now."

"You're more than that. You're flourishing."

"Huh?"

"Look at you. You're with one of the top firms in Boston, even if you hate it there. You're brave enough to do something risky to meet your goals. And you look ravishing tonight."

Warmth creeps up my throat and into my cheeks. "Guess I look okay—"

"Don't do that. You're stunning. Own it."

I don't know how to react to his seemingly genuine praise. It's nice and uncomfortable at the same time. So I mutter a strained, "Thanks."

He pulls out a small box from his jacket. "Size seven, right?"

"Not since the tenth grade."

He passes me the box. "Your ring size, June."

"Oh, right." I'd forgotten about this part of the ruse. When I open the box, it takes my breath away. "Wow."

"I hope it's okay. I've never bought one before."

A huff of a laugh puffs out of me. I can't stop staring at it. "Well, I've never gotten one before." The engagement ring is a huge emerald-cut diamond with tiny alexandrite stones down the sides of the band. "It's incredible. But why alexandrite?"

"That's the birthstone for June," he says, like I should have known.

I laugh hard, shaking my head as I slip it on.

"What's so funny?"

"My birthday is August eighth."

"Shit," he says with a laugh. "Seems like the kind of thing your fiancé should know."

"Yeah, but it's okay. We're new at this."

"Why did your folks name you June if your birthday is in August?"

"I'm named for my grandmother."

He slowly nods. "Also seems like something I should know."

"And what were you named for?"

Anderson smiles. "Where my parents met. Anderson, Indiana."

"Aw, that's sweet. Why were they there?"

"They were both just driving through—him for business, her with her parents. They met at the only diner in town and hit it off."

"Guess you never know where life will take you."

"That's for damned sure."

The trip is a quick ride to Beacon Hill, the most classic and expensive neighborhood of Boston. I'm a little surprised—I would have thought his parents would live outside the city. Brookline, maybe. The Park Street townhouse we pull up to is gorgeous, though. Rich red brick and trees lining the road.

I slip the ring on, and despite the wrong birthstone, it fits perfectly. "Honestly, I think the birthdate thing is kind of perfect. Tells the story of two people too excited about new love to get everything right."

"That's some good spin."

"Ready for this?"

"If you are."

I laugh, shaking my head. "Let's do it."

He jumps out of the car and tosses the keys to the valet on his way around the car in a move so practiced I would think he does it every day. He opens my door, and when I stand up, he says, "They'll already be watching from the window."

So, I put my hands around his neck and smile. "Then you should keep me warm."

He bends down for a sweet peck on the lips, and I'm surprised. "Don't look so shocked. We're getting married, remember?"

I giggle and feel the heat in my cheeks again. "This is going to be weird before it's over, isn't it?"

"No, of course not. Just two former enemies pretending to be engaged in order to pull the wool over the eyes of a man too controlling for everyone's own good. Not weird at all."

I roll my eyes, and he takes my hand to lead me into the building. "It's nice to know you're nervous, too."

"What makes you think that?"

"You ramble and you get facetious when you're nervous."

"Good that my fiancée knows me so well."

Which we do. As we walk through the halls, his hand warms my lower back, and I cannot explain why, but it doesn't bug me when he does it. The few times any other man has done it, I found it grating. But right now, I don't mind a little friendly guidance. The elevator takes us to the penthouse.

When we get to the door, he pauses. "Here we go."

"Yep."

But he doesn't move.

"Anderson?"

"Kiss for luck?"

I laugh. "Just knock, you big baby—"

But the door opens. A smiling older woman holds her arms out. She is dressed to the nines in a silk blouse and skirt that, on anyone else would look like office attire, but on her, I suspect it's her loungewear. Instantly, I have the impression that her ash blond hair would not be moved by the Boston breeze. Despite her snooty exterior, the warmth in her voice is unmistakable. "Anderson."

"Mom, hi," he says as he hugs her.

She looks over his shoulder at me, beaming. "And you must be June."

I smile and nod, unsure of what to say at the moment. She releases him, then scoops me in for a hug. "It's nice to meet you, Mrs. West."

She takes my hand. "Please, you must call me Kitty. Come in and meet the family."

"The family?" Anderson asks as he closes the door behind us.

"Well, when Elliot told me you were finally bringing a girl home, I assumed it was serious and that she should meet everyone."

I keep my face in a permanent smile, but it's strained. "*Everyone?*"

"Yes, of course, dear. This way."

I glance back at Anderson with my heart in my throat, and he gives a sheepish shrug. Neither of us expected this kind of reception, but it's not as though we can do anything to stop it.

The penthouse is a mix of old world and modern, with hardwood floors throughout and vast windows to absorb every possible view. Pops of blue show up in the occasional blue stripe or the overstuffed dining chairs. Everything else is beige or white. It's lovely, but frosty. Certainly not the kind of place to raise a son with a soul. No wonder he was so mean as a child.

But it seems incongruous with the sweet woman dragging me behind her and rambling about the architecture as I try to seem interested. She name drops designers as we walk, and though I do not know who these people are, I know enough to sound fascinated. The place must be three or four thousand square feet big, maybe larger. I cannot fathom how much it cost, but easily near ten million to be this palatial in this neighborhood.

Then we reach the living room. And I'm surrounded.

Dozens of people turn their gaze to us, and before long, Kitty is introducing me to Quincy, Heathcliff, Marylin, Theodora, and so many, many more. I cannot keep them all straight, and Anderson gives me a pained smile as he gets us both cocktails. When he delivers mine, he teases, "Mom, do you think she will remember everyone's names? Come on."

"Of course not," she says, smiling and rolling her eyes, "but your cousins came all the way from Brookline to be here, so I'm introducing her to everyone. It's just polite." She leans in closer. "It's the Mackenzies you should take note of, June. They aren't cousins—they're just friends, and they own the best boutiques in Boston and New York. Get in with them. You'll never dress out of season the rest of your life."

Oh, no. Did I commit some faux pas? "Is what I'm wearing okay?"

"I meant nothing by it. But aren't you a dear for worrying? No, you look terrific." If anyone else had said that to me, I would have thought it was an insult, but Kitty clearly doesn't have a mean bone in her body. Where the hell did Anderson get it from? "All I mean to say is, they will take care of you, if I let them. They love to dress the family. Oh, and speaking of the family …" she gazes over my shoulder.

Anderson's expression had been tight before. It's practically cement now.

I turn to see who has joined us, and in an instant, I know. The severe man stalking into the room is Elliot West. Has to be. He looks too much like Anderson not to be his father. This is where he gets his harshness. The man's very step stiffens my spine, no matter how relaxed I pretend to be.

"Dad. Meet June."

When he takes my hand to shake it, ice travels through my arm and down my spine. "A pleasure to meet you, Mr. West." Not sure if I'll get the chance to stop lying tonight.

Chapter 29

JUNE

"Call me Elliot, please. So nice to meet you, June." His eyes flicker at Kitty.

"Let's let them get acquainted, Anderson. I need your help in the kitchen."

Anderson's pained smile deepens. "Alright then, Mom. Be right back."

Why don't I believe that?

"Come with me, June. I'll show you the study," Elliot says, smiling. But his smile never makes it to his eyes.

I'm about to get grilled. This is what we've prepped for, and this is why I spent the last two days googling the hell out of Elliot West. I've boned up. Now it's time to see if my hard work pays off.

God, I hope it pays off.

The study isn't too far from the living room, so the din of chatter and soft jazz is audible until he shuts the door. Then the study feels more like a tomb. It's darker than the rest of the penthouse, with book-lined walls and two large blue leather chairs. A blue-shaded Tiffany lamp sits atop a small table between them.

"Please, have a seat."

I smile and nod, not really wanting to sit there until I do. The chair is far more comfortable than it looks. He sits, too, and I'm relieved. I half thought he might grill me while standing over me.

I'm not sure where to begin, so I go with, "You have a lovely home, Elliot."

"Thank you, but this is really our home away from home. We keep a place in the city for convenience. Our primary home is in Brookline."

I have no idea what to say to that.

"Anderson must be smitten with you for that ring to be on your hand."

Not a congratulations in the traditional sense. "I consider myself lucky to be wearing his ring."

"I would think so. You're a junior associate at your firm, correct?"

Of course he's looked into me. Why wouldn't he? But that doesn't make it any less creepy. "Yes, I am."

"A bright young woman, according to your transcripts."

How far back did he go? "*Bright* might be pushing it, but I worked hard in school."

"And you were there on a scholarship." He sits back, studying me. "Seems you turned a tough childhood into a goldmine."

"My mother raised me to believe that hard work could get me where I want to be in life."

"Hard work and a little luck, right?"

I smile, unsure where he's going with this. "We can all use some luck in our lives."

"And how do you like the law, since you made it your career?"

"It's like most careers, I imagine. Good days and bad. But there are more good than bad, so I stick with it."

"Tell me about the bad days."

This feels like a job interview where the interviewer has already decided they aren't going to hire me. But I push on after a breath to clear my head. "Well, to be honest, there are days when I am pushed to the limit of what I can tolerate."

"How does helping the rich avoid taxes push you to the limit?"

"That's just it—when I wanted to become a lawyer, I thought it was all money and glamor and catered parties … but I was naïve enough to have believed I'd get all of that by helping regular people. That's what all the television lawyers did." I run my finger around the rim of my glass. "Never thought I'd be getting there on the backs of those people. *My* people. But by helping the wealthy keep their wealth, that's exactly what I'm doing. When the rich avoid their taxes, the government must depend more on the money from everyone else. It increases the tax burden on regular people, and the truth is, I hate that part of my job."

He stares at me, and I can't tell if I've upset him.

But he doesn't look happy, and that panics me. "Meaning no offense, of course. I'm sure you pay your fair share—"

But a cool smile comes over him as he says, "No offense taken, June. It's refreshing to hear such an honest assessment of the situation from someone who straddles the lines of it. Tell me, do you want to continue the work you've accomplished?"

"No. I don't."

"What do you want to do?"

I smile, thinking about how he's the man between me and what I want to do. "For a while, I'd thought about going into photography. A creative career for an outlet."

"But … ?"

"But I have a law degree and I am capable of doing something useful with it. If I had my druthers, I'd work for the little guy. I'd help regular people get the justice they deserve."

"And yet, you have fallen for my son, a man who isn't in the business of helping regular people. Does that give you pause?"

Shaking my head, I can't help but think he's trying to trap me in the subtlest of ways. "Anderson's career is his own. I'd never think to tell him what to do, and god help the woman who tried. If he wants to help me in my crusade, I welcome the help, but I would never try to tear him away from his family's work. Though your firm caters to the upper echelons of society, you're also heavily involved in charity, and being able to make generous donations requires sizable funds. I might be an idealist in some aspects of life, but I am foremost a realist."

"That is very good to hear. Has he mentioned that I want him to take over?"

"We haven't spoken much on the matter, but I had assumed that to be the case. He's been groomed since birth for the role, and I cannot think of someone better suited."

Elliot smirks, and it's unsettlingly like Anderson's smirk, except it does not turn me on. But the smirk fades into something else. Hesitance? "No need to campaign for him, June. You're right. I have groomed him for the role. The reason I ask is, he will need a partner in this. Someone as dedicated to the firm as he is. Or at the very least, someone who understands what his work entails. That there will be long nights. Long weeks. Times when he cannot come home, no matter the reason. Running the firm must be his first priority. Not his wife. Not his family. It requires everything of him. He needs a strong partner who can weather that. Who understands the score. Is that something you can do?"

Not hesitance, then. Elliot wants to know if I'm willing to give up myself for Anderson's responsibilities. It would be easy to say yes and tell him what he wants to hear. It would all but slam dunk this whole thing. But what he wants is too much to ask of anyone.

The next woman Anderson brings home will be asked the same thing, and the woman after that, and the next one, and so on. Someone will say yes, and it will blow up in Anderson's face, along with the rest of the family. His child will be raised to be another Anderson, another kid who needed his dad around to make him a better person. I hate that Anderson was neglected. He might have been a happier kid. He might not have bullied me.

If I say yes now, Elliot will think this is okay. That this is how the world should work, because for him, it always has. I can lie about a lot of things. But not this.

"No, Elliot. I can't do that."

"Then perhaps it's for the best that—"

"What you ask for is too much. It's too much to ask for anyone who wants a true partnership in marriage. When I said yes to him, I said yes *to him*. Not to a legacy of cold, lonely dinners and children who don't recognize their father. Anderson grew up like that, and I won't continue it into our family. He deserves more. Our future children deserve more, and so do I. A parent is supposed to provide more for their child than they had, not perpetuate a cycle of loneliness."

He all but rolls his eyes at me. "You would say no to a lavish life of what you've seen around you? Of vacations around the world, multiple homes, all the clothes you could ever want. The best nannies for your children and the latest car under a big bow at Christmas? Gold and diamond—"

I laugh, shaking my head. "I'm not here to absorb his inheritance, Elliot. Anderson's financial situation is easier than most, but that's not what interests me about him."

"What then?" he growls.

"Him. Just him." I shrug. "I knew Anderson back in Appleton. Did he mention that?"

"Yes."

"He was so different back then. Kind of a dick, actually." I laugh at myself. "But I always knew there was something deeper beneath the surface. Then we ran into each other again at Boston U, and it was like the edges had been sanded down some. Not enough, so I kept moving. And then finally, when I ran into him at a charity ball, it was as though all the rough edges had been sloughed off, and what was left was the good man I knew was under all that bravado. He's kind. Thoughtful. Generous. Those qualities I want in a partner. I am grateful he had Kitty to instill that in him." I leave the obvious lack of his father out of the conversation, but we both know what I'm saying. Anderson has those qualities in spite of his father. Not because of him.

Elliot stares for a moment, contemplating something I'm sure I won't want to hear. "So, you would sign a prenup, then?"

Oh that? I laugh. "Happily."

His brows slide up. "If I happened to have a prenup ready to be signed here and now, you'd sign it?"

"Give me a pen, and I'll sign it."

Instead, he laces his fingers together like a villain and smiles. "It is a rare thing to meet a woman with your convictions, June. I don't have a prenup—Anderson hadn't mentioned that he'd proposed. He doesn't tell me much about his personal life," he grumbles the last part. "Not that I blame him. A man's personal life is his business, and I try not to interfere unless needed. He *will* be required to work long hours at the firm. That is the nature of the beast. How he works that out with you is between the two of you. I will not interfere."

Whoever Anderson actually marries owes me big time. I smile at Elliot, feeling a hint of relief. "I'm glad to hear that."

Someone knocks at the door, and Elliot says, "Enter."

When I see Anderson, I feel like the cavalry arrived just after I won the battle. But I'm still glad to see him. "Thought I'd check on everyone."

Elliot smiles at his son. "You've done well for yourself, Anderson. A word of warning, though. June isn't going to put up with your nonsense."

He chuckles. "Oh, believe me. I know."

Chapter 30

ANDERSON

I can't believe she's in one piece after so much time with Dad. Not red-eyed or shaky. In fact, she's smiling brightly. I always knew June was special, but I think I underestimated her.

Fuck, I think my crush on her has just grown. A lot.

Doesn't help that she's in that tight sweater dress and knee boots. It's not revealing at all, but it shows off her shape, and I can't help but think about her naked. Of course, I was doing that before I picked her up, but now it's much worse. The dress is a beige that could be mistaken for nude, so my mind keeps making her naked in my head. The boots? I want to see her in just the boots and nothing else.

The problem is, she hates me. I owe her

money. And cannot think of a way to seduce her yet. Spending time with her enemy's family is not the aphrodisiac I need it to be. Maybe we can get a drink after all of this and see where the night takes us.

Dad stands, and she follows suit. He cocks his head, then smiles. "Time for the dance."

"The dance?" she asks.

"The dance?" I ask flatly, trying not to whine.

He chuckles. "Yes, Anderson. The dance." Then he walks past us to find Mom.

"What dance?" June asks.

"It's a family tradition on my mom's side of the family. When they get together, there's dancing. It's just a thing they do, sort of a way to break the ice for the new people and reconnect with everyone." I shrug. "We can try to skip it, but they will hunt us down."

"Well, if it'll make a good impression on them, I'm game. I enjoy dancing."

"Oh. That's great." I put my arm out for her. "Shall we?"

She smiles and takes my arm. "Lead the way."

When I was a boy, I had fantasized about having a girl with me for the family dance. After

I met June, that fantasy was always her. Seeing her laugh and twirl and have fun with my mom's side of the family. They are much more easy-going than Dad's side. Still as proper as ever, but if someone spills their wine, it's more likely to earn a happy laugh than a scolding.

Taking June to the small ballroom, I eat up the look on her face. She lets out a nervous laugh. "Oh my god, you two were not exaggerating."

"No, we were not. This ballroom is smaller than the one at my parents' home in Brookline, but it suits our purposes." The ballroom is large enough for everyone to be on the dance floor at the same time, and with dark wood floors and ivory walls, it gives the impression of a dance studio more than a ballroom. Wide windows show off the city and a small band plays jazz standards in the corner.

"This is so much fancier than I'd expected, Anderson."

"Be glad we're not at their Brookline house. You'd have to wear a gown."

She laughs, and I take her in my arms. It startles her, but she presses herself to me in a stance, before we begin a turn around the dance floor. As we dance, it is so hard to remember the real reason she's here. That it's not for me. It's for the money. Any other person, I would want to keep things transactional between us. That's easier—less messy. No attachments is a simpler way of life. But if I'm honest with myself, I hate it. Simpler, yes, but meaningless. I want her here for me. It would be so easy to let myself get swept up in this farce—I want it to be real. I want all of this to mean something.

Funny how a family tradition I hated now gives me the chance to have June in my arms. Even if it's only for the money, at least I finally get to have her here like this. I get to hold her and imagine what it would be like if she were here because she wanted to be.

It's the fantasy I had as a boy, but it's tainted by our agreement. She'd never be here of her own accord. She hates me. I've given her no reason not to. But maybe if she has an enjoyable time, then she won't want to run away after all of this is over. If I can make this fun for her, then she might want to stay. Or maybe I'm just telling myself what I want to believe.

A slow version of, "There will never be another you," plays, and I worry she'll want to sit it out. But instead, she loops her arms around my neck, so I press against her low back, and we sway. This feels so right. I never want it to end.

June murmurs, "Been a long time since I slow-danced. Sorry if I step on your feet."

I laugh and she smiles up at me, and my breath catches in my throat as she presses her head to my shoulder. This is everything I have ever wanted. "You're doing just fine, June."

"Thanks. This is nice, Anderson. Your family is a little—"

"Intense?" I offer to mitigate her word choice.

She giggles. "I was going to say passionate, but yes, intense works, too. Explains a lot about you."

"How so?"

"Well, forgive the phrasing, but you're like a dog with a bone when it comes to going after what you want."

"You're not wrong."

"It's nice."

I gulp. "It is?"

"Since you stopped being an asshole, yeah."

I snort a laugh.

"This is not news to you."

She smiles again. "The point is, you come from passionate people, and that's a good thing.

It means that I know what you want. I don't have to guess with you, and that's a nice change."

Part of me hopes she can tell what I want, but the other part of me worries she'll think it's absurd. *Must change the topic.* "Other men leave you guessing?"

"Oh, definitely. They're all cowards. They don't tell you a thing upfront, like every interaction with them is a merger, and they're trying to get the best deal they can. It's exhausting."

Better to ask than to guess wrong. "So, what is it you think I want?"

She chuckles and whispers, "The account."

In that last three minutes, I'd completely forgotten about the account. She was the only thing on my mind. It was a nice three minutes.

"Right. The account." I twirl her, then bring her close. "Doesn't mean we can't enjoy ourselves, right?"

She smiles and comes close again. "Right."

I don't blame her for keeping her eyes on the prize. In her case, it's a literal prize. But her words bruise me. I didn't want to be brought back to reality. Not here. Not now. Maybe part of me wished she was in the fantasy with me, wishing this was real for her own reasons.

Guess it doesn't matter. I know what's on her mind.

The money. Not that I can blame her for that.

"Autumn Leaves" comes on, another slow version. "I've always loved this song."

She looks up at me. "Really?"

"I'm a sucker for a melancholic love song."

"You?"

"And what did you imagine I liked?"

She gives a little shrug with a smirk. "Out of this kind of music? Mack the Knife."

I laugh hard. Can't help it. "A song about a killer for hire? I'm flattered."

She beams up at me. "Or maybe Hard-Hearted Hannah."

"Another murderer?" I spin her and hold her tight and still, staring into her eyes. Her cheeks flush and her eyes fall to my lips. I murmur, "What must you think of me?" Then, I start us up again. Slower this time.

"I was thinking you'd like songs about people who know what they want and go for it."

"Hmm." I wonder if that's the real reason. "Suppose that's not so bad, then." Feeling her soft body against mine, a rush of heat shoots low. I'd been holding it back this whole time, but it's becoming impossible. Knowing what she thinks of me—and that it's not all bad—appears to be an aphrodisiac, and I struggle to keep things PG around my family for the moment.

"Never knew you were a secret romantic, Anderson." The way she says my name is too much. Like she's savoring every syllable.

"The Nearness of You," begins, and I'm sunk. Why is the band playing so many slow songs in a row? Doesn't matter. I'm struggling not to fall into the music. If I do, things between me and June are going to be much more complicated.

I swallow, trying to ignore the way my heart warms when she stays so close to me. Feels like I'm on a knife's edge, and I'm about to get cut. "We all have our secrets, don't we, June?"

"I guess we do."

As the band plays on, I hardly hear the music. Only the steady drumming in my chest. She and I fall silent, swaying to the rhythm. I don't know when the song ended or if anyone else is in the room. All I see is June. The way her lips call to me. The unsure look in her eyes as they keep glancing at my mouth. I am drawn to her—I don't care if this is real or not. The desire is plain on her perfect face. Just as I tip my head down for a kiss, the room breaks out into applause.

Apparently, the band is taking a break, and so are we.

She blinks and smiles around the room, but when she looks up at me again, there's that desire again. I don't know if it's real or if she's the world's best actress. Only one way to find out.

Chapter 31

JUNE

Why am I so warm right now? I can't catch my breath when I look at Anderson. It's so strange. He smiles down at me, and my first instinct is to smile back. Not to brace for an insult, like I always used to.

Things aren't … things are not the same as before, and I don't know what to think about that. But it feels good to smile at him.

He leans close to whisper. "We have some time before supper. I'd like to show you something."

"Okay."

He takes my hand, and it just feels right. Like our hands fit together as though we've held hands our whole lives. It's not awkward or uncomfortable. It's perfect, and it makes me want to follow him wherever he wants to take me.

Why am I having thoughts like this about Anderson West?

It's a startling change, and I'm not sure what's going on exactly. But I have to keep my wits about me. This is all just to get his account unfrozen. Right?

He leads me down some halls I missed on the tour, and before I know it, he stops in front of a large, dark wooden door. It stands out compared to the rest of the place, much like the door to the den his father had taken me to. Anderson pauses before opening it. "I've never brought a girl here before."

I laugh, trying to make light of everything, because he sounded way too serious when he said that and I'm nervous. "Is this your child-hood bedroom?"

He laughs, too, shaking his head. Why does he look so devilishly handsome when he does that? "No. Not hardly. It's just that, I want to take you here, but I'm concerned you'll think I'm being droll or funny. But this is my favorite place in the apartment, and I want to share it with you."

His words make my heart clench. "Oh. I'm flattered."

He opens the door. "Come with me."

I step inside, and I'm in shock. Books. Books as far as the eye can see. Dark wood all around, and a fireplace burns in the far corner. In front of it, two cozy leather chaises and a small table between them. Behind the chaises, a longer table for setting the next selections onto, I imagine. But there are shelves and shelves of books in all other directions, both lining the walls and free-standing.

Anderson places his hand on the small of my back to guide me in, and my body goes molten from his heat, while my brain tries to take in the sheer amount of books around me. I'm at a loss for words while surrounded by them. "What is this place?"

"A library," he says cheekily.

I snort a laugh and swat his shoulder. "I know that, smart ass. Oh my god, you even have one of those slide ladder things to get to the top shelves. Tell me all about this place."

"This apartment used to belong to my grandparents. Actually, they used to own the entire building. That's why, if you look down that way, you'll see the library—"

"It runs the length of the apartment, doesn't it?" I'm in awe. There must be forty rows of free-standing bookshelves in that direction. Maybe more.

He nods. "Yes, it does. Grandfather wanted every book in publication, so for a time, he bought them all. He believed knowledge was the most important thing, which makes much of his collection nonfiction. But Grandmother believed that knowledge without heart was dangerous, so she ensured that there was plenty of fiction, as well."

"She sounds wise."

"Truly, she was." He drifts from me to look at the books. But he doesn't look at them the way he looks at his car. This isn't just another possession to him. It means something to him. "When I was a kid, I used to come here, and I'd pretend my grandparents were here with me. I missed them. Grandmother, in particular. She was so smart and so kind ..." His voice trails off.

I rush to his side and rub his back. "I'm glad you had that in your life, Anderson."

He sighs. "Me too. After she passed, things weren't as ... warm ... here. Mom tried—she still tries, as I'm sure you noticed. But it's not the same. It'll never be the same." A little shrug. "I guess that's how things go."

"But there could be warmth here again. You have to fight for it."

He gives me a small smile. "I've had to fight for it my whole life."

"What do you mean?"

"This library was the only place I felt like I could be myself when I was a kid. The only place I could go and just be me. Most of the time, though, I could only do that alone. Dad … when he caught me with my nose in a book, if it wasn't the classics, or economics, or law, or something he cared about, then I was doing something wrong." He takes a moment, and this feels vital somehow, so I don't speak up. "I figured out that reading in here meant he wasn't likely to bother me, which made it the perfect place for me to read all those *sensitive* books, he called them. You know, books for kids, like *The Hardy Boys* and *Harry Potter*. Things he didn't give a shit about but taught kids how to be—"

"Kind?"

Anderson nods. "He thought all of that was a waste of time."

I am so confused. "But the way you treated me—"

"Was unforgiveable. Which is why I understand why you feel the way you do about me. I more than earned it."

"But if you knew better, then why did you do it? All this time, I thought it was because your dad neglected you—"

"Oh, he did." He sits on the edge of the table behind the chairs. "He was rarely around, and the few times he was, he spent them belittling what I liked. Mom told me that was just how he showed he cared, how he showed his interest in me. And I think I got it twisted that picking on people was how you express yourself, if you're a guy. Mom is kind. Grandmother is kind. But Dad and Grandfather?" He shrugs and winces. "That is how they express themselves—"

"Because they think being vulnerable is showing weakness." This is making too much sense.

He nods slowly. "And Dad is this titan of business, Grandfather, too. I had these impressive, powerful men to look up to, and they treated me like shit. So, I thought that's how impressive, powerful men were. I had no clue how to talk to someone I cared about. All these conflicting ideas … they really fucked me up."

He scrubs his hand over his face and through his dark hair, before letting out a nervous laugh. I find myself on my way to him without even thinking about it. "It's a bullshit reason to treat someone you like so terribly, but I didn't know how to talk to you, June. Not back then. And I hate who I pretended to be then. Hell, I hate who I wanted to be. I don't want to be my father. A wife shouldn't be a trophy you keep on a shelf and take out when you want something pretty to look at. My mother … god, she deserves so much more than my father has ever given her."

The raw emotion in his voice makes a knot form in my throat. I'm standing between his feet, close enough to feel the hurt radiating off this man. It's palpable, choking. I want to make it all better, but I need him to say the words. "Anderson?"

He rasps, "Yes?"

"You're saying that you treated me like shit for years because you liked me?"

He takes a long breath and lets it out slowly. "Yes. And now, I hate myself even more."

"What? Why?"

"Because here I am, whining about being a poor little rich boy to the woman whose life I have upended, when all I wanted to do was make her life better. Because I keep fucking up with you, June. It's un—

"Forgivable."

"Exactly, and—"

I take his face in my hands and pull him to me for a kiss. I'd hoped for more of a passionate embrace, but instead, all I get is a frozen Anderson. When I pull back, his eyes are enormous.

"Did I do something wrong?"

He shakes his head, blinking himself back to the present. "No, but I don't understand why you did that. There's no one in here for you to act for, June."

"I'm not acting, Anderson. I like you."

"You hate me."

I laugh and shake my head. "Not anymore."

"You mean that?"

I get half a nod in before he launches off the table and kisses me, wrapping me in his arms like he's afraid I might change my mind. He slants his mouth over mine, deepening the kiss, and I don't ever want to stop.

Chapter 32

JUNE

What am I doing? This is Anderson, the guy who … oh, fuck it.

The truth is, I don't really have much of an answer. I can hardly think with my blood thrumming and my body melting. My nerves are shredded from the conversation with his dad and the days I spent worrying about this charade. But what if it wasn't a charade? What if I let myself accept the truth?

I have a thing for my former bully.

Former, being the operative word. Besides, he kisses like his life depends on it, and I know what else he can do. Every kiss leads to something more in the moment—a gentle caress down my side, the clutching of his collar. His fingers sifting through my hair. A moan vibrating my lips against his. The need to press myself to him. To feel him. It's incredible—*he's* incredible—but as we make out, I'm dying for more.

Anderson kisses down the side of my neck, his breath warming the shell of my ear. "This was not what I had in mind when I invited you in here."

Oh, shit. Don't make me ask it. I cleared my throat. "Do you want to stop?"

"Fuck no."

"Thank god," I gasp just before he picks me up and sets me onto the heavy wooden table. "Um, but won't someone come in here?"

"No one comes down here anymore. Just me."

"But they could—"

Anderson presses a finger to my lips. "They won't. But if it makes you feel better …" He stalks to the door we came in and locks it, before joining me again. "Better?"

"Yes."

He smirks, and it sends that zap through me. "Glad to hear it." Then he slowly reaches up my dress as he kisses me again. Between soft lip bites, he murmurs, "Tell me if I'm taking this too far."

"Don't stop."

He kisses me harder as his fingers drag over my underwear. They slip to the side and scoot the thin fabric out of the way before his knuckles brush up against my center. "So wet for me already?"

"I like kissing you."

"Me, too." Then he drops to his knees.

"Where did you—"

He yanks me to the edge of the table and dips beneath my hem, while spreading my thighs wide.

"Oh my god, Anderson!" I gasp before he starts. Then his tongue runs up my pussy and I'm trembling already. I'm too close, too on edge, too on an actual edge, and I'm worried I'm going to fall on his head. His tongue has me shaking, and I can't hold back. "Gonna fall—"

"I have you. Just let go. Let me have you."

It feels like an impossible ask. To just let go means I'm not in control. The only other time I did that was also with Anderson, but that was a different circumstance, and I thought I'd never see him again. Now, though, things are different. I want this, and I want to keep seeing him. But that's the real reason I want him; I see him.

Who he really is. And I like him far more than I should.

I gulp and nod, not that he can see me. "Okay. You have me."

He pulls me just a little more over the edge, then wrecks me with his tongue. It's like he's counting my pulse with it, he moves so damned fast. My breath flies out in a keening wail, something animal and brief, as my climax picks up. I grab the back of his head to keep him on me, right there, right where I want him. It hits with enough force that sends my spine arching back. But he has me—his arms shoot up to keep me from falling. To let me ride it out on his face.

When I come back to earth, he stands up, kissing me long and deep, and when I taste myself on his lips, I want him even more. He murmurs, "I've been dying to taste you since the last time I did."

I whimper my thoughts in another kiss. I want this man, consequences be damned. "Anderson, fuck me."

He spins me around and on my shaking legs, I worry I'll fall, but he has me. When he bends me over the table, I'm losing my mind. I want this so bad. But then he stands me back up.

"Not like this." He takes my hand and

guides me to the end of one of the bookshelves, pressing my back to it. In a flash, he grabs my ass and lifts me up, and I let out a shocked whoop that makes him grin like a demon. Then he kisses me and grinds against me. His hard cock presses against my clit with every motion, and I'm on the verge again in a hurry. There's going to be such a wet spot on his damn pants, and I don't give a fuck. But this is not enough.

"I want you inside of me—"

"I don't have a condom. Thought this would suffice for now."

"I'm negative for everything, and I haven't been with anyone else since you, and I'm on birth control, so if you're good without a condom, so am I." I'd thought I'd seen lust on this man's face before. Nope. I am wrong. This bit of encouragement has unleashed some hormone-fueled beast.

He orders, "When your feet hit the floor, take off your panties." He sets me down gently while he unzips, so I scoot them off onto the floor. Then he picks me up again and I feel it— skin on skin. I have never moved this fast with a guy before. Condoms or no sex for the first few months. I'm always careful. Tonight, though, I don't fucking care. This feels right.

When he slides in, he's as careful as he can be. His muscles strain with every motion. The glide of him sends my eyes rolling back as he fills me up. Inch by inch, he's taking too long, and it sets my body alight.

"More, Anderson. I need more."

He thrusts up to the hilt, and I groan from the impact, while he lets out a primal growl that makes me want to hear it again. With his hands under my ass and my back on the bookshelves, he rolls himself up into me. I brace on his shoulders for balance, but I know he has me. I should have felt caged, trapped between him and the shelves. I didn't. All I felt was safe and cherished and wanted.

Pleasure winds so tight in me that it is almost pain. I wrap my legs around his waist to bring him closer, and he kisses me reverently. Like he is in awe of me. I never want this to end. But then his cock swells in me, and I worry that it will.

Anderson picks me up off of him as he pulls out. I whine my discontent. How can this be over? I didn't even feel him finish.

But then he turns me around to face the bookshelf. He leans in close, lifting the back of my dress. His hot breath sends a shiver from my ear down my body. "Brace yourself."

I grab both sides of the bookshelf, and he slams himself into me from behind, hard enough to shake the books. His girth grazes against my G spot on every thrust, and I'm practically speaking gibberish between curses. But when he reaches around for my clit, I lose my mind. My pussy clenches tight to him, throbbing and aching. "Fuck, And—oh, god!"

"That's it. Come on my cock," he demands.

He covers my mouth with his free hand, and I scream into his palm as I come all over him. But he doesn't stop. He doesn't even slow down. Every stroke is faster, hotter. More determined. Like he knows he's hitting my spot, and he'll never stop.

He drags another orgasm from me as he grunts in my ear, "That's my good girl."

My whole body arches back against him as he pounds into me and plays my body like an instrument. I'm lost to white hot flashes of ecstasy. He won't let me stop coming. Not yet.

"I'm going to come in you. Fill you up. Is that what you want?"

I can't speak. Only nod.

He growls in relief. "Fuck, yes." Just as his

cock thickens up, he slows down. "Just not yet. I like you squirming on me, baby."

I let out a whine, and I'm not sure if that's encouraging him to stop or to keep going. But with my core so wound tight, I can hardly breathe. Then he triggers another that makes me gasp for all the breath I've lost, and I'm more than squirming. I can't hold still—every part of me shakes violently as I come harder than ever on him.

He covers my back with his body, leaning as he pumps into me and plays with my clit. He rasps, "Love to make you come. Fuck, that's it, just like that, baby." His growl shreds me to my core as he comes inside of me, kissing and biting my neck like a rabid beast.

Chapter 33

ANDERSON

I point June to the library's bathroom, and while she's gone, I arrange the two chaises next to each other by the fireplace to work like a makeshift bed. Thankfully, we keep a few cozy blankets in here for when a reader doesn't feel like a fire, so I gather them there, too. I'm not ready to join the rest of the household right now. Not when I have June here, secluded in my favorite room.

She returns with a sly look on her face that thrills me. "You made a nest."

I chuckle and shrug. "Guess I did. Join me."

"Yeah, okay."

We lie down together, and I pull a blanket over us and spoon her with my arm over her waist as we watch the fire. Nothing has ever felt this good unless we were having sex. This is everything I want. Right here, right now. I bury my nose in her hair and breathe her in. This moment in time is everything.

And her perfection awakens my cock.

She wriggles against me there. "Already?"

"Can you blame me? Your ass is exquisite." And I've been dreaming of this day since I met you.

I'm trying not to get ahead of myself, but I can't help it. Having June want me of her own accord is all I've ever wanted. This wasn't for money, and she's sober, so there's no blaming it on a drunken mistake. She chose this. She wants me. The thought makes my chest ache in a way I've never felt before.

When June reaches back for my hip, I back off immediately. "Sorry. Don't mean to make you uncomfortable."

Her voice is soft. "I wasn't going to push you away."

"Oh?" What game is she playing at?

But her hand snakes between us, and she fumbles with my zipper. "I was hoping—

"Let me." I unzip, and she grabs my cock, stroking me. It's a strange angle, and I don't care at all. She has a firm grip, but her silken palm feels so damn good. Her touch would be enough to make me come if I didn't have more control than that.

When she turns around to face me, I don't know where she's going with this, but I want to go there, too. She bites her lip and smirks. "Stay just like that."

"Okay—"

She vanishes under the blanket, and I'm floored. She can't possibly want to—oh. Yes. Yes, she does. Her wet mouth is on me, and I'm going out of my mind. Her tongue slides up and down my length, before she takes me into her mouth fully, swallowing my cock.

My jaw grits, and I suck in a breath through tight teeth like a hiss. "Fuck, baby, that's so good."

She laughs with me in her mouth before she keeps at me, and I'm lost to it. To her. Whatever she wants, I'm down. I'd give this woman anything. Everything.

When her lips slide off me, I feel the loss keenly. "I want you inside me, Anderson."

"How?" I pant.

She scoots back up from under the blanket and gets into spooning position. "Like this."

As gently as I can manage, I pull her dress

up and her hips back before I explore her from behind. I want to make sure she's ready for me, and oh hell, she's so wet that my fingers slip into her. She groans for my touch, working against my fingers in little thrusts. "This is what you want?"

In a throaty moan, she demands, "I want your cock."

God, this woman is going to kill me. And I'm going to let her.

When I get into position, I plunge deep in one stroke, earning a growl from June and a gasp from myself. She feels too good. I don't ever want to stop being inside of her. Every thrust is magic between us. I grab her hip for purchase, and she rocks back to meet me each time I dive back in. She clenches around my cock like she's close again, and I need to feel that. I need to make her come on me.

My hand slides over her dress for her tits, and when I get there, she gasps light and feathery and arches to press her body into my hand harder. She is everything and more, and I cannot believe I am buried up to the hilt in my dream woman. It's unreal. I don't deserve this. She's going to come to her senses. She has to.

So, I'm going to make it count.

I tour her body, memorizing her soft curves as I reach between her thighs for her clit. When I get there, she mutters, "Oh, fuck yes." That's my girl. It's not three seconds before her body tenses and she cries out, coming on me in a fit of delicious agony. She jerks in my arms and still works herself on my cock, like she needs more.

I roll her onto her stomach, my fingers still on her clit, my shaft buried as deep as I can go. And still, she writhes on me. I hammer into her and try to ignore the pain in my balls as they beg for relief. Not yet. She's not done.

When June grips the arm of the chaise and shudders again, I feel it, too. Her body milking me. It's like she's pulling me over the edge with her. She lets out a strangled gasp. "Come for me."

My vision flashes black as I come in a roar. There's no holding this back. Not when that's what she wants from me. A shock of pleasure bolts through me, making me twitch and throb and spasm inside of her until I go weak from it and narrowly avoid collapsing onto her back. I flop over onto the second chaise, dying for breath.

Carefully, she turns onto her side. "Be right back."

I half-heartedly nod, too blissed out to speak. There are no words for what just happened. At least, none of which comes to mind. For once in my overly verbose life, I'm speechless. Utterly without thought.

Until I hear footsteps. It's not June—she hasn't managed to get up yet.

But a purposeful throat clearing tells me precisely who it is, and I yank the blanket over us before Dad sees anything he shouldn't.

Chapter 34

ANDERSON

His imperious tone tells me all about his judgmental thoughts. Thankfully, it comes from a distance, which means he hasn't seen anything. Probably.

"You have missed supper, but your mother wishes for your presence at dessert. Don't be late, and do be dressed."

This is bad. This is so bad.

I blurt, "We'll be there."

"Very good." His stiff tone is followed by fast and quiet footsteps, which means his previous loud footsteps were loud on purpose. When the door shuts behind him, my relief is nowhere in sight because she is going to be pissed.

June whispers, "Oh my god."

"I am so sorry—"

"I'll … I'll go clean up." She launches from the chaise nest for the bathroom.

I can hardly blame her. Glaring up at the decorative carved wooden ceiling, I am beyond frustrated with myself. I zip up and get myself presentable, but my mind races from self-loathing to cynical. Of course, Dad had to come and interrupt the best moment of my life. I should have known better than to think I'd get to simply bask in the afterglow with June.

Oh, shit. June. Is she going to freak out? Is she going to never speak to me again? That might actually kill me.

When she emerges from the bathroom, I can't get a read on her expression, so my heart drums. She nervously asks, "Can we get out of here?"

Okay, I enjoy hearing *we* out of her, but the rest is null. "I won't make you stay, but I would ask it of you."

"Your dad just caught us having sex!"

"He did, but he's not going to say anything to anyone."

She frowns. "What makes you so sure?"

"Because he's the type of man to be more

embarrassed about it than we are. Hell, he might even be jealous—"

"Jealous?"

"That we're young and can't keep our hands off each other."

"Oh." She almost smiles at that.

"He won't tell a soul, June."

Her shoulders slump. "Okay. But how can I look him in the eye after that?"

"To be honest, I'm asking myself the same question. I guess we muddle through?"

She sits next to me, and I'm relieved she hasn't run out the door yet. "This is humiliating, Anderson."

"It's not the best thing that's ever happened, but at least we had that before he showed up."

She smiles and tips her head to my shoulder. "Yeah, we did."

"So, that was good for you, too, then?"

She nods, and I can take a full breath finally. She's not about to run away if that was the case for her, too. "I wonder about something."

"What's that?"

"So, you liked me back in school, right?"

"Yes."

"And you just didn't know how to express it, if I'm following what you said before."

I nod. "I had no game and no good example of how to speak to someone I liked. In short, I was a teenage boy."

She giggles. "So, I wonder if the reason I can't stop thinking about you inside of me is because of fourteen years of sexual tension between us."

Her words make my cock ache. Even now, I want to fuck her again. Not that we have the time, and I don't think I could go again quite this soon after two rounds, but dammit, if I don't want to try. "Uh, that could be. So, do you think you're up for dessert with the family?"

She sighs. "Yeah, I think I can manage it. Just don't make me sit near your father. Ever."

I take her hand and kiss the back of it. "No worries. Pretty sure he wouldn't want that, either. Dad is … I never got *the talk* from him. In fact, he's never been the kind of guy to ask me about my personal life, aside from demanding I have a girlfriend."

"Who gave you *the talk*?"

I laugh, thinking about it. "Mom tried. But she got too awkward about it. So, our family physician made a house call for the occasion. He brought diagrams and pictures. It was all very clinical. Mom sat through it with me, in case I had questions for her, too, but she and I were both so red-faced through the whole thing, I couldn't bear to speak."

June laughs hard. "Oh my god, that's … I mean, it's great that she did that, but that had to be so painful."

"Oh yeah. I was twelve, I think, and I was so freaked out about it all that I didn't even try to sneak porn for a year."

"You were looking at that back then?"

"Before *the talk*, yeah. I had the internet and had found Grandfather's classic *Playboys* here, in fact. He kept them in the library, I think, in hopes Grandmother would never find them."

She glances around. "I noticed the library is organized alphabetically. Are they under P for *Playboy* or something else?"

"Under P for *Popular Mechanics*."

"Huh?"

I smirk, unable to stop myself. "Grandfather had slipcovers made for his *Playboys*—or maybe he fashioned them himself—so that they all look like *Popular Mechanics* magazines instead of what they are. When I found the magazines, I'd thought I'd learn about cars, but I learned about something else that day."

She giggles. "Oh my god."

"He was clever. It was a good way to keep Grandmother from figuring out he had them, because she hated all that stuff."

June takes a deep breath. "So, um, do you think we've dawdled enough? Should we go join them?"

"Not exactly. I should rearrange the furniture back to what it was." I get up and start, but she looks up at me with the strangest look on her face. "What is it?"

"I … I'm not sure where to start."

"Try the beginning." Her tone has me worried, so I sit next to her again. "What's going on?"

She runs her fingers through her hair, and they snag on a curl, so she gives up. "This wasn't what I thought it would be, Anderson."

I gulp. "And what was that?"

"I'd thought we'd come here, do our little act, and you'd get your account, and that would be that."

Shit. My heart sinks through the floor. "Are you saying you regret what happened in here?"

But she half-smiles and shakes her head. "Nothing like that. I'm saying I could never regret what happened in here. I like you. If you're game for it, I'd like to see where this might go."

I feel like a puppet with their strings cut, as all the tension leaves me. "Truly?"

"Yeah. But no more embarrassing your dad."

I laugh sharply and kiss her. "No more of that. I promise."

"Wait—how did he get in here, anyway? I thought you locked the door."

"I did, but I forgot about the door at the other end of the library. It's past the stacks down that way." I point toward the far end. "The library is so large that it needs two points of entry, even with all the windows. The second door was added a few years ago to keep the place up to code."

She rolls her eyes and shakes her head. "Well, let's not forget about that ever again."

"Never." I cup her cheek in my hand. "You mean it, though? You want to give us a shot?"

"If you do. Yeah."

I kiss her again, longer and deeper. If I'm not careful, we'll miss dessert. "Yes. Very much. But first, let's get the room back to rights and have dessert, so we might talk about this over some champagne at my place."

"That sounds like a good plan."

As we put the furniture and blankets back, I keep thinking I'm going to wake up. That I must have hit my head and I'm concussed in a hospital some place. That there is no way this is actually happening. "June?"

"Yes?"

"You really stopped hating me?"

She laughs. "I would have thought that was pretty clear by now. Yes, I stopped hating you."

I kiss the top of her head. "Thank you for that. I don't deserve it, and I know it."

"Shut up."

"What? I'm serious. I remember how I was to you, and I hate that—"

"No more self-flagellation, okay? I'm not ready to chalk it up to a, 'Boys will be boys,' bullshit thing, because as far as I'm concerned, boys should be held accountable, just like girls. And, Anderson, you have been accountable. You got me out of a questionable situation. You took care of me that night, and you've been trying to take care of things ever since. There's been apologies and penance, and I don't see the need to keep beating you up over everything." She takes my hands in hers and looks up at me with such sweetness in her eyes. "It's in the past. I'd like to think about the future."

For a brief moment, I let myself think about her like this in a wedding dress, and my heart stops. It's impossible not to think of it—she's wearing my ring. June Devlin would be the most beautiful bride there ever was. Now, I have to make that happen.

"Anderson?"

I blink myself back to reality and clear my throat. "Right. The future. I'd like that, too, June."

She gives my hands a squeeze. "Then we should get to dessert."

"Sounds good." I run my knuckles down her low back before settling my hand there. "Let's go."

Chapter Thirty-Five-June

The family dining room is a sight to behold. More of a dining hall, really. I'm not sure when night fell—sometime when we were in the library, but now, the dining hall's city view is lit up in the darkness. Floor-to-ceiling windows showcase Boston the way it was meant to be seen. It's gorgeous, but not as pretty as the chandelier over the table.

I can't tell if it's supposed to be nautical or not, but it's glass and kind of looks like some sort of deep sea creature, with blue and gray streaks in the glass itself. A marvel of balance and light—I'm not entirely certain how it's perched over the table. Looks like it might fall at any moment.

The table is long enough to host the entire extended family, which means there are empty chairs in a few directions. Even some that are paired. Thankfully, none of them are near his father. He doesn't even glance at us when we walk in, and I am grateful. We take a spot a good distance from the man, and Anderson chats up his cousin on the other side of himself, pretending we got lost in the library.

His mother, sitting at the opposite end from his father, smiles conspiratorially at me and says, "The library can be such a distraction. Don't worry, June, I won't hold it against you. I've spent days in that room myself."

I doubt she was doing anything in there like what we were up to. But given what Callie told me about her society's thoughts on affairs, maybe his mom was doing exactly that. All the same, I smile at her. "Thank you for the grace, Kitty."

She smiles warmly and motions toward someone, and before I know it, a group of servers come into the dining hall to deliver trays. One is placed before me on the place setting, and the server pulls the silver lid from it. On a small white plate is a ball-shaped chocolate sculpture, with dark chocolate ribbons on top and a white chocolate bowl base. Beneath the ribbons, is what appears to be a crème brule. It smells like Heaven itself.

Coffees are delivered afterward, and with no fanfare for such a sumptuous dessert, the family digs in, continuing their conversations. I'm in awe of the intricate thing on my plate, while everyone else acts like it's just another food. Everyone except Anderson, who beams at his mother.

Kitty smiles at him. "Thought you might enjoy a trip down memory lane."

He chuckles. "Thank you for this, Mom."

"Memory lane?" I ask, trying to figure out where to begin.

She explains, "I took Anderson to Paris after he missed out on his graduation trip, and he took ill with food poisoning the first day. Poor thing. We were scheduled to be there for a week, and he didn't feel well enough to do anything until the final day, when I took him to a patisserie. Ever since then, I've tried to recreate it, because he always says it was the best thing he's ever eaten. I think this is a fair approximation of what you ordered—"

"Looks just like it. You did well."

"Try it."

He lifts the dark chocolate ribbons and scoops the crème brule first. His eyes close when he tastes it. "This is it exactly, Mom. How did you do it?"

"Flew them in from Paris."

I laugh, but there's no joke on her face. "Wait, really?"

"I tried for years, but I gave up. Whatever it is French people do to dessert, I cannot replicate it. They are magic, pure and simple."

So, I follow his lead, lifting the ribbons and diving into the crème brule. It is light and ethereal with just a hint of sweetness. I want to eat this every day. "Oh my god, that is incredible."

Anderson tells her, "Thank you for this, Mom."

"I wanted to have something special for you for the first time you brought a girl home, and considering the ring on her finger, I'm glad I did it."

It's funny—I keep forgetting the ring is there. It fits on my finger like it actually belongs there, and I am way too comfortable wearing it. But who knows? Maybe one day it'll be there for an actual reason.

Anderson clears his throat and catches his father's eye. "Dad, thank you for finding us for dessert."

His father's cheeks go rosy, and it's all I can do not to join him. He gives a quick nod, then returns to his conversation.

I return to my dessert, focusing on the divine instead of the uncomfortable. His cousin— Evelyn, I think—asks about the ring, and I quickly recall the story we made up about our engagement. She oohs and ahhs as I embellish things a little more, and as it turns out, she's engaged, too. She insists, "We must decide on a date soon, so our dates don't conflict. Being that convention dictates our wedding dates must be at least six months apart, when were you thinking?"

"Oh, um, we haven't set a date yet. Have you?"

"We were looking at, well, next June. But I

doubt a woman named June wants to be a June bride—"

I laugh. "Eh, no. Maybe the December after yours. Or later. Right now, I'm so swamped with work, the idea of planning a wedding is too much."

"But you'll stop working to plan the wedding, right?"

I almost laugh, but then I catch the look on her face. *Oh my hell, she's serious?* "I wasn't planning on it."

"Right, right. You're a lawyer. Hard to peel any of you away from that profession," she says with a little shrug. "My Daniel wouldn't dream of ending his career. I swear, they will have to bury him in his office."

"We are a dedicated lot."

She goes on about wedding planning, and Anderson gives my leg a squeeze under the table. But before long, we're saying our good-byes and leaving it all behind. When we get outside, the brisk breeze nearly takes my breath from me. "So, how did I—

He wraps his arms around me and kisses me, long and deep. "You were amazing. The whole time, but especially when Jessalyn started going on about wedding stuff."

"Jessalyn? I thought that was Evelyn."

"Her mom is Evelyn."

I smack my forehead. "Pretty sure I called her Evelyn. She didn't even correct me."

He chuckles and kisses me again. "And she was either too in the bag to notice, or she was being nice about it. They know you were inundated by a bunch of strangers. We usually give people a year to know everyone by name. It's fine."

"Your family is such a weird mix of snooty and nice. I don't get it."

"That's Mom's side of the family. Dad's is all snooty, all the time." He waves to the valet, and they run to fetch his car. "You did really well tonight, June."

"Thanks. Still feel like an idiot with Jessalyn, but what's done is done."

"I'll text you her number, so you have it— she's easy going about most things, but she was serious about that wedding planner for you." He pats his pockets. "Oh hell. I think it fell out … probably in the library."

"Go on up. I'll wait out here and warm up in the car."

He smiles. "I'll be quick." He kisses me

again. "I could just buy another phone. That way, I don't have to leave you."

I giggle. "Okay, there's extravagant and there's frivolous, and that is definitely the latter. Go."

"Be right back." As he passes me, he gives my ass a smack.

"Hey!"

He grins back at me before disappearing into the building.

I think back to our evening and can't help but smile. I don't know what's to come for our relationship but I'm excited about it. Knowing him, I might not be wearing clothes for the rest of the weekend, and I am very okay with that.

A man in all black strolls down the sidewalk. His suit is well-tailored—it moves with him fluidly. Makes sense. In this neighborhood, I doubt anyone wears anything that isn't bespoke. A vehicle rumbles by, then stops in front of the building. One of those sprinter vans, black with tinted windows. Odd, but I imagine someone in the building is getting a late night delivery. Rich people can get anything they want at any hour, I'm sure of it.

The man in black's pace picks up as he comes near, and I smile at him and give a nod of acknowledgement. But he doesn't smile back. In fact, he walks faster. My pulse picks up, and I take a step backward. "Hello?"

When he's an arm's length away, he grabs a fistful of my hair and shoves something into my mouth. I punch him in the face, but he doesn't seem to notice. He grabs my arm and twists it around, so it's in the small of my back, and suddenly, there's something sharp at my throat. He growls, "Do not struggle, princess. I don't like cutting pretty girls, but I will."

Oh my fuck!

The van door opens in the back, and the man in black pushes me forward toward it. But I drag my feet—if I get into that van, I'll die. I know it. He presses the knife to my throat harder. "Walk."

"What do you want?" I ask against the gag.

He ignores me and shoves me inside the back of the van. Two more men in black are waiting for us, but they wear masks. There's four seats back there—three for them, one for me. This isn't just some random thing. They've planned this. I start to panic and struggle, but the door is shut before I can get back outside. The other two move just as fast as the first one. They throw me into one of the seats and tie my feet and wrists to it. The engine revs as they pull away from the building. I'm close to hyperventilating, and the first guy must notice, because he pulls the gag out of my mouth.

"What do you want?" I ask between fast breaths.

"I want you to breathe through your nose so you don't pass out and hurt yourself. No one pays for damaged goods."

"Where are you taking me? This is kidnapping."

"And to think, she's a smart lawyer," one of the other guys mocks.

"But I don't have any money. Is this because I'm in this neighborhood? I promise, you are barking up the wrong tree. I'm not from here. This isn't where I live. I'm just as broke as you guys probably are. You have the wrong woman."

The first guy smirks sinisterly. "And with that little speech, you're not hyperventilating anymore." He puts the gag back in, only this time, he ties it around the back of my head.

Okay, I can handle this. I just need to be able to talk myself out of being their target once he removes the gag again.

But then, he pulls out a blindfold, and the

panic hits all over. I try to thrash away from his hands, but he pops me in the back of the head. "Cooperate, and this will go much easier for you, Ms. Devlin."

Fuck. They know exactly who I am.

"Why?" My question is muffled and I sit still this time to let him get the blindfold on. No point in fighting this. Not yet. Save my fight for later.

"I'll assume you asked why this is happening. It's nothing personal against you. Just business. We're going to see if your boyfriend and his family will pay for your safe return. We'll see what loyalty really means to them."

This is business. Okay. I can survive a business transaction. That's all this is. Once it's settled … except, he's not really my boyfriend. Or my fiancé. We're whatever we are, but am I someone he'd pay for? Would his family?

"It's a pity the Wests aren't good at paying their bills, or we would have avoided all this unpleasantness in the first place. Understand, Ms. Devlin, we don't *want* to hurt you. But we will if we must. They have to know we're serious. We will do whatever it takes to get the money they owe us. If that means sending you back to them piece by piece to prove our point, then we will."

C hapter Thirty-Six-June

By the time the SUV stops, a cold sweat trickles down my back. My mouth is so dry from the gag, and my wrists and ankles are abraded by the rope on them. The vehicle smells new. Light and shapes stream in at the edges of my blindfold, and the longer I sit with it on, the more I wonder why these bozos didn't use a head bag. I've been counting the seconds and the turns, and I'm pretty sure we are still in Boston.

The tiny details are the only things keeping me from losing my shit right now. Paying attention to them instead of what might happen is the only option I have. Otherwise, I'll hyperventilate.

The problem is, I know too much about kidnapping and the fact that if you see the kidnapper's faces, there's a good chance they'll kill you. And I've seen one of their faces.

Maybe he's a mark. Someone they're using to get the job done, and he's the one they'll offload, not me. Only the others seem to take his orders. Which means he's in charge of this operation. Not good. Definitely not good.

"Ms. Devlin, we have arrived."

A moment later, the binds are cut. I fight the urge to rub my wrists or make any other sudden moves. It's hard though. I want to beat on the window and draw attention to myself and pray that someone sees and tries to help. But that also seems like a dumb way to die, so I don't.

The doors open and I catch a whiff of dank air. Humidity, motor oil, and exhaust. We're not in the open anymore. We're in an underground garage.

Oh, goody.

"Come along, Ms. Devlin." Two hands grab my arms and help me out of the vehicle. My ankle wobbles for a moment, but someone catches me. They don't use the opportunity to cop a feel, so at least they're not creeps about this. It's discombobulating to be led around while wearing a gag and a blindfold, but the pair walking me through the place are careful not to let me stumble. It's almost like they do this kind of thing all the time, and that thought is not making me feel better.

A door creaks open ahead, and it feels like a pressure change when it closes again. Where the hell are we?

"There are many stairs between here and our destination. Step lively and carefully."

My guides stay with me, one on each side. So, the stairway is wide enough for three people. The light has a hazy green glow and hum like bees—old fluorescents. A foul scent hangs in the air, like a building that hasn't been cleaned in a very long time. Musty and thick. It reminds me of the time I got stuck in the basement at my great aunt's retirement home.

That day was hell, and I hoped to never relive it. But I'd take that over this any day.

The stairs go on forever. Nine and then a landing, and we turn for the next batch. Eight stories down, until another door scratches the cement floor as it's opened. The door opener's footsteps sound far away in a hurry.

Was this a bomb shelter or something? Shamefully, I don't know much of Boston's history in that regard. But I know bomb shelters were a thing for a while in the fifties. Maybe that's where they're taking me. Someplace no one will ever find me.

No. Can't think like that. This will all blow over.

I hope.

Something clicks ahead, and then he says, "That's right, gents, over here." It's the same guy who grabbed me off the street—he's the one who has done all the talking.

They lead me toward the grabber, then plop me onto a hard wooden chair. The next thing I know, they're tying my ankles and wrists to the chair. After I'm bound, someone unties the gag, followed by the blindfold. It takes a few blinks before I realize I won't be seeing anyone anytime soon.

I'd thought it'd be a minute before my eyes adjusted to the light again, but I was wrong. One of those floodlights people use for interrogations is aimed right at my face. I can't see shit other than bright white light.

I smack my lips together a few times, surprised by just how dry my mouth is. It's hard not to panic right now. I've been transported to a destination that they obviously planned for. In fact, they've clearly planned all of this for a while now, since they know my name and my involvement with Anderson. If they think I'm this valuable to him, then they know about things from an outside perspective—they don't know we're not together.

Well, are we?

No, not the point. Life and death on the line. Can't focus on my romantic life at a time like this. I have to keep my wits about me and get answers. "Who are you? Why are you doing this?"

There's no answer. I don't hear footsteps, but I didn't hear them after we came in, either. It's like the men vanished into thin air. Like ghosts. There's a pleasant thought. I've been kidnapped by ghosts. Won't that be fun to explain … assuming I get out of this place?

"Anyone there?" I shout, hoping for an answer.

Nothing. Not even crickets.

Well, at least the interrogation lamp is warm. I need it down here—basements are cold. That's what I've decided this place is. A basement. Not a bomb shelter. A basement is survivable. A bomb shelter is a great place to leave a body. I am not a body. I am a person, and I will survive this.

I have definitely not been left here to die.

Okay. Let's forget the d-word for right now and focus on what's happened. I'm strapped to a chair in a basement after getting nabbed by a crew of thugs. The grabber said this is business, not personal. They haven't done anything untoward. Other than kidnapping me and threatening me with violence. Fine. It doesn't appear to be something sexual, either, which is a relief. If anything in this situation could be a relief … whatever, I'll take it.

How strong is this chair?

It's wooden—I can feel the woodgrain under my nails. Can I pry it apart? Should I bother to? If I cooperate, they are less likely to hurt me, right?

All the times I've heard about kidnappings for money, it's the cooperative captives that stand a better chance of surviving. And even though I know that, I can't help but try to pry my chair apart.

Tugging at the rope doesn't do anything but hurt my wrist. Flaking at the woodgrain with my nails only hurts my nails. I have no weapons on me, but I can't just sit here, either. If I fall over, will the chair break? Not likely—this thing reminds me of the chairs at Appleton. Thick wood designed to be abused by kids. Solid construction. No chance of breaking it on the concrete floor.

If I hop the chair toward the light and knock that over, will someone come? Do I want them to? Would the light start a fire? Not that there's much around me to burn. And I don't want to die of smoke inhalation before someone gets here to save me.

If they'd save me.

I huff and try not to panic. My thoughts keep circling the drain of doom, and I have got to think of something more productive or I'll lose my mind. Okay. The grabber said Anderson's family owes him money. If he wants to get paid, then they won't hurt me ... but also, why does his family owe him money?

That doesn't seem right.

Anderson's family doesn't owe anyone anything. They've been generationally wealthy for many generations. *Old money*, as they like to call it. None of this makes any sense.

Though, people can get stupid with money. Even people with lots of it. Maybe his mom has a gambling problem. Or his dad made some poor investments. Huh. Could it be Anderson's fault? Is that why his dad froze his accounts—to stop him from running up a tab with a bookie or something?

Whatever the reason is, I'm stuck here for now. I close my eyes and take a few deep breaths. Nothing good will come from panicking or trying to guess what's actually happening. The only thing I can do is focus on myself right now. More deep breaths and just let myself melt into the situation. Think of this as an opportunity to meditate in the absolute quiet or—

Who the hell am I kidding? I've been kidnapped. It's okay to freak out. I blow out one of those useless deep breaths and decide to scoot the chair away from the light. At least I can explore that way.

But when I try, I discover it's bolted into the concrete. Super.

-

Chapter 35

ANDERSON

Once I retrieved my phone, I dodged my family to get downstairs as fast as possible. Leaving a hot woman alone in the cold is not good form. But when I got outside, she wasn't in my car.

Odd.

I check in with the valet, but she was gone before he returned with the car. Searching my memory, I can't think of how I could have misinterpreted her saying she'd wait in the car. Maybe she went up to check on me and we missed each other?

"Thanks," I tell the valet, before I head up one more time. The elevator ride takes far too long for my liking, but it always does. It's an old building. It's just frustrating. Feels like every second away from June is a second wasted.

When the door opens, I take a breath and march back to Mom and Dad's and ring the bell. I doubt anyone will hear me knock—not with the band playing again. As their front door opens, I'm expecting Mom or the housekeeper. Not my younger brother, Cole. He's still wearing his coat.

He grins. "Holy shit, man, you're late!"

I laugh. "I was already here before. Pretty sure you're the late one."

He takes my hand and pulls me in for a hug, patting my back hard twice. "Get in here, old man."

"How the hell have you been, kid?"

"Oh, you know. Living life." He takes his coat off, hanging it in the nearby coat room. "I hear you're engaged … ?"

Right. The lie. "Uh, yeah. I am. In fact, have you been introduced to June yet? I think she must be around here someplace. She was supposed to wait for me in the car when I came back up to get my phone, but I think she must have come back up here to check on me."

"Ah, she probably got a load of our family and took off." He leans in and quietly says, "Not that I blame her."

"We can be a lot, can't we?"

He laughs. "Ain't that the truth? Guess I should show my face a little before jetting out of here—"

"Why the rush? You just got here. I'm sure Mom would love to see you for a bit."

He rolls his eyes and shrugs. "You know how things are, Anderson. This isn't exactly my scene."

No, it is not. His scene has been the party circuit for far too long. I love my brother, but he is the least reliable man I have ever known.

"How's work?"

"I don't want to talk about work." Translation … he got fired.

"Are you seeing anyone?"

"Pfft. I'm seeing everyone."

"That sounds," terrible, "exciting for you. I—"

"And I hear your fiancée is June, somebody. Didn't you used to have a crush on someone by that name?"

How in the *cocaine-fueled weekend* mind of his does he remember that? "Same woman, actually."

"Really? I'll be damned."

Most likely true. "I'm going to see if anyone has seen her, Cole. Excuse me—"

322

"Wait, hang on. You don't have a minute to catch up with your little brother?"

Shit. He wants money. This is awkward. To avoid eye contact, I text June while speaking to him. "I'd be happy to lend you—"

He laughs and puts his arm around me. "What makes you think I want your money?"

"Experience."

But he only laughs again and starts walking with his arm still around me, so I go with him. I have a sneaking suspicion he's building up to something big, and I'm not going to like it. He corners me near the kitchen, and the caterers make a ton of noise there. Ugh. He doesn't want anyone to hear him hit me up for money.

Cole says, "I'm not asking for a loan, Anderson. I'm done with all of that."

"Well … good for you. Got your shit together, did you?"

"Yeah. I've turned over a new leaf. They told you I passed the bar, right?"

"And that you hit the top one percent of the scores, but that doesn't mean anything if you don't do anything with your education, Cole."

He gives me an overly patient look. "That's what I'm doing, Blanderson. I'm joining the family business."

I laugh at first, unsure if he's serious, but when he doesn't laugh, I'm flabbergasted. "Childhood nicknames aside, are you serious?"

"I am. It's about time, don't you think?"

No. Good god, no. "Uh, wow. I suppose so. That'll be," a disaster, "great."

He grins. "Knew you'd be on board. Can you help me convince Dad not to throw me in the mailroom?"

"You know our father. He'll do what he wants. But he's not going to stick his son in the mailroom."

"Guess we'll see."

"Yeah, so help me find June, will you? She's the prettiest brunette you've ever seen wearing a beige dress with knee boots." Checking my phone, she hasn't texted me back. My message isn't even read.

He glances around the room. "Don't see her."

"No shit, Sherlock. She's not a caterer. She's a lawyer. Come on." I drag him with me through the soiree, but he gets snagged when some of our family gushes over him. With Cole being MIA for most family gatherings, I'm not surprised.

He's the fun one, the one everyone loves to

have around for weddings and birthdays, because he's usually tanked and eager to be the life of the party. They don't know about his stints in rehab or the times we've bailed him out of trouble. We keep that sort of thing within the family. Hell, I'm sure there are times my parents have helped him I don't know of, because the reverse is certainly true. They don't need to know about the time in Ibiza when I had to get him out of trouble with a DJ and his drug dealer. But that's the kind of thing you do for family.

All of that gets shoved to the side in my mind. I need to find June. My message is still unread, so I truck through the apartment fast. There's a limited number of places she could be. When I ask, no one has seen her since we left. I shouldn't be so worried—this is an obnoxiously safe neighborhood. In fact, part of me feels like I'm being ridiculous about it. But she hasn't answered my text, and that's not like her.

Did she get cold feet about us? Is there an *us* to have cold feet over?

Funny how insecurity creeps up at the worst imaginable times. It's terrible to think about it, but I'd prefer she had a family emergency over breaking things off. No. That's not true. I don't want anyone in her family to be in any kind of trouble. But that would be easier to swallow than the idea that she just ran off. Or that my family ran her off.

She didn't seem unnerved when we were outside, though. The kissing—that was real. So was everything in the library. There was no faking that. Maybe she's in the library, hoping for another rendezvous in there. The thought thrills me, so I jog down that way.

But she's not there.

This is getting worrisome. She's not the type to just bail. Unless …

Unless this has all been her revenge for what I did to her. Could she … no. She couldn't possibly … but it would be one hell of a punishment. A very deserved punishment. All those years, me acting like I hated her, only for her to make me care and then vanish on me?

Vengeance is best served cold, isn't it?

No. She isn't that person. She will be in the library, bedroom eyes and wearing nothing but her knee boots. I'm sure of it. I open and close the door behind me, just in case she's naked in here somewhere. "June? Are you here?"

A stifled "Oh my god," is giggled in a far corner beyond the stacks.

Swiftly, I walk in. "June, are you okay—"

"Not June," Jessalyn says as she comes around the bookshelves. She's straightening her skirt. Her hair is the least neat I have ever seen it, and her lipstick is smeared. "Um, Anderson, I haven't seen June since you left. Everything okay?"

"Uh, sorry." I can't help but chuckle at her predicament. "No, I can't find her. I'll be going now."

"Don't um, don't mention this to anyone. Please. I beg you."

"I didn't see a thing, Jessalyn. Have a good night. Sorry to bug you."

She smiles, and I dip out. I'm ten feet into the hall when I recall her fiancé wasn't at the party. Doesn't matter. Not my problem. I—

My phone buzzes with an alert. I got a text. Thank god—it's from June. But when I open it, it's a picture of her, tied to a chair in some place that looks like a basement. What in the fuck is going on?

-

Chapter 36
JUNE

It's all but impossible to do anything but sit here and freak out. I heard a click earlier—like the fake camera sound my phone makes when I take a picture. After that, an annoyed sigh. But when I called out, no one said a word. I don't know if I'm alone or not. These people move like cats, apparently.

Until they don't.

Heavy, echoey footsteps alert me to a presence, but I didn't hear the door scrape open. Must have come from another door. Sounds like boots, but I still cannot see them. And they're dragging something on the floor. A chair, maybe? They're close, too, so I guess they're behind the light.

Then I can see the outline of him. It's definitely a him, too—unless they're a beefy, broad-shouldered woman. He sits down, and I still can't see his face because he's right behind the light. I get only the shape of my captor and the faint distinctive sound of leather rubbing on leather. His coat.

And he's a big one. Like a breathing threat.

A deep voice rumbles, "How did you meet Anderson West?"

Well, shit. That's not exactly what I thought he'd ask about. What does he know already? They know my name. They think he and I are together. What does it matter how we met? Is this a test? To see if I lie to him? What would they do if I did? The man has no discernible accent—he sounds just like every other person in Boston.

My mouth is dry, and my head is spinning with questions. Fewer details seem the best route. I rasp out, "School."

A grunt of acknowledgement. "How long have you been together?"

"Not long."

"Would you say it's serious?"

"I'm wearing his ring."

He pauses. "Would you say it's serious?"

I thought I answered. What is he saying by asking it twice? "You just asked me that."

Another pause. "Would you say—"

"Yes. I would."

"Who is your best friend?"

I laugh. What the hell kind of question is that, under these circumstances? "I'm not sure I have one."

"Do you have pets?"

"No. What sort of interrogation is this?"

"Thorough. Do you have houseplants?"

This is so weird. "Why? Are you offering to water them for me while I'm here?" Okay, maybe it's not the best idea to smart off to your captors, but this line of questioning is just plain bizarre and it's setting me off.

"What is your banking pin?"

Well, that was a zig when I thought he was gonna zag. "It's four fives."

"Are you in love with Anderson West?"

I laugh, but the question takes the air out of my lungs. "Can't say."

"Can't or won't?"

This guy! I snap, "Not that it's any of your business, but I'm not sure."

"What grades did you get in elementary school?"

Elementary school grades? Seriously? Just before I answer, I realize what he's doing. It's two things—getting a baseline of my responses and to see what pushes my buttons. The answers themselves don't really matter, so long as they're honest. It's more about how I respond to them. If I lie, if I don't. If I have an emotional response or not. It's all a test.

It's like talking to the police after an accident they think you may have caused. Like when I was a kid.

I've done a lot to forget about what happened back then. Shoved it way back in the rear of my memory, but right now, I can't help but recall the accident. The thrashing. The panic. All the splashing—

"Could I get a drink? My mouth is—"

"What grades did you get in elementary school?"

That's a no. Super. The knot in my gut keeps growing. "Mostly A's. Why?"

"Have you ever gone hiking?"

Why did he have to ask about that? "Yes."

"Do you have any regrets in life?"

My jaw grits. "Yes."

He pauses again, but then his outline gets up and his heavy footsteps fall away from me. He didn't take the chair with him. It should be a relief that he's gone, but the truth is, having a person nearby was a strange sort of comfort after sitting here alone for so long. Even one as inscrutable as that guy.

It's not long before there's more footsteps. Lighter ones. A slender woman sits in the chair now, and she scoots it from the light some. I can't make out her face, but her clothes are in view. A pantsuit. Not expensive. More like a bank teller or a government worker. No coat on her.

"How did you meet Anderson West?" Her accent is more New York than Boston. That and her gender are the only differences between them, evidently.

"School."

"And how long would you say you've been dating?"

I pointed out the ring to the last guy, but she calls it only dating. Is she trying to trip me up? "We haven't been together for very long."

"But you're serious about him?"

She's asking the same kinds of questions, but in a friendlier way to make me more comfortable with her. Bad cop, good cop. God, I do not like cops. Not after what happened ... No. We are not thinking about that. I clear my throat. Am I serious about Anderson? That's the question right now. "Yes."

"Who have you told about your relationship with him?"

Is this the best friend question in a roundabout way? "Just a work friend."

"Does anyone depend on you? Family? Pets?"

"Not really."

"Would you mind sharing your banking pin?"

I huff. "It's four fives, but you won't find much in there."

"Are you in love with Anderson West?"

"I'm not sure."

"What were your—"

"Grades in elementary school like? Mostly A's. If you're going to ask the same questions as the other guy, you're going to get the same answers because I didn't lie to him. This is a waste of your time and mine. Can I get a drink? I'm parched. Gags will do that to a girl." I'm surly because I'm thirsty and trying not to panic, and being rude probably won't make me any friends, but to be fair, they were rude first, and I'm at the end of my rope.

Oh god. Rope. Rope in the water. Too short. Not enough. Fingers sinking—

"Do you hike?"

"Not anymore," I blurt. The panic is hitting me and I can't stop it this time. My toes tap in my shoes and I'm gripping the chair so I don't lose my fucking mind.

"Do you have any—"

"Regrets? Yes. Of course, I do. I'm an adult who learns from her mistakes. Do you have any regrets? Like treating me like a suspect when I'm the victim here?"

She pauses before standing up. Her light footsteps carry her away, but as she leaves, a faraway click happens before the bright light turns off. It's pitch black in the room, save for the rectangular outline of a door closing.

No, no, no, "Wait!"

But it's too late. I'm left in utter darkness.

Just like when I sank beneath the surface of the lake. Only this time, I know I'm breathing. I'm breathing and dry and not about to drown. My foot is in a boot and that boot is on a concrete floor, not dangling in the water. When I push off the floor, it's a floor. Not someone's hand.

Not Claire's hand.

I take a breath and try to slow it down. Hyperventilating will not help right now, but I'm not sure I can stop it, either. Get your shit together, June. I am not twelve. I am not being interrogated by the police about a prank gone wrong. This is not that. I am an adult who has been kidnapped. Not a child who made a mistake.

And I need to get the fuck out of here.

Okay. They're not going to leave me here. That much is certain. I'm not going to be abandoned down here to—no. Not the d-word again. I am not thinking about that or anything related to that.

Claire's face. Under the water. Lifeless.

I can't stop the thought. Can't make it go away. It's there. Right in front of me. No matter what I try to think of, she's right there. Just … there.

I wrench air into my lungs, before a sob wracks and takes it from me. I can't do this. This is going to kill me. I can hear her laughter. The sweet way she used to sing herself to sleep at night. It wasn't her fault the other kids liked to tease her. I tried to make them stop. I didn't even know what was going on until it was too late, and we were both in the water.

Summer camp was supposed to be fun and safe. Canoeing was one of the best activities there. But when twelve-year-olds decide to fuck with you, they don't play around. I'd seen Wendy and Pippa by the canoes earlier, but I hadn't thought anything of it. But those sisters were monsters, and I knew it and I should have done something.

When we got our boats in the water, I paddled with Claire because the other girls didn't like her. Pippa had made sure to help her with her life jacket, and I hadn't paid attention when Claire said it felt heavy. Said it felt like rocks were in there. But I was too excited to go out on the long trip to the island in the middle of the lake.

As we passed by Wendy and Pippa in their canoe, a pop rang out, and suddenly, our canoe sprang a leak between the shore and the island. Too far from safety.

We sank fast. We screamed. A lot. The counselor was already on the island—Becka had led the way. There supposed to be a counselor behind the group, too, but she wasn't there. I found out later that she had food poisoning. No one knew if that was intentional … but I think Wendy and Pippa did something to her food. I've always thought that. After everything else they did, why not that, too? Those girls were evil. Pure evil. And their parents were too rich for it to matter.

The more I think about it, the more I can't breathe. Just like Claire.

Tears stream down my face, and I can't stop seeing her in front of me. "I'm sorry, Claire. I didn't know."

Not that it matters now. In the water, I kicked and kicked, trying to get to the surface. My life vest was weighted, too, but I wriggled the clips open and got out of it, and swam for the surface. Someone threw a rope toward me, but it was too short and panic splashing made me sink. When I did, there was Claire. Dead.

I screamed underwater and thrashed for the surface, kicking Claire's body in the process. Sometimes I still feel that sensation when I'm in the water. The softness of it. Soft, but still solid. I knew right then what I'd done, and the thought made me blackout for a flash.

But it was that little extra push which got me back to the surface, like kicking off the bottom of the pool. She saved my life because I had her body to propel me upward. It was instinct—I was kicking wildly, didn't have a plan or a thought in my head. I didn't want to use her like that. It just happened.

I'm not in the lake.

Chanting that over and over is the only thing that will keep me from losing my shit right now. My face is cold from the tears dripping down it, but that doesn't matter because I'm not in the lake. I'm dry—face aside—and I'm not blacking out. That is not an option. I am present and I am not drowning and I am going to get the fuck out of here somehow.

Focus. Breathe.

If not for myself, then I'll do it for Claire. Because when I get out of here and I get my money, I'm going to open a firm to help people who get stepped on by everyone else.

-

Chapter 37

JUNE

Hours pass by. It has to be hours, because the only two things that have calmed me down are thinking about the firm I want to start and counting the seconds, and I've reached over eight thousand and that's over two hours. That is, if I've been counting actual seconds.

I haven't thought about Claire in so long that it feels fresh. Therapy—lots of therapy—helped me to stow those thoughts away for processing later because every time I thought about her as a child, I had intractable panic attacks. No meds touched them, so my therapist thought it best I lock the thoughts up for the time being.

Now, I can't stop thinking about her. But it doesn't have to be entirely for naught. Back then, it was a horror in the truest sense of the word. Still is. But if I can use that horror to bring some good into the world, then I will. I'll help people who have been wronged.

Maybe I'll track down Pippa and Wendy and make their lives a living hell while I'm at it. I'm sure I can dig into their family's financials and find something wrong.

"Claire, I will make them pay. All of them."

But to do that, I have to start with making Anderson pay. Oh, Anderson. God, could this be more complicated? Maybe I shouldn't have told them about our relationship. Maybe I should have kept my mouth shut. I don't know. It's hard to know what the best—

The rectangle of light says someone is opening the far door. A slim figure walks through it, and I'm not sure if it's better that it's the woman coming toward me right now, but it feels like it's better. Silly, really. She could have a gun or a knife or something. She's just as much of a threat as the big guy. But I still feel better that it's her.

An overhead light comes on—one of those humming fluorescents. It takes a minute before my eyes clear up and when they do, the woman is untying me. It makes me want to celebrate, but that feels premature. She's pretty, but plain. Brown hair, brown eyes, nothing remarkable about her at all. The perfect kidnapper.

And another face I've seen when I would prefer not to see them. One more person I can identify is one more reason for them to kill me.

When I'm untied, she says, "Follow me." Then she turns on her heel and heads for the far door.

I stand up and almost lose my balance. Pins and needles in my calf. "Leg's asleep. Just a moment."

If she's annoyed, she doesn't show it. She merely stands near the door, waiting. I hobble toward her as best I can and by the time I reach her, I'm awkwardly walking like a newborn horse, but I can travel. She gives a curt nod, then opens the door.

We're in a hallway. It's rudimentary and a little bare. It reminds me of the time I had to go through a mall's back halls because I got locked in after it closed and the security guard had to help me get out. But then we go through another door, and we're in a lobby with a bank of elevators. There's no outer door from the lobby, and no windows, either. But there are guards. Lots of armed guards. This place is a fortress.

Running is not an option. I want to ask a thousand questions, but I doubt she'd answer any of them, and I don't want to annoy her. Nervously rambling won't make things better.

Anyone who has a fortress in the middle of Boston—if we're still in Boston—is dangerous. I shouldn't have said shit about Anderson. Hell, I probably shouldn't be involved with him, either. Not if being involved with him gets me here. This is about his family. Not me. I don't have anything to do with anything this nefarious.

But I'm here and there's nothing I can do to change that right now.

The woman waits as an elevator door opens, and she gestures for me to walk in.

Sure. Why not?

She steps in, too, and presses her finger to a fingerprint reader. There are no buttons in the elevator. Top-notch security here. Great. The elevator trip goes on for a long time, and when it opens, it opens directly into a penthouse.

The skyline is unfamiliar, and I'm not sure if that's because it's Boston from an angle I've never seen or if I'm not in Boston anymore. All of the décor is hyper-modern, but classy. Less

Jetsons and more jet-set. I can't take much of it in, because it seems we're heading toward a man with his back to us, and I have a sneaking suspicion that he's the one in charge, so my panic threatens to rise again. After all, the other interrogators came to see me, but I had to come to see him. It's a negotiating tactic I studied, but I doubt there will be much negotiation today.

He stands by the window, overlooking the city like he owns it. For all I know, he does. A long table near the windows appears to be our destination. At least if I'm tied to a chair here, it'll be more comfortable than that damned wooden chair downstairs. These are overstuffed leather numbers like in boardrooms. The woman gestures at the one at the end of the table away from the man, so I sit. Thankfully, she doesn't tie me to it. In fact, there's a glass of water there.

Progress?

The woman leaves us behind, vanishing back into the elevator. I'm not sure if I should speak first or let him do the talking. But he doesn't. Not at first. Just as I draw a breath to say something, he says, "I'm sure you have many questions."

"Good guess."

His shoulders hop a little, like he's chuckling. But I don't hear anything out of him. Then he turns to face me, and I'm struck by him. He's a good bit older than I'd expected after all of this. I'm not sure how old he would be, but he has to be in his fifties. White, with shining green eyes and a pleasant smile. His brown hair has gray sideburns, and he's clean shaven. Handsome, classically so. He has a medium frame, and aside from the very expensive clothes, he looks painfully normal.

I'm a little disappointed. I'd thought for sure he'd be some Bond villain-type, with a strange facial scar and petting a white cat or something. Callie's influence, I'm sure of it.

He sits at the other end of the long table. "Feel free to drink that. I'm sure you're thirsty after your ordeal."

I reach for it, but then stop. "How do I know it's not poisoned?"

He laughs. "I suppose you don't." Suddenly, he gets up and comes toward me, and I brace for a smack for my insolence or something. But he takes a sip of the water instead. "Granted, you don't know me, but I'm not in the habit of drinking poison." Then he returns to his seat.

Ah, well. If they wanted me dead, I would

be. The water tastes like the best thing ever and I'm tempted to drink it all down, but I pace myself in case this is all I get. "Thanks for that."

"I am Andre Moeller. A friend of the West family."

"Then they need better friends."

He laughs again. "Truer words …"

"If you're their friend, then why take Anderson's fiancée hostage?"

Andre folds his hands on the table. "It is an unfortunate situation, but they owe me a debt. I need them to know I am serious about getting paid. You, my dear, are the bit of pressure I believe will inspire them to make good on said debt."

I find myself envious of Andre. At least he could figure out a way to get paid by them. "What makes you think I'm that valuable to the Wests?"

"Look at you. How could you not be?"

"Okay, sure, flattery is nice and everything, but you had me kidnapped, so I'm not going to blush and say thanks."

"You're spirited. No wonder Anderson likes you."

"Being nice after keeping me locked up in a

basement for hours is not going to level the playing field between us, Mr. Moeller."

He chuckles under his breath. "What makes you think we're on a level playing field, Ms. Devlin?"

Oh. There's the hint of a threat. To be honest, I'd expected worse. "Not a thing. But you're being nice to me, and I assume there's a reason for it."

"Of course. No sense in making this more unpleasant than it needs to be, don't you think?"

"Sure." But I'm not letting my guard down for anything. "If this is a simple business matter, then why not use the courts to enforce it?"

He smirks. "Because neither myself nor the Wests want the law involved in our dispute. Trust me."

Considering the circumstances, I did.

Chapter 38

JUNE

Things aren't improving, so I try another tactic. "I'm not sure what you want from me, but there isn't anything you can get from me here that I can't give you from my home. Surely, the threat of taking me away is just as effective as actually doing it."

He laughs much harder this time. "Ms. Devlin, I've never been fond of lady comics, but you are a talent."

A swing and a miss. "If—"

"How well do you know Anderson?"

Oh boy. There's no good answer to that question. Except maybe the truth? I mean, our past is sticky at best, but depending on what Andre knows, it might be the right option.

Pissing him off isn't going to win me a friend. Should I just tell him everything, blather on until I annoy him so he'll send me away? Would that even work?

Or should I tell him about the auction and let his imagination run wild, so he's distracted?

"We went to school together. Tonight is the first time I've met his family." Simple. Straightforward. No room for error.

"Hmm," is the only response I get out of him.

"Why me? The Wests have a ton of relatives —hell, I met a bunch of them tonight. I'm not attached to the family in any formal way. So, why me?"

"I told you. You are their collateral."

"Right, but why not anyone else?"

A hint of a smirk draws the corner of his mouth tight. "Are you saying you would wish this fate on a stranger?"

Don't like him talking about fate, like this is the end of the line for me. "I'm saying that strategically, it makes more sense to nab anyone but me. I like to play chess, and as a strategy, this one isn't a winner, so I'm just trying to understand."

"Glad to hear it. I play as well. Perhaps, one day we will play together. In the meantime, do not underestimate your value."

"I'm just surprised, is all. We haven't been dating that long."

"From the sometime after the Chamberlain Auction, according to my sources."

My face flushes hot, but there were two auctions that night. Hopefully, he means the first one. "Um, yes. A worthy cause, the Chamberlain—

"Yes, it is." He pauses. "But I'm not speaking of the public auction. I'm speaking of the private one."

Okay, that's a little too much honesty from my kidnapper. "Right well, we've been together since after then. Just a few weeks. So, see? Not a brilliant strategy for you."

He grins. "You blush prettily, Ms. Devlin."

"And easily, so it's no mean feat that you've managed it."

"The thing you're overlooking in all of this is that it's not the length of time that you dated Anderson. It is the quality of that time. I have never seen that boy as smitten as he is with you. He would do anything to get you back."

Okay, that's nice to hear, but hearing it from Andre and hearing it from Anderson are two different things. "Guess I hope you're right. Wait—you're not trying to hurt him, are you?"

He sits back, a curious look on his face. "And if I were?"

"Please don't. Whatever this is all about, there has to be another way to handle it. Anderson can be a jerk sometimes, but I'm sure whatever this is, he wasn't trying to hurt anyone."

"You have that much faith in him?"

I nod rapidly. "I've seen him at some of his worst times. It was never who he really was. He's a good man who had a lot of bullshit thrown at him from a young age, and he's struggled to make the best life he can since then. He deserves another chance. Please don't hurt him."

"You care a great deal for your fiancé."

"I do." To my surprise, it's true.

"Young love is sweetest when it's fresh. Do you—

"I have known Anderson since we were teenagers, Mr. Moeller. This isn't just young love or puppy love or some other diminutive thing you want to call it. This is real. It's solid. It's not going anywhere. I need him to be okay after all of this is said and done. So, you tell me what I need to do to make this right for you, and I'll do it. But let's be done with the cat-and-mouse crap and get down to business. Tell me about the debt, and we can settle this one way or another."

Again, he sits back, looking me over. "Big promises from a woman with less than four grand in her checking account."

"There are other ways to pay a debt."

"Are you offering to seduce me?"

I laugh at the thought and hope he isn't offended. "I was thinking more of favors from important people. My financials aren't great, but my clients' financials are, and if you've looked into me as much as I think you have, then you know that and you know who my clients are. They like me, Mr. Moeller. I save them from big bad Uncle Sam. So, if I ask for a favor, they are inclined to give it to me. That's how I've vacationed in some of the best villas in Tuscany and a few islands in the Caribbean. I'd be happy to extend those favors to you."

He smiles condescendingly. "Oh, that's precious. You think a vacation in Tuscany can balance what Elliot West has done? You truly do not know how deep this goes, do you?"

"I don't think a vacation in Tuscany would do much for you, but maybe some sweetheart business deals would, and there are other favors my clients would do for me as well. Government contracts I can make appear, things of that nature. But why don't you spell it out for me? What did Elliot West do that put such a bee in your bonnet?"

At that, he stares off out the windows, looking wistful. "It's a pity. Truly it is. You don't deserve to be here. I had considered taking Kitty instead of you—it's likely she knows what he's up to, so it seems more appropriate to take her instead of you. But she is a dear woman who I have known a long time, and I don't wish to trigger her heart condition any more than this situation might already. That said, the blame for all of this sits squarely on Elliot's shoulders, so perhaps taking her would have been better … you see, he has done a terrible thing, Ms. Devlin. Very bad. Something I hesitate to mention because the more you know, the more you're likely to suffer for his sins. Do yourself a favor and try not to get involved any deeper than you already are."

"You kidnapped me, Mr. Moeller. I'm as involved as it gets, I'd say."

He chortles. "Oh. No. You're not. This could be far worse than what you've already experienced. But I do not wish that for you. Not at all. Remain an innocent bystander—"

"No! I deserve to know why the fuck you took me!"

His eyes darken as he returns his gaze to me. It's strange—he looks like a completely different person when he's pissed off. "You're right. You deserve to know. But I will not be the one to tell you. I will not taint you with that knowledge. As I said, the more you know, the more risk you are at. Do yourself a favor when you leave here and break up with Anderson West. You'll stay safer that way."

"I don't remember asking you for relationship advice."

"I'm not offering you relationship advice. I'm telling you how to stay alive. This will only get worse before it gets better. *If* it gets better. You're a bright woman. Unless you have a death wish for you or your possible future children, you'll leave Anderson."

That takes the wind out of my sails. I rasp,

"You would threaten the children I don't even have yet?"

"Have you ever built anything, Ms. Devlin?"

I blink at him. "What?"

He gets up and paces in front of the city. "These windows are bulletproof. It's why I can stand here and watch the world in front of them without worry. When you build something, you must consider things from every angle. How fortified can you make it? How safe for those you love? Can you guarantee—except that you cannot guarantee a thing in this life. The glass is bulletproof, but what about a bomb? What about poison fed into the water pipes from several buildings away? Or a toxic gas? So on, and so on."

"What is your point? What does this have to do with Anderson?"

"I had another building before this one. Beautiful. Tall. Elegant. Bulletproof glass and filters on the water system to prevent toxins from coming in, all the latest in security. And do you know what toppled it?"

"Your ego?"

He laughs. "Termites. Billions of them. I have no proof that it was sabotage, but the infestation came from the inside and they ate their way out, so it's hard to think it could be anything else. When you build something, Ms. Devlin, you must consider every possible angle. Every threat." He turns to me. "If you build a family with Anderson West, the threat will come from inside the house. He will be the downfall of all you hold dear. Every West man is exactly the same. None of them are to be trusted. Mark my words."

My voice shakes, but I don't care. "You're the one who threatened my non-existent children, Mr. Moeller. Not Anderson."

"I build things. If your future children are a threat to what I build, I will end them just as easily as anyone else. Leave him and keep those future children safe from people like me. And people like Elliot West. That's the only way to keep what you build safe."

My skin crawls. I don't know what the hell kind of business this guy is in, but it's obviously much worse than I ever thought. That he'd lay a finger on children I don't even have is too much for me. I'm all for doing business dirty. We do what we have to, and I don't pretend I'm above doing things that are unseemly or pushing the law to its full extent to save my clients some money on their taxes. But there are limits. A lot of them.

Kidnapping is a big one. But hurting kids is a far bigger limit.

"I'll take your recommendation under advisement."

Chapter 39
ANDERSON

This isn't happening. This cannot be happening.

But the security guard plays the tape again for me, because I am beside myself. It shows June on the street after I leave her there. She looks so small by herself that it guts me. A black sprinter van pulls up, and a man in all black comes along, keeping his face turned. He knew where the camera was to avoid it. The amount of planning ... how did they know she would be there alone?

Or worse—were they watching us the whole time?

When he reaches for her, my fists clench. She fights. God, she fights, and a surge of pride shoots through me. But it's no use. This was too well-executed.

He pulls out a knife, and I want to scream. I want to kill him myself. The back of the van opens, and he manhandles her into it. Another person inside pulls her in, and the knife guy hops in after her, closing the door. No license plate. No nothing.

I've watched the video over a dozen times, trying to figure out what to do next. My first instinct is to call the police, but I know better. If this is a simple kidnapping for money, then calling the police is the last thing I should do. Most kidnappings fare better without their involvement. But I want them involved.

I want the damned army involved.

The Pentagon. Anyone who can get her back for me. I want to rain hell on these people.

The scent of stale coffee and staler donuts permeates the security office of the building. It's a dreary little room with some of the best trained people in the field. A table, monitors with live feeds, recording equipment, everything to keep the wealthy of Boston safe.

A lot of good it did June.

I force myself to ask, "Who knows?"

"Just me and Mike," George says. He feels guilty—he should—but these people are profes-sionals. They knew when George took his break, and they knew when Mike called his wife. It was the perfect time to grab June, and it just so happened to be when I lost my fucking phone.

Yeah. They are definitely watching us. Maybe even now.

"Any cameras in here?"

"No. That's against protocol."

Doesn't mean they're not watching. But if they're piped into the system, it'll make it harder to see into here. "What other rooms don't have cameras?"

"The residences, the bathrooms, and this room. That's all."

Mike jumps in, "But some of the residences have their own systems. They have their own personal security."

I'm familiar with that. Mom and Dad have their own private system. Huh. I'd forgotten that in the library. Doesn't matter. Not now. "Could someone tap into the private systems?"

They both shrug and George says, "Depends on the system, but yeah. I'd think so. If someone were motivated enough."

"Clearly, they are."

"Mr. West, how can we help?"

How can anyone? "I'm not sure. I've texted them back over a dozen times. No answer. Why send a picture and no ransom request? It makes no fucking sense!" I slam my fist into the wall, and thankfully, I picked the drywall and not the brick right next to it, or I'd have more than bloodied knuckles right now. But I don't even feel it. Just the trickle of blood down my fingers. "Sorry."

"Understandable," Mike says, probably thinking of his wife.

George suggests, "I know you said no cops, but have you thought of telling your father? He has a lot of friends in high—"

"Yeah. I have. But I keep thinking that the fewer people who know about this, the fewer people who can screw this up."

Mike nods. "True. But that's also the fewer people who can help."

"I know, but … I can't risk her. This is damn near the worst thing that could happen, and every move I make could be the wrong one." It's not just that. It feels like all my luck has turned to shit.

First, I have the most amazing night of my life with June at the auction, and then everything after that has flung itself off a fucking cliff. June, storming my office, rightfully demanding her money. My account being frozen because our CFO is being a jealous asshole, and then, my dad backing him up on it. The humiliation of having to tell her that my account is frozen because my father still thinks I'm a fucking child. And now, this.

I am not trying to make her problems about myself, but every problem she has is my fault, and I can't fix any of them, and I am so frustrated that I might actually strangle the next person who gets between us.

In short, my luck has run out.

So, I have to figure how to operate without it. "Play it again … maybe we missed something. This time, watch the edges of the screen."

They nod, and Mike plays the video again. No shadows at the edges. Nothing we missed. Fuck. It plays out the same every time. No one sees a damn thing. If someone had, they would have called the police by now. Or their own private security. Either way, nothing.

As much as I hate doing this, I have to tap Dad in. He has more resources than I do and far more money. Especially right now. Hell, maybe he has a clue as to what is going on. I almost laugh at the thought.

Our family has been in the entertainment and law industry for generations. We have always kept our noses clean and done things by the book. Elliot West is as likely to know about this as he is to know about the Yakuza. But he has friends who might be able to illuminate the situation. Entertainment is never that far from the seedy underbelly of the world.

A lot of deals go down at entertainment venues—clubs are great for being seen in public while not being heard. Same for concerts. Celebrities like to source bodyguards from less reputable sources, because those people are usually willing to do things others will not. Keeps them safe.

Right now, I'm wishing I had one of those disreputable bodyguards on June.

"Alright. Gentlemen, what do I need to do to ensure your absolute silence on this matter?"

They exchange a glance. George weakly says, "Don't get us fired?"

I almost laugh, but then Mike says, "We just found out my wife is pregnant again. I can't afford to lose this—"

"No one is getting fired, so long as you both keep your mouths shut. Don't even mention this to your wife. We don't know what's going on. I'd hate for anyone else to suffer the consequences."

He quickly nods. "Not a peep."

George agrees. "I won't say a word to anyone."

"Thank you both. Text me a copy of the video. I'm going to speak with my father."

"Will do," he sets about the task, as I run out of the security office for the elevator. As soon as the door closes, I slump on the wall. I know George and Mike can see me, and I don't fucking give a shit. Exhaustion has gut punched me, and I'm just done.

It's not the physical kind of exhaustion—I'm too wired for that right now. But my soul has been run over and backed over by a semi-truck. I cannot believe this is happening. I don't want to believe it. All I want to do is crawl into bed and spoon June until I fall asleep with my arms around her, so I know she's safe.

But none of that matters right now. Right now, I have to think about who would do this. That will tell me more about my next move than focusing on anything else.

Which begs the question, why the fuck kidnap a tax attorney?

Could it be a client of hers? Someone who didn't get the outcome they wanted? Pretty sure that's not the case. Otherwise, why text me her picture? Fuck, that picture grows rocks in my gut every time I look at it.

There is nothing in the picture to distinguish it from any other basement. Can't even see the walls, which has to be on purpose. Just a bright light shining on June, and she's tied to a wooden chair. Cement floor. No boxes or crates, no trash or debris. Only her.

This isn't sexual. If this was just about money, they would have sent a ransom request. This is personal.

Who the fuck did I piss off enough to do this?

I sniff and shake myself out of my self-pity spiral. Whoever did this for whatever reason, they're wrong. There is nothing I have ever done to warrant this as recompense. Maybe they have the wrong woman. Right now, I'm not sure if that would be better or worse.

-

Chapter 40
ANDERSON

When I get to Mom and Dad's door, it's open, and my gut clenches. What if something happened to them, too? Is the whole family under attack? I step to the side of the door, peeking in to look for enemies.

But then a caterer rushes through—another is holding the door open for them with their foot from the other side. They are taking their equipment out, since the party is winding down. My family must have left while I was in the security office.

I let out a breath in relief. Didn't know I could be more tense right now, but here we are. I shake loose of that particular fear and trudge into the apartment. I have to see Dad before he goes to bed. Or I'll wake him. I don't fucking care.

Mom yawns as she passes through the hall. Then she quirks a sleepy smile at me. "I thought you and June left already."

Do I tell her? Not yet. It's not that I don't trust her. It's just that there is no time. "I need to speak with Dad. Do you know where he is?"

"His private study, I think. He likes a bit of quiet and a shower after things like this. Otherwise, he doesn't sleep." She gives a sheepish shrug.

"Thanks, Mom. Goodnight."

"Goodnight, Anderson." She drifts down the hall.

The private study is at the other end of the apartment, so I run. Every second lost is a second June cannot afford. I bust into the private study's closed door, decorum be damned. "Dad, we need to talk."

He sits in his lounge chair. It's one of those zero gravity chairs that takes pressure off the joints. Well, I'm about to put a lot of pressure on him, so that seems appropriate. The private study has dark paneled walls and an enormous bay window overlooking the city. The city has never looked so grim from up here. But it swallowed June up, and I will never forgive Boston for that.

"What is this all about? I thought you left with June." A puff of cigar smoke leaves his mouth and nose, and now I know the real reason Dad has his quiet time and a shower before bed.

"She was kidnapped. I want to call the police, but I wanted to speak to you first. In case you have someone you think would be better—"

"Do not call the police," he says mildly, before pressing a button on his chair to sit up.

"Who then?"

Watching him sit up, it's strange. He's not surprised or upset or even confused. Merely annoyed. "Not the police."

"If you don't tell me who to call, I'm calling them."

"Put the phone down, Anderson."

"Why?" I snap.

"Because once you involve the police, it is all out of your hands. Do you want to lose control of this situation?"

I growl, "*I'm* not in control of this situation!" Showing him her picture, I bark, "*They* are!"

His lips flatten into a perturbed line as he sighs and shakes his head, exhaling smoke like an inconvenienced dragon.

This whole thing isn't upsetting him as much as it should. Especially considering how much he seems to like June. Why isn't he angry? Why isn't he on the phone to his connections right now?

Something inside of my gut twists and my mouth is dry as paper. "What do you know about this, Dad?"

"I don't—

"Who would do this? Why? What's going on?" I'm shaking from anger, and I don't want to take it out on my father, but he's not making this easy. I need answers now.

He sighs. "Nothing is for certain until they communicate their needs. That is the way of these things. Have they?"

"No."

"I presume you've reached out to them on her phone?"

"Of course."

When he stares out the window, his voice sounds hollow. "You don't stay on top of this business without making enemies, Anderson."

"What the fuck does that mean?"

"There is no such thing as having our wealth *and* having clean hands. Sometimes, things get … messy."

I am losing what little patience I had. "Explain what you're talking about. Now."

"We will do what we can to bring her back. I promise."

"That is not an explanation!"

He turns to me. "Whatever you do, son, do not call the police."

And at that moment, I know why. At least partially. It's not to protect June. It's to protect him. Whatever this is, it's his fault, and he knows it. He's done something deeply illegal, and June is paying the price for it.

Fuck that.

"Tell me what you know. Right now."

"I'll tell you this, she is safe. She—"

"Does she look fucking safe to you?" I shove the phone in his face.

He sighs again. His voice is flat. "Her clothes are in place. There are no visible marks. She's not even crying, though I imagine that is due to her fortitude and not her treatment. There are no obvious threats to her—no gun to her head, no water creeping in over the floor, etcetera. So yes, she looks fucking safe to me."

Never in my life have I been so close to striking my father. "How the fuck can you just sit there and act like this isn't a big deal? How are you so calm?"

He taunts, "One of us should be."

My fist balls up without a thought, but I keep it at my side. It is all I can do to keep emotion from my voice, but if I don't, he won't listen to me. He's never responded well to anything but logic or anger. "Tell me how to get her back."

"Find your calm. If your woman can maintain her composure under her circumstances, then you should be able to as well. It's embarrassing that you're so hysterical—"

"You think I give a shit about my composure right now?"

He advises, "If you do not keep your composure, Anderson, you will lose her. You will make a rash error in judgment and whoever has taken her will take advantage of that. They have the upper hand right now, it's true. But if you rush into this, they will keep it. They have you by the balls. Don't let them know it, or they will cut them off."

"If the next words out of your mouth are not useful, I will call the police."

Another sigh out of him. "The police will get her killed."

"Who the fuck kills someone when the police are involved?"

"Very dangerous people."

"Why is she with very dangerous people, Dad? Talk to me. Tell me what the fuck is actually going on!"

Again, he looks out the window. "No."

Talking to him is pointless. He's not helping. He's stonewalling me. Why? Who knows? Doesn't fucking matter. I have to get to June. "What the fuck ever, Dad. You won't help me? I'll help myself." I turn for the door.

"Don't forget what I said. No cops. They will get her killed."

I whip back around to him. "From where I'm standing, it sounds like this is all *your* fault. Not theirs. If she dies because of something you did—

"You'll what? Storm into my study and act like a petulant child who got his new favorite toy taken away?"

"I'll end it. All of it. I will destroy the firm from the ground up just to watch you suffer."

He scoffs. "You do that, and you lose everything, too."

"Mutually assured destruction," I tell him simply. "So, you better get off your ass and help with this, because I'm young enough to rebuild my life and you're not."

"You wouldn't dare, and even if you did, you don't know enough about what we really do to be able to destroy us."

"Don't fuck with me, Dad. You do not know how much I know. Calling the police might get June killed, but I doubt the same is true of calling the IRS."

His eyes bulge, and before he can say a word, I stomp out of his study, slamming the door behind me. It was a good bluff, if I say so myself. I do not know what Dad is really doing behind the scenes, but everyone fears the IRS, so it was a solid guess. But given his earlier intimations, it's not just tax evasion he's worried about.

Something else much bigger is going on, and June was taken because of it.

I march out of the apartment, ignoring the caterers as they finish the last parts of cleaning. Once I'm in the elevator, I take a breath and try to figure out my next steps. Only, nothing comes to mind other than the sight of June, tied to a wooden chair in a random basement somewhere I don't recognize. The sight of her like that is enough to make every other thought vanish without a trace. Just like June.

-

Chapter 41

ANDERSON

I'm so angry that I keep gripping my steering wheel too tightly and driving too fast. I have to slow down, or I'll get pulled over, and if I get pulled over, I'll spill it all. I know I will. The idea of speaking to a police officer without telling them exactly what's going on? Madness. I'd spill it all, and right now, I cannot afford to be that messy.

Dad was right about one thing. Police mean I will not be in control of the situation. They introduce too many moving parts. They have protocols they have to follow, no matter what. I, however, do not. I will do whatever it takes to get her back.

Part of me wonders if I shouldn't have pressed Dad. But he wasn't going to crack. That man never cracks. No matter how tough the negotiations, he doesn't budge. It is simultaneously frustrating and admirable and a quality I do not share with him. I have a strong spine, but right now, I'd give the kidnappers whatever the fuck they want.

Where am I even driving to?

The truth is, I don't know. I got into my car and started driving. Movement feels better than sitting around. Feels like progress, even though rationally, I know it's not. What are the odds I'll just find her walking along the side of the road? Zero. But movement still feels better.

Trying to think of what connections I have at the firm doesn't help. I'm the son of the man in charge, the heir apparent. But I've never been included in whatever the fuck Dad is actually up to. It's like I've been shielded from all the useful contacts, which makes me distinctly useless in a situation like this.

June has been taken, and I have no way of getting her back. I have never felt so goddamned helpless in my life.

I'm the guy who fixes things. Who makes things happen, even if I never get the credit. Shit like that doesn't matter to me. I like to help, no matter the circumstance. I do my best to take care of what needs to get taken care of, and now I'm the guy who sits around waiting for someone else to do what needs to be done. This is maddening.

When a text buzzes in, I slam on the brakes. Thankfully, at four in the morning, there's no one behind me. Hell, I don't even know what street this is. But I pull over and look at my phone. I don't trust my car to read it out loud— what if someone has my car rigged to scan my messages? What the fuck can I trust at this point?

The message reads, "Be at easterly side of Hell Gate Bridge tonight at ten. Wait for a red car."

That's it? That's all they have to say to me?

I text back, "What do you need from me?"

"Be there."

No ransom request. No payment of any kind. Not even art or someone else in exchange?

Maybe that's it. Maybe *I'm* the exchange. Okay, good. I'll go with them, and June can drive my car back to Boston and get as far away from these people as possible. She'll go to my Dad and they can handle this from there. This is progress.

Not that I want to be taken, but it's a hell of

a lot better than June being taken. But why not take me in the first place? They probably knew I'd put up more of a fight than she could. They had to take her to soften me up. To make me pliable. Fine, whatever. They win. I don't care, so long as she's safe. That's all that matters.

Should I call Dad to update him? No. If he thinks I'll be taken next, he'll have a fit and fuck this up. He was right about one thing—the more people involved, the worse the outcome. Even if he wouldn't be upset about them taking me, he'd be angry if someone moved against the family so boldly. My kidnapped fiancée he can take in stride, apparently. But taking his son would be an insult to his pride.

Good. Let's insult him.

Now that we have a time and place to meet, I could call the police. Get some backup … but it still feels like the wrong thing to do. And I don't have the kinds of friends one needs in a situation like this. Call Tag? I almost laugh at the thought. Tag is a lot of things, but backup in a hostage situation? Hell no. He's barely backup in a buffet situation. Cole? Equally laughable.

This is all on me. Just how I like things to be.

Heading home, I need to grab a few things. Oh, I'll let them take me. But that doesn't mean

I'll be a pleasant guest while they have me. My apartment is on the other side of Boston from here and the urge to speed hits again. I want to get there and get to the bridge right now so I can be there early.

But I can't risk speeding. No cops. In fact, I'm half-tempted to call a driving service for the trip to Manhattan to ensure I don't speed my way there. But if I did that, it would be another pair of eyes on the situation, and that's not an option. So, a lot of self-control is in order.

When I get home, I ignore the call of my bed. I'm exhausted and wired and shaky right now. Never been good at staying up all night, and by the timing of things, I doubt I'll get any sleep tonight, either. But, maybe grabbing a few hours would make me more clearheaded. God knows I need to be.

Not like I could sleep right now, anyway.

I bank the idea for later and flip out the painting on my wall. My wall safe sits behind the painting, and I press my thumb to it to unlock the door. It pops open. Inside is a load of cash and a selection of handguns, and I grab my favorite—the Sig Sauer P226. It's light enough not to weigh down my jacket, but heavy duty enough to make me feel better. It's also the one I'm best with at the range.

I've never considered myself a gun nut or into the culture of it at all. They're for protection, nothing more. Which means I also have a custom-made ankle holster for a pocket pistol. I prefer pocket pistols for ankle holsters because a pat down is more likely to not notice something that small, especially if it's tucked into my boot.

Though it's not the most comfortable thing I've ever worn, comfort is the last thing on my mind right now. I also grab the bear spray—it shoots farther than pepper spray and has the same effect on people as it does bears. I tuck the Sig into the internal pocket of my coat and the bear spray in the outer pocket, so if I get a pat down, they'll feel the can and think that's all there is.

I hope.

All of this preparation may be moot, though. If June is possibly in the line of fire, I won't take that chance. She is everything in this. I won't give them any reason to harm her any more than they already have. I'll go peacefully, if I must. But if I can defend myself once she's gone, I'll do it.

I dump my gym bag onto my bed and go

around my apartment, stuffing it with anything useful. Protein bars, bottles of water, cans of Red Bull, an extra scarf for June, a small first aid kit I keep in the bathroom, a telescoping baton, all the cash I have on hand, my passport —should I break into June's place to get her passport?

In what world do I think a passport will be useful right now?

I shake my head at myself and dump the bag again. I'm freaking out, not thinking clearly. Okay. Breathe. What do I need right now? It's then that my stomach growls, and that sensation fills me with a strange shame. How can I eat at a time like this? Has June eaten? Have they given her water? Fuck!

I rake my fingers through my hair and try to calm down. Repacking the bag, I keep everything but my passport. If they search me and find that, they'll think I'm going to take off. Though that's not a bad idea, if this situation is going to drag on—and I think it will—if I take off or if June does, I do not know how they will respond to that. Chase us down? Take my mother hostage? Hurt someone I care about?

The ball is in their court in all of this, and I can't rattle them right now.

With my bag packed and on my shoulder, I glance back at my apartment. Wonder if I'll see it again. Time's wasting. I want to be at the drop before they are, so I can scope out possible exits and get a feel for the place. I don't think I've ever been to Hell Gate Bridge before, but it's appropriately named.

But if I'm going to Hell tonight, I'm taking them with me.

-

Chapter 42
JUNE

Chapter Forty-Four-June

"The blindfold again? Really?" I huff as I get no answer from the woman. She merely ties it over my eyes. She does a better job than the guys did. Can't see a damn speck of light. Makes me wonder if this isn't her first time with a blindfold. Or if she uses them in her bedroom for fun. She certainly knew to pull at the edges of it to guarantee my blindness. Bet she's a top in the bedroom. Can't be a mousy little thing if you're a kidnapper.

It's so much more comfortable to think about lurid details like that than to focus on the existential terror of being transported again.

When I was upstairs, Andre had fielded a few calls, speaking Italian the whole time, so I had no idea what was being said. But the words were so similar to Spanish that I thought I might have had a hold on some of them. Not that my Spanish was great, but I spoke enough to get by on a Mexican vacation.

Buono—Bueno—Good. Banca—Banco—Bank. Some words needed no translation. Padre. Problema. Tempo. I had the feeling Anderson's father was running out of time to solve a problem with the bank, and if they cooperated, things would be good.

Strange how similar our problems were.

But now, being downstairs in the garage, our problems' similarities have ended. I'm not sure what's happening now or why I'm being transported. No one tells me shit. My hands are tied in front of me. I'm just a package, as far as anyone here is concerned. All I know is the woman and the big guy walked me next to a nondescript red sedan with black tinted windows. Older model. Nothing fancy. Not as nice as the sprinter van—not even close.

All of that makes me nervous. This is the kind of car you use to dump a body. Something unremarkable, so it goes unnoticed. I guess my status will be determined by where I ride. If I go in the trunk, I'm dead. I know it.

Once the blindfold is secured to the woman's liking, she says, "No. Not there."

"He said the trunk."

Fuck.

But she counters, "No point to that. She can sit in the back."

I love her.

"Moeller said she goes in the trunk. Easier when we get to where we're going. Simpler for the meet up. Pop it, and we go."

"If I get a vote—

"Shh," she says coldly to me. "Fine. Put her in the trunk. But if anything happens to her—"

"It won't."

As soon as I feel his giant mitts on me, I struggle. I can't help it. I'm about to die, and I'm not going to make that easy. But he lays me in the trunk. "See? Not so bad in there. Just be quiet and don't cause any problems and there won't be none for you, neither."

"Wait—"

But the lid shuts.

I take a breath and try not to scream. To my surprise, the trunk isn't as uncomfortable as I thought it would be. It's lined with blankets and pillows. This is their usual prisoner transportation car. Lucky me.

I'd pull my blindfold off, but I'm sure I'd be in trouble for that. Not that it matters anyway. Trunks aren't exactly made for sightseeing. But something in my mind flashes to an old book I read. It was a spy novel, I think. The spy was kidnapped and placed in the back, and there was a lever in the trunk for accidents, like if kids were playing in a car, so they could get out, and he used that lever to spring it open.

Where is that lever?

Feeling around, I pull my blindfold down a little to see, but I was right before. It's pitch black in here and there's no point in incurring the wrath of my captors if I can't escape, so I pull it back up. As I'm groping blindly, the car starts up.

Here we go.

Okay, no one has shot me, and I might be able to pull a lever to escape. Win-win. Keep looking. As I do, I grab onto something that feels like it might be a lever, except it's sharp. We hit a bump right then, and it cuts my palm. Dammit. It's not deep, but it hurts. Then again, if that's the worst injury I end up with over this, I'll take it gladly.

I press the wound to my coat, hoping to staunch the bleeding, but it's not bad and seems to end fast. Bet that was the lever. Someone cut it to make it impossible to use. Nothing else in the trunk would match the description I read in the book, so I'm not escaping anytime soon.

But at least no one has shot me. I'll take it.

I lay back and try to think of what to do next. Make noise when we stop? It'll attract the attention of the woman and the Big Guy first, and I don't look forward to their potential reactions. There's really not much more to be done, other than waiting.

Great. More of the same.

It was strange to watch Andre on the phone after our conversation. He seemed so adamant that I trust him about Anderson, so forceful about it. But when he was on the phone, he vacillated from laughing to threats with ease. Whatever he did professionally, it wasn't good. He sounded like a maniac.

But thinking about what he told me about the Wests leaves me confused. He said I didn't know who I was really involved with, and that if I stayed involved with Anderson, I would get into a lot more trouble than I was already in. Details? None. Just threats.

I defended myself and told him I didn't know anything, and he said he knew I wasn't involved, and that was why he was being so friendly about everything. I scoffed at that. "Getting threatened and kidnapped and tied to chairs is fucking friendly to you?"

He smiled at that. "Yes. Very." The man is a fucking sociopath.

I gulped. "Well, it's not where I come from, Mr. Moeller."

"You and I come from two very different places, then. It is plain by how you are that you don't know anything, Ms. Devlin. I beg you not to change that. Your ignorance is what keeps you from facing other consequences at the moment. It keeps you safe. From me. From others. We are exploiting that privilege tonight."

"What does that mean?"

"It means you will go home."

My whole body tensed with excitement at that. "Seriously?"

"Provided you continue to cooperate with us, yes."

"What, um … what else do you want from me?"

He smiled. "Let's have breakfast." He did something on his phone and within a minute, a feast was delivered to us. My mouth watered at the pastries and fresh fruit and scrambled eggs and coffee, but I didn't recognize the cup of what looked to be incredibly dark hot chocolate. He sipped that first, smiling, so I did the same. It was incredible. The richest chocolate I'd ever tasted. After that, breakfast was relatively pleasant, given the conditions. Might as well enjoy what could be my last meal.

After breakfast, he started his calls in Italian, and after a while, the woman came and took me to another part of the penthouse, where we watched TV. It was all so weirdly normal that I didn't know what to think of any of it. But I was wiped out from the stress and from being up all night, and I ended up dozing off in an easy chair. After all, these people could kill me at any moment, whether I was asleep or not. Might as well rest while I could.

When I woke up, it was to hushed voices in the other room and I was alone. I listened at the door, but it was more Italian. Shortly after that, the woman brought me a turkey sandwich and said to eat fast, because we had to be somewhere. On the way through the penthouse, Andre stopped us. "Remember what I said, Ms. Devlin. Remain uninvolved with the West family, or things will not be as easy on you next time."

I gulped and nodded, and the woman ushered me out.

It is all so strange. Nothing matches up to what I know about kidnapping. I mean, sure, they took me pretty easily, and they obviously know what they're doing in that realm. But I've never read a book, or a seen an interview with a kidnapped person who was treated so friendly, as Andre put it. And to be fair to him, the breakfast was spectacular. Sure, he's a sociopath, but he was nothing but respectful to me while I was in his presence. His staff was, too.

As kidnappings go, this could have been a lot worse. But then again, I'm in a trunk, and he might have let me believe I'm going home, so I didn't get hysterical. Guys hate that. But if they're not going to kill me in the trunk, then why put down blankets and pillows? The whole thing boggles me.

It was night out when I woke up, so it's late now. Maybe I should have been counting the seconds to calculate the distance to where they are taking me, but does it matter? They're taking me there regardless of whether I know where I am. More than that, I'm not sure where I was at Andre's anyway.

Guess I'm just trying to think of something to do. I hate not being able to do anything. All I know is, when the trunk opens, I am hitting whoever is there. The woman. The Big Guy. I don't give a fuck. They did this to me. They might not be in charge, but they are just as guilty as Andre, and I'm angry about all of this. They deserve my wrath as much as he does.

The car sounds change—we're on a bridge. Oh shit. What if … what if they're just going to dump the car in a river or the bay or something? Fuck. I turn around and kick at what I think might be the lever. My boot scrapes against the sharp end, but I keep kicking, hoping to pop the trunk. I kick again and again and it's useless, but I don't care. I can't drown. Not like Claire. She had her weighted vest to pull her down. I have a whole fucking car around me. Oh my god—

Just then, the car stops.

I freeze up, trying to listen for anything. Any indication that the car is in neutral and about to me shoved into the water. The doors don't open. They'd get out first. Even with the doors not opening, there's the scratch of footsteps on concrete, coming close. Then one of the car's doors opens.

The trunk opens, too, and I still can't see a damn thing. But I hear the woman from behind me say , "Get her out."

How can I get out if I can't see? But then the Big Guy roughly picks me up and sets me to my feet. With both my hands still tied together, I ball my fists and hit him. Again and again, I hit him. But he catches my hands, and murmurs, "Stop, June. I have you."

I know that voice.

The car's tires squeal behind me as it pulls away, and the blindfold is lifted. Anderson stands in front of me, and my mind resets. It's night still, and bright underneath the street lamps of some bridge I don't know.

But all I really see is Anderson. My voice shakes, "Are ... are you really here?"

He smiles and cups my cheek. "I'm here. I have you. You're safe now."

My body goes embarrassingly limp, and he catches me. Scratch that—I'll be embarrassed tomorrow. For now, I'll let him hold me up. It's all I want in the world.

Chapter 43

JUNE

After I can stand up straight again, Anderson asks, "Where would you like to go? My place? Your place? A hotel?"

"Where are we?"

"New York City. This is the Hell Gate Bridge."

"Oh." I look around, trying to find anything familiar. But I don't know the city well enough. "I've only been to Manhattan."

"It's close to here."

"If it's not too much to ask—"

"Name it," his voice is firm, like he's straining to speak.

I'm too worried about him to ask for the favor. "Are you okay?"

He laughs, shaking his head. "Pretty sure I

was supposed to ask you that." But then he buttons down his expression into something colder. "June, do I need to get you to a hospital?"

"No—"

"Did they hurt you?" His voice is barely contained rage.

I shake my head, as much to tell him as to remind myself. "Mostly just scared the hell out of me."

"Why is there blood on your coat, June?"

"Hmm?"

He points to a spot, and I glance down. I'm alarmed at first, but then my hand aches. "Right. I forgot about that." Holding up my hand, I show him. "Thought I could try to open the trunk with the emergency latch, but I think they sharpened the metal to discourage that kind of heroics. Just a scratch. I'll be fine."

Anderson takes a deeper breath now. I wonder how long it's been since he took his last one. "Would you like to stay in Manhattan? I'll book us a suite, and we can stay as long as you like."

"I'd like to go home."

"Then I'll take you there." He puts his arm around me and guides me to his car. I'm glad for how comfortable it is, because it makes it easy to fall asleep. When I wake up, we're already at my place. "June, I don't know where you're at in your mind, but do you want me to walk you up?"

Slowly, I nod, and a faint smile takes his lips.

The elevator ride up is silent. The last twenty-four hours have felt like a year, and I don't have much conversation in me. Neither does Anderson, it seems. Not that we should talk about what happened in an unsecure location.

When we get to my door, he asks, "If you want to be alone, I'll go. If you want me to stay, I'll stay. It's up to you."

"Would you sleep better in your own bed?"

"I'll sleep best knowing you're alright."

"Then, if you don't mind, would you stay with me?"

His shoulders slump a little at that. "I would be happy to."

We go in, and it's as if nothing happened. Strange. My place is a little messy, but I'm too weary to give a shit about Anderson seeing my mess. Though, it's nicer to think about that than it is to think about what just happened to me. What's a little embarrassment compared to being kidnapped for a day?

My head feels like mush and cotton candy, and I can't tell if I'm on the verge of breaking down or if I'm simply exhausted. But when I look at Anderson, I feel better and worse. Better because he's nice to look at, but worse because he looks so fucking worried right now. I mumble, "What is it?"

"Don't take this for bullying, okay?"

I laugh once and it sounds strange to my ears. Almost mechanical or something. "Sure."

"You look like shit right now, June."

"Gee, thanks."

But he comes close and studies my face. "Are you sure they didn't hurt you?"

I nod, and the bouncing makes me want to vomit, but I hold it back. "Other than the initial struggle—"

He growls. Like an animal.

"What was that?"

"Please go on."

Oh-kay. "Other than how it started, no one really hurt me."

"Did they …" His lips go tight. "Did they assault you? Sexually?"

"No! Nothing even close to that happened."

"You can tell me. It's okay."

Oh, this poor man. "Anderson, I swear,

nothing like that happened. My clothes all stayed in place. No one even said creepy things like that. This was business to them. That's all."

Once he believes me, it's like all the air went out of him. His face isn't tight from anxiety anymore, so when he goes slack, he looks like he's aged a decade in the last day. "It's hard not to let your mind go wild when you're worried about someone you care about."

It feels good to smile at that. "I'm not sure if I can eat, but—"

"What would you like?"

"It's almost three in the morning. Maybe breakfast? And I don't have any groceries—I was going to do my shopping yesterday."

He smiles. "I'll get waffles delivered."

"Sounds great. I think I need a shower. I feel gross in my dress and boots right now."

"No problem. I'll wait out here for the delivery." But he pauses. "Unless you feel shaky in the shower. I don't want you falling—"

"I'll be fine. But thanks." The truth is, as much as I find Anderson comforting, I just want to shower while knowing he's got my back by guarding my front door. It's stupid, maybe, but just knowing he's there to take care of possible intruders makes me feel better.

He smiles and nods. "Anything you need. Anything."

"I'll be out soon." In my bathroom, it's like time slows down. Catching a glimpse of myself, I realize he's right. I look like shit. Hollows beneath my eyes and my hair's a mess. But the worst part is my expression. I look like I've been through hell, and I can't make my smiling muscles work at all.

Why am I still in my coat?

When I go to shrug it off, though, I don't want to. It feels like taking away some layer of protection I need. But I don't need it now. I'm home. Anderson is out there to protect me. I'm safe.

Safety feels like a lie.

But I tell myself I have to do this, and I shrug off the coat. Unzipping my boots takes much longer than it should. More self-talk is in order. I'm not removing my armor. Just taking off my boots. I don't need them to keep me safe. I am safe.

Yep. Still feels like a lie.

I turn on the shower to the hottest setting and watch as steam fills the room. It's just me and my dress now. I can do this. But when I grab the hem, all my instincts tell me to leave it on. That if I take it off, then I'll be under attack. The room feels too small. Too tight. Can't breathe.

I get dizzy and remind myself to breathe. But my lungs don't get the message. I have to hang onto the sides of the sink and breathe while watching myself in the mirror, ordering Mirror June to breathe steadily.

Maybe I should have made Anderson hang out in here.

But that seems silly. I don't need a chaperone to shower. I can do this.

To do it, I hurl myself into the shower. As the water runs over me, I reach for the soap to make this fast, and when I try to rub it on my skin, I'm met by my sweater dress.

Right. That's still on me. Crap.

I blow out a breath and wriggle out of the dress, along with my undergarments. Much harder when they're wet, but I manage. When I'm under the hot jet of water, I hardly feel it. Maybe I'm numb or in shock or something. I dunno. But at least I can breathe in the shower.

Letting the water beat down on me, reality creeps in. I don't want it to, but I can't seem to stop it.

Oh, screw this. Maybe if I go see Anderson, I can keep my shit together.

I turn off the water and grab my robe, ignoring the pile of wet clothes on the floor. Tomorrow June can pick them up. I pad out to the living room and find him setting up the delivery waffles on my kitchen counter. "Hey."

"So, I don't know where you keep anything, but they came with butter and syrup, and bacon. Is that okay?"

"Sounds great. Probably. I don't think I have an appetite right now."

"That's fine. We can eat later."

I smile up at him. "You can eat now, if you want."

He smiles back. "Not hungry, either." Anderson puts the boxes into the fridge. "So, what do you want now?"

Flicking my eyes to the door, I see it's locked, but that doesn't feel like enough. So, I drag a chair in front of it and wedge it beneath the doorknob. I don't have any illusions that it would stop them, but that's not why. "This way, I'll hear if they try to come in."

He nods. "I'll stay out here, too, so—"

"No, um. Would you sleep next to me?" I

wring my hands, remembering the cut on my palm, and not caring at all.

"Of course."

I take his hand and lead him to my bedroom. When I get under the covers in my robe, he doesn't comment on it. Instead, he gets onto the covers and lets me keep them between us to spoon me. I take his arm and wrap it over my waist. Feels like where he belongs.

"Do you want to talk about it?"

I shake my head. "But if you want to—"

"It was hell. Nothing compared to what you went through, of course, but for me, this was my version of hell. Not knowing, not being able to help ... I never want to go through this again. I will do whatever it takes to avoid this happening again." He pulls me tighter to him. "Whatever it takes, June, I will keep you safe."

I'm not sure when I started crying, but when it streaks across my face sideways, I wipe my eyes. He presses a kiss to the back of my head, and that's just not enough. As I roll to face him, he murmurs, "I'm so sorry, baby."

But I kiss his cheek and cup the other one. "This wasn't your fault."

He blows out a breath. "I know. But it feels like it is."

I smile at that and kiss his cheek again, before pulling his arms around me and burying my face against his shirt. Anderson holds me tight, and it's just a few deep breaths of his scent, before I fall asleep in his arms.

-

Chapter 44

ANDERSON

Sleeping with June in my arms is damn near the best feeling in the world.

I cannot get over how good it feels to hold her. She doesn't wake until eleven, but I've been up for hours. Too wired still, I guess. When she stirs in my arms, I lean back a little to give her room. She smiles up at me, and it's like the sun is shining on my heart. "Good morning."

"Good morning," she says sleepily. And then her stomach growls like a beast, and she giggles.

"Think you can eat this time?"

She nods, still smiling.

"I'll be right back. You stay put."

"Shouldn't I be waiting on you? You're a guest—"

I laugh so suddenly that it takes the wind out of me a little. "June. You were kidnapped. Let me get you breakfast."

"Well, when you put it that way …"

Shaking my head at that crazy woman, I jog to her kitchen and work on heating the breakfast we ignored earlier. When she was taken, I truly was in hell. But now that she's here, I'm happy. Genuinely happy. Going from one extreme to the other is dizzying.

I deliver our breakfast in bed and sit near the end to give her space. "Do you want to talk about it?"

"No. Not yet."

I nod once, having expected that answer. It had surprised me that she wanted me in bed with her last night. I thought for certain she would change her mind or have some sort of trauma-induced panic attack and wake up screaming. But she didn't. She's stronger than I give her credit for, and I promise to myself to stop underestimating her.

Since I'd expected her to say no, I had come up with some unrelated questions to keep her occupied. "Do you think your upbringing affected your perspective on law?"

She laughs. "Is this your idea of a casual chat?"

"What's wrong with my question?"

"Sounds like a job interview."

I chuckle. "Admittedly, that's where I got the idea from."

She giggles around a bite of syrupy waffle. "Ah. Well, it's not a terrible question. And I think everything in your upbringing affects the rest of your life. Your career, your politics, it's all shaped by your childhood. For instance, I grew up poor, so I have a soft spot in my heart for the needy."

"Yet you work for the very wealthy."

"The needy can't pay my school loans."

I smile at that, even though the reminder stings. Can't ignore that elephant in the room, either. "Working on getting the money thing settled, by the way."

June laughs with exuberance. "God, I haven't even thought about that in the past day. I mean, not really. Funny. It was all I could think of before some guy stuck a knife to my throat."

A surge of rage floods through me, like my body thinks the guy is here right now. But I bank it for later. "Thought we weren't talking about that now."

"We're not. Just … funny how perspective changes in the blink of an eye."

She is more right than she knows. This whole incident has shifted my perspective on a lot of things. "Very true. I'm not sure I want the CEO seat at work. Not after all of this."

Her eyes widen. "Really?"

"I won't make my future family pay for my mistakes. Not in any way."

"That's smart of you. But I think everyone pays for the mistakes of the generation before it, no matter what you do."

"Doesn't mean I can't mitigate the possibilities of what that payment might look like." I scrub my hand over my face and try not to make her talk about things while talking about them. Maybe we can just keep talking around it until she's ready. "If I can make my children's lives safer, my wife's life safer, then that's what I'll do. If that means abandoning the C-suite, I'll do it. Or leaving the company entirely, I'll do it. I don't care about the company. I care about my family."

She smiles mischievously. "You don't have any of those things yet."

"But I will. I want that more than anything."

I want you more than anything.

June sighs. "You don't know what it's like to live without money and access and connections, Anderson. It's easy to say you'd leave all that behind, but in practice, it would be far harder than you think."

"I'm sure you're right about that. But I'd be willing to try." *To keep you safe.*

"What do you think your upbringing taught you about the law?"

I smile and sigh. "A lot of the technical. Dad was big on me learning about the law from a young age. He molded me as a boy to follow in his footsteps … but I never wanted to. It was a destiny decided by others. Nothing more."

She sets her waffle down and looks at me. "What would you do if you weren't a lawyer?"

The question makes my mind go blank, and I laugh. "You mean, what did I actually want to be when I grew up?"

She nods.

It's a fair question. But it's also an impossible one. "I don't rightly know. I was never given the option of being anything else."

June smiles. "Well, think about it and get back to me."

I grin. "Maybe a househusband."

She laughs sharply. "What?"

"I'm still young enough to be a trophy husband, and I could marry some rich, powerful woman, and raise our babies and—"

"And lose your mind from the boredom."

I laugh. "Yeah, okay. Not a serious thought, but now that I think about it, it doesn't sound half bad."

"Better than rescuing damsels in distress?"

"I would prefer my damsels were never in distress in the first place."

She sighs. "Yeah. Me too."

And we're back to this. But the truth of it is, I don't mind talking about what happened. I want her to talk about it. If not to me, then to someone. She went through something no one should ever go through. "Eh, June?"

"Yes?"

"Do you want me to call someone for you? Your mom or a friend or a therapist or—"

She laughs and grabs at her waffle again. It's slick with butter and syrup and seems to elude her fingers. "A therapist?"

"To help you process everything."

"No, but thank you. And not the others, either. Might be dangerous for them to know about this."

I shrug. "I know, but I don't care about

them. I care about you. If talking to them makes you feel better, then—"

"I won't put anyone else at risk, Anderson. You're sweet for suggesting it, but no. No one else should be in on this."

"You don't always have to be strong."

She gives a whimpering laugh. "You think I'm strong? I'm barely feeding myself a fucking waffle."

I pick up the waffle bite and hold it up. She surprises me when she eats it out of my fingers —I'd thought to hand it over. Her slick, sweet lips on my finger sends an ache through me. "Yes, you're strong. After everything you went through, and you're making complete sentences? That's strong."

She smiles and looks away. "I got into the shower in my clothes last night because I couldn't bear to take them off and forgot I had them on by the time I talked myself into going under the water."

"And you still did it. You're struggling, and that is strength. Weakness is giving up, and I'm pretty sure that's not in your vocabulary."

When she meets my gaze, I'm sunk. I know I am. This woman is in my fiber. "Thanks, Anderson. I think I needed to hear that."

My throat is dry from holding in everything I want to tell her, and I rasp out, "Anytime."

-

Chapter 45

ANDERSON

After I put the waffle boxes in the garbage, she yawns next to me in the kitchen. "Coffee?"

"I didn't think to make any. Want some?"

She smiles up at me. "I was offering to make it for you."

"But—"

"Please. Just let me do something, Anderson. Yes, I've been through some shit, but I need to feel useful."

Relenting, I hold out my hands. "I give up. Go ahead." The truth is, I am happy to see her want to do something for herself. She is one of the most independent people I have ever known, so I think it's a good sign.

The scent of fresh coffee brewing fills the air, and I wonder if this giant leap forward means she's ready. "June, do you want to talk about what happened?"

Her shoulders bunch up and she sighs. "I don't know."

"We can call someone in and—"

"You're the only person I know who would understand. And I'd rather talk to you, anyway."

It's nice to hear that second part. "Okay. How about I start?"

"You?"

I nod. To get this conversation started, I think I need to prompt her like a witness. Not that I do much courtroom work, but she's reluctant to say anything. "I had gone back for my phone and I ran into my brother Cole upstairs. Talked to him for a few minutes, hunted down my phone, and headed out. But you weren't there. After I searched around some and tried your phone a lot, I ended up in the security guard room. They saw me running around, and they'd hesitated to call the police, because they're good at their jobs."

Her plump lips smooth into a flat line. "Because the police can make things messy?"

"Exactly. One had gone on break, and the other was on the phone to his pregnant wife.

411

That's how they missed the abduction. For the team who abducted you to know that …"

She rubs her upper arms absentmindedly. "They're good."

"Exactly. Real pros. We watched the abduction several times, looking for anything. But the guy knew how to tilt his head to avoid the cameras, no license plate on the van, nothing to identify them. Do you remember anything identifying about them?"

June sighs. "I do. I could probably describe most of them to someone."

"Maybe I can call in a sketch artist. We can identify them and—"

"I don't think you need all that."

"Why not?"

"Because I know who took me."

I frown at her, because I'm lost. "But … you know them?"

She nods slowly. "Yeah, I—"

"I thought my dad was involved, but if you know them—"

"Because they told me who they are. Andre Moeller. Ring any bells?"

I lean back and try to think. "He's an old friend of my father's. But that doesn't make any sense."

"He said your dad owes him a lot of money. Said this was all just about business. Wasn't personal." She pouts. "Felt damned personal to me."

The one thing about all of this that has killed me since I got her back is not being able to casually touch her. But I will only touch her when she invites me to. She has to initiate it. I want her to feel like she's in charge of what happens to her body. She already had her autonomy taken from her. I won't do it again in any way.

But I am dying to touch her when she pouts over this. I want to comfort her and hold her and kiss the top of her head, while telling her everything will be alright. It's too soon, though. I know that. And she might not invite me to hold her ever again after all she's been through. Not that I could blame her for it.

After all, my father is the one who fucked everything up.

"I don't understand what's going on with everything. Dad … he demanded I not call the police. At first, he made it sound like it was to protect you, but it wasn't. It was strictly about protecting himself. He doesn't include me in on some things, and I always thought that was just business. I'm busy, he's busy. That's how things are. But after all of this … I don't know what to think. What else he's hiding?"

"Not to mention that it's super weird I was kidnapped and there was no ransom."

"That we know of," I add. "I'd like to think he squared up with Andre and that's why you were released, but I doubt it. Dad would have smugly called me to tell me to thank him or something. Tell me more about how things were on your end of it."

"Not much to tell. They kept me blindfolded for a lot. Interrogated me for a long time. Two of them, a man and a woman. I think they were getting a baseline to see if I was lying, because they kept asking the same kinds of questions. After a while longer …" The coffee's done, so she gets out two mugs and the cream. "They brought me upstairs to meet Andre in the penthouse. And before you ask, I didn't recognize the skyline. Anyway, he wanted to talk to me. I think … I think he felt guilty or amused, honestly I'm not sure. That guy seems like a sociopath."

"What did he do to you?"

She shrugs. "Had me kidnapped and gave me breakfast."

I snort a laugh. "No, I mean, during your conversation. Why do you think he's a sociopath?"

"It was just his vibe. He went from clearly angry and keeping it all in to a little flirty and extremely polite in a flash. He was so hot and cold and had no trouble going from one to the other. Not like he'd lost his marbles. More like he was in full control of every marble and ready to wield any of them at any time." She sips her coffee. "I don't know what his deal is, but it's not healthy."

My blood boils at the thought of her in the presence of someone dangerous like that. "I don't really remember him. Last I saw him, I was a kid."

"I still think it's weird that there was no ransom."

"Pretty sure he did it to show Dad he could do it. If he took someone closer in the family, that would have been a step too far in their game." I can't say the last word without every muscle in my body tensing. "This … they're playing at something. I'm just not sure what it is." I take a sip and a breath and try to sort through it. "There's also the distinct possibility that he took you off the street in front of their

415

home to show them that no one is untouchable."

Her eyes lift at that. "Because if they take me from their expensive, seemingly safe neighborhood, then they can get anyone?"

I nod. "Whatever the case, no one in my family is safe. Not while Dad deals with people like Moeller." And I mean to put a stop to that.

"It's, um …"

"What?"

"Do you think your dad had them do it? To scare me off of you?"

"No!" I almost drop my coffee at the thought, so I set it down and go to her, fighting the need to touch her still. But I need her to hear me on this. "Dad wasn't exactly surprised that this happened, but he was more resigned than anything else. Like this was the cost of doing business. Dad keeps secrets, but he's not a good liar. He would have screwed this up, if that were the case."

She sighs and puts her head on my chest, so I take that for permission to hold her, and she melts against me. It feels incredible that she's coming to me for comfort. I love it. But then she mumbles, "I'm sorry."

I take her by the shoulders to look at her. "What for?"

She sniffles and her eyes are a little pink. "I didn't want to think your dad would do this, but I had to ask. I didn't mean to offend you—"

A laugh pops right out of me, and I pull her in for a hug. "You didn't. I promise. All options are on the table until we figure this out."

"Thanks for understanding. This whole thing is just too weird. I keep spinning out, trying to figure out what I did wrong or—"

"You did nothing wrong." Other than pretending to be engaged to me. "Now, listen, I don't know what Dad is involved in, but I'm going to find out. I don't know how well either of us will sleep until we know what is actually going on."

She nods and holds me tighter, and damn, if that's not the best feeling in the world.

Chapter 46

JUNE

God, he smells good. It's not fair. I'm at my absolute lowest right now, and here he is, smelling like a million bucks. Or in his case, several million bucks.

I pull from the hug and smile at him, unable to stop myself from the smile. "Uh, so if we're going to pretend like this never happened, I'm going to have to get ready for work—"

"Eh, no."

"We're not pretending this didn't happen?"

"No. You're not going to work. You're playing hooky today."

I laugh. "I already missed yesterday and didn't get to call them, so—"

"On account of kidnapping," he says, like I don't know. "You get to take some time to deal with that, June. I'm guessing you never take days off as it is, right?"

"Well no, but—"

"So, they owe you some leeway. Take it. Please."

Why did he have to add the *please?* "Ugh. I'm such a sucker for a man who begs. Fine. I'll stay home today."

He grins. "That wasn't begging."

"I got a *please* out of *you*, of all people. I'm counting it."

His laugh makes me warm inside. It's like a cheat code to my body. Very unfair. "Call in with work, and we'll order delivery and have naps, and we'll figure things out as we go along. Do you mind if I shower?"

"You saved my life. Take all the showers you like."

His boyish smile kills me. "Hardly call it saving your life, but I don't mind the gratitude." He struts toward the bathroom, like he knows I'm staring at his butt through his jeans.

Of course, I am. But that's not the point. What is it like to walk around with his level of confidence all day long? I'll never know.

Doesn't matter. Gotta call Callie. She texted me a couple of times, and I'd ignored them until now, because I didn't know what to say. But a call will put her at ease.

She answers fast. "June, are you okay?"

"Uh, food poisoning. Atomic food poisoning. Somehow I got food poisoning, and then the flu or a cold or something. Can you let everyone know?"

"Do you need to go to the hospital?"

"If it gets worse, I will. For now, it's Gatorade and crackers."

She sighs. "Girl, you sound like hell."

"I feel worse." At least that part is true.

"Okay. Want me to stop by? Bring you something?"

"No, but thanks. I got everything delivered, and I'm sure I'm contagious—

"I'll stay far, far away. No problem, hon. Get some rest."

"Thanks. Talk later."

Okay. I don't like lying to Callie. But this is for her own good. Anderson is right—getting anyone else involved is only going to put a target on them, and I won't do that to her or anyone I care about. I hate that Anderson is involved in this at all. He doesn't deserve this, just because he's his father's son. It's ridiculous that he's gotten sucked into it. Or that I am sucked in because of my connection with him.

So, no more people added to the equation. The math is already bad.

The odd thing about being tied up in a basement for an unknown number of hours is how it clicks into your head afterward. Like, if I blink too long, I'm back there. If Anderson hadn't slept over last night, I never would have fallen asleep. Closing my eyes is dangerous to my psyche, and that's already feeling fragile right now.

At one moment, I'm fine. I feel normal. And then the next, I'm ready to rip the cabinet door off their hinges. I'm angry, but it bubbles up in weird moments, instead of being a constant. The irrational part of my brain wants to blame Anderson. To make him leave. That is what Andre said, isn't it? To un-involve myself with him? But this isn't his fault. He has nothing to do with any of this.

Besides, I don't want him to go.

He's been so kind and supportive and so sweet that it makes my teeth hurt. I love how he's been taking care of me. Giving me space, letting me breathe. He got waffles delivered, then brought them to me in bed. And he slept on top of the blanket, like a gentleman. Not to mention the fact that he came for me in the first place.

It makes me want to rip his clothes off.

That's what a hero should get, right? All the naked, sweaty good stuff? But he's being so good to me, and it worries me. Does he see me as a responsibility instead of a woman? Is that why he's being so perfect? Am I a project to him now?

I don't think I am, but I don't know. I'll give him the chance to make a move. If he doesn't, then maybe he thinks of me as ... what exactly? The woman he bought at auction, owes a lot of money to, pretended to be engaged to, then inadvertently got kidnapped? Huh. There really is no simple one-word title for all of that. I don't think *friend* really covers it.

When Anderson comes out of the shower with a towel wrapped around his waist and nothing else, my mouth waters. Can't be helped. It's just biological, right? No one should have that many abs. It's not fair, it's—"

"June, are you okay?"

"Um, what?"

"I said I needed some coffee before I got

dressed, and you just stared into space. Do you need to sit down? Are you dizzy?"

Great. "Not dizzy, just lost in my thoughts. I'm fine. Don't worry about me."

But he puts his big, hulking hand on my upper arm and looks deep into my eyes. "I will always worry about you."

Can't tell if that's a good thing or a bad thing right now, but he's almost naked and standing right in front of me, so that's a good thing. "Thanks."

He smiles sweetly. "Okay. Coffee, then clothes. Sorry about coming out here in just a towel. But I didn't think you'd want me running around in your robe."

I can't help but giggle at the thought. "The one with the embroidered flowers? No, please. Help yourself."

He downs his coffee and smirks. "Maybe next time. Be right back." As he makes his way to the bathroom, the towel drops, and he mutters, "Shit," before snatching it up fast to cover himself.

Not that I minded the view of his muscular ass. Why is he being so shy still? I mean, I get that he's trying to give me space and be polite, but I've seen him naked before. It's literally nothing I haven't seen before.

Crap. I'm a project to him. I cannot let that be the case. When he comes back out, I have to make a move.

He returns dressed. "Thanks. I feel like a person again. And I was thinking about something we could do today."

Me too. "What's that?"

He reaches behind himself and pulls out a bottle of red nail polish from his back pocket. "What do you think?"

"You need your pedicure touched up?"

He grins. "No. I was thinking I could paint your nails."

Is this a fetish or something? "What a random thing to do."

"When I was a kid, I liked to paint. For a while there, Mom and Dad went through a rough patch, so I started painting her nails to cheer her up. I used to be pretty good at it, if you want to give it a shot."

Oh my god. I'm not just a project. I'm a fixer upper. "You think my nails need—"

"No, no. Just thought you could use some cheering up."

He's right. If we're just friends now, I'm

going to need that. "Um, okay. Yeah. Sure."

"Great," he says, grinning. "I'll get it all set up." Then he vanishes back into the bathroom. When he comes out with his arms full of stuff, it's clear we're not just doing nails. He's giving me a DIY spa day. First it's the nails, followed by an eye mask, which triggers my trauma from the blindfold, so we move on to a shoulder massage while we wait for my nails to dry. He even agrees to watch a teen slasher for me.

It's amazing, but I feel bad. "You know you don't have to do all this, right?"

"Yes, well, my father is the reason you were kidnapped, so let me work out some guilt on the knots in your shoulders."

"You don't have to feel guilty about any of it —oh. That spot."

"On it."

I can't take advantage like this, so I turn around. "Anderson, stop."

"Why? Are you okay? Did I—"

"You're great. But I'd rather just hang out with you and eat too much Chinese food and watch some teenagers run from the guy with the machete. Is that okay?"

"Whatever you want, June."

We settle on the couch with our takeout

boxes and chopsticks and get into the movie, while I try to figure out how to make a move on him. Just as the protagonists run for the SUV and I'm about to scream, "He slashed the tires, just run!" Anderson says, "There is something I need to ask you."

"What's that?"

"I feel terrible about the money I owe you, and well, everything else, and—"

"Please stop assigning terrible feelings to things related to me. That's not exactly what a girl wants to hear."

He chuckles. "Point taken. You know I didn't know my father would have our CFO freeze my account, right?"

"Yeah. What about it?"

"With Dad's actual business practices coming to light, it's clear he's involved in some shady shit. But in the shower, I got an idea, and I want to run it by you."

-

Chapter 47

ANDERSON

"Hear me out before you say no," I begin, hoping she won't interrupt much. "This situation has been awful, to say the very least—"

"Yeah."

"And I think you should get something out of it."

Her brow lowers, almost like a curious frown. "Go on."

"Dad doesn't know you've been released, and to our knowledge, he doesn't know who took you."

"Do you want to call him or something?"

"I do. I really do. But I want to tell him the kidnappers are demanding four hundred K for your release."

She laughs. "Wait, what?"

"It's the perfect plan. He'll unfreeze my account so I can withdraw the money, and I'll just pay it to you, instead of Andre Moeller."

"You can't be serious."

"I am deadly serious, June. You deserve that and more."

"Yeah, I do, but—"

"And he will definitely unfreeze my account for this if I tell him I'm going to the police and the press otherwise."

She laughs, dragging her fingers through her hair. "You want to blackmail your own father?"

My jaw clenches. Can't be helped. "It's the least he deserves after all of this. This whole thing started with him. He should pay for what he's done."

She takes a deep breath and shakes her head. "This is crazy, Anderson."

"I might be crazy, but I'm not wrong."

Her head bobs from side to side, like she's considering it. "Okay, you're not wrong. He deserves to pay for what he's done, but—

"Most importantly, you deserve to finally be paid. You've been through enough with my family."

Her attention catches on that. "And after I get paid, what then?"

"Then you're free of us." Oh. Crap. I don't want that. "If you want to be, I mean."

"It's an interesting proposition. I'll have to fake being sick a while longer for work, though. Pretty sure your dad would get suspicious if I showed up at work before this was settled."

"How? He doesn't work there."

"No, but he's pretty well connected. If he wanted to keep an eye out for me, work is a good place to start, right?"

She has a point. "So, you take some time off. It's good for you, and you've earned it."

June smiles to herself. "I can't think of another way to get paid soon."

"That's the spirit. Just remember—he's earned this." I grab my phone.

"Don't do it just yet. I want a little more time to think about it."

I nod and set it back on the coffee table in front of her couch. Her place is much cuter than I'd expected from her, considering she appears utilitarian. But her apartment has all sorts of homey touches. The coffee table has flowers carved into the edges. Her bedspread has a sort of lacy trim on it. The place is girly, but not over the top. I like it. It's very June.

"Take all the time you need to think about

it. That said, the sooner it's done, the sooner this is over."

She smirks. "You know, for someone who resents his father's underhanded business dealings, you're not exactly an angel, either."

I laugh hard. "Never claimed to be an angel, June. And if I remember, you're a bit of a little devil yourself."

"I am a fine, upstanding woman who has never done anything sinful in her life," she says with far too much seriousness to be serious. Then, she giggles a storm, and I want to kiss her so badly for the silliness of the moment. But I don't. Can't impose myself on her right now. Can't …

Damn, I want her.

It's funny. Every other woman I've been with made a big deal about everything. Their hair, their makeup. That's the sort of woman I am expected to date. Someone to whom appearances were everything, because that's how things are in my world.

But it's never been that way with June, though. She doesn't care that I have no product in my hair, or that I'm casually dressed in the same tee shirt and jeans I've been wearing. Or, if she does, she doesn't bring it up.

Maybe because we grew up together? I don't know. But now, sitting across the couch from me in her pajamas with her curly hair loose and no makeup, she's perfect. Absolutely perfect.

Someone screams, and I jolt.

Which sends her into another giggle fit. "It's the movie, Anderson. It's fine—"

More deep breathing. "Sorry. I ... I'll clean up." I grab the spent Chinese boxes and head for the kitchen. Explaining my reaction is not on the list of top twenty things I want to do, so staying in the kitchen is a valid choice. Once I toss the empties, I take a minute to lean on the counter and breathe.

"What's wrong?"

I almost jump at her right then, but I'm okay. She's here. She's okay. Breathe.

When she places her hand on my back, it almost startles me. But then it feels nice. I've missed her touch. She quietly says, "You can tell me. If you want, I mean."

"It's the movie. I—"

"If you don't like horror, then why did you put it on?"

I explain, "Because everything in your watchlist is horror, so I figured that's what you like. And it's not that I don't like it. The genre doesn't bug me."

"Then what is it?"

I turn to face her, because I need to see her face right now. "When you were taken, I couldn't stop playing out scenarios in my mind of what was happening to you." I pause, because I am not about to tell her what I am worried about. No point in putting those thoughts in her head. It's bad enough that they are still in mine. Without getting into specifics, I go on. "Some of those scenarios involved screaming, and I just can't deal with that right now."

"Oh." Then she darts out of the kitchen.

Not exactly the reaction I'd expected. I follow her out and find her digging through the couch cushions. "Where is that damned remote?"

It's sitting on my side's armrest, but I'm enjoying the sight of her bent over the couch too much to tell her. "You don't have to turn it off. I just freaked out."

"Yes, I do." She keeps looking.

"It's fine—"

"It's not," she says firmly. "It's—"

432

I grab the remote and hand it to her. "Really, June. It's okay. Just had a bad moment."

She turns the TV to some music channel and looks up at me. "I don't want to be the reason you have a bad moment, Anderson. And what you said … I understand what it's like to have something bring you back to a bad moment. I prefer being the reason you have good ones."

I swallow, hoping we're on the same page about that. "You are."

"What do you mean?"

"You're the reason I have good moments. You're the reason …" I'm not sure what to say. The words catch in my throat. "June, since the auction, you're the reason I smile."

Her eyes dip to my mouth and her voice softens. "I am?"

"I haven't been able to think about anything but you since that night. It's why I—"

She hooks her hand behind my neck and pulls me down to her lips for a kiss. I'm surprised, and at first, I stiffen up. With everything she has been through, everything my father has put her through, I didn't know if she'd ever want to see me again. Much less anything else. But this kiss gives me hope.

She started this. She doesn't hate me.

It's hard to believe that, especially now. I've caused her pain so many times, and with Dad's involvement in her kidnapping, I couldn't blame her if she had hated me forever. So, this kiss means everything to me.

June backs toward her couch, but pulls me along with her, not breaking the kiss until she lays down. But she clutches onto my shoulders to pull me down with her, coaxing me to lie on top of her. Once I do, she takes my face in her hands again and kisses me. It's making me delirious.

I want this so much. But I cannot push her after what she's gone through. Lying on top of her in the cradle of her thighs, I'm at war with my body. My sac aches, my cock throbs, and my heart? My heart drums rapid fire. I breathe her in during our kiss, reveling in her sweet scent. The unmistakable perfume of her body permeates my senses, and if I'm not careful, I'll get lost in her.

Careful. Pull back.

I break the kiss, and her half-lidded eyes lift in concern. Clearing my throat, I tell her, "Let's take this slow."

"I am. My clothes are still on."

I laugh and kiss her again, happy to know where her head is at. It's been years since I've made out with someone on a couch. Seems so juvenile. But that's a part of the fun, too. Like we're two horny teenagers who can't stop kissing.

I balance myself on my left hand, and with my right, I grope her over her shirt as a test. I have to know where this is going. When I cup her warm breast over her shirt, she moans and arches herself against my palm. There's no hesitation in her at all, and that breaks the dam inside that's held back my passion for June.

-

Chapter 48
JUNE

I am going out of my mind right now. His kisses, his touch, it's all too much and not enough, and if we don't get to the good stuff soon, I might die.

He flicks his thumb over my hard nipple through my shirt, and I whimper in my mouth. Fuck, this man makes me crazy. He reaches beneath the hem and glides his hand up to my breasts. His growl sends a thrill through me. He runs his fingertips along the curve of my breast, before he holds me there. Warmth pools in my belly, and this is too delicious for words.

In response, I wrap him up in my legs and grind against him through our clothes. He works himself against me, and I wonder if he can make me come like this. I grab his ass and pull him tighter to me. His hard cock grinds against my clit through my pajama bottoms, and I'm sure I've made a mess of them. I'm so fucking wet right now. Can't even remember what it was I was so upset about earlier.

Oh yeah. Getting kidnapped.

But right now, that's the distant past. I have Anderson in my clutches, and I'm not letting him go. Not after he told me I'm the reason he smiles. That melted me on the spot. It wasn't just a line. The way he looked when he said it … a guy can't fake that earnestness. He actually cares about me. I'm not a project to him. I'm a woman he wants. He's put my fears about that to rest, and all that's left is us.

This is so good, and even with all the layers between us, I'm close. But I want more. I want the real thing with Anderson. And I want it now.

It's hard to pull back from our kiss with the couch arm against the back of my head, but I manage it. "Hey—"

He freezes. "Do you want me to stop?"

"I want you naked."

"Now?"

I giggle. "Yeah, now."

He leans back and strips fast, while I try to

do the same, but it's clumsy, since I'm trying to do it while lying down. He laughs and helps me out of my pajama bottoms after I get my shirt off, and then we're both naked. Anderson looks at me reverently, like I'm this special thing to him. There's no mood lighting—it's the middle of the day in my living room, for Pete's sake—and he can see everything, and it's like he's in awe of me. I'm not sure what to do with that, but I like it.

I wonder if that's the face I'm making at him right now. He's so handsome it hurts. He's got a jawline for days and an illegal number of abs, but neither of those is why I'm here. It's him. I'm so hooked on this man for so many reasons.

I want to watch him while we do this, and if I'm on my back, I'll close my eyes to relax into it. That won't do. "Sit up."

He does, and I crawl onto his lap, facing him. Once I'm straddled on top, I hang onto his thick shoulders for balance and ease myself onto his cock. He holds onto my ass, but doesn't push or pull me there. Just holds. He's being so gentle and sweet about everything that it makes me want to wreck him.

Slowly, my body reminds me. Even though

I've been resting, my body aches from the stress of everything I've been through, and somehow, that's made me tighter than usual. His proud steel feels so good inside of me, and I'm only halfway down. But when he pulls me in for a kiss, I lose my restraint entirely. Anderson wraps me in his arms, and his warmth takes me over. Then he slowly rocks himself in me, brushing against my G spot on every motion. I growl into his mouth, and that only spurs him on.

Soon, he groans against my lip, and I feel him pulse inside of me. I love that I can make him feel good. I feel strong from it. Powerful. Like I'm not helpless anymore. I know he treated me like I was fragile because, for a while there, I was. But right now, it's like he trusts me to handle things. Like I'm not about to break. And because he believes it, so do I.

I sit back to look at him, and his eyes rake all over my breasts and my face, like he's not sure where he wants to focus. So, I pull his hands from my ass to my tits, and his thumbs brush over my nipples while I ride him. He bites his bottom lip. Concentrating? Fascinated? I can't tell. But I like that look on him. Hell, I like every look on him.

I like everything about Anderson.

It's scary to think about, but I can't stop. There's no reason for me to think of him in a permanent capacity in my life, but how many other people can say they've been a constant presence? How many people have pushed me as hard as he has? How many people know me as well as he does? No one. With Anderson, I can be utterly myself without hesitation, and I really like that.

Even now, in the throes of passion, I'm not self-conscious or embarrassed by any of it. Not like other guys, when I worried about looking sexy or fucking like a porn star while we were going at it. My fake moans and expressions are a thing of the past. Anderson likes everything I'm doing. The proof is throbbing inside of me.

And I like everything he's doing.

He again pulls me tighter to him, and I can feel his heartbeat through our bodies. It's beating almost as fast as my own. At this angle, he digs against my spot harder, and the heat coils in me. When the drop hits, I come with a roar, thrashing on him until I can't move anymore. But instead of going harder at me so he can come, Anderson just holds me until I catch my breath.

When I do, I look into his eyes, and I don't

know what to say or think, as if I am capable of words or thought. This man is all there is in the world right now, and he looks at me the same way.

Anderson runs his thumb along my bottom lip and quietly asks, "Are you okay?"

My lips curve into a smile. "I can breathe again, if that's what you mean."

He softly chuckles. "We can stop, if you like."

"Why would we do that?"

"I don't want to push. You've been through—"

I kiss him to shut him up. "No more of that. Not right now. Just you, and me, and this."

He smirks slyly. "I was hoping you'd say that." He scoops his hands beneath my ass and stands, scaring the bejeezus out of me.

"What are you doing?" I squeak out.

"Better position." He turns around and sets me onto the edge of the couch, before kneeling between my feet and spreading my thighs wide. Then he yanks me to him to get just the right angle to penetrate me again.

I'm smooshed into the couch, but I don't even care. Especially not when he reaches down and circles my clit as he thrusts. "Oh my god, yes!"

"You like when I touch you and bury myself deep, don't you?"

"Yes!"

"I can feel it," he groans. "When I hit the right spot, you clench onto me. You're addictive, June."

I whimper and drive myself to meet his thrusts. I'm too impatient to wait for the next one, and I can't sit still. Not when it feels this fucking good.

But then he slows down and lays onto me. His head rests on my breasts, and he makes short thrusts like he can't hold still. It lights me up. I run my fingers through his hair, adjusting to the new angle. He doesn't hit as deep, but the head of his cock stays on my spot, and every little thrust is enough to ring my bell. When I come, it's smaller, but it triggers another. Feels like I'm a pinball machine. One orgasm bounces into another. I can hardly breathe between them other than to moan.

He rasps, "You mean everything to me, baby."

"You too," I pant out.

He groans, "I want this. Every day. All the time."

"Yes!" I whimper as I come yet again.

Without another word, he grabs my legs and swings us onto the couch, so I'm lying on it and him on top of me. He works himself in long strokes, while holding me close. His throbbing cock sets off another orgasm, and I grip his back with my nails. Just need something to hold on to, until finally, he pounds into me and comes. His grunts come from deep inside his chest and he shudders in me, before collapsing.

When I run my fingers through his hair, they come out wet from his sweat, and I'm thrilled to know I'll smell like him. I want everything he said. This. Every day. All the time. I never want it to end. After feeling so terrified for so long, I want the man who makes me feel safe. Who makes me come like a nympho. Who looks at me with awe.

I want Anderson West to be mine.

-

Chapter 49
JUNE

When I bought the oversized, extra deep couch, I told myself it was a waste of money. That it would only inspire me to lounge, and I didn't need any encouragement on that. But it was too comfortable not to buy it.

Today, I am so fucking glad I went with that instinct.

Anderson and I haven't left the couch all day, other than for bathroom breaks and snacks. We've found ourselves in a spooning position again, with him behind me and a blanket draped over our naked bodies. I love having him like this, even when we argue over Netflix.

"Okay, I know you're not down for screaming horror, but what about something more subdued? A master class in building tension and suspense?"

"What, like a thriller or a mystery or something?"

"I was thinking *Silence of the Lambs*."

He laughs. "Hmm…"

"It's barely horror, but fine. *Aliens*?"

More laughs out of him. "That is definitely horror."

"It's really more of a sci-fi, but sure." I think for a moment. "How about *Predator*?"

He hesitates.

"Oh please! It's definitely sci-fi."

"Okay. No horror, no sci-fi, nothing with cannibalism. Try again."

I huff, thinking. "How about *Parasite*?"

"The Korean film?"

"Yeah. Have you seen it?"

"No."

I grin. "We should watch that."

"No body horror either. I should have put that on the list."

I giggle at him. "It's not an actual parasite. It's a metaphorical parasite situation."

"Oh. Okay, yeah. Let's watch it."

But before I can turn it on, someone knocks at the door. Don't be Callie, don't be Callie—

"That'll be the pizzas I ordered," he says as he climbs over me and yanks his jeans up.

"When did you order pizza? Without asking me what I want?"

He smirks, and that knocks my annoyance down by five percent. He's too cute when he smirks. "Do you trust me?"

"Of course, but—"

"I've got this." He pulls on his tee shirt, then goes to the door while I remain hiding beneath the blanket. He mumbles something to the delivery guy, then closes the door, so I peek my head up. What he's holding doesn't make any sense. Three pizza boxes for the two of us.

"How much do you think I can eat, Anderson?"

He laughs. "I don't ever eat pizza, and when I do, I go a little overboard. Come on. It's way past lunchtime." He vanishes into my kitchen.

Alright then. I yank on some clothes, because it feels weird to walk around and eat without them, then join him in the kitchen. The boxes are open, and the pizzas look strange. "What, um, what's all this about?"

"So, because I go overboard on pizza, I like to make each half different. Left to right, we have half cheese, half pepperoni. The middle is half pineapple and anchovy and half veggie supreme. The third is half meat lovers and half vegan."

I am mystified. Looking up at him, I'm sure my face tells him my question.

He grins. "It's fun to mess with them. Dig in." He grabs a slice of each one, and I am fascinated to see him try to eat six slices. I snag a pineapple and anchovy and a vegan, and follow him out to the living room. He eyes my selections. "See? You have to start trusting me with these things."

"Okay. First, meat lovers and vegan should be illegal. It's naughty in a way that I can't wrap my head around. Second, how in the hell did you remember pineapple and anchovy?"

"That it's your favorite, you mean?"

I nod, too smiley to speak.

He hesitates and takes a bite of his slice before washing it down. "I remember the field trip we took, and how we ended up lost and at a Pizza Hut because it was the only restaurant around that all the kids were happy about and could take all of us. And everyone ordered their own pizzas, and you got pineapple and anchovy—"

"And it was the one time you *didn't* make fun of me for something."

He nods. "As much as I was an absolute dick to you—still sorry for that, by the way—I was intrigued. So, I ordered pepperoni because I wasn't brave enough to be that weird, but I watched you dig into yours with abandon, and you enjoyed it so much that I was jealous. After that fiasco, I tried it myself, and well, I've been hooked ever since."

I'm lost. "You couldn't order the kind of pizza you wanted? I don't understand."

"And that's what I like about you. It wouldn't occur to you to be self-conscious about your pizza toppings. You weren't afraid to be judged for it. You ordered it and enjoyed the hell out of it."

"It's pizza. It's meant to be enjoyed."

He leans close and kisses me, tasting like heaven. "*You* are meant to be enjoyed."

I don't know why, but that makes me giggle and blush. "Shut up."

He laughs. "You're so damn cute."

I cannot take his full attention right now or the fact that he remembered all of that, so I focus on something else or I will spiral out into wondering what that means. Why does he remember so much stuff that I tried to forget? That trip was a disaster for me. We were supposed to go to Six Flags, and somehow, we ended up at a Pizza Hut in a tiny town. It was one of the old ones that still needed remodeling. Crap, I'm spiraling. Whatever.

I was so disappointed and annoyed, but the kids in my class were worse. Whining to the teachers and chaperones and demanding to speak to someone over them. It was the first time I really understood the difference between me and them. All those factors made the day awful.

But for Anderson, it was the day to learn my favorite toppings.

"How long did you have a crush on me, Anderson?"

He pauses, no longer digging into his pizza. To my surprise, he's downed four of the slices already. "Pretty much from the day I met you. Is that a problem?"

I'm not even sure how to process that, but I laugh. "No. Not really."

"What is it?"

"I just ... I wish I'd known about your crush back then."

He slowly nods. "I wish I had been given the

tools to understand it back then. But being a kid and not understanding what I was feeling made for a bad time. If I could change that history, June, I would."

"I'm not sure I would."

"Really?"

"I mean, yeah, I hated you, but you pushed me to work harder. I wanted to beat you at everything. Every time I studied for a test, I wanted to make sure I got better grades than you, so I could rub your nose in it."

He laughs. "Well, okay. I'm glad I helped inadvertently, I guess."

"Speaking of grades and responsibilities, I am going to have to go back to work tomorrow."

"Why would you do something silly like that?"

I roll my eyes. "Because I have bills and—"

"And if you go back so soon, remember my father could find out you're not still kidnapped."

"Right. Crap."

"Besides, you are about to have enough money to quit that job." He has a point.

"Oh." I clutch my heart. "I cannot wait for that."

He smiles. "Me, too."

"Why you?"

"Because if you quit your job, then you have more time to spend with me. If ... if that's something you want to do."

I can't help smiling at his nervousness. "You want to spend more time with me, Anderson?" I'm gonna drag this out as long as I can stand it. It's fun to see him squirm.

"Yes. I do."

It's nice to be with a guy who doesn't play games. "I'd like that, too."

"Hold still." He reaches out and swipes his thumb over my jaw, then licks the sauce off. "You got messy."

I giggle at him. "You've turned me into a giggler. How did you manage that?"

"I don't know, but I'm very glad I did. I love hearing that out of you."

"So, if we're going to play hooky, what are we going to do with all that free time, sir?"

He smiles in a way that tells me he has only dirty thoughts. "I can think of a few projects. But I'll need your help with them."

"Oh?" I tease and set my plate down.

He sets his aside, too. "It's really more of a collaboration than a project." He leans over me, and I lean back. "We will have to work closely with each other. I'm afraid there's no other way."

"Sounds like a challenge," I say as I pull his shirt over his head. "But I'm a team player."

"That's a good thing," he says, slowly lifting my shirt and kissing my stomach. "But this will be a team of two only. No one else." His gaze is intense, and I can't tell if we're just playing or if he's asking me to be his girlfriend.

Whatever he's asking, the answer is yes. "I don't want to team up with anyone else."

He nibbles at my stomach, then slowly drags my pajama bottoms off of me, before resuming his position between my thighs. "That's good, because I'm about to get started with some research, and I'll need you to hold as still as you can." Then he lifts my legs onto his shoulders.

"No promises, boss."

"Oh, I like it when you call me that." He grins, then his head dips between my thighs.

I groan, "Keep giving me a reason to call you that, and I will."

He grunts and licks me all over. If this is what he wants to do for the next few days, I'm not going to argue.

Chapter 50

ANDERSON

Between bouts four and five, we ended up on her bed. We're both panting and tangled in the sheets and there is nowhere else I'd rather be. Except maybe right next to her. Instead, my head is at the foot of the bed and hers is on the pillows at the head. "You know, this is a good bed."

"It's held up so far, despite our best efforts."

"No, I mean, I like the mattress. I need one like this."

"Oh? Not as comfy?"

I shake my head. "Definitely not. Mine gives the best back support. Not comfort."

"We should get you a new one, then."

"But that means we have to leave this one, and I'm not ready for that just yet."

She giggles, and I'm such a sucker for that. "I didn't mean now. Besides, if we go mattress hunting, you know what we have to do, right?"

"Try them out?"

She grins and nods, then winks. Only, she's terrible at winking and her other eye half-winks, which cracks me up. She swats at my leg. "It's your fault I can't wink right now. I've lost all control of my muscles."

"Happy to be of service."

"Clearly. I've never had a guy so—"

My phone rings on her nightstand. She reaches for it, but I tell her, "Ignore it. Nothing is more important than what's right here, right now."

But she looks anyway. "It's your dad."

Shit. "Okay, toss it to me."

When she throws me my phone, it slaps onto my chest. "Ow."

"You said to toss it!"

"Not *on* me," I tease her and answer the phone. "Dad, hey—"

"Enough with the chitchat. What is happening with June?"

"Just a second. Let me get to where I can talk." I pop out of bed and slide my boxers on along with her embroidered robe that I hope I don't hulk out of, then go out to her balcony for some privacy and to make sure he doesn't hear her by accident. That's the last thing we need right now. Not if I'm going to blackmail him.

It's freezing out, but at least it's not raining or windy. Time to start the show. "I was just about to call you. I was contacted by the kidnappers."

"You were?"

"They want me to deliver four hundred thousand dollars to return her."

He sputters, "That is preposterous! No skirt is worth that kind of money!"

"The fuck you say?" I don't have to fake my anger now.

"You heard me!"

"What about Mom? Would you pay that for her?"

He huffs. "I'd pay anything for her. She's priceless. You know that—"

"June is going to be my wife, Dad. I'm not letting her rot in a hole somewhere because you didn't think she was worth it!"

"It's too much! Did you try to talk them down?"

"Talk them down? She's not a car! She's—"

"Yes, yes, your future wife," he says dismissively. "It's still out of the question. You were born with too much money to appreciate its value. You don't know what it is to put in a hard day's work and truly earn your money."

I laugh. "And you were what, a pauper when you were born?"

"I did not grow up with the wealth and privilege that you did."

We are getting off track and nowhere. So, I decide to take a different tactic. "I know it's a lot of money, Dad. I'm not that irresponsible. But I'm scared out of my mind. I'm sure you understand that. If it were Mom—"

"But it's not, and thank your lucky stars for that. She would never hold up under this kind of strain. Just think of your poor mother tied up. Her heart would give out."

Again, he's sidetracking me and taking control of the conversation. And now I know he's doing it on purpose. Talk about Mom to distract me and steer things back to how he wants them. Not happening. I sigh. "Well, I suppose I could always go to the police and the press and tell them everything that's happened, couldn't I? That way, we can get a proper manhunt going at taxpayer's expense and no one would have to pay a dime—"

"You will do no such thing!" he spits.

Good. I have his attention. "Dad, they want the money, and after our last conversation on the matter, I have a feeling you know more about all of this than you're telling me. So, what is it you're not telling me? I have the right to know what kind of business we are in. You want me to be CEO? Then I need to know what this is about. Why did they take her?"

"Anderson, I will tell you everything in due time. I've been planning to let you in for years. But now is obviously not the right time—"

"Why the hell not?"

"On the phone?" He scoffs. "You're smarter than that."

He wants to talk to me in person? I take a beat to realize why he won't say anything on the phone. My phone could be tapped. So could his. No point in dragging that issue on, then. He's too smart to come clean about anything over the phone. Hell, he might suspect I'm working with the police. I've brought them up too much. But they're my only real leverage against him at the moment, so I can't hesitate to use them if I need to.

"Fine, whatever. Dad, are you going to unfreeze my accounts or not?"

"*You'd* pay for her out of your own money? I thought you wanted my money."

"I would do anything for that woman. I don't care where the money comes from. It doesn't matter to me. I just have to keep her safe." After a conversation of lies, it feels good to tell the truth.

He grunts, surprised. "I'll think about solutions, Anderson. In the meantime, don't do anything rash. Do not call the police or the press. Don't post about it on your social media. Absolute silence is just as much a weapon as a gun, and it will protect her just as well. If they catch wind of you going public, they're liable to make an example of her."

I know it's not real. Not anymore. She's safe in her bed. I can see her right now. But the thought of kidnappers making an example of June makes me want to punch something.

Specifically, my father.

After a lifetime of lectures on business, the law and the media, the berating, the arguments, I still don't know what my father is up to. It twists the knife that, on top of everything else that's happened, he's still a mystery. My own father.

I hate this.

"I won't go to them. Yet. But if you drag your heels on this, you'll leave me with no other choice."

"You will ruin the family if you do that."

"You think I fucking give a shit?"

He laughs. "Yes. I do. Why do you think a woman like June is after you, son? For your sparkling personality? Say you do it. You go to the police and they save her at the expense of tanking the firm and putting me in prison and freezing all our assets. How will you keep her by your side when you have no money?"

I could drive to their apartment and punch his lights out and be back before midnight. But if I do that, he won't unfreeze my accounts. I might consider it worth it, if I didn't need desperately to pay June back. So, I swallow it down.

"Dad, you have until tomorrow afternoon at two to get my accounts thawed or give me the money. I have to get the money to them by four. Please decide faster than that. Gotta go." I hang up, because I'm done talking to him. If I had my druthers, I'd never speak to him again.

-

Chapter 51

ANDERSON

I almost don't want to face her after all of that. How do you say, "My father thinks you're after me for my money and also you're not worth four hundred thousand dollars?" But I'm not holding anything back from her. Not ever.

I open the sliding door and she looks up at me with expectant eyes. "So. How did it go?"

"Not as well as I'd hoped. But not terribly."

"How so?"

I strip off her robe and get under the covers next to her. I want to be close to June and being in bed with her feels so right. "Told him I'd just heard from the kidnappers, and they want four hundred thousand dollars for you. He's acting like that's too much money—"

"I don't blame him."

I laugh, but she's serious. "June, I'd pay anything to have you by my side. Safe, I mean. All that. Anyway, he said some unflattering things about you, and—"

"Like what?"

I do not want to tell her. "He thinks you're with me for the money—"

"But I told him I'd sign a prenup." She frowns. "That makes no sense."

"Huh. In the moment, I'd forgotten about that, but you're right, it doesn't. Maybe he thinks I'm too emotional to realize that, and fair play to him, he was right. Why would he say that, then?"

"Maybe he's playing on your insecurities?"

I sigh, thinking. "Maybe. Hard to know with him, I guess. Anyway, I didn't outright say I was blackmailing him, but I clarified that if he doesn't get off his ass, I will happily see the firm burn down around me by calling the police and the press in on this. I gave him until two tomorrow afternoon to move the needle on things."

"That's what you wanted. Right?"

"Yeah."

"Then why do you look so dejected, Anderson?" She knows me well. Too well.

"I hate this."

"Well, I don't think you're supposed to enjoy blackmailing your own father—"

I laugh. "No, not that part. Actually, I sort of get a kick out of doing that part. But it's all the secrets I didn't know we had. All the lies. The backroom deals ... the man is no saint, I know that. I'm not naïve. But I never thought it was anything this seedy."

"How do you mean?" She takes my hand in hers, and it's nice to feel that kind of support. Especially after never having it.

"We're in the media. We help people in entertainment law. It's supposed to be fun and light and breezy. Parties and meeting celebrities. Yachts and award shows. And I find out my father is doing things that, evidently, warrant kidnapping."

She shrugs. "Okay, I can see how that would be jarring."

"And there's nothing I can do about it. He won't tell me shit, so I can't help him get out of the situation. It's ... it's a lot. To be honest, I'm not sure I would help him get out of it. Not after the way he's been about you."

"It's a shit ton of money, Anderson. I don't like his attitude either, but I get it."

I shake my head. "Yes, it's a lot of money. A life-changing amount of money for someone without money. For us? He could drop that kind of cash on a vacation and not think twice. I've seen him do it." My jaw tightens in anger. "For him to all of a sudden be worried about money means there is something even bigger going on. I aim to find out what the fuck it is."

She sighs and rubs my arm. "Do you think you might be more angry about the fact you feel your father is a stranger than about the money?"

"It's more the money than the other thing, but the other thing is there."

"Why is the money a bigger problem for you?"

I turn to face her and touch her cheek. She leans into my palm and kisses me there. "Because the money is about you, baby. When he has the chance to help you, and he doesn't jump at that chance and take it?" I shake my head. "Fuck that guy."

"That guy is your dad. I know you're angry with him about this, but he's still your dad."

"Is he?" I huff a laugh. "All I've ever gotten from him were lectures and nagging. He's never shown me who he is, other than a series of lessons, one after another, on the rare occasion he was around."

She gulps and frowns. "Do you think that maybe stealing a chunk of money from him isn't the right way to get to know him?"

"We're not stealing. It's my money. I'm just trying to get back control before he was planning to give it to me."

"Okay, true." She pauses. "Tell me about him. You don't talk about him much. Or your mom, for that matter. But the other night at their place, you seemed like you were having a good time with your family. Why the disconnect?"

It's a good question. She's too observant, but I don't hate that about her. I like that she knows me. "My mom was around a lot. Dad, not so much. Lots of nannies, too. When Dad was around, it was lesson, lesson, lesson. If I didn't immediately memorize whatever he talked about, I was in trouble. If I didn't have great grades, trouble. Didn't dress the way he liked, more trouble."

"Why do you think he was so hard on you?"

"I'm not sure." I take a beat and try to organize my thoughts on it all. But it's hard. "When I was young, I didn't understand it. Dad was this odd man who came around sometimes to yell at me. Then I saw my friends with their dads, and it wasn't like that. At least, not when I was around. They joked and played sports. Had fun being guys. I think Dad missed the fun gene somehow."

She smiles and clings to my arm. "I guess that happens."

"Whatever the case, everything was rules with him. If you didn't follow the rules, he didn't like you. So, I tried. I wanted to make him happy. Every kid wants their father's approval. At least when they're young. It was a rare moment I ever felt like he approved of me. Or even liked me." The words keep pouring out. "I've never really talked about this. Thanks for listening."

"I'll always listen to you, Anderson. I'm happy to do it."

"It's strange to say it, but I could never meet his expectations, and now, knowing what I know … that he's doing something incredibly illegal, I'm sort of glad that I've never met his expectations. If I did, what kind of man would I be?"

She holds my arm tighter. "You're not him, and that's a good thing. Let's just be happy about that."

The problem is, I feel shattered in a way. "I know he's not responsible for the version of him I've made in my head. It's not fair to hold anyone to that kind of standard. But it feels like I had this picture of him in my mind, and now, pieces of that picture are being replaced by rotten versions of them. Does that make sense?"

"Too much sense, to be honest. But until you know what he's doing, getting sucked into that quagmire isn't going to help you. Can you put a pin in it until you actually know what he's up to?"

"If it were your dad, could you?"

She chuckles. "No, I guess not." She pats my leg and presses herself to me. "I enjoy having you here."

I laugh at the abrupt change of topic. "That's good. Because I enjoy being here."

"What I mean is, this feels nice. Not the kidnapping and blackmail and lying, but having you here in bed with me. Just chatting about the day's problems and trying to figure them out together. I've never really had that."

"Me either. You're right. It feels good to have this. But I hate that it took all of this to get us here."

June shrugs. "It's not exactly a fairytale—"

I laugh hard. "Uh, no. No, it's not."

"But if I get you at the end of the day, then I'll take it."

I derisively tell her, "You say that like I'm some kind of prize—"

"Baby, you are. Haven't I made that clear yet?" She looks in my eyes and crawls on top of me. "You are a prize. And I won you, and I'm not letting you go."

"Well, then …" I pull her to my lap while kicking the blanket out from between us. I need her on me. "Claim your prize."

Her lips skate over mine, and all that other stuff feels insignificant. A kiss from June makes everything better. Even me.

Chapter 52

ANDERSON

I lean in to kiss her again. Before she can take the lead, I slip my tongue past her lips. I know I'd told her to claim her prize, but I'm not in the mood to be claimed. She's mine. I won her. And I will do the claiming tonight.

The temptation is too great for me to be gentle this time. The only thing that's made any sense in the last week is June. Everything she is. Everything she could be. This woman is my world, and I will do anything to keep her. She is mine.

Reaching between us, I press the heel of my hand to her clit through her pajamas, earning a surprised whimper. She's tender after all our fun. So am I. But we're not quitters.

I need more.

With that, I grab the front of her top and rip down the middle, exposing her tits and shredding the thing from her. She gasps and braces. "The hell?"

"You're mine," I murmur against her neck, before I bite her there.

She lets out a cry and clings to me, wrapping her legs as much as she can around my waist, despite the pillows behind me. She kicks one from the bed in the process. We're making a mess, and we're just getting started.

I lick the teeth marks I left in her skin, and she shudders. But I pick her up and march to the nearest wall with her legs still belted at my waist. She grunts when her naked back hits the wall, and I kiss her harder for it. It's just like when we were in the library, and that bookshelf held us up. I'm aching to be inside of her, but her pants and my boxers are in the way.

I resent every piece of clothing between us.

I set her to her feet and jerk her pants off as fast as possible, while she groans. A rip of the thin fabric tells me my patience has evaporated. I am ravenous for this woman.

She fusses at me, "What are you doing? Those pajamas were expensive."

"I'll buy you new ones," I say right before I

take her breast into my mouth. Her back bows, thrusting her nipple into my mouth. But I back off and reach between her thighs to cup her pussy. "I'll buy you a whole damned store of pajamas, and do you know why?"

She gasps and tries to ride my hand. But I pull it away. She has to learn I'm in control of this one. "Why?"

"So that I can rip them off of you." I stroke each side of her pussy, dodging her clit entirely.

Her fast breaths make her breasts rise and fall. "Don't buy me pretty things ... only to destroy them."

"Anything between you and me is disposable, baby. Anything."

She tries again to ride my hand, but I pull away. "Why are you teasing me?"

"We have gone at each other over and over today, and each time, I've taken care of you." I grab her shoulders and turn her to face the wall. "This one is just for me."

She lets out a breathy moan, then braces on the wall.

Fuck, her ass is incredible. "When I touch your pussy, baby, are you going to be wet for me?"

"Yes," she whispers.

I pull her hips back and reach between her legs again, driving my hand up until I get to her there. She's so wet, and it's all for me. I slide a finger into her, and June shakes. Her G-spot is rough and every time I touch her there, her fingers grip at the wall as if there's something there to hold on to.

Enough of this.

I shed the boxers and, unlike every other time, I thrust straight home. She gasps so hard that it sounds almost like a scream in reverse. But I know my girl can take it. I grab her hips and pound into her. Deeper. Harder. Until her body quakes with my thrusts. I need this. Need to mark her as mine in every way possible.

I need to cover her body with mine.

Leaning onto her back, I take her wrists and pin them to the wall. Then I drive myself into her, savoring every rough gasp. She bounces herself at me, meeting my thrusts. It feels incredible to have June want me. She's as hungry for me as I am for her. It's intoxicating. Magical. Something I never dreamed I'd ever actually have.

And I will never let her down again.

I will protect this woman with everything I have. Connections, money, my life, all of it is hers. There is nothing I wouldn't do for her. Whatever she wants, she will have it. Nothing else matters. Just her, right now, arching back for more of what I want to give her.

Is this what love is? How could I possibly know for sure?

All I know right now is she's close. Her pussy clasps onto my cock, and her sounds are ragged and breathier than before. If I see her face right now, I'm sure her cheeks are pink and puffed. She gets this rosy glow that is so alluring that when I see it, I'm almost on the edge myself.

She sobs out, "Baby, don't stop!"

"Never," I growl.

"Just like that, oh fuck," she squeaks the last two words out as her body goes rigid.

I release her wrists and she gasps when I grab her hips to hammer into her harder. When she cries out, it's brutal, like she's coming with every part of her body. Even her back muscles go tight. Her hot, wet body tries to pull me over the edge with her—pulsating against my shaft so much that I could.

But I'm not done with her yet. We need to be safer, though.

The moment her back muscles release, I pull

out and pick her up before she falls over. She gasps, "What're you doing?"

"This." I carry her to the bed and drop her onto it, enjoying her surprised giggles and bouncing. Then I grab her legs and yank her to the edge, before thrusting straight in again. Her back bows and her eyes roll back atop pink, puffing cheeks. Before she can speak, I've got her legs against my chest, shaping her body like an L against me. I kiss the inside of each of her ankles while I pound into her.

This angle is better. It makes her tighter, and I can see the front door through her open bedroom door. Against the wall was fun, but I need a clear line of sight. It's bad enough that she's only on the fifth floor of her apartment building. High, but not high enough to keep someone from using her bedroom balcony to get in. Her building is brick. Pretty, but vulnerable. Too many hand holds. A skilled free climber could make it up here in a matter of minutes.

Her sounds become something deeper, and I glance back down at her. She's touching herself, the naughty girl. I swat her hand away, and she gives me a pouty, wounded kitten face. Fuck, she's so sexy I can't stand it. "That's my job." I thumb her clit while I work her with my cock. "See? Mine."

"Mm, you were distracted."

She's not wrong. I hate I was distracted. But it's hard not to think about what could happen right now. Things are precarious, and I'm not used to that. I've always rolled with the punches because I'm lucky and I can get out of things pretty easily most of the time. Now, with her to consider, I can't stop thinking about the possibilities of how it could all go wrong.

But I have to keep my head in the game, and right now, I'm playing to win.

I bend forward, leaning over her, so she's bent in half. The fit is intense like this—tighter and somehow wetter. My balls draw up and surges of pleasure wash through me. "I'm not distracted now."

"Fuck, baby, you're so deep!"

I slow down to drag this out, and she trembles violently. When I kiss her this time, I can hear it—she can hardly breathe. My cock is so sensitive at the moment that I feel her spot against the head. "You're going to come for me again if I keep this up, aren't you?"

She hisses, "Yes!"

"But I told you, this one is for me," I

rumble, dipping in when I speak and pulling all the way out after every sentence. "Just for me. You're not supposed to come when it's just for me. You're supposed to take it. But I feel you are right on the edge again. Shaking like a leaf."

Her face is red and glistening with sweat, and she's never been more enchanting. She whimpers, "Mm, hmm!"

I lean to her ear and demand, "Come for me," before I bite her earlobe.

Her head digs into the mattress as she writhes beneath me, her body jerking and quivering and clasping all at once. I brace my weight off her to let her breathe, and the sounds she makes are unholy, until she screams my name in the middle of them. Can't hold back anymore. Pleasure shoots through me, pulling me into her, knocking me off my balance until I have to lean over her again, giving her all of me.

That's exactly what I want. To give her all of me.

I devour her with kisses and carry her up the bed. She is limp and wrung out and falls asleep on my shoulder in seconds. I whisper against the top of her head, "I will keep you safe, love. No matter what."

. . .

Chapter Fifty-Five-Anderson

"You sure about this?" June asks.

Mostly. "Dad won't know that you've gone back to work. He's powerful but doesn't have spies in every law firm in town. It will likely be fine."

She looks so cute when she's nervous. It's a shame it's not over something petty. She's right, this is something we cannot afford to screw up. But it's sheer paranoia to think he has spies where she works. "Guess I'm just worried. Always feels like when things start to turn around, they go to shit."

I smile at her and kiss her forehead. "You better get going, or you'll be late."

"What about you? Doesn't he hate it when you're late?" she asks, pointing to the clock on the wall.

"Sophie's isn't far from here. I'll be fine. I could walk you to work—"

She laughs. "Thanks, but no. That might give things away."

One more for the road, then. I kiss her until

my balls ache, and I hate when she pulls away. But she's smiling, and I did that. I made her smile, and it's the best feeling I can have while wearing clothes. She leaves, and I go the other way, and it thrusts the opposite feeling through me. I hate to leave her, but I have to.

Brunch with Dad will not wait.

Sophie's is yet another hoity-toity place he likes. The place has long been rumored to be a favorite of local high-end criminals, possibly run by them as a front for money laundering. But that's just old Boston lore. Lots of places have that reputation in the city. It adds to their mystique and makes a lot of them into tourist destinations.

It's a small, brick building with private, soundproof dining rooms perfect for birthday parties and bribery. Or, in my case, blackmailing my father into giving me access to my money. The hostess takes me back to our private room. Dark stone flooring, no windows, ivory walls with decent artwork. The table has a black tablecloth on it and two place settings. The room has space for several small tables like this one, but we are the only patrons. It is almost awkward, but Dad doesn't seem to notice. His martini is half drained.

A server delivers a very old scotch for me without taking my order. This isn't his move, though. It's Dad's.

After the server leaves and the door closes completely, I take a whiff. It's the good stuff, and I am not one to turn that down, so I take a sip. Heady, smoky, entirely too expensive. "What's the occasion?"

"Can't a father spoil his favorite son?"

I laugh at the characterization. "*I'm* the favorite?"

"For now."

I shrug and sip again. "Thank you."

He nods his head once. "Your mother is well, thank you for asking."

"Is it too much to assume that if she weren't, then you would tell me?"

A gentle lift of his eyebrows is all I get from him to say I was right about that. "Our last conversation was less convivial than I would like, Anderson. For the part I played in it, I apologize."

I choke on the scotch, and it takes a moment for me to make words again. "Did you just apologize to me?"

"It has been known to happen from—"

"No. No, it has not."

He almost shrugs. "Apologizing can easily become a bad habit, and you know how I strive to avoid that." He is doing this to drive me crazy. I know he is. Talking in circles is something of an art form for Elliot West.

"Let's not get off-topic—"

"Did you know Cole will be joining us at the firm?"

"Yeah, he mentioned—"

"Yes. Not yeah. You're not some uneducated street urchin."

I stretch my hands instead of letting them ball up from tension. A fist feels stronger. It's my first instinct. But he trained that out of me at a young age. According to him, a fist is the refuge of those who aren't smart enough to fight with their words. I ignore his correction. "Cole told me the night of the party, when June was taken." Maybe if I add that part, he will explain why we are here.

A line forms between his brows as a pensive expression takes hold. "You know, there's something about all that which strikes me as convenient."

"The kidnapping of my fiancée is convenient?" Huh?

"You can't get your money. You yell at me. I

don't budge. Then your fiancée is kidnapped, so you need your money. Kidnapping is a very—"

"Let me stop you right the fuck there. You have seen what I've seen. You know what's going on here. How the fuck can you accuse me of anything like that?"

He held his hand up to silence me. "Ah, ah. I am not accusing you of anything. Merely pointing out how things might be."

"You're making shit up, so you don't have to give me my money."

"I don't have to give you your money at all, Anderson. Do not forget this."

"Guess you don't mind if the police and the media find out about everything going down at the firm, eh?"

His eyes flicker with something I have never seen before with him. I'd seen it with only a few people in person, and even now, some primal part of me goes into a hyperaware state. The flicker is pure rage. The kind of rage I've seen when a client had to get dragged into rehab against his will before his next concert tour. The kind of rage that hits right before a fight breaks out in a frat. It's mindless and has no thought of consequence. Seeing that look in my father's eyes sends a shot of frost through my veins.

But he neutralizes the expression and trades it for apathy. His voice is flat. "You are capable of many things, but hurting your mother is not one of them, and I promise you, that would hurt her. More than you know."

He will never give me what I want if I push any harder. I have to make him think of the future. Of what he's standing in the way of. Otherwise, he's going to feel attacked and shut down. Since he's brought her up twice now, I ask, "Do you think she likes June?"

"She seems to, yes. Why?"

I shrug as innocently as possible. "I'd like to think of them getting along. Planning our wedding together. Becoming friends while playing with our children. Mom was always so good with kids."

He huffs a bitter laugh. "Are you going to name one of them after me while you're at it?"

"Hmm?"

"This allusion to our future together to pull on my heartstrings?" He shakes his head, smirking. "Well done."

"I am merely working with what I've got." Which admittedly isn't much right now.

He sighs, folding his arms over his chest. "You can have the money."

I close my eyes, trying not to let him see the relief wash through me. "Thank you."

"But first, there is something I require of you."

I fight the urge to grit my teeth and snarl that it's my fucking money. That will not get me what I want, and I know it, but this cranky old bastard makes it impossible not to want to. My jaw clenches no matter how much I fight it. "What would that be?"

"Something you will not like but is necessary for the firm's continued success."

"Details, old man."

He chuckles. "So anxious to get started?"

"She doesn't have a lot of time!"

He shrugs at that. "There are several details of the business I have kept you from, Anderson. Things which you did not need to know about. I drew lines in the sand I vowed not to cross until you were old enough to understand them. I had hoped to keep you clean a little longer ... but now, I do not have a choice in the matter. It is time for you to get your hands dirty."

"Fine, I'll intimidate someone for you, whatever. Just get to the point."

He pauses. "Or, you can stay clean longer if you would be willing to forget about June."

Chapter 53

JUNE

Okay, June, everything will be fine. It's been my mantra all morning, getting me through the elevator ride. Ever since I left Anderson, I've needed pep talks, mantras, and everything else to get me to put one foot in front of the other. It's been hard not to have him right next to me on my trip to work. I keep jumping whenever someone moves near me or turns a corner too fast. When I saw a jogger, I nearly belted him.

No one is coming to kidnap you again, and even if they do, it probably won't be the worst thing in the world. The first time has to be the worst time, right?

Weird that I get comfort out of that thought, but I do. I didn't see it coming the first time, and that was not the kind of surprise anyone wants. But now, I think I'd handle it better. I've been there and done that. The only person with cause to kidnap me is Andre, and though he is a sociopath, he doesn't seem to want to hurt me, so I'm probably in the clear. Ish.

Still, though, blackmailing Elliot gives me pause. I fight not to text Anderson to call it off. It's wrong. I know it is. But I need the money. For that matter, I earned it. It's mine. But it still feels wrong to let Anderson blackmail his father for it, no matter how terrible Elliot is.

As soon as the doors open, I half expect to be bombarded by everyone in the office. But thankfully, no one is at the door. They're buzzing about, getting things done. Like I should be.

As soon as I put my bag down at my desk, though, Garrett's voice calls out, "Oh my god, she *is* alive!" He rushes over from the direction of the breakroom behind me, but I spin around to stop the hug I know is incoming.

"Still too fragile for a hug. Might throw up on you."

He stops in his tracks. "Ew. Are you sure you should be at work?"

I shrug and give a wan smile. Maybe I'm playing this up too much. I don't know. But after being absent so long, it feels like the right play.

"Don't want to eat up all my PTO. But I'll go home if I can't make it through the day."

He smiles. "Well, I am glad you're doing well enough to be here, even if it's just for a few hours. Did the doctors say what it was exactly?"

"Some wicked combination of food poisoning and flu."

"What ancestor did you piss off to get stuck with that?"

I chuckle, shaking my head. "Whoever it is, I spent days over the porcelain apologizing to them."

"Do you need a soda? Crackers?"

"I'm good. I don't want to eat much of anything, actually."

He nods knowingly. "Went to Mexico for vacation once. Ended up sicker than a dog for a week. The best, worst diet I was ever on."

I laugh again and hold my stomach. "I bet."

"June, is that you?" Madi's voice cuts right through me from behind, making me hate whoever invented the open floor plan for offices. That trendsetter is the bane of my existence. What I wouldn't give for a door I could slam in her face.

When I turn around, I begin, "Hey, Mad—"

"You look like shit!"

Nice to know she thinks that's appropriate to tell someone who's been sick. Especially since I haven't been. "Nice to see you too, Madi."

"Did you lose weight from your illness?"

No. "Yes."

"It shows. Never thought I'd say this to you, but I think you've lost too much weight."

"That answers all the questions I didn't ask."

She looks taken aback. "Well, I didn't mean anything bad by it—"

"You told me I look like shit, and you never thought I'd be too skinny, but now I am. Exactly what part did you not mean bad?"

She flutters her eyes, and it's like her brain is resetting. Garrett, on the other hand, snorts to keep his laughter down. Madi recomposes herself. "Are you certain you should be back so soon, June? You don't seem like yourself at the moment. You're sniping at me. It's unprofessional."

"What you've been saying about my appearance is unprofessional, Madi. I am pretty sure HR would not enjoy hearing what you've told me, but I'd be glad to tell them myself, and Garrett is a fantastic witness, wouldn't you say?"

She stammers over a few syllables, then mutters, "I was merely expressing concern.

You've been absent so long, I think you've forgotten how people speak to one another."

"No, I haven't," I tell her as I sit at my desk. "What I have forgotten is my ability to let your bullshit slide off my back. I'm not doing that anymore. So, keep your inappropriate comments about my body to yourself, and we won't have an interesting chat with HR. Got me?"

"Wallace will hear about this—"

"Good. Tell him. Or would you like me to?"

She huffs, spins on her heel, and stomps away.

That felt so fucking good.

Garrett stares at me, mouth open for a few seconds. "Don't turn me into HR for this, but I kind of want to kiss you for that."

I laugh. "Get in line." I'd kiss me, too, if I could.

"Seriously, you are my new fucking hero."

"Mine, too."

I turn to the voice and find Callie there, beaming at me with her arms open. Before I can speak, Garrett says, "She's strictly no hugging right now. Still vommy."

Her arms drop. "I'll wait for my hug, but holy shit, that was awesome."

"You heard us?"

"Saw the whole thing, June. Never thought being sick would turn you into a badass."

I laugh, shaking my head. "Just figured I am done with the bullshit around here. I thought I was going to die, but I didn't, so no more of that. Madi's crap isn't going to go the way she wants it to any longer. I'm done." It's true, all of it. But for very different reasons than Callie and Garrett think. That's okay. They don't need to know. They're safer this way.

If I get my money—no, *when* I get my money—it doesn't matter what Madi says or does in retaliation. I'll be gone.

"Shit, I'm late for a meeting," Garrett grumbles as he gathers his laptop. He gives my shoulder a squeeze. "Glad you're back and better than ever, June. Missed you." He jogs down the hall.

And Callie takes his seat. Her voice is low. "Now that we're alone, what the fuck is actually going on?"

"I told you. Food poisoning and flu. It's a rough—"

"Cut the crap, June. Tell me the truth."

Why is she pressing on this? "I am. What—"

"You look fine. Maybe a little tired, but I

know you. It's not like you to ignore my texts and my calls. It's not like you to miss work for an illness. Normal June would have gone to the hospital if she were this sick. Normal June doesn't show up to work smelling like a man's cologne. Most importantly, Normal June doesn't come to work with a hickey."

I grab my phone and turn the camera to selfie mode to see what the hell she's talking about. "What? Where?"

She grins. "I knew it."

"Huh?"

"You wouldn't have looked for a hickey if you didn't think there was the possibility of one. It's Anderson, right?"

I take a breath and blow it out slowly to stall. If I tell her I've just been in bed this whole time with Anderson, she'll think I've lost my mind. And I hate lying to Callie. Plus, she's smart enough to know to keep her mouth shut about the truth. It might be nice to have someone to talk about it other than Anderson. He's amazing, but I want a neutral party's opinion on everything …

Crud. Here goes nothing.

"We should go somewhere private, Callie."

She grabs my hand and yanks me into one

of the empty offices, drawing the blinds. "What—"

"You know, with all of our empty offices, you'd think we could have our own, right?"

She huffs and rolls her eyes. "What happened?"

I sigh, and we sit on the couch. "Keep your voice down when I tell you these things, okay? I don't want anyone running in here or listening in through the thin walls."

"You got it."

"So, Anderson asked me to pretend to be his fiancée …" I tell her everything. To her credit, she manages to keep her squeal inside when I tell her about the ring. And the kidnapping. "… so right now, he's blackmailing his father for access to his own money. Which is ridiculous, right? I mean, it's his. Not his dad's. But he has to play by his rules, or he might not get the CEO gig. It's complicated and weird, and I just want off this roller coaster already."

"Can I say something now?"

"Yes."

"Holy fucking shit."

I laugh. "In a nutshell, yes."

Her perfect posture crumbles under the weight of it all, and she slumps back. "That's crazy, June. All of it. And here I thought food poisoning combined with the flu was the worst thing you could go through. Boy, was I wrong."

"I'm sorry for all the lying—"

She waves her hand at me. "Don't even. We're good. I appreciate you keeping me out of the loop until now. I'm mildly worried about being in the loop at all, but I did press you about this, didn't I?"

"Sorry for that, too."

She smiles sweetly at me. "Not at all. Just makes me wonder what Elliot West is into, you know?"

"Yeah. I keep thinking about that, too."

"Obviously, it's not all media and tech. Or if it is, it's the seedy, violent parts of those industries. If he owes this kind of money, the kind of money that gets you kidnapped, there is something violent happening."

"You really think so?"

She nods. "Without a doubt. It's good that you're getting out before you get too attached to Anderson. Sounds like that whole family is bad news."

"Wait, what do you mean?"

"A fish rots from the head. If Elliot is this corrupt, Anderson likely is, too."

I shake my head. "This has been all new information for him, Cal. He had no idea any of this was going on."

Her lips form a line and she grunts, "Hmm. If you say so. Either way, it's good you're not into him—"

I give her a helpless smile.

"Crap. You are, aren't you?"

I nod and sigh. "I think I'm falling for him. No. I know I am. Whatever is going down, I'm in it for the long haul."

"Well, if you're going to do something stupid, do it smart." She cracks her knuckles and smiles at me. "Do you own a gun?"

I laugh. "No!"

"We should fix that. Also, we should get you a smart ring—"

"A what?"

She flashes her hand out to me, pointing to the pearl ring I've always envied. "If I turn the pearl on this, it sends a signal to a satellite to alert my private security team in case I need to be found."

"You're kidding."

"Absolutely not. I had debated giving it to you the night you had your auction, but if you were kidnapped that night, doing so would have breached my contract if they found you instead of me, and they wouldn't have helped you." She shrugs.

"Why do you have any of this?"

"My family has a lot of money. People do stupid things for a lot of money."

She is not wrong. "Tell me more."

-

Chapter 54

ANDERSON

I had vowed to do anything for June, and I meant it. But I didn't want to ride with Moss to northern New Jersey.

Moss is a big guy who works for the firm. I never thought to ask what he does—he works with Dad, almost in an assistant capacity. He shows up to the office sporadically, and when he leaves, Dad is almost always more relaxed. When I first noticed the pattern, I briefly joked to myself that they were having an affair. Now, I know better.

Moss is Dad's muscle.

"Security guard," Dad had said at Sophie's. But we both knew what he meant by that. Moss beats people up for Dad. Something I find repellant. Businesses should not require violence. But I had agreed to this, promising I'd see it done.

I really wish they were having an affair. It would be far less dangerous to everyone.

Moss' car is a black lowrider Escalade. Not exactly the slyest of cars. Seems like a bad fit for the job to me, but what did I know about it? Last I'd seen, Moss drove a BMW, so it's odd he'd pick this thing for a mission. But again, this is not my area of expertise. If I planned to rough someone up—or is it a shake-down?—I would drive something like a white Civic or another plain, invisible commuter car. Something unremarkable seems best for hiding. But he's the expert, I guess.

Moss is huge, too. There is nothing subtle about him. Bald. Six and a half feet tall and probably half as wide, all muscle. White with the ends of tattoos creeping up from his shirt collar when he's in a suit. It's strange seeing him in a suit, like seeing a bear in a cage. His suits are tailored and expensive, so they fit, but they don't *fit* him. The civilized world is not his natural habitat.

Today, his tattoos are better hidden by a black turtleneck sweater and a black leather coat. It's frigid out, and evidently, even bad asses don't like the cold. But his clothes fit him. He's in his element, driving on his way to beat someone up, and that makes me want to jump out of the car to get away from him.

Moss has an air of danger about him. Always has. Even when I met the man, smiling and suited, I knew he was off kilter somehow. Meat hooks for hands, I remember shaking his hand and thinking I never wanted him near me again. But I meet a lot of people I don't like. That's just business.

Now, I get to find out exactly what kind of business I am actually in.

"I understand you're doing this for your girl," Moss says. His accent is a little different than I remember. His voice is still sandpaper in a garbage disposal, but there's a hint of something else to it. Still rough, but not Bostonian.

Also, why the fuck does he know that? "Dad read you in?"

"I know all the family secrets, Anderson."

"That makes one of us," I mumble angrily.

"Don't worry. It's safe with me."

Every other time I've been around Moss, it was either the day I met him or at big functions, where I did my best to avoid being in his presence. I wasn't afraid of the man—I just didn't like him. Sitting in his lowrider, I realize why. The flicker of pure rage my father displayed at Sophie's today is a constant presence in Moss' blue eyes. Icy, like a wolf.

Today just keeps getting better.

"It is not so bad, is it? Taking a ride to Jersey, seeing the sights."

"The sights? Highway is a sight to you?"

"Could be worse."

"How's that?"

"I could be taking you out here to dump your body."

Everything in me stiffens as I furtively look at him.

A harsh laugh bursts out of him as he cracks up at his own joke. "I kid, I kid."

I try to laugh, too, but I am out of humor. And patience. I just want this over so I can pay June and get this thing between us to be done. We can move on after this. Hell, maybe I can leave the firm behind and keep Dad out of my life. With June at my side, I can do anything.

Moss pulls me from my fantasy that will never happen. "Everyone sees me as the bad guy, but I am only your father's errand man. I do not make the calls. He does. I carry them out. It is only business. You must remember this." The longer he speaks, the more I hear the accent. Italian, by way of Italy, not New York City. I'm used to hearing the city's Italian accent around Boston—plenty of New Yorkers come to town for various reasons. But true Italian is not as common.

"Where are you from, Moss?"

He smiles slyly, eyes on the road. "Here and there."

"Sure. Why must I remember it's only business?"

He takes a beat. "Because when you are with me in this car, this is what we do. This is what I drive when I do your father's errands. Not all business in this car is pleasant. But it is only about the numbers. It is not personal."

"I'm sure it feels personal to the person whose face you rearrange."

He laughs at that. "You are right."

So, that's what we're up to, eh? He admits it? Which means I'm going to see him beat the crap out of someone today. Stellar. My stomach knots at the thought.

I kind of wish I'd worn a wire because that was a three-word confession that could land my father and Moss in prison. But the big guy gave me an uncomfortably thorough pat down before he let me into his car. No wire would have escaped his nimble fingers. Not that I blamed him for it. If I were in his line of business, I would have done the same thing.

But I guess I'm in his line of business. I sigh at myself. "Is this what you like doing, Moss?"

He shrugs his boulder shoulders. "It is what I am good at."

"That sounds like a curse."

"Only to someone who cannot appreciate my gifts. Your father does, though. I am surprised he let you in on this one. Your father has shielded you from so much of the world for so long that I thought he might end all of this before you succeed him. Guess not."

I gulp. "What is it we're doing, exactly?"

"No *we*. Me. You will watch me work."

"Lucky me."

"You like to watch, eh?" He laughs at his joke. "If you like watching, then I know a fantastic titty bar near our destination with the best buffet you have ever seen—"

"No, thanks. I already ate." The thought of eating with Moss in a strip club is enough to turn my stomach.

"Then, while I eat, you can just watch the

girls. They are nasty ones. They like each other. Put on a very good show."

"I have somewhere to be after this. Didn't Dad tell you? I have to get the money to the kidnappers for June."

He nods along. "Oh, si. I forgot. Titty bar next time, then."

With any luck, there won't be a next time. Whatever this shit is, it ends the moment I'm in control of the firm. Hell, I'll shut us down before I perpetuate whatever the fuck this is. I don't care if I end up living in a box on the street so long as violence is not a part of my life.

We pull up to a bay of docks in an industrial area. He parks the car between some others like he wants to tuck in and hide the vehicle. This is an unexpected visit from Dad's enforcer. We're catching these people off-guard for a reason. Why? Would they attack us otherwise? Fan-fuck-ing-tastic.

I'm not sure if that's what I was expecting, but I didn't have much in the way of expectations going into this. Just spending the time with a guy I do not like and heading off to do something illegal. My luck has officially run out.

It's a gray day with an icy, stinking wind. Everything seems wet outside. New Jersey is a decent enough state, but I could never imagine living here. Even the nice places seem sketchy.

The docks are not one of the nice places of New Jersey.

I follow Moss to the rear of the SUV, and there, he opens the door. He lifts a gray blanket that blends in with the interior so well that I didn't realize it was there. Beneath the blanket are guns.

Shit.

He passes me a Glock 9mm. "You know how to use this?"

I pop out the clip and check the chamber. "Yeah. I do."

He grabs a second gun for himself and a file folder, then grins. "Let's get this party started, eh?"

-

Chapter 55

ANDERSON

He turns to lead the way, tucking the file folder into his jacket. But I grab his arm. The look he gives is curious. "What is it?"

My mouth is dry, and my head spins. It's hard to say the words because I never thought I'd need to say them. "I'm not killing anyone."

He grins. "It is as I say. You watch. That is all."

Feels like an elephant is sitting on my chest. "I won't … I won't be a party to murder, Moss."

"Is that what you worry about?" He speaks to me like I am an overwhelmed child. "No, no, Anderson. We are only here to make sure someone will pay their debt. That is all."

"Then why the guns?"

"Insurance that they are intimidated."

"Brandishing is a crime—"

He laughs heartily. "If that is the only crime we commit today, it is a good day. Come, come. We go have a, eh, conversation. That is all."

"No guns?"

"Only if they are necessary. Your father is a bastardo, but he does not like the violence."

Cold comfort. But likely the only comfort I would get today. I huff. "Let's go, I guess."

He grins again, then leads the way. The ground crunches underfoot, a mix of dirty snow and gravel on top of worn-out pavement. If the breeze didn't chill me, the happy jaunt in Moss' step would have. The man is practically giddy at the thought of intimidating people.

Am I that different?

I like to intimidate people, too, but in a professional setting where there are rules to play by. This is not the same thing. But come to think of it, is it all that unfamiliar? They owe us something. We are here to collect. That's just a simple transaction, like any other time I've had to ensure a witness' cooperation or tried to get an injunction. I want something, and I work to get it.

Trying to couch this in terms I prefer is not helping my stress level. Not when I feel the weight of the Glock in my pocket. This is a fucking nightmare. Except I can't wake up.

We're heading for a warehouse. I'm not sure which one. There are several lined up next to each other. Must be a slow day for the rest of the businesses around because there's no one outside. I don't know if that's good or bad. Or maybe, that's why Moss picked now for this. No witnesses.

Perfect.

Moss leads me to the warehouse on the far end, the one closest to the actual docks themselves. The water carries the fresh scent of dead seals or something equally horrid, and I fight back a wave of retching. My nerves are already frayed. I don't need that, too. He smirks as he holds the door open behind him. "Here we go."

The warehouse looks like every warehouse I've seen on television. Crates and boxes line the walls, and a few stand haphazardly in the middle. A forklift sits idle. The rear of the warehouse is a gaping open wall that overlooks the harbor. Three men in heavy coats stand around looking at a phone, and by the sounds of the video on it, they're watching porn together. They haven't noticed us.

One of them grunts, "See, I told you she could take it—"

"Ah, but Bobby, can you?" Moss taunts.

The three men jump so fast at the sound of his voice that it scares me. Not their jump but the fact two of them reached for their pockets the moment they were spooked. They're carrying, too.

Better and better.

"Moss, uh, hey," Bobby says, stuffing his phone in his pocket. He looks like every other white guy in his thirties who works manual labor. A little scruffy, a little dirty, built by hard work with a layer of fat on him. "What are you doing here?"

"Come now. Are we to play that game?"

Bobby slowly takes a step backward. "I ain't playin' no games, Moss. Honest."

"Then you have the two-hundred-and-fifty g's my boss is waiting on?"

We're here to intimidate a guy for a quarter of a million dollars? That's what my father thinks risking my life is worth? It's beyond insulting.

"I, uh, I don't have it, but I can get it," Bobby stammers. It doesn't go unnoticed that he's backing away while the two who grabbed for their pockets stand firm. Concerned but firm.

I like watching nature documentaries. It's a hobby of mine since I can't get into the outdoors as often as I'd like. Sometimes, those documentaries show animal attacks. It's a part of nature, and I understand it. I don't like those parts, but they are like trainwrecks, and I can't look away. It might be started by blood in the water or the spotting of a lame straggler in the pack. There is always a moment right before the attack begins when it seems like it might not happen. The predator appears to consider a different option, but in reality, he's sizing up his prey.

Right now, that's what this feels like. We're being sized up. For all my hours in the gym, my practice at the gun range, and my sharp suit and coat, I look like prey to these guys. I do not like it.

So, I stand taller. Slowly, so I don't spook them. They don't know me. They don't know what I'm capable of. It's all I have going for me at the moment. That, and the Glock. I'll let Moss do all the talking so I remain a mystery. I'd like to think that worries them enough to keep this from getting out of control.

"That is what you say last time, Bobby. And the time before." Moss cracks his knuckles and stretches. "I like you, Bobby. It is why I let you string along. But my boss? He does not like you. He grows impatient with my patience. He says Bobby is not a good man. Do not let him get away with it this time."

"Come on, Moss. You know I'm good for it."

"What I know is, if you keep this up, you lose more than your money. You lose your valuables."

"I ain't got nothin' worth that kind of money—

Moss says no more. He holds out the file folder from his jacket. He doesn't hand it over to Bobby. Instead, he makes Bobby come to him for the folder. The squirrely man creeps between his associates to grab the folder, then retreats a little as if Moss will spring on him at any moment.

Bobby opens the folder, and his face drains of color. His gaze is a mixture of shock and anger. He rasps, "Never thought Elliot West would go after my kids."

It's a knife to my gut. I try to contain my shock—if I show it, they'll know I'm not some silent killer here to back Moss up. But fuck, Dad's threatening kids? Jesus. What the fuck is going on with my family?

Moss says nothing, either. He just stands there like some immovable object instead of a person. Considering he was giddy about everything else, I get the feeling he might not be thrilled about threatening children, either. Or maybe he's content to let the pictures do the talking.

Bobby shakes his head. It's not anger in his voice anymore. It's resignation. "I shoulda known not to get in bed with Elliot West. He's a fuckin' animal. I'll get ya the money, Moss. Let me make a call."

Moss merely nods.

His men relax, shoulders slumping in defeat. I don't know what's in those pictures, and I don't want to know. This shit ends the moment I'm in charge. I wish I could promise that to Bobby right now. I feel bad about this. Sick, actually. But the worst of things is over, and I'm relieved. Tucking my hands in my pockets—

"Gun on the suit!" one of the goons shouts as he points at me.

"What? No, wait—"

But it's too late for explanations. Everything

happens so fast. The goons grab Bobby and dive behind the nearby crates, and Moss grabs me and does the same. We're behind a cluster of them, affording us more protection than what the other guys have since they're in the middle of the warehouse.

I shout, "I didn't mean—"

But gunshots ring out anyway. Doesn't matter what I meant. Doesn't matter who I am. My fancy degrees and expensive cars mean nothing. At this moment, the only thing that counts is tiny metal projectiles seeking something solid to bore a hole into, and I am their target.

Moss returns fire, then grins at me. "Flashed your piece."

"I didn't mean to!"

He laughs, ducking a shot. "Tell them that."

"I'm trying!"

"Does not matter now, eh?" He shoots at them again. A man screams in pain, and it sends a spike of ice up my spine. He scans out, still smiling. "Bobby, I warned you—"

A few shots ring out, all the while, Moss laughs. I'm enraged by his cavalier attitude. "What the fuck is funny?"

"They think we will be shot by them. It will

not happen."

"Huh?"

"These good crates. Better than theirs. Read." He leans up and shoots again. More screaming.

I don't want to know what just happened, so I read. The side of the box had a label for some sort of manufacturing company. "So?"

"They make steel gears for machinery. Bullets do not like steel. Is why I picked this spot to speak to Bobby."

He knew. The motherfucker knew we'd end up in a fucking shootout. I'm enraged by this, but it doesn't matter right now. There's still a hail of bullets fired off at us now and then.

Moss gloats, "I have them pinned down behind crates for soda." He laughs. "It is almost unfair—"

"No fucking shit!" Part of me wants to push him out into the bullets and let them have him. But I can't rely on their goodwill not to shoot me, too. "How do we get out of this?"

"It would help if you stop hiding and start shooting."

"I'm not killing anyone!"

He laughs. "With your aim, I am certain you are right. But it keeps them distracted while I reload." He shoots until the gun empties. "Your turn."

Fuck. I pull my gun out and wave it at the edge of the crate, earning a barrage of bullets aimed my way. Even though they nick the edge of the crate only, my heart is racing. Just a matter of time before one side runs out of bullets. I keep myself mostly covered by the crates as I stand and fire, aiming for their legs.

Whatever this is all about, I'm in it now.

When they stop firing, Moss stands at my side. "We finish this, eh?" The hulking piece of shit actually fucking winks at me before grinning and opening fire on them again. A ragged grunt comes from someone over there, and he strolls straight at them, a man on a mission. Three shots ring out in quick succession. "It is done."

I'm lightheaded. Adrenaline slammed into me at some point, and now, my hands shake. Slowly, I stand on boneless legs. Moss leers over three bodies on the floor. All with head wounds. My voice is empty. "You killed them."

"Before they could kill us. It is a good day," he says proudly, shoving his gun into a holster.

"I don't…I'm not…" Can't tell if I'm going to throw up or if I'm going to blackout, but either one is on the table.

Moss comes to me, throwing his arm over my shoulder to walk me out. "Put your gun away before we are out of the warehouse."

Didn't realize it was still in my hand. It takes more effort than I'd like to admit to get it back in my pocket.

Moss claps my chest. "You did good. Come now. We go. Business over."

"You have no idea."

He laughs, shaking his head. "Your father did not say you are funny. I will tell him. I will tell him all about his brave son who shot at our enemies and made jokes. He will love it. You are just like one of us now. He will be pleased, eh?"

There was a time when I would have wanted Dad's approval. But my father lords my money over my head. He acts as though June is disposable. He blackmails people with the lives of their children. Dad's approval is nothing but a felonious disgrace.

My ears still ring from the gunfire as Moss gets me into the car. He turns the radio on and sings along for a verse. For a murderer, he has a nice voice.

-

Chapter 56
ANDERSON

On the elevator ride to Dad's floor, I want to rage. At Moss. At how long the elevator takes. Even when we get out and I see his secretary, Margaret, I want to shout at her when she tells us he's waiting for us. This secret is eating me from the inside out, and it's been less than a day. We came straight from the warehouse to Dad's office, and I am ready to explode.

Walking into Dad's office, I am overwhelmed by the need to scream at him. I glare at the old man and snap, "Get out."

"This is my office—"

"Moss, get out."

He must look to Dad for direction because Dad nods toward the door. But I don't see it. All I see is the devil in the CEO's chair. My chair.

When the door closes, I slam my fists on his desk. "The fuck!"

A tight little smile comes over his face. "Tell me all about it, son."

"You set me up!"

"To understand what this business entails? Yes. I did."

"You made me an accessory to—"

"Anderson. You cannot be this naïve. Not anymore."

"Naïve?" I ask, panting. "I may have shot people today, Dad! Because of you! Because to you, I'm worth risking to get back a quarter of a million dollars! No wonder you didn't want to pay up for June! You're a cheap son-of-a-bitch

"Ah, ah, don't speak of your grandmother that way—"

I lunge over his desk and grab his collar, shaking him. "The fuck is wrong with you!"

He glances at my wrist with mild disdain. "Are you done yet?"

"I haven't even gotten started!"

"You realize, of course, that Moss is on the other side of that door still, and if I needed him to, he would come in here and remove you. I do not wish that to happen, but it will if you do not unhand me. Now."

Moss, who shot and killed three people today. My father is threatening me with that guy. Fuck this shit. Fuck all of this. I need … June. I have to get her the money.

With shaking hands, I release him. "Why? Just tell me that."

"First, you will tell me how today went. Sit. Would you like a scotch?"

"No."

"Go on, then."

I gulp against a dry throat as I sit. "We went to New Jersey like you wanted. We spoke to Bobby, and he pussyfooted around until Moss threatened his children. Things seemed like they were settling down, and I relaxed, tucking my hands into my pockets. Which exposed my gun and made them think I was going for it. The situation devolved into a shootout. We're alive. They're not."

His smile deepened but only a fraction. "Sounds like you handled yourself as best you could."

"It is your fault three men are dead, and that doesn't even bother you, does it?"

"That's where you're wrong, Anderson."

Does he have a spark of humanity in him? "It bothers you they're dead?"

"No, not that part. It is not my fault they are dead," he says, shaking his head. "If Bobby had paid his debts, then his children would still have a father. It is his own fault he is dead."

I grip the arms of the chair. "You made me an accessory to three murders. And you're not even bothered by it?"

"It was high time you understood what it is we really do."

"No."

He smirks. "No?"

"It is not time for me to understand any of this. There is nothing to understand. My father thinks I'm worth nothing, and—"

"You are worth *everything* to me, Anderson," he growls. "You are my legacy! If I have to twist your arm to get you to understand that, then I will!"

"My DNA is all over that warehouse, Dad. How am I going to be your legacy when I'm in a federal prison?"

At that, he laughs and sits back. The very picture of unbothered once more. He turns his laptop to face me. On it is full-color CCTV footage of the warehouse. Seeing myself there turns my stomach. It really does happen just as fast as I remember it. Things are fine, and then they are not.

Dad says, "It is good you got out from behind the crates. Most men don't their first time."

I say nothing, my attention rapt on the footage. It's impossible not to flinch when Moss shoots the three in the head. All three were injured by that point, so it was easy for him. Then he collects me, and we leave.

A cold sweat breaks out over my entire body. "Why are you showing me this?"

"I don't think you will end up in a federal prison, Anderson. This is the only footage of what happened, and I have it."

This means if I don't play ball, Dad will send me to federal prison with this footage. He holds all the cards now. He's blackmailing me. Turnabout is fair play, or so they say.

I rake a hand through my hair. "What about DNA? Or the bodies? Or—"

"Keep watching."

After Moss and I leave, a team of people in black come in and take the bodies, cleaning the blood and making it appear as if no one was ever there. The warehouse is left with only crates and a forklift.

Dad says, "I do not leave things to chance. It's bad business."

My mouth is dry, and my knuckles ache to punch him. To wipe that smug look off his old face. But I have to keep my eye on the prize. "I need the money for June."

"Ah yes, of course." He bends down to his side, and I half expect him to sit up with a gun and shoot me. Instead, he pulls a small black duffle bag onto his desk. It sounds heavy for its size. He unzips it to show the contents. Stacks of hundred-dollar bills in bands. "Four hundred thousand, as agreed upon. Feel free to count it."

"I will."

"Don't trust your old man?"

I yank the bag from him. "Why should I?"

"Because I got you the money. From my own accounts. Not yours. You have access to yours again, by the way. A gift from me to you."

"It's not a gift to give me access to my own money."

"In your case, son, it is," he says with a sigh. "But that's neither here nor there, and I refuse to split hairs over trivial matters. What I meant is the cash is the gift. Something to appease your worries that I am heartless when it comes to

June. I'm not. I like her. She's a good fit for you. For this … life."

"How dare you say that about her?" I hiss. What a wretched thing to say of her. I hate him. Everything about him. I don't like him liking her. I don't like him thinking about her at all. She is above him. Better than him.

Better than me, too. I'm pretty sure she didn't kill anyone today.

He calmly says, "I mean it as a compliment. She is practical. Smart—"

"Why did you risk my life for so little money, Dad? If I'm your legacy, then tell me why." Even with everything else, as much as I hate him, it stings that he put me in harm's way for what amounts to less than he spends on vacation.

He steeples his fingers and sighs. "Every day in this life is a risk. It could be for a small sum or for everything we have. But breathing while holding so much in my hands is a risk. It is not the money that makes the risk worth it. It is maintaining our reputation. Bobby didn't owe much. But if I let his debt slide, the next guy will want the same consideration. And the next, and so on. Before we know it, this life is over. The firm collapses. Hundreds of people are out of work. We are poor ... reputation is everything."

"How do you build your reputation on this if the bodies aren't found?"

"They will be. When I want them to be."

I try not to let my mind wander into the specifics of that, but I can't help it. Where does he keep the bodies in the meantime? What cursed refrigerator houses Bobby's body? What are the names of his two dead friends? But the most important question of all has nothing to do with any of that.

How am I getting out of this?

"Shouldn't you be going, son? Don't want to miss the kidnapper's cutoff time. No telling what they might cut off."

Right. Still playing that role. Without a word, I nod and take the money. No point in counting it right now. I have to pretend I'm in a hurry.

As I reach the door, he says, "The first time is always the worst, Anderson. It gets easier from here."

The first time murdering people or the first time paying a ransom for the woman I love? I don't ask the question. Dragging out a conversation is the last thing I want to do. Just being in my father's presence is enough to make me want to peel my skin off. I feel like I'll never be clean. The men's screams replay in my mind again and again. All I do is nod once and walk out the door.

Chapter 57

JUNE

Friday nights used to be date night. I miss those days. Tonight, instead of a date, I got a text from Anderson. "Meet at your place at seven."

How romantic.

But I can't give him crap for the brevity of the text. Whatever has happened today, it can't have been good. He's been silent most of the day. No texts, no calls. Today was the day he was going to get the money from his dad, and since he's been quiet all day, I assume it went badly. What if Elliot figured out our scheme and refused to give him the money? Or maybe something else went wrong. I won't know until Anderson gets here.

He knocks on my door, and I leap to my feet. Anxiety has ridden me hard today, and I need answers. When I open the door, though, all urge to grill Anderson evaporates. He looks awful. Handsome but awful. Anderson is drenched. Dark smudges sit atop his cheeks like he hasn't slept in weeks. His lips are tight. His eyes take the cake, though. Almost hollow-looking.

I know guys hate talking about their feelings, but I can't help but blurt, "What's wrong?" as I close the door behind him.

He sets a bowling bag on my table. "You have your money."

"In cash? I thought it would be a wire transfer or something—"

"Cash."

He kicks off his shoes and takes off his coat before wandering into my bedroom. My doorway frames him when he turns to me. "Can we talk?"

I race to be at his side, and he motions for me to follow him to the bed. We arrange ourselves until I'm on my back, and he's on his side, facing me. It's how we lay for so many days in my bed while I was pretending to be kidnapped. We would talk for hours like this until we couldn't take it anymore and had to get naked. I hope that's where this is heading, but I doubt it. "What do you want to talk about?"

"Today … things went bad."

"Do you want to tell me?"

He shakes his head. "Can't. Won't."

"Can I kiss you?"

Tension breaks on his face as he smiles sadly at me. Then he leans down for a kiss. It's brief and chaste, but god, I needed it. "Sorry, I didn't kiss you when I came in."

"It's fine, Anderson. You're sort of freaking me out."

"Sorry. I don't mean to."

"What can you tell me? Start there."

He sighs and lies back, so I crawl onto his shoulder and cram myself into the nook there. It's nice to just lay and listen to his heartbeat and breaths. Sets my mind at ease better than Xanax. He says, "I need to get away from my family, June."

Well. Anxiety is back. "What? Why?"

But he shakes his head. "Without getting into details, they are not good people."

"But everyone I met was perfectly nice and—"

"My dad. It's him. He's the problem." His

jaw is tight when he says this, and I get the impression things are worse than I thought.

"Oh."

He takes a deep breath to calm himself. "Dad is a monster. He is just as bad as Andre Moeller. Maybe worse. I don't know enough about Andre to say for sure. But Dad is … in a similar line of work, I think. I want no part of it."

"But how would you extricate yourself from him, Anderson? He's your father. You work for him—"

"The company pays for my apartment, my life … I don't know. I've built a reputation as a decent attorney, but I've done that on the back of West Media. Everything I am is tied to him, and I hate it. So, maybe I'll try a different industry. I don't know. But I have to get out."

He's panicking. I feel it coming off of him in waves, and he's threatening to make me panic, too. So, I take a different course of action. "Anderson?"

"Yes, baby?"

"Whatever you choose to do, I support you."

He pauses, and when he finally looks at me, it's all nerves in his eyes. "And if that meant I was poor, you'd—"

I laugh and throw my thigh over his. "You think I care about your money? Honestly?"

"I didn't mean to be offensive, just that—"

I kiss him. He's stunned, I can tell. He hardly moves when I do it. But as the kiss deepens, Anderson strokes my cheek. I smile up at him after. "Yes, I'd support you even if it meant you were poor. Money is not why I like you." But *like* has not felt like a sufficient word for days now.

"Why then? Without that, who am I?"

I fling myself on top of him, straddling his waist. "You are Anderson West. The boy who made my life a living hell when we were kids because he had a crush on me and didn't know what to do with that because he was never properly shown affection. The guy who went to my alma mater to follow me there, I suspect. And the man who won a sex auction just to keep me safe. Anderson, your money makes a lot of things easier for you, but it doesn't make you who you are. If things were harder for you, then you'd work harder." I shrug. "But money does not define you. Your father does not define you, either. You do."

He grabs the front of my shirt and pulls me down to his lips. "I needed to hear that."

"I will tell you that whenever you need to hear it."

He smiles up at me and kisses me again. But this time, the tension in his lips is gone. I let him wrap me up in his arms. It feels so good to be held by him after all of this craziness. It's all I ever want to do. But as the kiss goes on, I want more.

I want everything he has to give me.

"Anderson?" I ask between kisses.

"Hmm," he murmurs against my jaw.

"I want you."

He looses a breath as he stares into my eyes. For a moment, it's like everything stops. There is nothing outside of my bed and this man beneath me. But then he grabs my hips, and everything starts again. Our kisses. My heart. My fingers argue with his shirt until I give up and remove my own instead. He shrugs out of his shirt, and I finally have his skin on my palms. His carved muscles make me crave him even more.

I kiss his shoulder while he shucks my pajama bottoms off. Then I kiss and bite my way down his body before I unbuckle his belt and work on his jeans. He helps me get them off, and suddenly, I have the world's hottest man naked on my bed. I'd pause to appreciate the sight, but I need him now.

Instead of pausing, I climb back up his body and trail my tongue up his length. He has the most enticing vein pattern on his cock, and I take my time to memorize it. He hisses a breath when I get to the tip. I love that sound. But Anderson is too impatient for a blow job and grabs my shoulders to pull me up his body. He rolls me onto my back, climbing over me. I'm breathless with need, and all I can think of is Anderson.

When he's on top of me, I feel so protected and small and cherished. I love it. Clasping my hands onto his neck, I pull him down for a kiss, and his tongue dances with mine as his hand trails over my tits and lower. He reaches between my thighs, and I yelp in his mouth.

His touch makes my pulse thrum in my clit. My hips keep jerking to and from his fingers as I grind against him. He growls when he slides two fingers into me. Warmth pools in my belly as he works me over, building the orgasm quickly. I can't help it. Can't slow down even if I wanted to. His touch is too good. Everything with Anderson is too good.

Just as I crest up into my climax, he slows

down to draw it out. He's figured out exactly how to play my body in the days we spent in my bed, and he's using that to my advantage, knowing I'll come even harder this way. But as he slows, he kisses me gentler. Sweeter. His tender touch keeps me high, but these kisses make everything warm and low. My body tenses, and just before I come, he says, "June, I love you."

His words push me over the edge, and I come so hard I see stars. I scream out, "I love you, too!" as I orgasm all over his hand. Ecstasy fills me from toes to skull and beyond, like I've turned inside out on his fingers, but in the best way possible. As my body shakes, he kisses me again as he nestles on his knees between my thighs. I need this so bad. I've felt so disconnected from him all day. This will fix everything.

He rubs his wet thumb over my bottom lip as he stares into my eyes. "June, I love you more than anything—"

"You must if you're willing to betray your family for her."

We both jump at that, and his father stands in my bedroom doorway. Anderson throws the blanket over me, then snaps, "What the fuck are you doing here?"

"I came for what's mine." He grabs the little black bag from my table and leaves.

Thank you for reading Highest Bidder! Can't wait to find out what happens next? **1-click Bidding War now!**

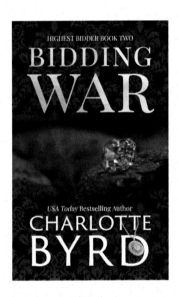

I never expected to meet the love of my life while auctioning myself off the to the highest bidder.

Anderson West is the heir to a billion dollar

fortune and I had to work my butt off for everything I have.

At school, he was my bully.
In law school, he was my rival.
In the real world, we fell in love. Hard.

Our relationship should have been a fairy tale.
But his controlling father turned it into a scan-
dalous headline.

The world is full of dangerous men and the
most dangerous ones work for the Wests.

After loosing my job, I have to work for his family's biggest rival and play a dangerous game of
chess.

When someone comes after me, Anderson takes
his life, and I become an accomplice in covering
up a murder to protect the man I love.

Is this the end of us or is it just the beginning?

1-click Bidding War now!

Want more of June and Anderson (and another STEAMY chapter)? **Read the FREE Bonus Chapter now!**

———

Please take a moment to leave a review on Amazon! Reviews help me find new readers and they can be as short as a sentence. Thank you!

———

If you find any mistakes or typos, please write to me directly so I can make changes immediately instead of through Amazon. My email is charlotte@charlotte-byrd.com

About Charlotte Byrd

Charlotte Byrd is the bestselling author of romantic suspense novels. She has sold over 1.5 Million books and has been translated into five languages.

She lives near Palm Springs, California with her husband, son, a toy Australian Shepherd and a Ragdoll cat. Charlotte is addicted to books and Netflix and she loves hot weather and crystal blue water.

Write her here:

charlotte@charlotte-byrd.com

Check out her books here:

www.charlotte-byrd.com

Connect with her here:

www.tiktok.com/charlottebyrdbooks

www.facebook.com/charlottebyrdbooks

www.instagram.com/charlottebyrdbooks

Sign up for my newsletter: https://www.
subscribepage.com/byrdVIPList

Join my Facebook Group: https://www.
facebook.com/groups/276340079439433/

Bonus Points: Follow me on BookBub and
Goodreads!

Also by Charlotte Byrd

All books are available at ALL major retailers! If you can't find it, please email me at charlotte@charlotte-byrd.com

Highest Bidder Series
Highest Bidder
Bidding War
Winning Bid

Hockey Why Choose
One Pucking Night (Novella)
Kiss and Puck
Pucking Disaster
Puck Me
Puck It

Tell me Series
Tell Me to Stop
Tell Me to Go
Tell Me to Stay
Tell Me to Run
Tell Me to Fight
Tell Me to Lie

Tell Me to Stop Box Set Books 1-6

Black Series
Black Edge
Black Rules
Black Bounds
Black Contract
Black Limit

Black Edge Box Set Books 1-5

Dark Intentions Series
Dark Intentions
Dark Redemption
Dark Sins
Dark Temptations
Dark Inheritance

Dark Intentions Box Set Books 1-5

Tangled Series
Tangled up in Ice

Tangled up in Pain

Tangled up in Lace

Tangled up in Hate

Tangled up in Love

Tangled up in Ice Box Set Books 1-5

The Perfect Stranger Series
The Perfect Stranger

The Perfect Cover

The Perfect Lie

The Perfect Life

The Perfect Getaway

The Perfect Stranger Box Set Books 1-5

Wedlocked Trilogy
Dangerous Engagement

Lethal Wedding

Fatal Wedding

Dangerous Engagement Box Set Books 1-3

Lavish Trilogy
Lavish Lies

Lavish Betrayal
Lavish Obsession

Lavish Lies Box Set Books 1-3

Somerset Harbor
Hate Mate (Cargill Brothers 1)
Best Laid Plans (Cargill Brothers 2)
Picture Perfect (Cargill Brothers 3)
Always Never (Cargill Brothers 4)
Kiss Me Again (Macmillan Brothers 1)
Say You'll Stay (Macmillan Brothers 2)
Never Let Go (Macmillan Brothers 3)
Keep Me Close (Macmillan Brothers 4)

All the Lies Series
All the Lies
All the Secrets
All the Doubts

All the Lies Box Set Books 1-3

Not into you Duet
Not into you
Still not into you

Standalone Novels
Dressing Mr. Dalton

Debt

Offer

Unknown

Made in United States
North Haven, CT
25 April 2024

51773047R10328